THE FRONTLINE FUGITIVES

BOOK III

G.I. GANGSTERS & COLLABORATORS

by Nick Jacobellis

The Frontline Fugitives Book III: G.I. Gangsters & Collaborators

Copyright ©2016 by Nick Jacobellis

ISBN   978-1-7333516-0-7 (print)

          978-1-7333516-1-4 (eBook)

Book design by www.StoriesToTellBooks.com

Cover design by Chris Jacobelis

Badge Publishing

E Mail: info@badgepublishing.com

www.badgepublishing.com

THE FRONTLINE FUGITIVES

FUGITIVES

BOOK III

G.I. GANGSTERS &
COLLABORATORS

CONTENTS

INTRODUCTION

The Frontline Fugitives Book III G.I. Gangsters and Collaborators is a plot driven, police procedural historical fiction war story, that takes place in the European Theater of Operations (ETO) in 1945. In Book III, Jim Beauregard and Al Parker are serving with the U.S. Army Criminal Investigation Division (CID) in Paris, France. In addition to a number of new characters, Book III also includes a cast of supporting characters who are carried over from Book's I & II.

As soon as they arrive in France, Jim and Al find the local CID Agents and their counterparts in the Paris Police actively engaged in several major investigations. As a result, there is no time to see the sights. Instead, Jim and Al join their fellow CID Agents and several Paris Police Investigators in the field, while a major effort is being made to locate and arrest U.S. Army personnel and French civilians who are involved in the thriving black market, including AWOL soldiers and French collaborators.

Serving as a U.S. Army CID Agent was critically important to the war effort, because there was a serious crime problem in Paris. In addition to having enough deserters living in Paris to fill the ranks of a U.S. Army division, CID Agents, Allied Military Police and the Paris Police had to deal with a thriving black market. This resulted in the theft of several thousand U.S. Army vehicles and large amounts of U.S. government property by Army personnel. CID Agents and their counterparts in the Paris Police also conducted a wide variety of criminal investigations that involved other matters.

Specific details about the crime problems in Paris, as well as the number of AWOL troops in the ETO, was not something that the War Department wanted the folks back home to hear about on a regular basis. This was the case, because it would be hard to expect the American people to abide by strict rationing regulations, when a small army of American soldiers were making a fortune, selling stolen Government supplies on the black market.

Bear in mind, that the American people lived with rationing and without certain items, to insure that Allied troops did not have to make such sacrifices when they served during a world war. Even though a black market of sorts existed to some extent in the United States, what transpired in France when Paris was liberated in August of 1944, proved to be a much larger crime problem.

In order to understand the significance of this crime problem, consider that a pack of American cigarettes was selling on the streets of Paris in 1945 for $2.00 dollars. During World War II, the same pack of American cigarettes sold for 5 cents in a U.S. Military Post Exchange, also known as the PX. Even in the United States, a pack of cigarettes cost between 12 to 15 cents during the war years. Some of the other popular items that were sold on the black market in Paris were, U.S. Army food rations for $2.00 dollars, a pound of stolen Army coffee for $10 to $15 dollars, a five gallon (Jerry) can of stolen U.S. Army gasoline was worth $100 dollars and a crate of fifty U.S. Army (heat resistant) Field Ration Chocolate D Bars was worth $300 dollars.

Needless to say, these were highly inflated prices, when you compare what these sought after products were selling for in the United States during the war. In comparison, one pound of coffee sold for 30 cents, a chocolate Hershey Bar cost 5 cents and a gallon of gasoline sold for 17 cents in the United States in 1945. Even at 30 cents a gallon, black market gasoline was also significantly less expensive in the United States, compared to the cost of black market gasoline in Europe. Despite the fact that a two to four ounce Chocolate D Bar was larger in size than a "civilian" chocolate candy bar, the price of a D Bar on the black market was still incredibly expensive. It is also important to remember, that with the exception of some basic operating expenses, black market operators made huge profits, because the items they sold were all stolen to begin with. (The reference sources for this information are listed in the footnotes for this book. Additional facts were provided by The National Archives and The National Museum of American History Behring Center.)

While Book III is a "cops and robbers" story about the pursuit of American and French criminals in Paris in early 1945, The Frontline Fugitives Book IV is more of a war story that is in line with the theme of "Cops in a Combat Zone" from Book II.

A NOTE FROM THE AUTHOR

As I mentioned in the Introduction for Book III, the U.S. Army had a major problem in the European Theater of Operations with the theft and sale of stolen military supplies. This crime problem existed for several reasons. One of the main reasons involves the negative impact that the German occupation had on France, especially Paris. After four long years of being occupied by the Germans, France was forced to cope with massive shortages of the critical necessities of life. These items included food, fuel, coal, cigarettes, coffee, soap, shoes, clothing, blankets and medical supplies. Certain luxury items were also incredibly expensive and highly sought after.

Life in France became even more demanding, when the pro Nazi Vichy French Government was unable to import goods from locations that were under Allied control. The destruction of critical infrastructure and the shortage of transportation, also had a negative impact on the ability of products to be delivered to markets throughout France. This was especially the case, when it came to being able to deliver food and other sought after items to a major city like Paris. The French were also victims of the so called "spoils of war." In other words, there was very little left for the French, after the Germans took what they needed and wanted from France.

Once the Allies landed in France on June 6, 1944, the U.S. Army represented the largest source of supply for the critical necessities of life and various sought after "luxury" items in the European Theater of Operations (ETO). As a result, Quarter Master supply depots, military transportation companies (truck and rail lines), as well as Petroleum Oil Lubricant (POL) Dumps became targets of U.S. Army personnel who elected to operate on the black market.

One famous CID investigation involved the theft of an entire train that was loaded with U.S. Army supplies in France. Another famous CID case involved the theft of supplies from trains that were traveling through France. Even when Military Policemen were stationed as guards on these trains, G.I. Gangsters found a way to steal supplies from the military railroad cars. I mention these cases to show the level of determination that G.I. Gangsters had, when it came to stealing government property, that could be sold on the black market.

As a point of information, the term G.I. Gangsters and G.I. Racketeers was coined in a Yank Magazine article dated May 4, 1945 by Staff Writer Sergeant Allan B. Ecker. This article provides a detailed account of black market operations and other crimes committed by U.S. Army personnel in the ETO during World War II. This included crimes committed by serving U.S. Army Officers, Non Commissioned Officers and enlisted men, as well as by Army personnel who were AWOL and listed as deserters. Some of these G.I. Gangsters were so bold as to impersonate U.S. Army Military Policemen.

The deserters who lived in Paris committed crimes in order to survive and prosper, while they remained Absent With Out Leave aka AWOL. While some of these deserters earned enough money committing crimes in order to survive, other G.I. Gangsters made more money than they could spend. This translated to deserters and other Army personnel making the equivalent of thousands of dollars, while operating on the black market.

In order to understand the significance of this problem, we have to examine this issue from a 1944 and 1945 economic perspective. According to an article written by Malvern Hall Tillit for Barron's National Business and Financial Weekly on April 2, 1944, an unmarried U.S. Army buck private earned just under $500 a year, after paying for certain basic expenses. While a corporal reportedly earned $612 dollars a year after basic expenses, sergeants made between $767 and $1188 a year after basic expenses, depending on their specific rank. Even though married military personnel and personnel with dependents earned a bit more, no military salary came close to providing the amounts of money that could be earned by operating on the black market.

Other types of crimes, including acts of violence, also occurred in Paris after the city was liberated by the Allies. In fact, there were instances when Paris appeared to be more like Chicago in the roaring twenties, than a quaint European city that was liberated in August of 1944. These acts of violence involved armed U.S Army deserters attacking other AWOL troops who were members of rival gangs. Some G.I. Gangsters survived life on the run, while living as wanted men, by committing burglaries and armed robberies.

Whether they worked alone, in small numbers, or in larger organized gangs, the active duty soldiers and the deserters known as "G.I. Gangsters and G.I. Racketeers" operated with virtual impunity, until they were brought to justice by U.S. Army CID Agents and the Military Police. The Paris Police were also involved in keeping the peace and interacted with Allied Military Police on a regular basis.

In an effort to honor the contribution that was made by Allied law enforcement personnel during World War II, every effort was made to base the fictional cases portrayed in this book on historically accurate events. Book III also addresses a variety of issues that were just as relevant in 1945 as they are today. Just as in Book I and II, Book III also addresses the issue of racism. The issue of racism had to be included in this book, because the U.S. Army was segregated during World War II. The fact that white troops and soldiers of color often fought, died and were wounded on the same battlefields, did not change official U.S. Army policy until 1948.

*In order to be historically accurate, this book series uses the words negro and colored to refer to African Americans, because these words were commonly used in the early and mid 20th Century. Even though the "N Word" was used sparingly, this word was used in certain key scenes because it is historically accurate to do so. This book also includes other examples of prejudice, slang words and language that was commonly used in 1945 and at other times in the 20th Century.

Despite the fact that segregation existed, African American U.S. Army personnel served in a variety of all "colored" non combat and combat units during World War II. This included serving in services of supply and transportation companies, as well as in artillery, military police, armored and infantry units. African Americans also served in the U.S. Army Air Forces as fighter pilots and ground crew personnel. The all "Negro" fighter pilots known as The Tuskegee Airmen and The Red Tails became famous as a result of their outstanding service during the war. (The name Red Tails refers to the tail section of their fighter planes that were painted red to identify their aircraft.) Other all "colored" U.S. Army units also distinguished themselves while serving in World War II. As a result, Book III includes several primary and secondary African American characters who help tell an important part of this story.

Book III also explores the different personal and professional relationships that developed between the various characters. This includes the relationship between friends and colleagues, superior officers and subordinates, fathers and sons, men and women, cops and criminals, as well as between the Allied troops who served together.

One very important change that occurs in Book III involves the evolution of certain primary and supporting characters. While Jim Beauregard and Al Parker are still the same hard charging lawmen depicted in Books I and II, they both have new hats to wear in Book's III and IV.

Now that he has been promoted, Lieutenant Colonel James Beauregard is serving as the Commanding Officer of the Paris CID Office. While performing his new duties, Jim interacts with the Paris Police, U.S. Army Counter Intelligence Corps (CIC) Agents and French Army Intelligence Officers. Even though Jim is quite capable of making command decisions on his own, he relies heavily on respected colleagues like Lieutenant Al Parker, Major Tommy Savino, Captain Don Lorenz and (French) Chief Inspector Francois Dumont, to help plan and execute investigations, surveillance operations, undercover operations and enforcement actions.

The fact that Al Parker is now a commissioned Army Officer means that he is now part of the Paris Office CID command staff. As a result, Al is forced by his new status as an Army Officer to direct others in the field. This proves challenging at times for the hard charging New York City cop turned Army CID Agent, who prefers to take the lead and go in first. The reputation that Al Parker earned, while serving with Jim Beauregard and others during the pursuit of Ivan Larson and Shorty Mc Ghee, also enables him to be accepted by the white Army Agents and MPs who are stationed in Paris.

Having Al Parker's youngest son Cal assigned to the Paris CID Office also creates certain challenges for both father and son, especially when Cal volunteers to work in an undercover capacity. Al and both of his sons, who are severing in the U.S. Army during the war, are also forced to deal with issues involving racism.

In order to create the right backdrop for this story and describe life in

Paris during and after the German occupation, various French characters are included in Book III. These fictional characters help provide a "French perspective" to this story. Chief Inspector Francois Dumont and his squad of Paris Police Inspectors/Investigators represent some of the main supporting French characters in Book III. It's through the cooperation of the Paris Police, that the American CID Agents are better able to navigate their way through Paris in search of criminals. This relationship proves to be an effective way to conduct investigations, because a number of French citizens and criminals are actively involved with the American troops who operate on the black market.

Gabriel "Gabby" Allaire is Francois Dumont's brother-in-law and the owner of The Paris Cafe. During the German occupation of France, Gabriel Allaire was an active member of the organized resistance. This character is one of several in Book III, who represent the rather impressive number of French citizens who refused to submit to Nazi rule.

After being wounded during the liberation of Paris, Gabby continues to serve by using his contacts to provide intelligence information to his brother-in-law and his American friends in CID. Thanks to Gabby, his cafe becomes the "home away from home" and the preferred hangout for U.S. Army CID Agents, U.S. Army Military Policemen and members of the Paris Police.

Michelle Dumont is the Chief Inspector's daughter. As the back story describes, while working for the Prefecture of Police in Paris, Michelle served in the her father's resistance unit that was comprised of French policemen. Michelle Dumont's character is a tribute to the French women who served with great distinction in different capacities during the war. Several other female characters, who represent a cross section of society in 1945, are also included in this book series.

In order to add to the historical accuracy of Book III several characters representing French Army Intelligence are included in this story. It was equally important to include characters who represent the collaborators, who worked with Section IV of the German Gestapo and served the pro Nazi Vichy Government. This included Frenchmen who served in the Vichy para military unit known as The Milice.

Another issue that is addressed in Book III, involves how much life has not changed since the 1940s, when it comes to how good investigators solve crimes. Even though they did not have access to the crime fighting technology that we have in the 21st Century, the law enforcement officers of the 1940s were just as successful in bringing criminals to justice. The way World War II era CID Agents worked undercover, recruited informants, gathered evidence, made arrests, conducted surveillance operations and got the charges dropped against AWOL soldiers who cooperated with the government, was no different than how such matters are handled in "modern times." In other words, much of what happened in the so called "good old days" is still going on today.

*The names that were used in this book series to identify different primary and secondary fictional characters were selected because I liked the sound of these names. With one exception, the names that were given to fictional characters have no connection to any "real life" individuals from the past or present times. As a tribute to my father's best friend, from his days growing up in the Flatbush section of Brooklyn, I named one of the CID Agents Sam Carubba. In real life, Sam Carubba was a decorated U.S Army soldier, who served in the 7th Armored Division during the war in Europe.

While every effort was made to make The Frontline Fugitives Book Series as realistic and historically accurate as possible, it is important to remember that this is a fiction story set in the European Theater of Operations (ETO) in 1945. As a result, certain liberties had to be taken, in order to combine fictional characters and a fictional plot with historically accurate events that occurred during World War II.

DEDICATION

This book series is dedicated to those who served in military and civilian positions and protected the United States and our allies during World War II. Clearly, the victory that was achieved in 1945 was made possible, because law abiding people banded together to engage and defeat the Axis forces. I would especially like to thank my father, Ben Jacobellis and my father-in-law, Louis Evangelista for their service to our nation and for all of the assistance they provided, in helping me to understand what life was like before, during and after World War II.

Special thanks also go to my wife, my sons, all of my loved ones and close personal friends. Their support and encouragement means more to me than they will ever know. Last but not least, I would like to thank Almighty God, for blessing me, protecting me and inspiring me throughout my personal and professional life. My Guardian Angel has also worked 24 hours a day 7 days a week to keep me safe, before, during and after my rather adventurous law enforcement career.

CHAPTER 1

SHOTS FIRED

Based on a lead that was provided by undercover CID Agent Cal Parker, two U.S. Army CID Agents and a Paris Police Inspector were assigned to search the 18th Montmartre arrondissement of Paris, for the deserter and black market operator identified as Corporal Eddie Finch. According to Agent Cal Parker, Eddie Finch was making deliveries for a group of G.I. Gangsters, that was run by another AWOL American soldier by the name of Sergeant Charlie Monacco.

After working throughout the night, CID Agent Hank Blair, Agent Chris Jacko and Paris Police Inspector Patrice Goulet spotted Corporal Finch, as he parked a stolen U.S. Army ambulance near the famous Moulin Rouge cabaret. The time was 0420 hours in the morning.

As soon as Corporal Finch jumped out of the cab of the Dodge 4x4 WC54, the deserter opened the back doors. A split second later, a young French civilian approached the back of the vehicle, looked inside and handed Corporal Finch an envelope, that was quickly tucked into the deserter's field jacket pocket.

While the two CID Agents sat in the black Citroen sedan with their counterpart from the Paris Police, Agent Blair looked into the back of the vehicle at Agent Jacko and said, "As tempting as it is to take Finch now and nail that French civilian for buying stolen government property, we better do like Major Savino said and wait until we get help from some MPs. Even the Chief Inspector said we should make every effort to get some help, before we move in to arrest a guy like Corporal Finch."

"I know, but if we can't get some MPs to give us a hand, we're not letting Finch get away," remarked Sergeant Jacko.

After asking Inspector Goulet how he thought they should proceed and hearing the experienced Paris cop agree with the need to follow orders, the veteran French police investigator continued and said, "Our superiors had good reason to be concerned for our safety, when we were warned about this deserter's intentions, to use a pistol and a hand-grenade to facilitate his escape, if he is ever confronted by the authorities."

While Chris Jacko sat in the back of the Citroen sedan, with a pump action Winchester shotgun in his lap, he looked up and down both sides of the street before he spoke up and said, "Unfortunately, there's never a cop around when you need one."

"The good news is, Finch is acting as if it's business as usual. That means he doesn't know that we're on his tail," responded Hank.

Authorizing CID Agents to wear civilian clothing over their Army uniforms and work with the Paris Police in a civilian vehicle, made it possible for the Americans to blend in when they conducted surveillance operations. It also paid to work with the local police, because they were considerably more familiar with Paris. Experienced police detectives like Patrice Goulet also assisted the American Agents, by identifying the French thieves who worked with G.I. Gangsters.

While a bone tired Agent Jacko covered his mouth when he yawned, Hank Blair tapped Inspector Goulet on the side of his right arm and said, "Look, Patrice, the plot thickens."

The presence of a French Citroen delivery van coming to a stop, next to the back of the stolen U.S. Army ambulance, was a clear indication that an exchange was about to be made. While the two Army Agents and Inspector Goulet continued their surveillance, AWOL Corporal Finch and his two French associates transferred ten cans of gasoline from the ambulance into the Citroen delivery van.

While Agent Jacko quickly looked around for some MPs and saw that there were none in sight, he leaned closer to the front seat and said, "Still no MPs in sight. That means we follow this asshole until we can get some help."

After turning to his left to face Inspector Goulet, Hank remarked, "Even though I hate to let those civilians get away, the smart move is to follow Finch, until we can get some MPs to give us a hand."

As Inspector Goulet put his car in gear and prepared to follow the stolen American Army ambulance, he spoke in a confident tone as he continued looking straight ahead. "I agree. Taking your AWOL Corporal off the streets is what we came to do."

Now that the exchange was made, the two Frenchmen drove away, while Finch secured the back of his vehicle and returned to the cab. After looking to his left, Finch put the Dodge ambulance in gear and began driving to his next stop.

While Inspector Goulet began to follow the stolen ambulance, CID Agent Chris Jacko leaned closer to the front seat again and said, "If Eddie Finch is as crazy as Cal's informant says he is, we're in for a fight, when we take this AWOL G.I. into custody."

While Hank Blair looked at his watch and made an entry in his notebook, Inspector Goulet continued to follow the stolen Army ambulance through the Montmartre Arrondisement of Paris. As soon as they spotted a pair of U.S. Army MPs sitting in a Jeep, Hank turned toward Inspector Goulet and said, "What'a you say we get some help from those MPs?"

"An excellent idea," responded Inspector Goulet as he downshifted the manual transmission while the Citroen sedan proceeded through the intersection.

By the time the French sedan came to a complete stop, Hank had removed the civilian hat and jacket that he wore over his Army uniform. While the stolen ambulance continued driving away, Hank held up his CID badge and spoke fast as he called out to MP Sergeant Rusty Morgan. "Hey, Sarge, can you give us a hand stopping that stolen ambulance. It's being driven by a deserter wanted for selling stolen gas, but be careful, 'cause this AWOL G.I. is known to carry a forty five and a grenade!"

The moment MP Sergeant Rusty Morgan called out, "Follow us," the MP Private sitting in the driver's seat put the Jeep in gear and drove off with the siren on. When another pair of U.S. Army MPs spotted the pursuit taking place, they joined in as well.

As soon as the American military police began their pursuit, a French policemen walking his beat with another gendarme, turned to his partner and said, "The Americans have turned Paris into Chicago."

As soon as Eddie Finch heard the siren and he looked in the side mirror, he felt a twinge a fear, when he realized that the military police were hot on his tail and closing fast. Within a few minutes of making his first delivery of the day, Eddie Finch had two MP Jeeps and a civilian car pursuing him and his stolen ambulance through Paris. The fact that he was carrying a stolen .45 caliber pistol and a hand-grenade would only add to his troubles, when the Army prosecuted him for deserting his post in time of war and being involved in the black-market. In order to prevent this from happening, Eddie Finch would have to make a clean getaway.

After driving down a very narrow side street, Eddie Finch saw his opportunity to escape, when he turned the stolen ambulance to the right and blocked the road. As soon as Corporal Finch jumped out of the vehicle, he took cover behind the front of the ambulance and opened fire with his forty five. The second several bullets struck the lead MP Jeep, the MP Private driving the vehicle instinctively turned the Jeep out of the line of fire and skidded to a stop. Immediately after MP Sergeant Rusty Morgan and his partner jumped out of their Jeep, they took cover behind their vehicle and returned fire with their .45 caliber Model 1911 pistols.

While bullets fired by the Army cops struck nearby, Eddie Finch had his pistol reloaded and emptied another seven rounds at the MPs as fast as he could pull the trigger. The exchange of gunfire became even more intense, when the MPs in the second Jeep, followed by the two CID Agents and Inspector Goulet, arrived on the scene and began firing at the deserter.

When 12 gauge pellets from Chris Jacko's Winchester shotgun hit Eddie Finch in his left ankle, the deserter knew that it was time for him to make his move, or end up in the stockade. After reloading his pistol with his last spare magazine, Eddie Finch fired three shots at his pursuers, before he slipped the forty five into his waistband and removed a hand-grenade from a side pocket on his field jacket. The fact that Finch kept a can of gasoline inside the cab, insured that once the grenade went off, the explosion would ignite every drop of fuel in the WC54. Once the stolen ambulance was engulfed in flames, Eddie Finch would be well on his way to making a successful escape.

Immediately after Eddie Finch pulled the pin, he tossed the grenade through the open driver's side door of the stolen Dodge ambulance, before he took off running. As soon as Agent Jacko spotted the deserter take off, he stood up behind the right front fender of the Citroen sedan and called out, "He's making a run for it. Let's go!"

Just as Chris Jacko started to run after the armed deserter, the cab of the ambulance exploded in a huge fireball that turned night into day. In the process of being blown off his feet, Agent Jacko sustained a few minor burns, a concussion and several shrapnel wounds. While the fuel cans in the back of the ambulance exploded and other MPs and French Gendarmes responded to the scene, Hank Blair and Inspector Goulet pulled Chris Jacko away from the inferno. Once they got Chris behind the Citroen sedan, Hank and Patrice knelt by his side and began to administer first aid to the wounded Army CID Agent.

Despite the fact that the burning ambulance was blocking the narrow side street, MP Sergeant Morgan began organizing the search for the armed deserter. After directing two Jeep loads of MPs to circle around the block, to try and cut off the deserter's escape, Sergeant Morgan jogged over to where Hank Blair was kneeling next to the wounded Army Agent and said, "As long as that burning ambulance is blocking the street, our options are limited, as far as going after that SOB."

While Hank continued to use his handkerchief to apply pressure on Chris Jacko's head wound, he looked up at MP Sergeant Morgan and said, "The good news is that my shotgun toting partner is sure he wounded AWOL Corporal Finch."

"That should slow the bastard down," responded MP Sergeant Morgan as he holstered his forty five.

The sound of two different types of sirens approaching the area brought Hank Blair to remark, "Here comes the fire department and one of our ambulances."

While Hank continued to apply pressure to the Sergeant Jacko's head wound, Inspector Goulet slipped a French Gauloises cigarette in between the wounded agent's lips. As soon as Inspector Goulet offered Chris a light, the veteran Paris Police Inspector remarked, "When I was wounded in the last war, one of our doctors offered me a Gauloises and told me that a strong

French cigarette would help me forget about the pain. Unfortunately, my friend, it did not work, but I appreciated the gesture."

Patrice Goulet got the reaction that he was looking for, when Chris cracked a smile as he removed the French cigarette from his lips and said, "You're right, Patrice. It doesn't do shit for the pain, but you made me smile and right now that's almost as good as a shot of morphine."

"That's what friends are for," responded Patrice, before he used an American Zippo lighter to light one of his own cigarettes.

As soon as Paris firefighters arrived to extinguish the vehicle fire, Hank looked at the injured CID Agent and said, "Hang on Chris. The ambulance just turned the corner."

While an American military policeman and a uniformed Paris cop held back a small crowd of local residents, the driver of the U.S. Army ambulance shut off the siren, once his vehicle arrived on scene. As soon as the ambulance came to a stop, an Army medic jumped out and applied sulfur powder to the CID Agent's head wound.

While the fire was being extinguished, MP Sergeant Rusty Morgan looked down at Hank Blair and said, "As soon as the fire is under control, I'll get some men ready to conduct a foot search of the area."

While an Army medic finished bandaging Chris Jacko's head wound, Hank stood up and thanked the MP Sergeant, as he reached into his coat pocket and removed a photograph of AWOL Corporal Finch. After handing the official Army photograph to MP Sergeant Rusty Morgan, the senior CID Agent at the scene continued and said, "In the meantime, Sarge, do me a favor and show this photograph of AWOL Corporal Finch, to every MP and Paris cop who is available to go with us, when we search this neighborhood. Inspector Goulet and I will join you in a minute."

As soon as MP Sergeant Morgan remarked, "Will do," he walked over to the MPs and French gendarmes who were securing the crime scene. While MP Sergeant Morgan showed the other MPs and the French policemen the photograph, Hank Blair and Patrice Goulet walked behind the Army medic, as he helped Chris Jacko into the back of the ambulance.

After Hank closed the back doors and he hit a door twice with a closed fist, the ambulance left the scene, just as the Paris firemen finished putting the vehicle fire out. With their guns drawn and held at the ready, CID

Agent Hank Blair, Inspector Patrice Goulet and Sergeant Rusty Morgan led a mixed contingent of Allied MPs and Paris Policemen on a foot search of the area.

Chief Inspector Francois Dumont of the Paris Police was born in 1895 and served in the French Army during World War 1. After the war, the highly decorated soldier returned to Paris, where he immediately followed in his father's footsteps and became a policeman. Because he came from a family of policemen, that included his father, grandfather, several uncles, brothers and cousins, Francois was well cared for and protected during his career. The fact that he had a large number of family members and friends serving as French cops, came in handy when the Germans occupied France in 1940 and various resistance units began to form.

Unlike other French Policemen who went along with the German occupation, Francois Dumont, along with his family members and friends, risked their lives to resist the enemy in every way possible. Even his daughter Michelle served in the resistance in and around the City of Paris. The fact that Michelle worked as a secretary for the Vichy appointed Prefecture of Police, also gave her direct access to information that proved to be very useful to the freedom fighters of France.

After meeting with Sergeant Cal Parker in a safe location, Major Tom Savino and Chief Inspector Francois Dumont responded to the crime scene, in time to see the remains of the destroyed ambulance being taken away. As soon as Major Savino pulled over and parked the CID staff car, he spoke as he opened his map case and pointed to the section of Paris, where the search for Corporal Finch was taking place. "We've been through this neighborhood a dozen times and there's still no sign of AWOL Corporal Eddie Finch." Then, after brief pause, the second in command of the Paris CID Office remarked, "Where the hell can this guy be?"

When the Chief Inspector responded he faced Major Savino and said,

"Even though our men do not believe that Corporal Finch was seriously wounded, he will still need medical care. Finch will also likely walk with a limp for some time, which should make it easier for us to find him, once he leaves wherever he is hiding."

After closing his map case, Major Savino continued and said, "This is a real mess, Francois. These AWOL G.I.s, who are involved in the black market, are operating in Paris, like the gangsters did in the states during the roaring twenties."

"That is the reason why they are rightly referred to as G.I. Gangsters," responded Francois.

"That name fits them well," remarked Major Savino.

In an effort to shed a more positive light on the current conversation, Francois responded and said, "Hopefully, we will hear more from Sergeant Parker. After all, it has only been 24 hours, since he recruited Corporal Greene to work for us."

"You're right, Francois. We can't rush these things," said Major Savino, who quickly added, "As my father always said, "If it's meant to be, it will happen."

"I agree," responded the Chief Inspector.

After arriving in time to see the destroyed ambulance removed from the crime scene, Major Savino put the staff car in gear and prepared to drive past the side street where the shootout took place. As an American MP stopped traffic, so the CID car could proceed, Major Savino waved to the military policeman, as he and the Chief Inspector headed over to their next stop.

After checking his watch, the Chief Inspector, turned toward the Major and said, "As soon as we get to Gabby's place, we can call the office and check on the status of our manhunt. Once that's done, we can finally have some breakfast."

"Next stop, The Paris Cafe," responded the Major.

The day Benny Greene explained why he returned to the warehouse, with his truck still loaded with stolen government property, AWOL

Sergeant Harry Moffett accepted his explanation and was happy to hear, that the only colored driver in his gang wasn't arrested. Moffett was twice as grateful that nothing happened to his truckload of stolen cigarettes. After hearing Benny's initial report of what transpired, Moffett asked Benny if he new anything about the soldier, who warned him that the military police were coming his way?

"Yes I do, Sarge," responded Benny, who quickly added, "He's a colored boy like me, so I hope you don't mind that I gave him a ride to a cafe, where he was gonna meet a French girl that he's sweet on. He met her when he got a pass from a friendly doctor in one of them convalescent hospitals. The day he warned me about them MPs, he just left the hospital on his last three day pass, before the Army plans to send him back to his unit. That means he has to decide real quick, if he's gonna go AWOL, or go back on the line." Then, after pausing for a split second, Benny did exactly like he was told and added, "Between you and me, Sarge, I don't think he's going back."

Under the circumstances, Moffett wanted to know more and wasted no time in asking, "What unit is this G.I. from?"

When Benny responded he repeated everything that Cal Parker told him to say. "He's from one of them colored tank units. He got two Shermans shot out from under him in one day and the damn Army sent him back into combat in a third tank, that was just patched up after its crew was killed. He said you could still smell the dead bodies of the crew that died inside that tank, even though the maintenance boys repainted the inside of that Sherman. The Army really pissed him off, when they put him in charge of a crew that ain't never been inside a tank before."[1] Then, after pausing for a split second, Benny added, "Sure enough...within twenty four hours, everyone in his crew was either dead or wounded, after they ran into one of them bigger Kraut tanks. Even my buddy ended up in a hospital in Paris, after he was thrown out of what was left of his tank."

After lighting a Lucky Strike cigarette, Moffett asked Benny what this tank commander's name was. Without hesitating, Benny responded and said, "Sergeant Andy Carter, but he told me his friends call him Doc, 'cause he's real good at fixing cars and trucks."

Because they were swamped with orders to fill, Sergeant Moffett told Bennie to get back to work. As Bennie walked away, Moffett called out, "Are you sure this colored tank commander will be in Paris for three days?"

"That's what he told me, Sarge," responded Bennie.

"I think I should meet your friend and buy him a drink for helping us out," said Moffett, before he asked Bennie if he knew where they could find the tank commander who came to his rescue.

When Bennie responded he sounded as confident as ever when he said, "Doc said if I was in the neighborhood, I could find him in the cafe where I dropped him off. He said he plans to spend most of his time in Paris drinking wine, in the cafe where his girlfriend works as a waitress." Then, after a split second pause, Benny did his best to sound as polite as possible when he said, "Excuse me for asking, Sarge, but would you mind if I brought my buddy a few cartons of smokes, that he could sell to raise some extra cash while he's on leave. I'm sure he'll need the money, if he decides to go AWOL."

After hearing what Bennie Greene had to say, Moffett remarked, "If we get all our work done today, we can meet your friend tomorrow. Instead of giving him cigarettes to sell, I'll give him a cash reward, for coming to your rescue and saving an entire truckload of smokes from being seized by the MPs. If I like what he has to say, I'll also invite him to join us. If he agrees, he can tag along with you, until he's good enough to go out on his own."

When Benny Greene woke up the next day, he was hoping that Moffett was still interested in meeting the soldier, who warned him that the military police were coming his way. After hearing the morning news, about the manhunt for an AWOL soldier who got into a shootout with MPs, Harry Moffett approached Benny, while he was drinking his morning coffee and said, "As soon as you clean this place up, I want you to go to that cafe and find your friend. If he's there, call me and I'll swing by."

Even if Harry Moffett never asked to meet Cal Parker aka Andrew Doc Carter, a team of CID Agents and plainclothes Paris Police Inspectors were assigned to follow Benny Greene, back to the garage that the Moffett gang used as their base of operations. As important as this investigation was to Army CID, Chief Inspector Dumont also had a personal interest in this case, because the American deserters that Benny Greene worked with, were associated with two brothers who collaborated with the enemy during the occupation of France. The worst of the two brothers was a Frenchman by the name of Pierre Mollet.

In order to further this joint investigation, Chief Inspector Dumont allowed his daughter Michelle to work undercover and act as Sergeant Parker's French girlfriend. Doing so, allowed Sergeant Parker to relay information to Army CID via the Chief Inspector, without raising any suspicion. This would be especially critical, if and when Sergeant Parker was contacted by the AWOL former supply sergeant identified as Harry Moffett.

Chief Inspector Dumont allowed his daughter to serve in this capacity, because Michelle was no stranger to danger, after having served in the resistance and in the fighting to liberate Paris in August of 1944. The Chief Inspector also saw the way Sergeant Parker and his daughter Michelle looked at each other, when the young agent was introduced to his undercover girlfriend. As far as Francois was concerned, this exchange was reminiscent of the way, that he and his wife Annette looked at each other when they first met. The fact that CID Agent Calvin Parker was a Negro also did not concern Francois, or anyone else in his family.

In addition to worrying about one of his agents working in an undercover capacity, Major Tommy Savino wondered how Cal's father would react, when he learned that his son was in harm's way. As soon as he parked the CID staff car, by the back entrance to The Paris Cafe, Major Savino remarked, "It's gonna be another long day, Francois,"

As soon as Major Savino and the Chief Inspector exited the staff car, Francois responded as he walked toward the trunk. "As my father used to say, "It's better for policemen to be busy than bored."

"Wise words from an experienced member of the French Surete," said the Major, as he opened the trunk and removed a wooden crate, that was filled with items from the commissary and the Post Exchange (PX). By the time Francois removed another wooden crate filled with canned food and tobacco products, his brother-in-law Gabby Allaire opened the door and held it open as he said, "You two must be hungry and in need of some hot coffee, after searching Paris for another troublemaker."

"You said it, Gabby," remarked Major Savino, as he followed Francois into the warm kitchen as he said, "But first we have to finish delivering a trunk full of supplies, to our home away from home in Paris." With help from Gabby, Major Savino and the Chief Inspector unloaded the rest of the supplies from the trunk of the CID staff car. Once the highly sought after food products and other supplies were brought into the kitchen, a grateful Gabby Allaire, invited Francois and Tom to have a seat, while he made them a breakfast, that would enable them to get through another busy day.

While serving in the Invasion of Normandy, France, Corporal Charlie Monacco was promoted to the rank of sergeant, after he led the men in his reconnaissance unit through a well defended German position. Even though he had a promising career as a soldier, the ex-con from Connecticut lost his stripes, when he had a run in with a young lieutenant, who should have never been given a combat command.

Charlie Monacco's sergeant stripes were returned, when the same officer that he had a run in with, froze again in combat and caused his squad to sustain additional casualties. When nothing happened to this Army officer, who was shipped off to a post in England, Charlie Monacco took a major hit in the morale department. Good men were dead and wounded because an incompetent officer was allowed to serve in combat. To make matters worse, it was well known, that this officer's father was a general, who was determined to have a son, who was just as decorated as he was.

In a way, it wasn't this young officer's fault, that he was forced to accept a transfer to duties that he had no interest in performing. The simple truth was, that this young Army officer, who spoke fluent French and German, was better suited to perform the duties of an intelligence officer. When his father intervened and got his son a combat command, the young officer became a nervous wreck, because he knew that he would never be able to live up to his father's expectations. Everything from that point on was downhill all the way.

After this incident, Charlie Monacco became a disgruntled non-commissioned officer, who decided to take care of himself and his closest Army buddies. When Charlie began to make this transformation to being a non conformist, he reverted back to a life that involved cutting corners and taking advantage of the system. He took this course of action, because unlike the young officer who proved to be unfit for a combat command, Charlie Monacco didn't have a father who could protect him when and if he screwed up.

While fighting in the Bocage Country, Sergeant Charlie Monacco and the men in his unit were earning more than their Army pay, by stripping dead and captured Germans of everything of value and selling enemy weapons, medals, bayonets, helmets, flags, watches and rings to rear area support troops. The ex con from Connecticut really hit pay dirt, when he turned his squad of riflemen into a scavenging band of G.I.s and filled two M3 Half Tracks and three GMC trucks with the contents of a captured German supply dump. The fact that this raid also led to the recovery of twenty cases of French champagne, eight cases of French cognac, six cases of wine, medical supplies, numerous war souvenirs and a large supply of French cheese, added to the value of the recovered valuables.

Charlie Monacco made the connection of a lifetime, when he met an Army Air Forces Liaison Pilot, who agreed to broker the sale of the entire load of war trophies and a good portion of the captured liquor, to a troop carrier squadron that was based in England. The day a U.S. Army C47 landed in an open field in France, the Liaison Pilot was on hand to take his cut, when the representatives of the troop carrier squadron paid for the planeload of captured supplies and equipment. In addition to receiving a partial payment in Allied Military Currency, known as Invasion Notes, Charlie and his men received ten cartons of hard to get premium brand cigarettes, two leather flight jackets and several bottles of scotch. As far as the Army aviators were concerned, this was an especially cheap price to pay for a planeload of captured German pistols, rifles, bayonets, helmets and other war souvenirs. The fact that this trading material didn't cost Charlie and his any money, meant that everything of value that they received in return was pure profit.

Immediately after watching the C47 take off, the Army Liaison Pilot told Charlie to let him know when he had more merchandise to sell. Now that their business was concluded, the Liaison Pilot started the Piper Cub's engine and took off to fly an artillery spotting mission.

While splitting the proceeds with his men, Charlie began to think of other ways to make money, while he served as an American soldier in the European Theater of Operations. Charlie solidified his plans, when he sustained multiple shrapnel wounds in his right leg while fighting in France. After getting an infection, that resulted in a high fever, Charlie underwent a second surgery that extended his stay in an army field hospital.

While recovering in the 4th Convalescent Hospital in Senoches, France, Sergeant Monacco decided to go AWOL in late October of 1944.[2] Even though Charlie wasn't fully recovered, he decided to join four other G.I.s, who recovered from their wounds and were tired of waiting for the U.S. Army to provide transportation back to their units, or to a Replacement Depot. One of the reasons Charlie and the other men went AWOL, was because many believed that the Germans were finished and the war would be over by Christmas.

Before traveling to Paris, Charlie stocked up on cigarettes and stole a stack of leave slips, that could be easily forged to prevent being picked up by the military police. All four of the soldiers who went AWOL with Charlie, remained with him and became the core group of soldiers, who helped him build a successful black market operation.

After stealing a Dodge WC54 ambulance, Sergeant Monacco and four other AWOL G.I.s drove to the destroyed farmhouse, where Charlie and the men in his old unit stopped for the night, before they continued fighting the retreating Germans in France. While using a pick and a shovel, Charlie recovered several items of value, that he buried before heading back into combat. These items included, bottles of liquor and a number of .50 caliber metal ammo cans, that contained captured war souvenirs. Inside these cans were a Remington Model 1911 .45 caliber pistol, eight captured German pistols with holsters and spare magazines, several boxes of ammunition, a German flag and various pieces of jewelry that Charlie took from dead Germans. Charlie also found the French painting that he liberated from the Germans, that was carefully wrapped in two rain coats.

Thanks to one of the men he went AWOL with, Charlie learned how easy it was to obtain fuel that was otherwise thought to be difficult to obtain. After being briefed by Private George Zangolas, Charlie told his men to wait behind a long line of parked U.S. Army trucks, while he went to meet the non commissioned officer in charge of the local Petroleum Oil and Lubrication (POL) dump.

The day that Sergeant Monacco met Master Sergeant Clyde C. Nelson, the two men became instant business associates. Charlie facilitated this arrangement, when he handed the senior non commissioned officer an unloaded 9mm German Luger pistol and said, "A buddy of mine by the name of George Zangolas asked me to stop by and say hi."

When Master Sergeant Nelson repeated the name George Zangolas, as if he was trying to recall if he remembered meeting this soldier, Charlie remarked, "I understand if you can't remember, George. A lot'a guys must come through here to get gassed up."

"You're right about that," responded the Master Sergeant.

As Charlie continued, he handed the senior NCO in charge of the Petroleum Oil and Lubrication (POL) Dump a black leather clam shell German Luger holster that contained a spare magazine. "The main thing, Sarge, is that me and my buddies wanted you to have this, because you and your men make it possible for us to fight the Krauts."

While Master Sergeant Nelson continued to admire the captured pistol, Charlie Monacco asked if the Army was still refueling vehicles and five gallon Jerry cans without a written request to do so. After thanking Charlie for the highly sought after war trophy, Master Sergeant Nelson slid the pistol back into the holster and answered the question in a friendly tone of voice. "Well, Sarge, it's like this. The situation has changed since you and your buddies were driving the Krauts back to the Fatherland after we landed in France. Back then the fighting was so intense, our troops didn't have the time to fill out requisition forms."

After placing the holster containing the Luger on the front seat of his Jeep, Master Sergeant Nelson paused long enough to bite a piece off a plug of chewing tobacco, before he continued and said, "Now that the situation has calmed down a bit, I need a written request signed by an officer to hand out fuel, engine oil and lubricants."

"I was just curious what the rules were, because I just got out'a the hospital after being wounded," remarked Charlie.

After Master Sergeant Nelson casually looked around, he paused long enough to spit some tobacco juice on the ground, before he faced Charlie Monacco and said, "However, since I can't be expected to know the name of every officer in this man's Army, I'll be obligated to give you all the gas you request, when you present me with the proper paperwork."

Charlie made an even better friend out of the senior NCO, when he motioned him over to the back of the vehicle. While Charlie walked with an obvious limp due to his wounded leg, he opened the double barn doors, leaned inside and removed a Nazi flag, that was draped over a wooden crate filled with liquor bottles. After handing the enemy flag to the senior NCO, Charlie remarked, "You'd be doing me a favor, Sarge, if you take this booze off my hands, 'cause me and my men have more than we can drink and can always get more. As far as that Nazi flag goes, I'm sure you have a place back home, where you can hang this Swastika."

After admiring the captured flag, Master Sergeant Nelson remarked, "You're no ambulance driver."

"No I'm not, Sarge," responded Charlie, who went on to explain how he got tired of limping around a convalescent hospital while he recovered from shrapnel wounds in his leg. When Charlie continued he said, "As far as my four buddies are concerned, they got tired of waiting around the same hospital, for the Army to return them to their old units, or to the repo depo. Besides, the way we hear it, the war is supposed to be over by Christmas." [3]

As Charlie continued, he sounded like a man who was dead sure of himself when he said, "Since the Army doesn't seem to be in a hurry to send my buddies back into combat, they decided to see the sights in Paris, while our Uncle Sam gets his act together. When I heard what they were planning to do, I figured I'd go with 'em. I also plan on making some dough while I'm on vacation. If you're interested, I'd like to cut you in for a piece of the action. If not, you'll never see me again."

After spitting another mouthful of tobacco juice off to his left, Master Sergeant Thompson extended his hand and said, "I'll fill every vehicle and Jerry can that you bring me, as long as you treat me right."

As Charlie shook hands with the Master Sergeant at the POL Depot, he introduced himself before he continued and said, "Once you take that box out of the back, I'll introduce you to the rest of my men."

Immediately after Master Sergeant Nelson stashed the box containing the liquor and the Nazi flag in the back of his Jeep, he walked Charlie over to the driver's side of the ambulance. When Charlie opened the door and started to get inside, the senior NCO remarked, "By the time you come back I'll have a stack of requisition forms that you can take with you. All you'll need then is some Jerry cans and a truck and you'll be in business, because fuel is selling like hotcakes on the black market. I can start you off with four cans, but you'll have to get the rest on your own. I'll also top off your ambulance."

★ ★ ★

After Private Zangolas, Private Smith, Private Badger and Private Owen met with Master Sergeant Nelson, Charlie and his AWOL buddies drove to Paris. Once they arrived, they raised the capitol they needed to live life on the run and go into business, by selling Charlie Monacco's supply of captured German pistols to rear area soldiers on leave. Charlie also raised some additional cash by selling the jewelry that he took from dead Germans. Later that day, Charlie met the owner of a Parisian cafe by the name of Raymond La Salle. Instead of waiting to sell their supply of stolen gasoline for the full market value of $20 dollars a gallon, or $100 dollars for five gallons, Charlie accepted $70 dollars a can from La Salle, providing that he purchased all four cans.

Raymond La Salle proved to be an excellent contact in Paris, who was actively involved in black market operations. With help from La Salle, Charlie and his men were well fed and given a place to stay. Two days later, La Salle arranged for Charlie and his men to rent a garage, that was large enough to accommodate their living quarters, a decent size storage area and several stolen vehicles.

After delivering Master Sergeant Nelson his cut for the fuel, four more Jerry cans were topped off and immediately sold to La Salle. Even though this type of vehicle couldn't carry as much as a cargo truck, Charlie and his men learned early on, that the MPs in Paris rarely if ever paid attention to a Dodge ambulance. As a result, their stolen WC54 proved to be the ideal vehicle to use, to make some of their smaller deliveries.

After a week of working together, La Salle introduced Charlie Monacco to a man by the name Marcel Badeau. Marcel was a former French policeman and famous resistance fighter, who was now devoted to making a fortune on the black market. Once they joined forces, Marcel and his men, along with Charlie Monacco and his gang of AWOL G.I.s, stole two U.S. Army GMC trucks and a dozen Jerry cans. Next came their first truckload of Army rations, a Jeep and another Jerry can. Business was good, very good.

In early 1945, Charlie Monacco and his fellow AWOL American soldiers, in conjunction with the French thieves that they fell in with, were making money hand over fist on the black market. While Charlie and his men were responsible for stealing the most sought after government property, Marcel Badeau and his men were responsible for selling this merchandise on the streets of Paris and splitting the profits with their American partners. Maintaining this arrangement, enabled Charlie and his men to avoid the additional risks of getting arrested, during the delivery phase of their black market activities.

Once they started working together, it also became clear, that Charlie and Marcel had a shared hatred for the American deserter known as Harry Moffett and his French partner, a man who collaborated with the Germans during the occupation of France. Even Pierre Mollet's brother Antone was a well documented collaborator, who remained heavily involved in black market activities after the Allies landed in Normandy and liberated Paris.

The fact that the Mollet brothers were wanted by French authorities did not deter them from remaining in Paris. One reason for this, was because in 1944 and 1945 Paris had become a city that was filled with thousands of deserters and criminals of all kind. If several thousand military and civilian policemen were unable to cope with the widespread problem of desertion, the black market and other criminal behavior, how could they be expected to find two French fugitives, in a city that was filled with its fair share of wanted men.

After hearing Marcel talk about his hatred for the Mollet brothers, Charlie decided to locate Antone Mollet as a favor for his friend and business associate. Charlie decided to locate the younger of the Mollet brothers, because Pierre was considerably more well known and feared by many. Rather than risk failing in his mission, Charlie and AWOL Private George Zangolas decided to go after the easier of the two targets.

While meeting with Marcel in his warehouse office, Charlie reached into his shirt pocket and removed a slip of paper. As the AWOL American Army Sergeant handed the handwritten note to Marcel, he spoke in a friendly tone of voice when he said, "I guess now is a good'a time as any to give this to you. Consider this a belated Christmas gift."

After reading the note Marcel seemed a bit confused when he looked at Charlie and said, "This is an address in the Latin Quarter."

"A very special address," remarked Charlie, who continued in a matter of fact tone of voice as he pointed to the note. "Hold onto your hat, Marcel, because I have some good news for you and your band of former resistance fighters."

While Charlie saw that he had Marcel's undivided attention, he continued and said, "After listening to you go on and on about how much you and your resistance buddies want a piece of Pierre Mollet's ass and another piece of his brother's rear end, I decided to find the big prick's little brother, as a favor to my French Allies. I figured, if you kept an eye on Antone Mollet, he would eventually lead you to his older brother. Once you take care of Pierre Mollet, that fat slob Harry Moffett will lose his big bad French thief for a partner. Even losing Antone Mollet would cripple a good portion of Moffett's ability to operate. The day that happens we'll both have something to celebrate."

"Are you sure you found Antone Mollet?" asked Marcel.

While speaking in a very confident tone of voice, Charlie responded as he pointed to the note that Marcel held in his right hand. "If you're looking for a short guy with jet black hair, who's missing the tip of his left index finger and looks like the guy in the picture you showed me, you'll find him at that address. Also, be advised, that when me and George found Collaborator Number Two, he was with three other French guys who look about as legit as we do, so be careful."

Marcel was still shocked and remarked, "You found Antone Mollet?"

While Charlie responded to Marcel's last comment, he acted as if what he accomplished was no big deal. "I don't know why you seem so shocked? All it cost us was a hundred gallons of gasoline and ten cartons of American cigarettes to find the little prick. As tempted as we were to bring him back here to meet you in person, we figured you and your men would prefer to keep an eye on little Antone, so he can lead you to his big brother."

As Marcel held up the handwritten note, he never sounded more sincere when he looked at Charlie and said, "I owe you more than you know, my friend."

It took Marcel and his good friend Charles Garnier less than two hours to confirm, that Charlie Monacco and George Zangolas located Antone Mollet at an address in the Latin Quarter. After calling eight of their men into the area, a twenty four hour watch was placed on the location where Antone was residing.

As fifteen year veterans of the Paris Police, who went on to serve in a more frontline capacity after the German invasion of France, Marcel Badeau and Charles Garnier were also familiar with two of the three French criminals, who were now involved with Antone Mollet. Since a great deal was at stake, Marcel decided to remain with his men and personally supervise the surveillance operation.

"Can you believe this turn of events?" said Marcel as he faced Charles Garnier, while they kept an eye on Antone Mollet's new hideout.

"Joining forces with the American deserters has worked out better than we expected," responded Charles Garnier, as he continued observing the location that they had under surveillance.

"Yes, it has," said Marcel, who quickly added, "Once we find Pierre Mollet and the men who served with him in the Milice, we will have our revenge."

CHAPTER 2

A LONG NIGHT IN PARIS

Eddie Finch was lucky that he made his way into the basement of Raymond La Salle's corner bar, where he and the other members of the Charlie Monacco gang often hung out, without being spotted by the military, or civilian police. Clearly, had his escape taken place during a different time of day, this would not have been possible.

In addition to being excellent customers, Eddie Finch and the other members of his gang, made sure that the owner of this bar was well supplied with stolen American cigarettes, food and gasoline. Even when two U.S. Army Military Policemen entered his establishment, Raymond La Salle remained as cordial as any other Frenchman, who preferred to have American troops in Paris, as opposed to the Germans.

After offering the two military policemen something to eat and drink, Raymond La Salle reacted in the appropriate fashion, when he was asked if he had seen a wounded G.I. with an obvious limp, or if he knew an AWOL American Corporal by the name of Eddie Finch. As soon as La Salle shrugged his shoulders and shook his head from left to right, he put on a good show when he responded and said, "No, Monsieur, I have not seen an American who is limping at this hour and I do not know this man you call Finch, but if I see your wounded Corporal I will call the police."

Even if the Allied military police wanted to conduct a more thorough search of the premises, Raymond La Salle was able to behave as if he had nothing to worry about, because the wounded deserter was hiding in the false wall behind his wine cellar. La Salle was able to maintain this level of confidence, because the Germans never located this false wall, when he worked with the resistance and he smuggled black market items into Paris during the occupation.

After passing on another offer of having something to eat and drink, the two military policemen left the corner bar and continued their search of the neighborhood. As tempted as he was to let Eddie Finch out of the secret room, La Salle chose to call the French girl who lived with Charlie Monacco, to get a message to the man in charge, that one of his men was wounded and in hiding. -

The last thing that Charlie Monacco wanted to hear, was that Eddie Finch was on the run, after he shot at four U.S. Army MPs, two CID Agents and a Paris cop, before he blew up a Dodge 4x4 ambulance that was loaded with stolen gasoline. The fact that Eddie Finch was wounded and in need of medical attention complicated this already messy situation even more.

As soon as Paulette contacted Charlie by phone, he made arrangements to have Eddie patched up by the AWOL medic who was a member of their gang. In order to make this possible, the AWOL medic known as Doc Peterson, wore civilian clothes when he went to care for the pistol packing grenade throwing deserter.

After filling a small suitcase with medical supplies and a change of clothes for Eddie Finch, Doc Peterson left the warehouse dressed like a Frenchman and headed over to La Salle's bar. As soon as the AWOL medic left the warehouse, that they used as their headquarters, Charlie Monacco opened a carton of Lucky Strike cigarettes and removed a pack while he considered his options.

After removing a Lucky Strike from the pack, Charlie used his Zippo to light the unfiltered cigarette, while he considered the trouble that this incident would cause for him and his men. As Charlie exhaled a long plume of cigarette smoke, he regretted the day that he let greed get the best of him, when he allowed Eddie Finch to join his gang. While Charlie continued to smoke his cigarette, he remembered the day when Finch showed up at his warehouse and he explained that he had a falling out with Harry Moffett and was looking for a new place to hang his hat. Instead of sending Finch on his way, Charlie transformed into a typical G.I. Gangster, when he pointed to the stolen Army truck and said, "Does the truck and whatever you have in it come with the deal if I bring you in?"

After Eddie Finch motioned Charlie to follow him to the back of the truck, he dropped the tailgate and pulled back the canvass top, to show that the deuce and a half was filled with crates of stolen premium brand American cigarettes. While Charlie looked inside the truck, Eddie remarked, "The truck is yours, as long as we split the value of the smokes, that we can sell on the streets of Paris for two bucks a pack."

As Charlie offered his new driver a Lucky Strike cigarette, he spoke as he admired the deuce and a half that was in very good condition and said, "Forget about selling smokes by the carton or the pack. I got a French partner who'll take the entire load off our hands, as long as we give him a break on the price. This way, we make a few bucks less, but we don't have to risk getting caught selling stolen cigarettes, off the back of the stolen Army truck to French civilians."

After shaking hands and agreeing to the terms of their working relationship, Charlie pointed to his warehouse and said, "Once you get your rig inside, I'll introduce you to the boys." As soon as Eddie Finch went to get into the cab of his truck, Charlie grabbed him by the arm and said, "One more thing. All bets are off, if I find out that you're still carrying a forty five and a fucking hand-grenade. The Frenchmen we're in business with are all former members of the resistance and take care of security. All we do is liberate government property and deliver it to our French partners. That doesn't mean that we don't keep some hardware around, in case we have to do battle with the competition. It means, I'll tell you when you need to carry a gun. If you don't like that deal, you can go back to work for Harry Moffett, or go out on your own. The choice is yours."

Even though Eddie Finch had no intentions of following Charlie Monacco's instructions, he did his best to sound sincere when he responded and said, "OK, Sarge, I'll stash the pistol and the grenade."

After hearing Eddie Finch agree to his terms, Charlie pointed to the open door to his warehouse and said, "Put your truck in the barn."

While Charlie watched Eddie Finch handle the deuce and a half as if it was a midget racer, he was equally impressed that his new driver came bearing gifts, when he asked to join his gang. The fact that Finch stole a truckload of stolen cigarettes from an overweight rear area slob like Harry

Moffett, also appealed to Charlie. Charlie also hated Moffett's French partner, because it was well known that he collaborated with the Germans during the occupation of France. Harry Moffett's French partner also had a brother who was easy to dislike with a passion.

While it was true that Eddie Finch had a screw lose and should have been sent home as a psycho, Charlie knew that his new driver was an experienced crook, who managed to avoid getting picked up by the MPs, while working on the black market for several months. The fact that Finch was a former Quarter Master Company truck driver, who knew his way around Paris and the surrounding area, was another reason to bring him into his organization. Charlie felt this way, because the rest of his men were frontline combat troops, who either went AWOL from hospitals or overstayed their leaves in Paris.

As Charlie crushed the remains of his cigarette butt out in a nearby ashtray, he stopped thinking about the past and focused on the situation at hand. While blowing up a stolen Army ambulance, that was filled with cans of stolen Army gasoline would be front page news, getting into a shootout with Army cops and being responsible for sending a CID Agent to the hospital, was definitely bad for business. Even the local French Police had a reason to seek revenge, because Finch also shot at one of their men as well.

Charlie also knew that the word was out, that a new commanding officer was on his way to take command of the CID Office in Paris. This rumor turned into a well publicized fact, when Yank Magazine and The Stars and Stripes Newspaper published articles, about the highly decorated Lt. Colonel James Beauregard and other members of his staff, including his executive officer and the Negro First Lieutenant, who would serve as the CID Liaison Officer to the French Police.

These articles served as a warning to U.S. Army personnel, that CID was beefing up its efforts to effectively deal with the problem of desertion, the black market and other criminal activity in France. As far as Charlie Monacco was concerned, any Army cops who pursued two fugitives from New York City to Europe and successfully engaged a German SS unit in order to make an arrest, would have no problem tearing Paris apart, to arrest G.I.s who were committing crimes in France.

Now that the military and civilian authorities started a massive search to locate Eddie Finch, Charlie decided that it was time for him to face the fact, that his days as an AWOL G.I. were numbered. Even though he was only in business for a few months, Charlie Monacco made enough money to live quite well, for a man who was Absent Without Leave from the U.S. Army. This included, living in first class accommodations, while eating the best food available, having access to a fully stocked bar, a closet full of custom made suits and a black Mercedes Benz sedan. Charlie also had an exclusive relationship with a beautiful French girl. The fact that he took care of her immediate family, which included employing her younger brother, further cemented their relationship.

When his girlfriend Paulette entered the warehouse using her key, Charlie remarked, "Give it to me straight, baby."

As Paulette put her black leather Hermes handbag on the corner of the desk where Charlie was standing, she spoke with a sense of urgency in voice when she said, "Peterson just arrived at La Salle's cafe and is taking care of Eddie in the secret room behind the wine cellar. The military police came by once, but left after asking a few questions. A few minutes ago two gendarmes were posted on the corner. This will make it harder for us to bring Eddie from the basement until they move on."

When Charlie asked how bad Eddie was hurt, Paulette responded and said, "He was shot in the ankle. Peterson said Eddie will need time to heal before he can walk without a limp." The next time she spoke she snuggled up to her lover and said, "There is something else that you must know." As Charlie looked at the young French girl, who was four years younger than he was, she went on to say, "Marcel told me that the MPs and the Paris Police know all about Eddie Finch and that he works for you."

While Charlie looked out of the open office door into the warehouse, he wondered if it was all worth it. Even though Charlie was in possession of a warehouse that was filled to the brim with crates of stolen Army property, including a fleet of stolen Army vehicles, he would trade it all for an honorable discharge and the ability to live happily ever after in France with Paulette.

After offering Paulette a cigarette, Charlie took one for himself before he offered her a light. As soon as he put the end of his Lucky Strike into the flame, he took a long drag and spoke as he snapped his lighter closed and slipped the Zippo into his pant's pocket. "The MPs and the Paris cops will likely make our lives miserable for a while. That means we need to lay low. Tell the men I want everyone to take some time off with pay until they hear from me."

Just as Paulette started to leave the warehouse office, Charlie spoke up and said, "Before the men leave I want every truck loaded to the gills. I also want you to call Marcel and ask him to meet me here later tonight."

As soon as AWOL Sergeant Harry Moffett arrived at the cafe, where Sergeant Andy Doc Carter liked to hang out, Benny Greene introduced his boss to the soldier who came to his rescue. "Doc, this is my boss, Sergeant Harry Moffett."

While Cal stood up to meet the subject of his investigation, Moffett appeared to be in good spirits when he extended his hand and said, "It's nice to meet you, Doc."

Once everyone took their seats, at a table in a quiet corner of the cafe, Benny Greene proved once again that he was a tremendous asset to Army CID, when he looked at Cal and said, "Sergeant Harry wants to thank you for warning me about those MPs."

"Don't mention it, Benny," responded Cal, who quickly added, "Cause I got no use for MPs, any more than I have for some of the officers in this man's Army."

So far, Harry Moffett liked what he was hearing. The former supply sergeant was even more impressed with Cal Parker, when the young CID Agent pretending to be a disgruntled tank commander, described what life was like fighting the Germans, in an armored unit that was filled with inexperienced crews and tanks, that were easily taken out of action, by more powerful Kraut weapons.

After hearing what Sergeant Andy Doc Carter had to say, Harry Moffett did his best to sound like a "Dutch uncle" when he said, "I know how you feel. You should'a seen the sad sacks the Army stuck me with when I landed in Normandy. Between our losses in North Africa and over in Italy, the Army started scrapping the bottle of the barrel, when they geared up for D

Day, but enough about my time in the service."

For someone who never worked undercover before, Cal Parker had no problem coming across like the genuine article. His cover story received the right amount of support, when Michelle Dumont delivered another bottle of French wine and an extra glass to the table. After Cal introduced his girlfriend to Sergeant Moffett, Michelle made sure that the black market operator noticed, the way she slid her hand across the back of Cal's neck, before she went back to work.

As soon Moffett raised his glass of whine and said, "The drinks are on me, boys. Cheers," Cal explained that he was torn between staying in Paris and going back to his old unit. Cal finished his remarks, when he pointed to the bar where Michelle was working and he said. "And she's the reason why I'm very tempted to stay in Paris."

After pausing long enough to sip some wine, Harry looked across the table at Cal and said, "I could use a good man like you, Doc. If you decide to come on board, I'd like you to work with Benny until you learn the ropes." When Moffett continued, he glanced over to where Michelle was tending bar and said, "Meaning no disrespect, Doc, but I'd go AWOL for her too."

To encourage the Negro tank commander to join his gang, Harry Moffett removed a thick bankroll from his pocket and peeled off a nice stack of French Francs. As Moffett handed the money to the man that he believed was a soldier by the name of Andy Doc Carter, the AWOL supply sergeant said, "This is for saving a truck load of very valuable merchandise and keeping Benny outta the stockade, but bear in mind, this is chicken feed, compared to how much you can make working for me." Then, after pausing to finish his wine, Harry Moffett spoke as he stood up in preparation of leaving. "Speak now, or forever hold your peace, Sergeant."

Cal Parker played his part just like the actor Jimmie Cagney did in gangster movies. As the undercover agent stood up, he tossed some French money on the table and put the rest of the cash in his right side pant's pocket as he said, "Mind if I say goodbye to my girl before we go?"

"Make it quick, Doc. Benny will be waiting for you out front. While he takes you back to your new home, I have some business to attend to," responded Harry Moffett as he stood facing his new recruit.

While two teams of CID Agents and Paris Police Inspectors followed

Harry Moffett, CID Agent Mike Mulligan and his French partner kept an eye on Cal Parker and Benny Greene. Just to be on the safe side, Inspector Goulet remained positioned across the street in a corner store, to protect the Chief Inspector's daughter. -

Because Eddie Finch was still a wanted man on the run, MPs, CID Agents, and their Paris Police counterparts were actively searching the city, for the pistol packing grenade throwing deserter. The military authorities were so aggressive in their tactics, that some G.I.s were stopped two and three times in one night, in order to confirm their identity.

In addition to the aggressive uniformed foot patrols, MPs in Jeeps pulled military vehicles over, to inspect the vehicles and determine if the occupants had a legitimate reason to be in Paris. Even the Paris Police were in on the search for the man who shot at American MPs, two CID Agents and Inspector Patrice Goulet, before he used a hand-grenade to blow up a stolen U.S. Army ambulance.

After searching Paris for several hours, the military police and Army CID had a dozen American soldiers in custody, who overstayed their leave by a few days, or had been AWOL for some time. In addition, MPs recovered two stolen Jeeps and a truck that was loaded with stolen Army rations and cigarettes.

CHAPTER 3

I'VE HAD ENOUGH

Marcel Badeau was a Parisian, who had no desire to serve as a policeman, in a city that was occupied by the Germans in 1940. As a result, at 37 years of age, the Paris Police Inspector found his duties far too distasteful to execute. This was especially the case, when some members of his department did the bidding of the Nazis and others did their best to keep the peace, while not overtly taking sides with the enemy.

Even though Marcel knew, that men like Francois Dumont were actively involved in resistance activities, he was determined to engage the enemy in the most violent fashion possible, even if he had to give up his police career to do so. As someone who had no love for communists, or the pro Nazi Vichy Government, Marcel Badeau left Paris and traveled to the countryside, to join one of the more aggressive resistance units. With the help of another like minded Paris policeman by the name of Charles Garnier, the fifteen year veteran of the Paris Police became a member of The Maquis.

Even when they were hunted by the German SS and the Milice, Marcel and Charles never wavered in their determination to rid France of its enemies. Because of their police experience, Marcel Badeau and Charles Garnier were asked to serve as resistance unit commanders. When they weren't executing raids and ambushes, with the precision of a well trained commando team, Marcel, Charles and the Maquisard fighters under their command, stole supplies and lived the life of wanted men. The night the Allies landed in Normandy, France, Marcel and his men were busier than ever killing Germans. The day Paris was liberated, Marcel and Charles were leading their men in fierce battles against the enemy in other parts of France.

After being inducted into the Armee Francaise, Marcel, Charles and some of their best men returned to Paris in late September of 1944. While serving under the French Army Intelligence Officer who commanded their resistance unit, Marcel and his men were given a new mission to perform. Their assignment was to serve in an undercover capacity and infiltrate the black market in order to achieve two goals. In addition to identifying Allied troops and French civilians who were involved in the theft and sale of stolen military supplies, Marcel and his men were to use their newly acquired underworld contacts, to locate certain enemies of France. Even though Marcel and his men preferred to serve in uniform and kill Germans, once the targets of their top secret mission were identified, they enthusiastically accepted the new assignment.

By the summer of 1944, the people of France, in particular the residents of Paris, were in dire need of the necessities of life and longed for the luxury items, that people had access to before the German occupation. The only entity that existed after the liberation of Paris, that was capable of providing the necessities of life and a number of sought after "luxury" items, was the United States Army. This situation existed, because the Americans were delivering massive quantities of supplies into France, that were just as desperately needed and sought after by French civilians, as they were needed by the Allied troops who were fighting the Germans. In fact, the amount of supplies that were being stockpiled in Allied supply dumps was so staggering, it seemed as if there was more than enough to go around. Unfortunately, certain active duty military personnel, as well as AWOL soldiers and French thieves, were stealing and selling enough government property on the black market, to cause a shortage of critical supplies, in areas where combat units were deployed.

After receiving a call from Paulette, Marcel arrived on time to meet privately with his American friend and business associate. When Charlie Monacco asked his French business partner not to say anything to Paulette, Marcel suspected that their conversation was about to get serious.

The fact that Charlie hated the AWOL American black market operator, who was in business with the main target of Marcel's intelligence operation, made it possible for French Intelligence to "allow" Sergeant Monacco and his men to continue to operate. This was done for several reasons, including because French Army Intelligence knew, that rival groups of black market operators were known to do battle from time to time, to protect their territory. If this happened, French Intelligence wanted to be present, when AWOL Sergeant Monacco and his gang clashed with the gang that was run by AWOL Sergeant Harry Moffett and the collaborator Pierre Mollet.

Charlie Monacco was also an unwitting provider of reliable intelligence information, about other black market operators, who were actively working throughout France. The AWOL American Sergeant really proved to be a valuable asset, when he located Antone Mollet and three French criminals who served as truck drivers for his black market operation. Even though Marcel and his men had not yet located Pierre Mollet, they were confident that the day would come, when Antone Mollet would lead them to his older brother. They came closer to achieving this goal, when Marcel and his men followed Antone Mollet to a garage, that was a long walk from his apartment.

The day Marcel and his men started watching this location, they were elated and surprised to see Gregorie Petit and Benard Allard drive a Citroen delivery van out of the garage and wait until Antone Mollet secured the door before getting into the vehicle. When the delivery van drove away, Marcel signaled his men, who were positioned on bicycles and in two vehicles, to follow the Citroen while he and Charles Garnier remained behind to observe the garage.

After turning to face his friend and second in command, Marcel remarked, "All we need now is to find Pierre Mollet, Jerome Paget and Edouard Tasse and we can move against these traitors."

Marcel's plan was to tell his cousin Paulette and her American lover, who he and his men were really working for, once they completed their mission. When this happened, Marcel also hoped to help Charlie resolve some of his legal problems with the American Army. Now that Marcel and his men were on the verge of closing in on Pierre Mollet and his fellow collaborators, it was just a question of time, before Charlie Monacco and his men would learn, that their French associates were only pretending to be a gang of resistance fighters turned thieves.

While Charlie Monacco closed the tailgate on the truck that was parked closest to the warehouse doors, he looked at Marcel and said, "Don't try to talk me out of this, Marcel. I've had enough. Besides, I always knew this day would come." Charlie then walked over to the cab of the GMC truck, opened the driver's side door and removed a medium size square package, that was wrapped in brown butcher block paper and secured with string.

After handing the package to his French partner, Charlie sounded like a typical American who was clueless when it came to fine art when he said, "This is the painting that I told you about. Needless to say, I know more about horse racing and shooting craps, than I do about the stuff that hangs on the wall in an art gallery. Besides, Paulette said this painting belongs to the people of France. If that's true, then they should have it back." Then, after pausing for a split second, Charlie remarked, "Even if I wanted to sell it, I wouldn't know what the damn thing is worth."

While Marcel held onto the valuable piece of French art, that was stolen by the Germans and recovered by Charlie on a combat mission, he looked at the American deserter who was also a highly decorated soldier and said, "No one will believe that an AWOL American soldier, who has excellent contacts on the black market, would pass up the chance to sell such a valuable piece of art work."

"You're right, Marcel, no one will believe it," remarked Charlie, before he continued and said, "But the simple truth is, I made enough money running this racket, to set myself up in a legitimate business in Paris after the war, so why be greedy. Besides, I'm no art thief and neither are you. After all, before you turned into a first class black market operator, you were a resistance fighter and a cop to boot. Now you're on your way to becoming a rich man and to tell you the truth, the Allies owe you for what you and your men did when the Germans occupied France."

Charlie Monacco's success as a black market operator really took off, when Raymond La Salle introduced the AWOL American Sergeant to Marcel Badeau in October of 1944. In a matter of weeks, Charlie and his small tightly knit group of AWOL G.I.s became considerably more successful, once they went into business with Marcel and his men. The fact that they were partners and friends, who would become members of the same family, when Charlie married his cousin Paulette, made it even easier for Marcel to do as Charlie requested. Because of their relationship, Marcel also felt comfortable offering Charlie advice. "One thing is certain. If Eddie Finch is found dead, the American military police will consider you their prime suspect."

While Marcel held the paper wrapped painting in his left hand, he continued and said, "The problem, my friend, is that according to my contacts, Chief Inspector Francois Dumont and a hand picked team of Paris Police investigators have been assigned to work with your American CID men. I know Dumont and I assure you, that he will do everything possible, to assist your military police and make all of our lives miserable, until Finch is found and that pig Mollet and his American supply sergeant for a partner are taken into custody."

Even though he was set in his ways, Charlie decided to humor his French partner and remark, "And you know all this because?"

Without hesitating, Marcel responded in a tone of voice that was laced with complete confidence. "Because my good friend Charles Garnier has been keeping his older brother Paul, the policeman and his family, in American cigarettes, food, soap, warm clothing and medical supplies, so we can have a direct contact with the Paris Police. Based on what Charles has learned from his brother, Chief Inspector Dumont and his men are filling French jails with every petty thief, shopkeeper and even some prostitutes who are known to do business on the black market. Dumont is taking his mission so seriously, he closed three cafes where stolen American cigarettes were being sold. Everything that Dumont and your military police are doing is being done to get people to talk. It is therefore, only a question of time, before someone will lead the American Army to your doorstep."

"That's exactly why I might as well turn myself in before they find me," responded Charlie, who quickly added, "If I wait for them to come looking for me, they could easily find the cash and valuables that I have stashed for me and Paulette to use, to start a life for ourselves once this war is over."

"I wish things were different, my friend," remarked Marcel.

"Me too," responded Charlie.

After offering Marcel a cigarette, Charlie took one for himself and accepted a light from his French partner before he continued and said, "I know what you're thinking. Why now? For starters I'm hoping they'll go a little easier on me if I turn myself in and face the music."

As soon as Charlie finished speaking, Marcel took a drag on his cigarette then remarked, "What do you think will happen once you surrender to the American military police?"

"If I'm lucky I'll get busted to buck private and be given a chance to return to a combat unit," responded Charlie, who went on to say, "Based on what I'm hearing, the Army is still hard up for riflemen, especially experienced soldiers. Who knows, maybe some of the medals I got will help convince the Army to go easier on me. The fact that I went AWOL while I was still a patient in that convalescent hospital, instead of abandoning my post under other circumstances, might also go in my favor. One thing is certain, Marcel. If I wait until the war ends, I'll lose whatever leverage I have, which may not be much."

Even though Charlie made perfect sense, Marcel had a few questions for his American friend and business partner. "Tell me, my friend. What will you do when you are asked about Eddie Finch and all of the stolen supplies that the U.S. Army will assume you must have in your possession? The Army will also ask you about the other AWOL Americans, as well as the Frenchmen who worked with you on the black market. I also would not be surprised if they asked you to surrender all of the money that you made selling stolen property. Do you really believe the U.S. Army will allow you to say nothing, then give you a rifle and return you to the front line?"

Without changing his position Charlie remarked, "As far as Eddie Finch is concerned, he can fend for himself. I'm not lifting a finger to help him. All I ask is that you get him out of La Salle's basement and drop him off on the street. If he doesn't get killed by Moffett and Mollet, he's bound to get picked up by the MPs, once they see him limping around. As far as this stuff goes, take half for you and your men and use the contents of one truck to take care of Paulette, her mother and her brother. I'm hoping the Army will go easier on me, when I turn the rest of this merchandise over to Uncle Sam. I'll also leave some cash in the safe that the Army can have, once I give the MPs the keys to this place. As far as you and your men are concerned, we never met. As far as my men are concerned, I paid the few that I still have working for me off, now that I do most of my work with you and your men. Once they finished loading these trucks, I told them that I was turning myself in. I suggested they do the same."

After pausing for a split second to admire all that he had amassed in the way of stolen merchandise, Charlie faced Marcel when he continued and said, "I also need you to do me a personal favor. I left the engagement ring that I intended to give to Paulette in a box filled with cash, under a loose floorboard in the bedroom closet in my apartment. Give her the cash and the ring as soon as I'm gone and tell her that we're officially engaged. I'll write her a letter using her mother's address as soon as I can."

Marcel had one last suggestion to make before he let Charlie Monacco execute his plan. "There is of course another path that you can take, one that will allow you to remain in France as a free man, providing that you survive the war."

"What's that?" asked Charlie.

"You can fight for France," responded Marcel who quickly added, "My cousin is a Major in the French Foreign Legion. The Legion is well known for accepting men into their ranks who have a troubled past. The fact that you are a well trained, highly decorated soldier will make you an attractive candidate for recruitment."

While Marcel continued, he dropped his cigarette butt on the warehouse floor and crushed it under the heel of his shoe. "The risks you will take while fighting in the Legion, will be no different than the risks you will take, if you are lucky enough to be returned to a combat unit in the American Army. If you join the Legion, you can also earn the right to a new life as a citizen of France, without any risk of the American Army sending you off to jail in disgrace." Then, after pausing for a split second, Marcel added, "If you wish to make a life with Paulette and you have no problem returning to the war, joining the Legion offers you the best chance of achieving that goal."

The only thing that Charlie Monacco knew about knew about the French Foreign Legion was what he remembered from watching the movie "Beau Geste," starring Gary Cooper, Ray Milland and Robert Preston and the movie "Under Two Flags," staring Robert Colman and Claudette Colbert. After hearing what Marcel had to say, Charlie did his best to sound grateful when he responded and said, "Thanks for the suggestion, but I'll take my chances with the U.S. Army."

"Your other option is to let me take you to the Swiss border," said Marcel, who went on to say, "My older brother Michel is a French Customs Officer in the town of Annemasse. During the German occupation, Michel and every member of our northern Customs force risked their lives to work with the resistance. It was as a result of their assistance, that we were able to smuggle Allied aviators, Jews and others who was being hunted by the Boche into Switzerland.[4] With the money that you have saved, you can live a good life in Switzerland until it is safe to return to France. If you give me a few days, I can get you documents that will show that you are a Canadian citizen who survived the German occupation. I can even have Paulette join you, once my contacts in Geneva help you get settled."

"That's a tempting offer, Marcel," responded Charlie, who continued and said, "The problem with that plan, is that I might get homesick and want'a visit my old stomping grounds. As long as I'm in Dutch with the U.S. Army, I'll never be able to return home without getting arrested. That means I need to face the music and take whatever comes my way."

Marcel had been around strong willed men long enough to know, that Charlie Monacco was never going to change his mind, or the course of action that he intended to take. With nothing else to say, Marcel extended his hand in friendship and remarked, "I will do as you ask my friend, but before you surrender you will have supper with me."

"I guess I could use a good meal before I walk the plank," remarked Charlie.

CHAPTER 4

BACK IN ACTION

As soon as they arrived in Paris, Lt. Colonel James Beauregard and Lieutenant Al Parker were met at the airport by Staff Sergeant Mike Mulligan. Sergeant Mulligan was a familiar face, from the day when a CID led patrol pursued Ivan Larson and Francis Shorty Mc Ghee during the Battle of the Bulge.

Immediately after both officers enthusiastically greeted Staff Sergeant Mulligan, the former airborne MP, who was now serving as a CID Agent, spoke while he loaded their luggage into the trunk of the Army sedan. "You and Lieutenant Parker couldn't have arrived at a better time, Sir. We're busier than ever."

As soon as Sergeant Mulligan closed the trunk of the staff car, he continued as he faced the two Army Officers. "Major Savino wanted me to let you and Lieutenant Parker know, Sir, that Hank Blair and Chris Jacko pursued a deserter, who was delivering stolen Army gas out'a the back of a stolen ambulance. This happened earlier this morning in one of the more colorful neighborhoods of Paris. During the chase, this AWOL G.I. drove down a narrow side street and blocked the road with the stolen WC54. After he opened fire on our agents, as well as on four MPs and one of the French cops who works with us, he made his escape when he used a grenade to blow up the ambulance."

When a concerned Lt. Colonel Beauregard asked if anyone was hurt, Agent Mulligan responded and said, "Chris Jacko was taken to the hospital with a concussion, minor burns and some shrapnel wounds, but from what I heard, he'll be OK, Sir."

After hearing what Sergeant Mulligan had to say, Lieutenant Al Parker remarked, "This place is like the wild west."

"You're right about that, Sir," said Sergeant Mulligan

When Al Parker asked if they had the gunman identified, Sergeant Mulligan responded as he faced the man that he came to admire, while pursing the fugitives Ivan Larson and Francis Shorty Mc Ghee behind enemy lines. "Yes, we do, Lieutenant. His name is Eddie Finch. He's an AWOL Corporal who works for an AWOL Sergeant by the name of Charlie Monacco. Based on what we know, Sergeant Monacco started out small, but is now running with a gang of French thieves. This combined group of G.I. Gangsters and French crooks work out of a warehouse somewhere in Paris. As far as we know, they operate a fleet of about fifteen stolen Army vehicles, minus the one that Corporal Finch blew up."

Sergeant Mulligan then turned to face Lt. Colonel James Beauregard and added, "Major Savino would like to brief you and Lieutenant Parker in the field instead of in the office, Sir. Between the search for Eddie Finch and the raids that we need to execute, we have another busy night ahead of us."

After turning to face Al Parker, the new Commanding Officer of the U.S. Army CID Office in Paris remarked, "You ready to go to work, Al?"

As soon as Al responded and said, "Yes, Sir," Lt. Colonel James Beauregard turned to Sergeant Mulligan and said, "Lead the way, Mike."

Even though they were exhausted from traveling from New York to Paris, the two men who truly loved being cops in civilian life, as well as in the Army, sat in the khaki colored Army sedan and were transported by CID Agent Mike Mulligan, to meet Major Tommy Savino and Chief Inspector Francois Dumont of the Paris Police.

In order to conduct a briefing in the field, Major Savino had Sergeant Mulligan transport Lt. Colonel Beauregard and Lieutenant Parker to the cafe that was owned by Chief Inspector Dumont's brother-in-law. As soon as the staff car arrived at the rear entrance to The Paris Cafe, Major Savino and Chief Inspector Dumont stepped outside into the cold, to greet the two Army Officers.

Immediately after Major Savino welcomed Jim Beauregard and Al Parker to Paris, he introduced the two Army Officers to Chief Inspector Francois Dumont. While the new Commanding Officer of the Paris CID

Office shook hands with the Chief Inspector, he addressed the veteran French policeman in a very friendly tone of voice when he said, "I'd appreciate it, Chief Inspector, if you call me, Jim."

Long before Jim and Al returned to Paris, the Chief Inspector heard and read about the outstanding piece of police work that they performed, when they pursued two fugitives from New York City to a battlefield in Europe, in December of 1944. The admiration that the Chief Inspector had for his American Allies, also extended to Major Savino and the other agents assigned to the Paris CID Office. As a result, it was easy for the Chief Inspector to operate on a first name basis with his counterparts in CID. "Only if you call me, Francois," responded the Chief Inspector.

"It's a deal, Francois," responded Jim.

Al Parker was just as friendly, when he extended his hand as he said, "My friends call me, Al."

"It is nice to finally meet you, Al," responded the Chief Inspector, who continued and said, "We have much to discuss, but we must also take the time to have supper, because we have a long night ahead of us."

After inviting Sergeant Mulligan to come inside and have supper with the Chief Inspector's driver, Major Savino held the door open as Jim, Al and Francois entered the cafe. As the American CID Agents and Francois Dumont walked into the warm kitchen, the Chief Inspector's brother-in-law and his kitchen staff were preparing food, while listening to the BBC's European Service Radio Network.

It was through the British Broadcasting Corporation, that Allied Intelligence sent coded messages to the resistance units operating in France. The most famous message of the war in Europe, was sent in two parts and was comprised of lines from the Paul Verlaine poem, Chanson d' Automne (Autumn Song). When the first message was repeated in French over the BBC, the words, "Les sanlots Des violins De l'automne" or "Long sobs of autumn violins" confirmed, that the Allied Invasion of Normandy was going to be executed in a matter of days. When Allied Intelligence had the BBC broadcast the second coded message from Autumn Song, that included the words, "Blessent mon coeur D'une languer, Monotone," which meant, "Wound my heart with a monotonous languor," members of the French Resistance knew exactly when to spring into action.

Even though they had no idea if the invasion would be a success, members of the French Resistance, including Francois Dumont, a number of the policemen under his command, his brother-in-law Gabriel Allaire and a small army of patriotic French men and women, did everything that was expected of them and more to assist the Allies. Clearly, a portion of the success of Operation Overlord, was due to the contribution that was made by the brave members of the French Resistance.

★ ★ ★

While Sergeant Mulligan and Police Inspector Philippe Leblanc would eat their supper at a table by the back door, Francois led his American colleagues deeper into the kitchen. As soon as Gabriel "Gabby" Allaire stopped stirring a large pot of stew, he welcomed his guests as if they were old friends. The fact that they would be dining on U.S. Army Field Ration Type C Meat and Vegetable Stew, was evident by the opened cans that rested on the counter next to the stove.

Immediately after directing his guests to a private table in the back of his restaurant, Gabby and his head waiter, served a supper that consisted of a large pot of stew, a tray of French cheese, two loaves of freshly made sliced French bread and three bottles of wine. For dessert, they would feast on a tin of freshly baked chocolate chip cookies, that were provided by an American commissary sergeant. This particular Army cook was indebted to Major Savino, for making it possible for him to keep his stripes, after he was picked up in a raid. In fact, it was through this commissary sergeant, that Major Savino was able to get his hands on a steady supply of U.S. Army food items, that went to the Chief Inspector's family, including to his brother-in-law. The other sought after items, that ended up in the storeroom of The Paris Cafe, were purchased in the PX by Major Savino and other generous CID Agents. This included American tobacco products, chewing gum, chocolate bars and soap.

The most recent supply of American goods were delivered earlier that day, when Major Savino and the Chief Inspector stopped by to have a late breakfast, after participating in the search for AWOL Corporal Eddie Finch. After arriving at the rear entrance of The Paris Cafe, Major Savino and the Chief Inspector delivered cans of assorted U.S. Army C Rations, five pounds of American coffee, two sacks of flour, two pounds of sugar, two cases of condensed milk, a box of cigars, a dozen chocolate bars and three cartons of Camel cigarettes to a very grateful Gabby Allaire. As far as Major Savino was concerned, this was the least he could do, given the fact that he and his men considered Gabby's cafe to be their favorite hangout in Paris. From an official perspective, the Major justified his actions, by documenting the valuable intelligence information that Gabby and his contacts provided to Army CID and the Paris Police. Naturally, all of these items were greatly appreciated, because Paris was still a city that was dealing with food and other shortages in early 1945.

As the man who walked with a limp, after being wounded during the liberation of Paris in August of 1944, finished filling their glasses with wine, Chief Inspector Dumont looked up at his brother-in-law and said, "You have a business to run and we have criminals to catch."

"I know when I am not wanted," joked Gabby, before he looked directly at Jim and Al and said, "I hope you will consider The Paris Cafe to be your home away from home, while you are stationed in France." Then, after pausing for a split second, Gabby added, "Please do not hesitate to ask, if there is anything else that you need. In the meantime, I will leave you to enjoy your supper, while you discuss matters of great importance."

Because he was a regular at The Paris Cafe, Major Savino proved that he was on a first name basis with the Chief Inspector's brother-in-law when he spoke up and said, "Thanks, Gabby."

While Gabby returned to the kitchen, Francois passed the tray of cheese and sliced French bread around the table. Once they began to eat their supper, Jim and Al could tell by the reception that they received and the supply of U.S. Army products on shelves in the kitchen, that The Paris Cafe was a cop hangout, where one hand washed the other. When Gabby walked by their table on his way to the bar, Jim proved that he had no problem with this arrangement, when he called out to their host and said, "Excuse me, Gabby, but would you have time to join us for coffee and dessert before we go back to work?"

No one on the face of this earth was able to express gratitude better than a Frenchman. While Gabby stood near their table, he seemed genuinely honored, to be invited to have coffee and dessert with the American Colonel, his two officers and his brother-in-law, before they executed a series of raids throughout Paris. "It would be my honor, Colonel," responded Gabby, before he walked over to the bar and began checking stock.

As Gabby went to work behind the bar, Chief Inspector Dumont looked at Jim and said, "You just made a friend for life, Jim. My brother-in-law has helped us solve more crimes than you can imagine. As Tom will tell you, Gabby will continue to do the same for you and your men."

"That's good to know, because we can use all the help we can get," responded Jim.

As the Chief Inspector continued, he looked across the table and said, "During the German occupation, Gabby was one of the most active members of our resistance unit. He worked day and night for us and used our family farm to hide Allied agents, shot down Allied airmen and French Jews from the Germans, as well as from our own people who collaborated with the Nazis. Thanks in large measure to Gabby and the small group that he worked with, everyone we helped was successfully smuggled out of France to England. How Gabby survived without getting arrested by the Gestapo and the Milice is considered a miracle by those who served with him."

"I can tell he's a good man," said Jim, who quickly added, "I also know from the briefing that we received before we left the states, that we owe you and your men a great deal as well."

Immediately after hearing such a generous compliment, the Chief Inspector held up his wine glass and proposed a toast. While Jim, Al and Tom raised their glasses in the air, the Chief Inspector spoke up and said, "Un problème partagé est un problème réduit de moitié, which means, a problem shared is a problem halved. As Allies, that is exactly what we are doing by pursing criminals together in France."

"Here, here," responded Jim, a comment that was echoed by Al Parker who remarked, "I'll drink to that."

As the four men continued to eat their supper, Major Savino asked the Colonel and Al Parker if they received the cable that he sent to the states before their scheduled departure. "No we didn't, Tom," said Jim Beauregard, who quickly added, "Al and I left New York a day early, but we ended up losing a day, when our plane needed to be repaired, before we crossed the Atlantic."

Jim knew Tommy Savino well enough to know, that he had something important to say, but that he seemed a bit reluctant to discuss whatever it was. In order to make it easy for his second in command to continue, Jim looked across the table and said, "What's up, Tom?"

As soon as Major Savino swallowed a spoonful of stew, he took a quick sip of wine before he responded and said. "The message that I sent to New York explained that CID Agent Calvin Parker has infiltrated a gang of AWOL G.I.s who are operating on the black market."

"That's great news," responded Jim.

"There's more, Sir," remarked Tom Savino, who wasted no time in looking across the table at the recently promoted Lieutenant Al Parker and said, "I have to tell you, Al. Your son Cal is a definite chip off the old block. As soon as Cal reported for duty, he was anxious to get to work. After I issued him his CID badge and ID, I gave him a map of the city and a .32 caliber Colt pistol that was easier to carry than his forty five. Before I gave him any cases to work, I wanted Cal to serve as my eyes and ears, while he became familiar with different sections of Paris. After I briefed him about some of our investigations, I told Cal to call in twice a day, for as long as he was on this scouting mission. I also had Cal change the insignia on his uniform, so he would look like a tanker from his old armored unit and not like an Army cop."

As proud as Al was to hear such kind words spoken about his youngest son, he knew there was a lot more to this story. While the others continued to eat their supper, the Major went on to say, "Once Cal learned the general lay of the land, I asked him to concentrate his surveillance activities in the 18th Arrondissement, a district of the city where American black market operators and their French contacts are very active. Two days later, Cal observed a young Negro G.I. park a deuce and half and deliver cartons of American cigarettes to two men dressed in civilian clothes. When Cal spotted a pair military policemen on foot patrol turn the corner, he walked over to this G.I. and warned him that two MPs were coming his way."

As much as Al did not want to interrupt a superior office, he couldn't resist and said, "Excuse me for interrupting, Sir, but why would Cal do a thing like that?"

Even Jim Beauregard was a bit taken back by Cal's actions and remarked, "Al's right. Why didn't Cal call the MPs over to help him arrest that solider?"

Immediately after Jim Beauregard and Al Parker reacted the way they did, Tommy Savino held up his right hand and said, "You and Al are right, Sir. What Cal did was very unorthodox, but once you hear why he did what he did, I think you'll agree that he took the right action."

After hearing Jim remark, "Go ahead, Tom," Major Savino sipped some wine before he continued. "When I briefed Cal about the black market problem in Paris, I told him that many of these G.I. Gangsters are working with some very talented French criminals. While some of these gangs are small in size, others are large and very well organized. The larger gangs operate fleets of stolen Army vehicles, that haul stolen gasoline, cigarettes, food and every other sought after item to their black market customers. Some of these crooks are so brazen, they're selling stolen government property right on the streets of Paris. The theft of cigarettes alone is so serious, that some our combat troops have been forced to smoke captured German cigarettes, to augment their weekly ration of American smokes. [5] Worse yet, we can't control this problem, even though we have some 4,000 MPs and a contingent of overworked CID Agents assigned to police Paris. Even with the help of the Paris Police, we have our hands full, dealing with AWOL G.I.'s and the crimes that are being committed by some of our troops. And that includes the black market."

"Tom is correct," interjected Francois, who quickly added, "The problems caused by the shortage of so many necessities of life and certain so called luxury items, has created a demand for everything that is sold on the black market. The French citizens and those who have deserted their post, rely on the black market for the things that cannot be purchased through legitimate channels."

As soon as Francois finished speaking, Major Savino picked up where he left off and said, "As soon as Cal warned this Negro G.I. and he asked him for a lift, this grateful AWOL soldier and Cal drove off in what turned out to be a stolen GMC truck. Initially, Cal identified himself as a Sherman tank commander, who was in the process of getting discharged from a con-valescent hospital and was deciding whether he should return to his unit, or go AWOL and remain in Paris with his French girlfriend. Cal became convinced that he was onto something, when this G.I. tried to talk him out of going AWOL and encouraged him to return to his unit. When Corporal Benjamin Greene continued, he admitted that he was AWOL from the 514th Quarter Master Truck Company and that he was planning to turn himself in, so he could be a soldier again. After hearing more about the black market operation that this AWOL G.I. was involved with, Cal identified himself as a CID Agent and placed Corporal Greene under arrest. Cal then asked the AWOL Corporal if he was willing to help CID make a case against the black market operators that he worked for?"

"It sounds like young Mister Parker is involved in one hell of an adventure," remarked Jim.

"Yes he is, Sir," responded Major Savino before he continued and said, "Cal said he took the action he did because he was raised to follow his instincts. To be more specific, Cal had a gut feeling that this particular AWOL truck driver was a good kid, who made a stupid mistake when he overstayed his leave and went to work for a black market operation. Cal also said that Corporal Greene seemed very sincere, when he encouraged him to return to his unit, instead of going AWOL. Benny Greene also sounded like he was telling the truth, when he told Cal that he was planning to turn himself in, so he could return to being a good soldier. In addition, Cal knew that if he arrested this AWOL G.I., while he was making a delivery, the rest of his gang would hear about it. Once that happened, it would be a lot harder for us to go after the other members of this gang, especially the men calling the shots."

"I assume there's a happy ending to this story?" said Jim.

"Yes, Sir, there is," responded the Major, who quickly added, "Cal proved that he made the right call, when Corporal Greene eagerly agreed to help us make a case against AWOL Sergeant Harry Moffett and the other members of his gang. Corporal Greene also provided us with some other worthwhile information, that Francois and I will brief you and Al about, before we go any further with what we have planned for tonight."

As concerned as Jim was for one of his agents, he agreed with the actions that Major Savino and Cal took when he said, "This sounds like good police work to me. A little unorthodox, but it's still good police work. It also sounds like Corporal Greene is the perfect candidate to help us infiltrate a group of G.I. Gangsters operating in Paris."

Immediately after hearing what Jim had to say, Major Savino remarked, "A gang that also happens to be involved with some very nasty Frenchmen." Jim Beauregard had worked with Al Parker long enough to know, that he was having some difficulty accepting the fact that his youngest son was in harm's way. Because he was genuinely concerned about his good friend from the PDNY, Jim turned to Al and said, "Are you OK, Al?"

Al knew that he wasn't doing a very good job of concealing the concern that he had for his son. Al also appreciated that Jim picked up on the fact, that he was worried about Cal. After turning to face the man who was his friend and his commanding officer, Al remarked, "The cop in me also knows that this is good police work, but the father in me is concerned about my son."

Under the circumstances, Jim Beauregard decided to make Al feel better by saying, "Like the Major said, Al. Your son Cal is a definite chip off the old block."

Once Al had a chance to think about how he reacted, he did his best to make light of the situation when he joked, "If Cal's mother finds out that he's gone above and beyond the call of duty and worked undercover, I'll be sleeping on the couch when I get home."

As everyone at the table smiled and laughed, Jim Beauregard patted Al on the top of his left arm and said, "Thanks, Al. We needed a laugh."

While the three American Army Officers continued eating their supper, Chief Inspector Dumont spoke in his signature calm tone of voice and said, "I know exactly how you feel, Al. I say that, because my daughter Michelle is also involved in this case and is working undercover in the cafe, that is being used as the location, where your son can relay information to us." Then, after pausing to sip some wine, Francois went on to say, "You would think that I am used to her risking her life, because Michelle also served in the resistance during the German occupation. My daughter also carried messages for me and my men during the fighting to liberate Paris. When I saw Michelle reloading the pistol that I gave her, to carry for protection, I knew that my daughter did more than carry messages. As worried as I was at the time, I was never more proud of Michelle, for she was helping to rid Paris of the Boche."

After pausing for a split second to sip some wine, the Chief Inspector continued and said, "Unfortunately, a good parent is always worried about their children, no matter how old they get. In fact, as my father used to say, until they are blessed with their own children, they cannot begin to comprehend what we go through as parents."

"You're right about that, Francois," said Jim.

Al agreed and added, "The only problem we're gonna have when they have kids of their own, is that we'll have our children, plus our grandchildren, to worry about."

As soon as Jim and Francois agreed with Al, Major Savino looked at Al and said, "Feeling better, Al?"

"Yes I am. Thanks for asking, Sir," responded Al Parker.

Now that the tension was broken, Jim continued as he looked across the table at Major Savino. "What happened next, Tom?"

When Major Savino responded, he seemed to be in better spirits when he said, "We have a lot to discuss, Sir, so I recommend that we eat our supper before it gets cold, while the Chief Inspector and I fill you and Al in on what we have planned for tonight."

"Shoot," was all Jim said as he picked up his spoon and continued eating.

As soon as Tommy Savino swallowed a spoonful of beef stew and wiped his mouth with a napkin, he continued with his briefing. "Once Corporal Greene agreed to work for us, Cal called in and gave me a detailed briefing. After I met with Cal and Bennie Greene, I asked Hank Blair, Chris Jacko, Mike Mulligan and Mike Butler from our office, along with Francois and two of his men, to meet us at a remote location along the perimeter of Le Bourget Airport. While we met with Cal and Corporal Greene, Cal repeated what he previously reported. This included describing every aspect of the black market operation that Corporal Greene works for, that's run by the AWOL supply sergeant Harry Moffett. In addition, Cal relayed what Benny Greene told him, about an AWOL Corporal by the name of Eddie Finch. According to Benny, Corporal Finch used to work with his gang, before he had a falling out with Sergeant Moffett over money. To get back at Moffett, Finch stole a deuce and a half loaded with cartons of American cigarettes and went to work for another gang, that's run by an AWOL Staff Sergeant by the name of Charlie Monacco."

While Tommy Savino leaned closer to the table, he spoke loud enough to be heard over the soft music that was playing in the background. "Benny Greene also told us, that Finch is a crazy SOB who carries a stolen Army forty five and a grenade. According to Benny, Finch told everyone that he worked with, that if he ever got cornered, he planned to use his forty five and the grenade to make his escape. Benny also told Cal, that he recently saw Finch, driving a stolen Army ambulance in the 18th Arrondissement, including in the vicinity of the Moulin Rouge Cabaret."

After pausing to take a quick sip of wine, Major Savino continued with the briefing. "Due to the severity of this information and the need to make every effort to get Finch off the street and in custody, Francois and I assigned Hank Blair, Chris Jacko and Inspector Patrice Goulet, to look for this AWOL Corporal. Because we're strapped for personnel, we also instructed our men, to make every effort to get help from some MPs when they arrested Finch. Unfortunately, even with help from four MPs, Finch proved impossible to apprehend, after he opened fire with a forty five and used a grenade to set a stolen ambulance on fire, that was blocking a narrow side street. Even though we know he was wounded in the exchange, Finch managed to get away and hasn't been located, despite our combined efforts to find him. Unfortunately, Chis Jacko was injured, when he attempted to pursue Finch, just before the grenade detonated and set an ambulance filled with cans of stolen gasoline on fire."

Jim Beauregard proved that he understood why Finch managed to escape, when he spoke up and said, "Mike Mulligan told us a little about this incident and what happened to Chris on the way over. The good news is, Chris wasn't more seriously injured. As far as Finch is concerned, sometimes bad guys get away, especially when you go up against a crazy bastard, who opens fire with a forty five and throws a hand-grenade into a vehicle, that's loaded with cans of gasoline." Then, after a brief pause, Jim added, "Under the circumstances, things could'a been a lot worse."

After hearing what the new commanding officer for the Paris CID Office just said, Francois Dumond spoke up and said, "Our sentiments exactly."

Since Jim sensed that Tom and the Chief Inspector had a lot more to say, he looked across the table at his second in command and said, "Please continue, Tom."

As soon as Tom finished eating a spoonful of stew, he took a sip of wine and continued with his end of the briefing. "According to the plan that we put together, we had two teams consisting of CID Agents and the Chief Inspector's men follow Benny Greene, when he returned to Moffett's warehouse, with his truck load of stolen merchandise in tact. Before we sent him on his way, Benny was instructed to tell Moffett that he was unable to make the rest of his deliveries, because another soldier warned him, that two MPs were heading his way, after they observed him delivering cartons of cigarettes to some of their French customers. We also told Corporal Greene to tell Moffett, that to make sure he wasn't being followed, he drove all the way out to the airport and waited a while, before he returned to their warehouse. This would explain why Bennie was gone for so long."

After hearing Jim remark, "This is gonna make one hell of a chapter in my book," Tom cracked a smile before he continued and said, "We also instructed Benny to ask Moffett for permission, to give the G.I. who warned him about the MPs a few cartons of cigarettes, that he could sell to make some money. Cal came up with this idea, because he figured AWOL Sergeant Moffett might like to thank the soldier, who kept one of his driver's out of the stockade and prevented a truckload of stolen cigarettes from being seized by the MPs. In addition to watching the warehouse where Moffett's black market operation is located, we put teams on Cal and the cafe where he was supposed to be spending time, while he decides to go AWOL, or return to his unit."

While Jim, Al and the Chief Inspector continued eating their supper, Major Savino sipped some wine before he went on to say. "To prepare for the possibility that Moffett might agree to meet with Cal and recruit him into his gang, I made arrangements for a personnel file, a medical file, an Army ID card and a set of dog tags to be put together using the name Sergeant Andrew Carter. Before Cal went undercover, as a Sherman tank commander from the 761st Tank Battalion, I also had someone from Army Intelligence brief him, about the current position of his old unit. In addition, I had an Army doctor we know, sign a three day pass for Cal, in the phony name he's using on this undercover assignment."

Jim was impressed and proved it when he remarked, "It certainly sounds like you covered all the bases, before you sent Cal on this mission."

"Thank you, Sir," responded Tommy Savino, before he continued with his briefing. "The good news, Sir, is that just as we hoped, Moffett took the bait and met Cal at the cafe where Cal's French girlfriend works as a waitress." "That is good news," remarked Jim.

Even the proud father spoke up and said, "That crazy kid. He pulled it off."

While Jim grinned and patted Al on the back, Major Savino went on to say, "Earlier today, one of our teams followed Benny Greene, to the cafe where Cal said he would be spending the bulk of his time, while he's on leave. Once Benny filled Cal in on his conversations with Moffett, Cal got a message to Michelle Dumont, who relayed the information to her father. Shortly thereafter, two of our men in separate vehicles, followed Moffett to the cafe where he met with Cal and Benny. Once Sergeant Andy Doc Carter was recruited into Moffett's gang, AWOL Sergeant Moffett was followed to a brothel, that's run by a Madam who worked with the French resistance. Thanks to Gabby, we were able to meet with this Madam privately and learn more about AWOL Sergeant Moffett. Immediately after Cal passed the good news to Michelle Dumont, he left the cafe with Benny Greene. From there, they were both followed back to Moffett's warehouse."

Tommy Savino proved that he knew how to give a detailed briefing, when he handed a small notebook to his commanding officer and said, "Later in the afternoon, Benny took Cal out on his first run and made deliveries to a number of locations in Paris. Every one of these locations is listed in that notebook, Sir." Then, after a brief pause, Tom added, "Thanks to Chief Inspector and his men, we were able to identify several French crooks and local businessmen, who took delivery of stolen U.S. government property."

While Jim examined the list of entries, he sounded like a cop who was frustrated by the crime problem that plagued France and other occupied cities during the war when he said, "The black market problem in major cities like Paris is the best kept secret of the war."

As soon as Jim handed the notebook to Al, the New York City

Policeman, who was now serving as a Lieutenant in CID, agreed and quickly added, "The people back home would not be very happy, if they knew that truck loads of supplies, that are heavily rationed in the states, are being stolen by our own troops and sold on the black market, instead of being supplied to Allied soldiers in combat."

After agreeing with the comments made by Jim and Al, Major Savino looked at his French counterpart before he faced his commanding officer and said, "The Chief Inspector should take it from here, Sir, so he can brief you and Al on the French side of our joint investigation."

As soon as Chief Inspector Dumont said, "Thank you, Tom," he looked directly at Al Parker and began his part of the briefing by saying, "I must tell you, Al, that your son is not only a very brave young man, but his actions have enabled us to do more than identify the activities of AWOL American soldiers, who are operating on the black market."

While Major Savino ate his supper, Chief Inspector Dumont continued as he removed a photograph from his suit jacket pocket and presented it to Jim Beauregard. "This is a photograph of a French collaborator by the name of Antone Mollet. In addition to committing acts of collaboration, Antone Mollet and his older brother Pierre operated on the black market during the German occupation of France. Because they were collaborators, they were protected by the Boche. As a result of what Sergeant Parker has accomplished, while working with Corporal Greene, we are able to confirm, that the Mollet brothers are still actively involved in the black market, only now they work with a gang of AWOL American soldiers."

As the Chief Inspector continued, he removed another photograph from his suit jacket pocket and presented it to Jim Beauregard. "This is a photograph of Pierre Mollet. Pierre Mollet is a pimp, a murderer and a traitor to France, who ran two brothels that catered to Boche officers. During the early days of the German occupation, Pierre Mollet was approached to see if he and some of his prostitutes would cooperate with the resistance. This request was made, because we knew that women in this profession, would occasionally hear things of importance from their Boche customers. When Pierre Mollet declined to cooperate and said that he wished to remain "neutral," two of our resistance contacts recruited four of his girls to work for us. Two weeks later, Mollet agreed to work with the resistance. We should have known better than to trust him, but the men who approached Mollet believed him, when he explained that he had a change of heart. Unfortunately, what we did not know at the time, was that Pierre Mollet was working for Section IV of the Gestapo. We learned of his treachery, when the two resistants who approached him were arrested by the Germans, after they left a meeting with Mollet. Fortunately for many people, both of these men died bravely and did not reveal any information about resistance activities to the Gestapo."

While Jim handed the two photographs to Al, Chief Inspector Dumont looked at the two American officers who were new to Paris and said, "I pray that you will forgive me, for discussing such distasteful matters while we enjoy our supper, but as policemen we are used to such topics intruding into our lives, including when we should be taking time for ourselves."

After hearing Jim Beauregard remark, "Please continue, Francois," Al handed the photographs back to Francois just as the Chief Inspector continued with his end of the briefing. "Of the four brave women who continued to work for us, even after it became known that Pierre Mollet was a traitor, two were arrested by the Gestapo and were never heard from again. The third girl was found shot to death. We believe this girl was murdered, because she was a favorite of a German Colonel, who was a heavy drinker and had as you say, a big mouth. Because of her work with the resistance, we learned many things of value from this Boche officer, that were passed on to Allied intelligence."

While Francois continued, he put the two photographs back into his suit jacket pocket. "The fourth girl, who happened to be the youngest, was badly beaten and thrown from the back of a moving truck in the early hours of the morning. Before she died, she told two of our policemen that Pierre Mollet had her arrested by the Gestapo. While she was being tortured, she spit in Mollet's face and admitted that she worked with the resistance, to rid France of collaborators like him and his brother. Because of his close relationship with the Gestapo, it made no sense to arrest Pierre Mollet at that time. Instead, I passed the information on to Allied Intelligence and added the charge of murder, to the list of crimes that Pierre Mollet would one day be charged with."

After pausing to sip some wine, Francois went on to say, "Pierre Mollet gained even more favor with Section IV of the Gestapo, when he hid dozens of wealthy Jews throughout Paris, only to deliver them into German hands. Pierre Mollet's level of collaboration impressed the Gestapo so much, that in 1943, this traitor to France was made a commander in the fascist French para military unit known as the Milice."

After pausing to take another sip of wine, Francois went on to say, "When Pierre Mollet served in the French Army during the last war, he was like Hitler and never rose above the rank of corporal. But because he collaborated with the Boche during this war, he was placed in command of one the most ruthless Milice units that served the Nazis and Vichy."

"This guy sounds like a candidate for a firing squad," remarked Jim.

Despite his obvious hatred for Pierre Mollet and his closest associates, the Chief Inspector remained amazingly composed when he responded and said, "Pierre Mollet will not be alone when he faces a firing squad, because the traitors who served in his Milice unit, also committed numerous atrocities against French civilians and members of the resistance. In fact, Pierre Mollet's Milice Unit acted more viciously at times than the Gestapo."

"That takes some doing," remarked Al.

"Yes it does," responded Francois as he picked up a bottle of wine and removed the cork.

While Chief Inspector Dumont refilled everyone's glass with more wine, Jim spoke up and said, "I'm curious, Francois. Why would the Mollet brothers remain in France and risk being arrested, when they had every opportunity to leave the country before Paris was liberated?"

"An excellent question," responded Francois, who went on to say, "I suspect one reason is because Pierre Mollet has a grand, or as you say, a big ego. I also know, that he has no respect for the police and was a man of no importance until he became a ruthless fascist. In the process of becoming a traitor to France, he made a small fortune and continues to do so, by operating on the black market. As far as Antone Mollet is concerned, he follows his older brother."

After hearing Jim's question and what Francois had to say, Al remarked, "Whether the Mollet brothers are lucky or good at what they do, they've managed to operate for some five months without getting picked up."

"That is correct, Al," said Francois, who quickly added, "We must never underestimate the capabilities of adversaries like the Mollet brothers, especially Pierre Mollet."

As soon as Jim asked when Francois first heard that the Mollet brothers were still operating in Paris, the Chief Inspector washed down a spoonful of stew with a sip of wine, before he responded and said, "After your troops landed in Normandy, I began receiving intelligence information that Pierre Mollet was still operating on the black market in and around Paris. This information came to me from two individuals. One was a prostitute. The other informant was the youngest member of Pierre Mollet's Milice unit. This young man was badly wounded and was being cared for in a hospital in Paris. According to his mother, her son made a terrible mistake when he joined the Milice. Due to his age and the fact that he had no father to guide him, I took the time to get to know this boy. He grew up quite a lot while lying in that hospital bed. Once he realized the poor choices that he made, he had a great deal to say about Pierre Mollet and the other members of his Milice unit. To reward him for his cooperation, I saw to it that he received clemency and was properly cared for."

After pausing to take another sip of wine, Francois continued and said, "In order to understand what I am about to discuss, you need to consider, that long before June of 1944, Paris was starving and in need of a great deal of assistance from the Allies. This situation existed for various reasons relating to the war. This is why to this day, one pack of your American cigarettes are being sold on the streets of Paris for as much as $2.00 dollars. American coffee is $10 to $15 dollars a pound. A five gallon can of your gasoline is being sold for $100 dollars. Fifty of your D Ration chocolate bars sell for $300 dollars and your tasty American Army rations are selling for $2.00 each. In fact, the black market is still thriving, because the situation in Paris in particular has not improved all that much, even though many months have past since the German occupation ended."[6,7]

When Jim spoke up and said, "Two bucks for a pack of smokes and a C Note for five gallons of gas....unbelievable," Francois paused to eat another spoonful of stew.

As soon as Francois took a quick sip of wine, he continued with his end of the briefing, while Jim and the others continued eating their supper, "As soon as your troops advanced deeper into France, the prostitute that Pierre

Mollet would often visit by surprise, relayed to me, that the Mollet brothers were working with a group of AWOL American soldiers, who were stealing all kinds of sought after items from your supply depots. When I sent one of my men to debrief her in more detail, she showed him the supply of American cigarettes and food that was given to her by Pierre Mollet. Unfortunately, we were unable to learn more, because Mollet stopped making surprise visits to this particular prostitute."

As tired as he was, Major Savino proved that he was invigorated by the conversation that was taking place, when he perked up and interjected, "Thanks to Cal and Benny Greene there's light at the end of the tunnel, Sir."

While Major Savino continued eating his supper, the Chief Inspector picked up where he left off and said, "As a result of the efforts of Sergeant Parker to recruit Corporal Greene, we also learned that Pierre Mollet is using the name Pierre Boucher. Even though your Corporal Greene only saw the Mollet brothers once, we know from the description that he provided to us, that Pierre Mollet has changed his appearance by growing a mustache and a beard. Now that we know this, it will be easier for us to find him."

As the Chief Inspector dipped a piece of bread into his bowl of stew, he quickly added, "We also know from Corporal Greene, that AWOL Sergeant Moffett bragged to his men, that Pierre Mollet will never double cross him, because he knows that his French partner did business with the Germans, when he was involved in the black market, before the Allies landed in Normandy."

When Francois paused to eat some of his stew soaked bread, Al Parker remarked, "Based on what you said, Francois, it sounds like we need to have a private talk with AWOL Sergeant Moffett."

After pausing to sip some wine, Francois looked directly at Al and said, "Thanks to your son and Corporal Greene, that is exactly what we intend to do before midnight tonight."

As soon as Jim offered a Lucky Strike to his counterpart in the Paris Police, he took one for himself, while Al Parker produced a box of wooden matches and offered both men a light. After Jim Beauregard and the Chief Inspector thanked Al for the light, Jim looked across the table and said, "When do you recommend that we move against AWOL Sergeant Moffett and his associates?"

Without hesitating, Chief Inspector Dumont responded and said, "While Tom and I would like to continue this joint operation until we can locate Pierre Mollet, we cannot afford to risk Sergeant Parker's life, or Corporal Greene's life beyond tonight. Pierre Mollet is ruthless and could learn of Agent Parker's true identity at any time. Should that happen, he would likely harm Corporal Greene as well. Even my daughter Michelle could be in danger, if Mollet and the AWOL Sergeant Moffett suspect her of working with Sergeant Parker and Corporal Greene."

After pausing to take a drag on his cigarette, the Chief Inspector continued as he tapped the ash from his Lucky Strike into a nearby ashtray. "We also cannot continue to assign the number of men that are required to follow Sergeant Parker and Corporal Greene, while also keeping a watchful eye on my daughter and various locations and subjects of interest for much longer. This is why Tom and I feel strongly, that we must move against these individuals and every location that we are watching before midnight tonight."

As soon as the Chief Inspector stopped speaking, Tommy Savino added, "As if we are not busy enough, we also need to find the deserter who shot at our men and used a hand-grenade to blow up a stolen Army ambulance on a Paris side street. We also have to start looking for the gang that AWOL Corporal Finch went to work for, after he left AWOL Sergeant Moffett's black market operation."

The moment Chief Inspector Dumont's brother-in-law approached the table, all four men stopped talking about official business and thanked their gracious host for a wonderful supper. Immediately after Chief Inspector Dumont checked his watch, he looked across the table at Jim Beauregard and said, "We have just enough time for coffee and some of those delicious American desserts before we get back to work."

As soon as Jim remarked, "Only if Gabby joins us," Gabby smiled wide then said, "Your coffee and dessert is on the way, Colonel."

While Gabby returned to the stove in the kitchen, Jim looked at his second in command and said, "What do you and Francois have planned for tonight, Tom?"

After removing a map from his pocket, Tom Savino passed the map to

Jim Beauregard and said, "As you and Al can see, Sir, I circled the locations that we are currently watching. Once we finish our coffee, we'll be meeting MP Captain Dave Thompson. Captain Thompson and two dozen of his MPs are assigned to assist us tonight when we execute our raids. The Chief Inspector also arranged for ten uniformed gendarmes from his department to assist us and his men."

As Jim and Al leaned closer to each other and examined the map, Major Savino went on to say, "While you and Al take one of our teams and raid Moffett's garage, the Chief Inspector and I will raid the brothel where AWOL Sergeant Moffett likes to spend his free time. The rest of our teams will hit the other locations at the same time." Then, after pausing for a split second, Major Savino added, "With your permission, Sir, we'll execute the raids at 2330 hours."

When the waiter and Gabby returned with their coffee and desert, Major Savino spoke as he removed a folded sheet of paper from his pocket and handed the list to his Commanding Officer. "This is a list of the men who will be assigned to each raiding party. I included the address of each location to be raided and identified the name of the CID Agent and the Paris Police Inspector who will be in command of every arrest and search team. I also listed the number of CID Agents, MPs and Paris policemen that have been assigned to each raiding party."

After reviewing the list and handing the paper to Al Parker, the new Commanding Officer of the CID Office in Paris looked at his executive officer and said, "You and the Chief Inspector are to be commended for a job well done. When this is over I hope you two can take some time off. You guys look beat."

While Major Savino responded and said, "Now that you and Al are here I'll try to do just that, Sir," Gabby poured Cognac into the five empty glasses, that were positioned on the nearby tray and handed each of the American agents and his brother-in-law an aperitif.

As soon as Gabby excused the waiter and he joined his guests at the table, the Chief Inspector raised his glass and relayed a perfect toast. "To our war on the black market. May we be safe and victorious in the performance of our duties."

In order to be considerate of their gracious host and French Allies, Jim stood up and raised his glass as he proposed another toast. While everyone present stood up with their glass in hand, Jim looked at Gabby and Francois and said, "To our French Allies. Vive la France!"

CHAPTER 5

IT'S TIME TO ROUND UP THE USUAL SUSPECTS

After surviving the fighting that took place in France, in the Huertgen Forest and during the now famous Battle of the Bulge, Sergeant Wilbur Carlton and Private Shelby Wilmont of the 28th Infantry Division, were both wounded in January of 1945 along the Ill River near Maison Rouge. Once their shrapnel wounds healed, Sergeant Carlton and Private Wilmont received a seventy two hour pass and traveled by train to Paris. As soon as they arrived at the most popular destination for leave in the ETO, the two soldiers who served together, ever since they joined the Pennsylvania National Guard, decided to celebrate the fact that they were still alive.

As far as soldiers go, Wilbur Carlton was known to be a tough son of a bitch, who lost and earned his sergeant stripes back more times than anyone else in the entire division. During the fighting in hedgerow country, the man who was busted to buck private in England for being in a drunken brawl, was promoted back to squad leader, when he led his men on a rampage through the German lines. By the time his squad made it to the Huertgen Forest, Wilbur Carlton had developed a reputation for not taking prisoners, even when German troops tried to surrender. His campaign to kill every German in sight continued, when he and his men found themselves fighting a determined enemy, during the Battle of the Bulge and in the area known as The Colmar Pocket.

As the shorter of the two men cleaned his eye glasses, Sergeant Carlton looked at his young friend and joked, "You might not want to clean your glasses until after we find a French broad to screw. This way, if she's ugly, you won't know the difference."

If there was one reason why Private Shelby Wilmont was still alive, it was because Wilbur Carlton treated him like the little brother he never had. Even though Private Wilmont was as dumb as a fence post, he was smart enough to do everything that his buddy Will told him to do.

When two uniformed Paris Policemen found the badly beaten body of a young French girl on Rue Froidevaux, by the Cimetiere du Montiparnasse, they immediately called their headquarters. Within a matter of minutes, a pair of American military policemen arrived on scene, followed by French Police Inspector Andre De La Fontaine and a U.S. Army ambulance crew. By the time Inspector De La Fontaine examined the body of 18 year old Marie Marchand, Sergeant Sam Carubba, the duty agent for Army CID, arrived in a khaki colored 1941 Ford staff car.

As soon as Agent Carubba stepped out of the Army sedan, he noticed that an older Frenchman, who walked with the aid of two canes, was standing off to the side with a pair of uniformed Paris policemen. While Sam walked over to where the Paris Police Inspector was standing, MP Corporal Tommy Baines greeted the former MP, who was now serving as a CID Agent and said, "Hi Sarge."

"Hi, Tommy," responded Agent Carubba before he addressed the criminal investigator from the Paris Police and said, "I got here as fast as I could, Andre. What's up?"

"This is a bad one, my friend," responded the Inspector Andre De La Fontaine, who paused for a second while he referred to his notebook and said, "Her name is Marie Marchand. She is 18. Before she passed out, she said she was on her way home, after working in the cafe where she is employed, when she was attacked by two American soldiers."

While a pair of U.S. Army medics prepared to transport the victim to the hospital, Inspector De La Fontaine put his notebook away when he continued with his briefing. "According to your medical personnel, she has been badly beaten and raped."

As a policeman from Baltimore, Maryland, who was performing his military service as a cop in the U.S. Army, Sam Carubba had no love for anyone who physically or sexually assaulted women. After looking down at the victim, Sam faced Andre and said, "By any chance was she able to give you a description of her assailants?"

"One was tall and one was very short and young," responded the 46 year old French Police Inspector, who fought for France during the armed conflict known as The Great War. When Inspector De La Fontaine continued, he pointed to the 52 year old Frenchman who was standing nearby and said, "Mr. Jerome Tiernay was on his way home from work, when he witnessed two American soldiers engaging Miss Marchand in conversation. When she tried to walk away, the taller of the two soldiers threw the cigarette that he was smoking off to the right, before he grabbed her arm, spun her around, struck her repeatedly and threw her to the ground. While Mr. Tiernay went to call the two Paris policemen, who he knew were posted on the corner one block to the east, he looked back and saw the shorter of the two soldiers kneeling over the victim, while his friend stood nearby and took a long drink from a bottle. After emptying the contents, the taller soldier threw the bottle over the wall into the cemetery. I have a man posted there, so we can recover the broken bottle as evidence. Unfortunately, Mr. Tiernay is a disabled French Army Lieutenant, who was seriously wounded while fighting in the trenches in 1918. As you can see, his injuries make it extremely difficult for him to walk, so it took some time for him to get help."

"Anything else?" asked Sam.

"Yes," said the French Inspector, while he motioned Sam to follow him into the street as he continued and said, "After hearing what Mr. Tiernay had to say, I asked one of your MPs to use his helmet to cover the remains of the only cigarette found in the street near her body."

As soon as Sam knelt down in the street, he lifted the MP helmet high enough off the ground to examine the unfiltered cigarette butt. After lowering the helmet back down to preserve the evidence, Sam Carubba looked at Inspector Fontaine as he stood back up and said, "Why anyone would beat and rape a nice girl in this town, when there's over two hundred brothels in Paris and some 6,000 registered prostitutes in this city, with a few thousand more working without a license, is beyond me."[8]

"I agree, my friend," responded Inspector Fontaine, who paused for a split second before he added, "This is one of those tragic crimes that certainly defies logic."

While the two medics and the two MPs carefully placed the victim on a stretcher and covered her with an Army blanket, Sam Carubba and Inspector De La Fontaine stood off to the side and held the back doors open on the Dodge WC54 Ambulance. Once the victim was placed inside, Sam asked the MP Private who he never met before, to ride in the back of the ambulance and stay with the girl, while he interviewed the witness. As soon as the MP Private acknowledged the order, Sam shut the back doors, before he turned to MP Corporal Tommy Baines and said, "Stick around, Tommy, I might need your help."

While the U.S. Army ambulance drove away from the crime scene, MP Corporal Baines responded and said, "Will do, Sarge," as Sam Carubba approached the area on the sidewalk where Mr. Tiernay was standing next to the two uniformed French policemen. After being briefed by Inspector De La Fontaine, Sam Carubba decided to give their witness the respect that he was due, because he was a medically retired French Army Officer, who was permanently disabled in the same war that crippled his father's left hand.

The moment Sam presented the witness with a casual salute, their witness did his best to stand up straight. While the American CID Agent presented his credentials, he spoke in fluent French and said, "Allow me to introduce myself, Lieutenant. My name is Sam Carubba. I'm a Staff Sergeant in the United States Army, assigned to perform the duties of an Agent with the Criminal Investigative Division."

The last thing that Mr. Tiernay expected, was to meet an American soldier who spoke French like a native. While Sam Carubba put his identification away, Mr. Tiernay congratulated Sergeant Carubba on his command of the French language. When the curious witness asked if Sam learned to speak French in school, Sam responded in a respectful tone of voice and said, "I learned French long before I went to school, Sir. You see, my mother is French. She was a nurse during World War 1. She cared for my father when he was wounded. From the day I was born my mother spoke to me in English and French. I also spent time with my grandparents here in Paris, when my father worked at the American Embassy. My father always said, that the best thing about getting wounded, was meeting my mother and falling in love with her."

"Have you been a policeman for very long, Sergeant?" asked Mr. Tiernay.

"Before the war I was a policeman in Baltimore, Maryland," said Sam who quickly added, "Once I joined the Army, they made me a military policeman assigned to Company A of the 709th MP Battalion. I was transferred to CID a few weeks ago."

"So you are no stranger to police work?" remarked the man who survived years of war, only to be severely wounded in the summer of 1918.

"No, Sir, I'm not," responded Sam before he went on to say, "I guess you can say, the only good thing about my job, is when I get the opportunity to bring criminals to justice."

"I hope what little I know can be of some assistance," said the old soldier who quickly added, "My only regret, Sergeant, is that I was unable to go to the aid of the young woman who was mistreated by two of your countrymen."

Rather than continue this in the street, Sam asked Mr. Tiernay if he would join him and Inspector De La Fontaine, while they conducted a search of the immediate area for the men responsible for this atrocious crime. As soon as the disabled combat veteran agreed to do whatever he could to help, Sam pointed to his staff car and said, "This way, Sir."

While Sam held the left rear passenger side door to his staff car open for their witness, he turned to Andre and said, "Can your men secure this crime scene until I can get another CID Agent out here?"

"Of course," said Andre, before he addressed the two uniformed French cops in their native language and instructed them to secure the scene of the crime until another American CID Agent arrived.

While the two uniformed Paris policemen acknowledged their instructions, Sam turned to U.S. Army MP Corporal Tommy Baines and said, "Let's see if we can find the bastards who did this. Who knows, Tommy, we might get lucky."

"Sure thing, Sarge," responded the 21 year old MP who survived D Day and saw some ground combat when he helped liberate Paris in August of '44.

Sam then walked over and picked up the MP helmet that was covering the cigarette butt in the street. After using his pocket knife to slide the cigarette butt into an empty envelope, Sam placed the evidence in his coat pocket as he stood up and handed the helmet to the MP Corporal. "Thanks for the use of your helmet, Tommy."

"Any time, Sarge, responded the young MP.

After facing the two uniformed Paris policemen, Sam spoke in French and said, "Il est temps rassembler les suspects habituels." As the two French policemen smiled and nodded their heads in agreement, Agent Carubba looked at MP Corporal Thomas Baines and said, "In English that means, "It's time to round up the usual suspects."

"I'll be right behind you, Sarge," responded MP Corporal Baines as he sat behind the wheel of his Jeep.

"Thanks, Tommy," responded Sam as he closed the rear door on his staff car before he addressed Andre again and said, "You might as well jump in with me, Andre, while we canvass the area. Your men can watch your car until we get back."

While Sam opened the driver's door of his car and got in behind the wheel, Inspector Fontaine opened the front passenger door, as he he told the two French cops that they were welcomed to sit in his car until he returned. Even though the two Paris policemen were like other cops, who were used to standing and walking for hours in different types of weather, they were grateful for the chance to sit in a car and get out of the cold.

After thanking the Inspector for the use of his car, Andre called out, "You are welcome," in French, as he sat in the front passenger seat of the U.S. Army sedan and closed the door. A split second later, CID Agent Sam Carubba, along with his French counterpart and their witness, drove away from the scene of the crime followed by MP Corporal Baines in a U.S. Army MP Jeep.

After walking two blocks from where they assaulted the 18 year old French girl, Sergeant Wilbur Carlton and Private Shelby Wilmont stopped at a corner cafe to get a drink. Even though he was an uneducated kid, Shelby Wilmont was looking to be reassured that they did the right thing, when he turned to his buddy and said, "I kind'a feel bad about what we did to that French girl."

"Why?" remarked Sergeant Carlton, who quickly added, "These French broads screwed every German in sight for years. That's why I'm not paying for it. She also pissed me off, when she said that we were acting like pigs instead of liberators."

"But she was just a kid, Sarge," responded Private Wilmont.

"So are you," remarked Sergeant Carlton, who paused to light another cigarette before he exhaled a lung full of smoke and said, "The least that bitch should'a done was give it up to you voluntarily, after all you've been through, to free her cute little French ass from the fucking Krauts."

Private Carlton sounded like his conscience was getting the best of him when he continued and said, "I didn't want it that bad, Sarge. She wasn't even awake half the time. I could'a waited until we found a girl who liked G.I.s. Heck, I would'a paid for it."

Once again, Sergeant Carlton acted like he knew what was best for the both of them and remarked, "I told you, kid. We're not paying for it. The most I'll go for is a pack of smokes, maybe two, but that's it."

After driving through the immediate neighborhood, Sam Carubba spotted two American soldiers leave a corner cafe who loosely matched the description of the two subjects. "Heads up, Andre," remarked Sam, before he continued and said, "Check out the two G.I.s who just came out of the cafe on the corner. The shorter one looks like he was kneeling in dirt."

After turning sideways in the front seat, Andre asked their witness if he thought the two American soldiers, who were standing in front of a nearby cafe, could be the two assailants? While Sam pulled the Army sedan over the curb, Mr. Tiernay responded and said, "They are the right size, but I was too far away to get a look at their faces. Besides, they were facing away from me at the time." Mr. Tiernay then remembered something of critical importance and sounded a bit excited when he quickly added, "Excuse me, Sergeant, but there is something else that you must know. When the taller one raised his bottle to take a drink and he threw it over the wall into the cemetery, the shoulder patch that he wore on his uniform looked as if it was red in color."

After hearing what their witness had to say, Sam instinctively knew that they just located the two soldiers who assaulted Marie Marchand. He came to this conclusion, because the two suspects they had under surveillance, were wearing the red keystone shaped shoulder patch of the 28th Infantry Division on their uniforms.

As soon as Sam shut the engine off, he turned to his right and said, "Are you ready, Andre?"

Andre De La Fontaine had been a cop long enough to know what needed to be done next. While the veteran French cop opened the passenger door to the unmarked U.S. Army sedan, he looked at his American counterpart from CID and said, "Oui, mon ami."

After signaling MP Corporal Thomas Baines to follow them across the street, Sam led the way as he approached the two suspects while they walked toward another cafe. While coming up behind the two men, Sam reached into his right side pant's pocket and gripped the leather bound blackjack that he carried, when he patrolled the streets of Baltimore before the war. If these soldiers proved to the men they were looking for and they resisted in any way, Sam had every intention of taking them into custody, so they could stand trial for sexually assaulting a female French civilian.

The second Sam placed his left hand on the back of the taller man's shoulder and said, "Hold it up, you two, CID," Sergeant Wilbur Carlton immediately turned and went to attack the Army Agent. Even though Sam Carubba was a tad shorter in height, he responded to being assaulted with ferocity. After blocking his assailant's punch, Sam knocked his attacker unconscious with one blow to his forehead with his leather coated blackjack. By the time Sergeant Carlton hit the ground, Private Shelby Wilmont was in custody and confessing to raping a French girl.

While Inspector De La Fontaine handcuffed Private Wilmont, MP Corporal Baines held back the crowd of Allied troops on leave, as well as some French civilians. Just as additional Allied MPs and uniformed French Police responded to the scene, Sergeant Carubba had a dazed Sergeant

Carlton handcuffed and was lifting him off the sidewalk.

With blood streaming down his face, Sergeant Carlton screamed, "Shut the fuck up, stupid," as he was led away to a nearby MP Jeep, while Private Wilmont repeated how sorry he was for hurting that French girl.

As soon as the two prisoners were taken away, Sam turned to Inspector De La Fontaine and said, "What do you say we buy our witness a drink before we head back to the office?"

"You are a Frenchman at heart, my friend," remarked the Inspector, who quickly added, "I will get us a table, while you help Mr. Tiernay across the street."

As soon as Sam Carubba and Inspector Fontaine returned to the CID Office to write their reports, Lieutenant Carl Miller from the 709th MP Battalion Headquarters called to inform the CID Duty Agent, that a shootout just occurred in the 14th Arrondissement between two groups of AWOL G.I.s. While Sam wrote the address down, the MP Lieutenant remarked, "Standby, Sam. I have another call coming in from an MP at the scene."

After taking the other call, Lieutenant Miller got back on the phone and said, "Sergeant Dalton just called in to report that Agents Coppola and Angelone heard the shots being fired and responded to the scene of the crime. Both of your agents are heading up the search for the two gunmen, who fled the area on foot when their getaway car wouldn't start."

"Thanks Lieutenant," responded Sam, who quickly added, "I'm on my way as well."

As soon as Sam hung up the phone, he stood up and turned to his left, to where Inspector Fontaine was sitting at the desk next to his and said, "You're not gonna believe this, Andre, but two groups of AWOL G.I.s just had a shootout in front of the Cafe Le Dome. Two AWOL Americans and three French civilians were wounded."

While Andre stood up and followed Agent Carubba to the door, the experienced Paris policeman remarked, "Forgive me for saying so, Sam, but these AWOL soldiers of yours are giving the American Army a bad name.

Someone needs to tell these men, that they need to be shooting at the Germans, not at French civilians, or at each other."

As the two men left the office, Sam responded and said, "You're right about that," as he shut the lights and closed the door to the office.

★ ★ ★

While Jim Beauregard, Major Savino, Lieutenant Al Parker, Chief Inspector Dumont, Sergeant Mulligan and Inspector Goulet were leaving the back entrance to The Paris Cafe, an unmarked U.S. Army sedan drove up and came to a stop. As soon as Sam Carubba got out of the staff car, the CID Agent spoke as he saluted his new commanding officer. "I'm Staff Sergeant Sam Carubba, Sir. I'm the Duty Agent tonight. Major Savino told me that I could find you here with Lieutenant Parker and the Chief Inspector, until it was time to execute a number of raids throughout Paris."

After returning the salute, Jim wasted no time in asking, "What's up, Sam?"

Jim Beauregard knew that he was being briefed by an experienced law enforcement officer, as soon as Sam responded and said, "An 18 year old French girl was badly beaten and raped on Rue Froidevaux by the Montiparnasse cemetery. She's in bad shape, Colonel, but she'll survive. The good news, Sir, is that thanks to a credible civilian witness, Inspector Fontaine and I, along with MP Corporal Thomas Baines, were able to locate two G.I.s, who matched the general description of the two assailants, when we canvassed the immediate area. When the subject identified as Sergeant Wilbur Carlton attempted to assault me, I had to use some force to take him into custody, Sir. The shorter of the two assailants, a Private by the name of Shelby Wilmont, confessed on the spot. We also recovered a broken pint bottle of Napoleon Brandy, that our witness said the taller of the two assailants drank from and threw over the wall into the cemetery. The same subject also threw a cigarette butt in the street that we recovered as well. This cigarette butt matched the brand of smokes that we found in Sergeant Carlton's possession at the time of his arrest."

"I see you've had a busy night," remarked Jim.

"There's more, Sir," responded Sam Carubba, who quickly added, "As

soon as Inspector Fontaine and I got back to the office, I received a call from
an MP Lieutenant that all hell broke loose, when two AWOL G.I.s opened
fire on two other deserters at the Cafe Le Dome, on Rue St. Dominique
in the 14th Arrondissement (Montparnesse). Sergeants Angelone and
Coppola, along with a squad of MPs and Paris cops led by Inspector
Fontaine, are searching the area for the two gunmen who fled the scene on
foot. As soon as I finish briefing the Colonel, I'll return to join the search."

"How bad was the shootout?" asked Jim.

"Five wounded, Sir. Three civilians and two AWOL G.I.s," responded
Agent Carubba before he continued and said, "Based on what I heard so far,
one of the wounded soldiers went AWOL from a rest camp, after receiving
a Dear John letter from home. This G.I. wasn't armed and is cooperating,
Sir. He's only been AWOL for about two weeks, so he could get off pretty
easy, as long as he agrees to return to his unit. The fact that he's willing to
help us nail the group of deserters that he fell in with, should also go in his
favor."

"Good work, Sam. Carry on," responded the new commanding officer of
the Paris CID Office.

"Yes Sir," said the 25 year old CID Agent, as he saluted his new CO,
before he got back in his staff car and left the area.

While Sam Carubba drove away, Jim turned to his second in command
and said, "Sergeant Carubba's a good man. We're did you find him?"

"He was an MP with the 709th MP Battalion here in Paris," responded
Major Savino, who quickly added, "We ran into him after he shot a deserter who was carrying a captured Kraut pistol, while he was burglarizing a
civilian home. When Sam ordered the AWOL G.I. to stop and he went for
his gun, Sam put a .45 slug in the guy's leg. By the time Hank Blair and
Chris Jacko arrived at the hospital, where this prisoner was being patched
up, Sam convinced the deserter, that it was in his best interest to cooperate
with CID. Based on his cooperation, we locked up a small group of deserters who committed a number of burglaries in Paris. Once I heard that Sam
was a cop in Baltimore before the war, who spoke fluent French and lived in
Paris when he was a kid, I offered him a job in CID."

"I'm glad you brought him onboard, he's an impressive young man,"
responded Jim, who paused briefly while he changed the subject and said,

"As far as tonight goes, I want everyone involved in these raids to be careful and watch what they're shooting at if they get into a gunfight. This is Paris, not the Battle of the Bulge."

As soon as Tom Savino acknowledged the order, Jim checked his watch, before he looked at the others and said, "We have twenty five minutes to get into position, size up the situation and hit every location at 2330 hours."

When another U.S. Army staff car drove up and stopped behind The Paris Cafe, Major Savino remarked, "Here's your ride, Sir and he's right on time."

While CID Agent Hank Blair exited the staff car and went around the front of the vehicle, to hold the passenger door open for his commanding officer, Major Savino continued and said, "If you follow us, Sir, we'll take you and Al to the location where Captain Thompson his waiting with his MP's and the Chief Inspector's men."

"OK gentlemen, let's go," remarked Jim Beauregard, before he greeted Sergeant Hank Blair with a smile and a hearty handshake. The last time Jim saw Hank Blair was when they were lying next to each other in a field hospital, after being wounded while pursuing Ivan Larson and Francis Shorty Mc Ghee behind enemy lines.

While Sergeant Blair stood by the open front passenger side door of the khaki colored Army staff car, Jim seemed genuinely concerned when he said, "How's your foot, Hank."

"Good as new, Sir," remarked Agent Blair, as his Commanding Officer sat in the front passenger seat of the vehicle.

Immediately after Agent Blair closed the front door on the Army sedan, a smiling Al Parker enthusiastically shook hands with the young CID Agent and said, "It's good to see you, Hank. We have a lot to catch up on."

Once Hank opened the back door and Al went to sit in the back seat, Hank Blair remarked, "Congratulations on the promotion, Lieutenant," before he closed the door and walked around the front of the staff car and sat in the driver's seat.

While Hank put the staff car in gear and began to follow the other vehicles, Jim Beauregard used his Zippo to light a cigarette, before he cracked the window and said, "Tell me, Hank. Do we ever get to sleep around here, or do we just work until we drop from exhaustion?"

While Hank glanced over to the man that he followed behind enemy lines, to pursue two fugitives during the Battle of the Bulge, the young agent sounded very gung-ho when he responded and said, "Paris is non stop action, Sir. I wouldn't have it any other way and neither would the other men. Besides, Major Savino said that we can sleep when the war is over."

CHAPTER 6

A BUSY NIGHT IN PARIS FOR ARMY COPS AND PARIS POLICEMEN

The second they spotted an American soldier nervously looking around, as he left the entrance to an apartment building and slipped a .45 caliber pistol under his coat, Sergeant Salvatore Coppola turned to his partner and said, "That must be the guy we're looking for."

"I agree," responded Sergeant Anthony Angelone, who quickly added, "In addition to the fact that he looks guilty as sin, I'll bet he has no authority to be carrying a gun in Paris."

"I wonder where his friend is?" asked Sal.

"My guess is they split up once they took off," responded the CID Agent who everyone called Ange.

While the two Army Agents, who served as Military Policemen before Jim Beauregard had them transferred to CID, remained in the doorway of a nearby apartment building, they watched the subject of their foot pursuit enter a cafe and take a seat at an empty table. "Let's go," said Sergeant Angelone as he and his partner left their position of cover to make their arrest.

While acting as if they were drunk, the two CID Agents entered the cafe, just as a waiter delivered a glass of wine to the subject of their manhunt. After intentionally bumping into the table where the armed AWOL G.I. was sitting, Sergeant Coppola excused himself, while Sergeant Angelone drew his .45 caliber pistol and shoved it into the suspect's neck and said, "CID asshole. Move and you're a dead man."

Once the prisoner was disarmed and handcuffed, the two CID Agents, whose fathers worked with Jim Beauregard and Al Parker in the New

York CID Task Force, escorted their prisoner out of the cafe. While Agent Angelone flagged down a Jeep carrying two American MPs, Agent Coppola continued searching their prisoner more thoroughly.

Just as a second MP Jeep arrived in front of the cafe, Sergeant Angelone leaned closer to their prisoner and said, "Things will go a lot easier on you if you help us find your friend."

As someone who knew that he was facing hard time, for violating several sections of the Articles of War, Nathan Gromley limited his response to saying, "Go to hell."

"You first, prick," responded Sergeant Angelone as he forcefully pushed his handcuffed prisoner down into the front passenger seat of the first MP Jeep that arrived on scene.

While Sergeant Angelone climbed into the back of the first MP Jeep with the other MP, his partner called out, "I'll follow you in the other Jeep," as he climbed into the back of the second MP Jeep that arrived on scene.

After logging their prisoner, Sal Coppola and Anthony Angelone met Sam Carubba as they left the 709th MP Headquarters in Paris.

"I heard you guys got lucky and nailed one of the gunmen," remarked Sam.

"Luck had nothing to do with it, Sam. It's what they call good police work," responded Sergeant Angelone.

"Any news on the one that got away?" asked Sal.

After shaking his head from left to right Sam said, "Nothing yet, but the night is young."

As soon as Lieutenant Carl Miller left the MP Headquarters in an obvious hurry, Sergeant Angelone spoke up and said, "It looks like the Lieutenant has some news for us."

"I'm glad I caught you guys before you took off," said the MP Lieutenant.

"What's up, Lieutenant?" asked Sam.

Without hesitating, the MP Officer responded and said, "The other AWOL G.I. who did the shooting tonight was just spotted going into the basement of an apartment building, two blocks away from the Le Dome

Cafe." While he handed Agent Carubba a piece of paper, Lieutenant Miller added, "Here's the address, Sam. Some of my men, along with Inspector Fontaine and a few Paris cops have the building surrounded and are waiting for you to arrive."

"Thanks Lieutenant," responded Sam before he turned to the others and said, "Let's go!"

When Charlie Monacco had a hard time sleeping he decided to leave Marcel's safe house and get on with the business of turning himself in to the military police. After washing up and giving himself a quick shave, Charlie put on his uniform and left the apartment so he could surrender to the first MP he could find.

Due to the time of year, it would be a while before the sun would shine this early in the morning. After closing the top button on his winter coat, Charlie decided to smoke a cigarette while he made his way to the corner where a pair of MPs were sitting in a Jeep. After taking one last drag on his Lucky Strike, Charlie Monacco field stripped his cigarette, as he walked across the street like a man who was resigned to accept whatever came his way. The moment Charlie spotted the MP driving the Jeep put the vehicle in gear and begin to drive away, Charlie called out, "Hey MPs hold it up."

As soon as the MP sitting behind the wheel put the Jeep in neutral, his partner stepped out of the vehicle and said, "What's up, Sarge," when he spotted the staff sergeant coming his way.

"My name is Staff Sergeant Charlie Monacco," responded Charlie, before he paused for a second and said, "I'm AWOL from the 4th Convalescent Hospital in Senoches, France and would like to turn myself in."

"This is a first for me," remarked the shocked MP Corporal, who quickly added, "I never had someone who was AWOL turn themselves in."

Under the circumstances, Charlie acted like turning himself in was no big deal when he remarked, "Do you guys mind if we get something to eat before you take me in. My treat."

Once the MP Corporal gave his prisoner a quick but thorough pat down, he pointed to the front passenger seat and said, "Have a seat, Sarge," while his partner jumped into the back. As the MP Corporal walked around to the driver's side of the Jeep, he did his best to sound appreciative when he said, "Thanks for the offer, Sarge, but we can't make any stops once we take a prisoner into custody."

While the MP Jeep drove through Paris in the early hours of the morning, Charlie wondered if Marcel was right and he should have joined the French Foreign Legion, or taken him up on his offer to go to Switzerland. If he was lucky, he would return to a combat unit and survive the war. If things worked out differently, he would end up in the stockade, until he was shipped home to serve the rest of his sentence in a federal prison.

As soon as the assignments were handed out, the staff car driven by Hank Blair, that contained Jim Beauregard and Al Parker, was escorted to the vicinity of Moffett's warehouse, by a Jeep carrying two MPs and a black Peugeot sedan carrying two uniformed French policemen. Once the three vehicles arrived at their destination, they came to a stop on a dark street in the business district. As soon as Jim, Al and Hank exited the staff car, Jim spoke just above a whisper when he faced Al and said, "Don't worry, Al. Your son and his undercover partner will be in safe hands in a few minutes."

As the two Army Officers, along with Hank Blair, the two MP's and the two French cops approached an unmarked French police car, CID Agent Bill Hayes and Inspector Girard Dupray exited their vehicle and met the rest of the raiding party on the sidewalk. Once the introductions were made, Agent Hayes provided a quick briefing to the two Army Officers and the men who were with them. While doing so, the 30 year old cop from Dallas, Texas, who was now serving as an Army CID Agent, explained how Agent Parker was just observed smoking a cigar in front of Moffett's warehouse and relayed the pre-arranged signal, that there were ten AWOLs inside beside his informant."

After checking his watch, Jim asked Agent Hayes what the set up was in Moffett's warehouse and how he recommended that they make entry. As Agent Hayes pointed down the long dark street that ran perpendicular to the subject location, he sounded like a veteran street cop when he answered his commanding office. "Moffett's warehouse is the one on the corner, Sir. Sergeants Butler and Fermi from our office are covering the front and west side. Inspector Dupray and I have been covering the east side and the back of this location."

After turning to face Lt. Colonel Beauregard and the other members of the raiding party, Agent Hayes continued and said. "With your permission, Sir, I'd like to post two men behind the warehouse to cover the back door and the alley. Major Savino also provided us with an old beat up but still serviceable deuce and a half that we recovered a week ago. This truck is parked nearby and will enable us to make quite an entrance, when we use it to crash through the large wooden doors of Moffett's warehouse."

While facing Lieutenant Al Parker and his new commanding officer, the CID Agent from Dallas explained himself further and said, "According to a message that we received from Sergeant Parker, we have no choice but to come in like gangbusters, Sir, because Moffett makes the man on duty at night, place a large wooden beam across the inside of the double wooden doors."

It was clear to everyone present, that Lieutenant Al Parker wanted to be one of the first members of the raiding party to enter Moffett's warehouse, when he spoke up and said, "With your permission, Sir, I'd like to ride in the deuce and half."

Under the circumstances Jim knew that it was futile to prevent Al from going in with the initial assault team. When Jim asked Agent Hayes who was assigned to drive the Army cargo truck, the Dallas police detective turned CID Agent pointed to himself and said, "That's my job, Sir."

"OK, Bill, but Lieutenant Parker will ride up front with you, while I ride in the back with Hank Blair, the two MPs and Inspector Dupray. Our French Allies in blue will cover the back door to the warehouse. I also want the two CID men covering the front of the warehouse to head around back to help the two gendarmes. Once we make entry, Inspector Dupray and Agent Blair will go with us, while the two MPs will cover our backs and keep anyone who gets past us, from escaping through the big hole that we're gonna make in those barn doors. Then, after checking his watch, Jim looked at Sergeant Hayes and the other members of the raiding party and said,

"Let's get into position. We go in five minutes."

After arriving at the apartment building that was surrounded by American, British and French Military Policemen, along with several uniformed Paris policemen, Sam Carubba led the way as he approached MP Staff Sergeant Steve Dalton and said, "Thanks for holding the fort for us until we got here."

Steve Dalton was an MP Staff Sergeant who served as a cop in New Orleans before the war. After arriving in France, Staff Sergeant Dalton was assigned to patrol the streets of Paris. One of the military policemen that he worked with was Sam Carubba.

As the tobacco chewing MP faced his old Army buddy, he spoke with a Cajun accent that was hard for the other members of Sam's team to understand. "You're just in time, Sam. We just finished surrounding the building. It looks like the guy we're looking for was wounded, 'cause we found a blood trail leading into the basement. We also had two civilians report, that they saw an American soldier who matches the description of one of the gunmen, limping as he walked toward this building."

After looking in the direction of the Cafe Le Dome, Sam turned back to face Sergeant Dalton as he addressed the military policeman. "That explains why the second gunman didn't get very far." Then, after turning to face Sergeants Angelone and Coppola, Sam added, "Fortunately, Ange and Sal nailed his buddy in a cafe three blocks from here."

After being involved in the arrest of the other gunman, Sal Coppola spoke up and said, "Does anybody know what this guy is carrying?"

"A small caliber pistol. That's all we know," responded Sergeant Dalton.

Sergeant Anthony Angelone was a lot like his father and could always be counted on to crack a joke at the right time when he remarked, "If we wait any longer to go after this guy, he'll bleed to death, or die from lead poisoning."

Sam Carubba also had a sense a humor and proved it when he removed an Army issue flashlight from his coat pocket and handed it to Agent Angelone as he said, "Thanks for volunteering to lead the way, Ange. The rest of us will be right behind you."

This was one of those times when even a Cajun like Steve Dalton could be clearly understood when he cracked a smile then said, "He got you that time, Ange."

"Me and my big mouth," remarked Agent Angelone as he slipped the flashlight in his coat pocket and drew his .45 caliber 1911. While Agent Angelone held the pistol by his right side, with the barrel pointing toward the ground, he seemed to be in exceptionally good spirits, when he faced the men who were following him in harm's way and said, "Let's get this guy."

Inside Moffett's warehouse Cal Parker and Benny Greene were playing cards in the office, while nine AWOL soldiers got some sleep and one was on guard duty. When the deserter on guard duty entered the office and asked if the new driver known as Doc Carter and Benny were ever going to hit the sack, Cal played along and said, "Not as long as I'm winning and Benny is losing." Cal then added, "Besides, Moffett said we won't be making a run to the POL dump to pick up fuel until tomorrow afternoon."

While Jim and Al stood by the side of the U.S. Army cargo truck, Jim checked his watch before he looked at Al and said, "Don't be too hard on Cal. You've done some crazy stuff in your day as well." Then, after pausing for a split second, Jim added, "Remember what my son Michael pulled, when he left a nice warm hospital bed before his wounds were healed, so he could rejoin his unit, in time to fight in that frozen hell hole around Bastogne?"

Jim and Al had been partners and good friends long enough to be able to speak honestly and in the frankest of terms to each other. Al proved that he appreciated what Jim was trying to do, when he looked at the man who was his friend, his partner and his commanding officer and said, "You're right. What Michael did was both crazy and very gung-ho. In fact, all four of our boys are doing some crazy stuff while fighting in this war…and God love for 'em for being who they are, 'cause that's why we're gonna win and the enemy is gonna lose."

After cracking a smile, Jim remarked, "Look who they take after."

"That's exactly what my wife's gonna say when she hears this story," remarked Al.

A split second later, their friendly exchange was interrupted by Agent Bill Hayes saying, "It's time to go, Sir."

While Al opened the passenger side door to the Army truck, he faced Jim and said, "Thanks," before he climbed inside the cab.

"You're welcome," responded Jim in a friendly tone of voice, before he joined the rest of the men, as they took positions in the back of the truck. Once Jim signaled Al to proceed, he climbed inside and sat next to Sergeant Blair.

Meanwhile, in another section of Paris, Sergeant Angelone glanced back at the men who were lined up behind him and said, "Here goes," as he slowly opened the door and entered the pitch black apartment building. Between the blood trail and the statements from two French civilians, every member of the search team was about as certain as they could be, that a wounded American soldier, who was armed with a small caliber pistol, took refuge in the basement of the building that they were about to search.

After crouching down behind the best cover available, Sergeant Angelone pointed his pistol into the darkness and cocked the hammer, while he held up his flashlight and called out. "Army CID! You're completely surrounded. Drop the gun, put your hands up and call out to us, but don't move until I tell you to do so!"

When no one responded, Sergeant Angelone got an idea and tried a different approach when he called out, "OK, Pal. You give us no choice. We have an MP with a German shepherd outside that's waiting to be let off the leash. Once Rin Tin Rin enters this basement, we're gonna let him take a big piece out'a your ass before we pull him off."

Immediately after Ange called out, "OK, bring that new dog down here right now! It's time he earned his keep!" a voice called out from the darkness and said, "Hey, CID, hold off on that dog! I give up! I'm putting my gun down and I'm standing with my hands up!"

After hearing Sam Carubba whisper, "Nice work, Ange," Agent Angelone aimed his flashlight in the direction of the wounded AWOL G.I.s voice. As soon as he illuminated the suspect, Agent Angelone used a commanding tone of voice when he called out, "Keep your hands in the air and walk slowly toward the light. If you try any funny stuff, you will be shot!"

Once the suspect got closer, Sergeant Angelone continued to hold his light on the wounded AWOL Sergeant, while Sam Carubba, Sal Coppola and Staff Sergeant Dalton moved in with their guns drawn to take the soldier into custody.

While AWOL Sergeant Alan Beaver was searched and handcuffed, Inspector Fontaine patted Sergeant Angelone on the back and said, "I will have to remember that trick, about calling for the German Shepherd to be brought in. After living in a city that was occupied by the Boche, I know from experience, that everyone is afraid of those damn dogs."

The second a loud crashing noise was heard and a U.S. Army cargo truck came barreling through the wooden double doors of the warehouse, Cal Parker drew the Model 1903 Colt that he carried under his Ike Jacket and pointed the pistol at the deserter on guard duty. "Army CID! You're under arrest!" yelled Cal. As soon as Cal relieved the stunned AWOL G.I. of his M1 Carbine, he slipped his pistol into his pant's pocket, before he cycled a round into the chamber and ordered the prisoner to place his hands on top of his head.

By the time the other deserters woke up and scrambled out of the back room to see what the commotion was all about, the raiding party led by Jim Beauregard had everyone surrounded and in custody. As soon as Cal Parker escorted his prisoner out of the office, he spotted his father patting down a half dressed prisoner, as if he was back on his beat in New York City, only this time his dad wore the uniform of a U.S. Army Officer.

When Jim Beauregard saw Cal emerge from the warehouse office with an AWOL G.I. in custody, he turned to the MP Sergeant in charge of the detail and said, "Sergeant, take that prisoner off Agent Parker's hands."

"Yes Sir," remarked the MP Sergeant as he complied with the order and he took custody of the deserter who was disarmed by Cal Parker.

The moment the ten handcuffed AWOL American soldiers were escorted past Cal Parker and Benny Greene, the last deserter in line made the fatal mistake of calling out, "You niggers are dead men once Moffett and Mollet find out you're with CID."

After hearing the last deserter in line threaten Cal Parker and Benny Greene, a pissed off Jim Beauregard called out, "Hold it up, Sergeant." While the MP Sergeant abruptly stopped the prisoners from moving any further, Jim Beauregard turned to Al Parker and said, "Lieutenant, I think we need to have a talk with the last man in line. You can use the warehouse office to conduct your interrogation."

As soon as Al said, "Yes, Sir," and he took custody of the last prisoner in line, Lt. Colonel Beauregard greeted Cal Parker with a smile and a hearty handshake as he said, "Well done, Cal. We're all proud of you, especially your old man."

"Thank you, Sir," responded Cal before he introduced Lt. Colonel James Beauregard to Benny Greene. "This is Corporal Benny Greene, Sir. We couldn't have done this without him."

As soon as Corporal Greene snapped to attention and saluted the new commanding officer of the Paris CID Office, Jim returned the salute, before he addressed the AWOL soldier who recently changed sides and became one of the good guys again. "You did an excellent job for us, Corporal. How would you like to remain assigned to CID until we address your AWOL charges? Besides, you need to be protected as long as Moffett and Mollet are on the loose."

After seeing the young Negro Corporal smile and remark, "Yes, Sir. I sure would, Colonel," Jim Beauregard motioned Cal and Benny to meet him off to the side of the warehouse with Agent Hayes and Inspector Dupray. By the time Al Parker escorted the deserter with the big mouth into the warehouse office, Jim was standing in a huddle with other members of the raiding party. After quickly lighting a cigarette, Jim looked directly at Benny Greene and said, "What can you tell us about the AWOL G.I. who just threatened you and Sergeant Parker?"

The thought of going from being an AWOL soldier to a member of Army CID in the span of a few days, made Corporal Benny Greene feel like he just earned a battlefield commission. When Benny answered the Colonel's question, he did so like a young man who knew exactly what he was talking about. "His name is Earl Johnson, Colonel. He's from Biloxi. He was one of Moffett's men in his old unit. They went AWOL together."

After looking at Cal Parker, the 20 year old Benny Green faced the Colonel from CID as he continued and said, "I told Cal all about him, Sir. Johnson is the one who picks up Sergeant Moffett's money from Pierre Mollet's right hand man, a Frenchman by the name of Duval."

As soon as Inspector Dupray heard what Benny just said, the experienced Paris Police Investigator spoke up and said, "Excuse me, Corporal, but do you mean Henri Duval?"

After hearing the question, Benny shook his head up and down and responded in a very respectful tone of voice and said, "Yes, Sir."

While Cal faced Colonel Beauregard, he confirmed what Benny had to say and added, "Duval never comes here, Sir. In fact, according to what Benny told me, the Mollet brothers only came here once and when they did, it was at night and they didn't stay long. As far as we know, Sir, Pierre Mollet and his brother Antone let Sergeant Moffett run this end of the operation. In addition to being Sergeant Moffett's right hand man, Earl Johnson is the paymaster for this gang of AWOLs and the main contact with Pierre Mollet's men, in particular Henri Duval."

In an effort to let his new Commanding Officer see how valuable Benny Greene was to this investigation, Cal turned to his undercover partner and said, "Tell the Colonel what you told me about what these guys have been stealing and selling on the black market through the Mollet brothers."

After facing Cal for a split second, Benny let his facial expression relay how much he appreciated the opportunity to brief the new Commanding Officer of the Army CID Office in Paris. Even though Benny Greene wasn't highly educated, he proved that he was worth his weight in gold as an undercover operative, when he began his briefing by saying, "Like I told Sergeant Parker, Sir. Every AWOL G.I. who works for Sergeant Moffett has been using stolen Army trucks to deliver everything from stolen Army gasoline to cigarettes, rations, medical supplies, blankets and clothing to different locations in Paris. When they make these deliveries, Earl Johnson runs the show and Duval is always waiting with his men to take possession of the trucks. Even the deliveries that I made with Sergeant Parker, were to customers that belonged to Henri Duval." Then, after a quick pause, Bennie added, "I was also told to forget that I heard the name Mollet. As I told Cal, I mean Sergeant Parker, the one night that Pierre Mollet and his brother came around, I was on guard duty when Corporal Johnson told me to open the doors and let them drive into the warehouse. At the time I didn't know who they were, Sir. Later that night, I heard Johnson joking around with Sergeant Moffett about how the name Pierre Boucher was perfect for Pierre Mollet, because that name meant butcher in French."

As soon as Jim asked how Benny knew who Johnson and Moffett were referring too, Benny responded and said, "Well, Sir, that was easy. You see, Colonel, it was Johnson who made some comment about how Antone Mollet would look a lot different if he grew a beard like his older brother. That's when I also heard that the Mollet brothers were wanted for being collaborators." Then, after a brief split second pause, Benny went on to say, "I almost forgot, Colonel, but Sergeant Moffett also said that the name butcher in French fit Pierre Mollet like a glove, because he was one ruthless son of a gun."

When Cal spoke up and prompted his sidekick to tell the Colonel about Johnson's apartment, Benny remarked, "Thanks for reminding me, Sarge," before he faced Lt. Colonel Beauregard and said, "Like I told Sergeant Parker, Sir. Corporal Johnson has an apartment in the Latin Quarter. I know about this place, because I helped Johnson move some of his belongings out'a the back room of this warehouse where he used to sleep. He uses this apartment on his days off." Then after another split second pause, Benny added, "As crazy as this sounds, Sir, even AWOL G.I.s who work in the gangs that are involved in the black market get days off."

As soon as Al Parker led his prisoner into the warehouse office, the father in him slammed the door loud enough to cause his prisoner to try and pull away as he remarked, "Hey what gives. I want'a talk to a white officer."

The moment Al felt his prisoner try and break free from the grip that he had on his arm, he yanked Corporal Johnson back and slammed him into the wall next to the desk as he said, "Resisting arrest are you? We'll see about that." Al then grabbed the AWOL G.I. by the nape of his neck so hard his prisoner grimaced in pain, as he was forcibly pushed down into the wooden chair that was positioned in front of the large wooden desk.

As Al Parker made eye contact with the prisoner, he leaned over and grabbed Johnson by the throat and said, "You listen to me you AWOL piece'a shit. That young CID Agent with the sergeant stripes on his arm that you threatened happens to be my son. If he so much as catches a fucking cold and I think you're responsible, I'll find you no matter where you are and I'll cut your dick off with a rusty dull knife. The same goes for Corporal Greene. If any harm comes to that kid, I'm coming after you. Do I make myself clear?"

The moment the office door swung open and Jim Beauregard entered the room, Corporal Earl Johnson called out, "This nigger assaulted and threatened me, Colonel."

While Jim stood in the open doorway, he did his best to sound official when he asked, "Is there a problem here, Lieutenant?"

As expected, Al Parker responded as if he and his commanding officer weren't friends. "When the prisoner resisted arrest, Sir, he had to be restrained."

The second the enraged prisoner vaulted out of his chair and screamed, "Who you gonna believe me or this nigger?" Al Parker shoved Corporal Johnson back down in his chair.

While Jim Beauregard approached the prisoner, Earl Johnson was convinced that a high ranking Army Officer with a southern accident would take his side and see to it that his colored lieutenant was arrested for mistreating a prisoner. No one was more surprised than Earl Johnson, when Lt. Colonel James Beauregard towered over him and said, "You're one stupid redneck son of a bitch who doesn't know when to shut the hell up."

As Jim continued, he spoke in a raised tone of voice while he pointed out the office door into the warehouse. "You threatened two of my undercover agents in front of a room full of CID Agents, MPs and a French cop and you have the balls to make accusations against one of the most highly decorated officers in this man's army; a man who served in combat during World War 1, as well as in The Battle of the Bulge."

While Earl Johnson looked up at the Negro Lieutenant, Jim Beauregard continued addressing the prisoner in a stern tone of voice, when he continued and said, "While you and your friends deserted your rear area tit jobs and were making a fortune selling stolen Army supplies on the black market, this man was killing Germans. Do you know how I know this.... because I was with Lieutenant Parker, when he risked his life to take on a reinforced squad of German SS troop, in order to save his unit and arrest a cop killer, who tried to surrender to the enemy, to avoid being captured by Army CID."

After removing a pack of cigarettes from the prisoner's shirt pocket and handing him one of his own smokes, Jim offered Johnson a light while he continued and said, "You're in a lotta trouble, Corporal, so if you want me to add additional charges to your court martial for threatening two undercover agents, I'll be happy to do so. It's up to you." Then, after lighting one of his own cigarettes, Jim looked down at the prisoner and said, "If Lieutenant Parker said you resisted arrest, then you'll be charged with that offense, as well other charges involving the theft of government property, war profiteering and dealing with French criminals who collaborated with the enemy during the occupation of France."

While the prisoner took a drag on his cigarette and he considered his options, he looked up at Al Parker before he looked up at Jim Beauregard and said, "I guess I did pull away from the Lieutenant." Then, after he paused long enough to take another drag from his cigarette, Earl Johnson looked up at Jim Beauregard again and said, "I might be a redneck but I'm no fool, Colonel. I know when the deck is stacked against me. I'll play ball. All I want's know, Sir, is what's in it for me if I do?"

As soon as Jim took another drag on his cigarette, he addressed the prisoner in a businesslike tone of voice. "Right now you're looking at hard time and being shipped home with a dishonorable discharge that will haunt you for the rest of your life. If you cooperate to our satisfaction and I mean to our complete satisfaction, I will personally recommend that every consideration should be made to mitigate the charges against you, but I stress that this will only happen if you give us everything we want and then some. Do I make myself clear?"

After pausing to take another drag on his cigarette, Johnson behaved like every other prisoner who submitted to being arrested and decided to cooperate with the authorities, in exchange for leniency when he said, "What do you want'a know, Colonel?"

As soon as Jim turned toward the door and he called Sergeant Cal Parker and Corporal Benny Greene into the room, he faced the prisoner and said, "You can begin by apologizing to Lieutenant Parker, Sergeant Parker and Corporal Greene for your rude behavior."

When Sam Carubba visited the wounded AWOL G.I.s at the hospital, he found AWOL Private Everett May not to be in a talkative mood. Private May knew that he was in a great deal of trouble, because he had been AWOL for several months and was captured by MPs immediately after getting into a shootout with other armed deserters. AWOL Sergeant Alan Beaver was is even more trouble, because he was one of the G.I. Gangsters who initiated the attack, that wounded two other deserters and three French civilians.

Fortunately for CID, AWOL Sergeant Thomas Drilling was willing to cooperate. While Inspector Fontaine checked on the status of the wounded French civilians, Agent Carubba listened and took notes, while Sergeant Drilling explained what transpired at the Cafe Le Dome. "In a way, this was all my fault," remarked the AWOL Sergeant, who was shot with a small caliber bullet in his right shoulder as he dove for cover when the shooting started.

"How's that?" asked Sam.

Sergeant Drilling sounded like a man who was telling the truth when he continued and said, "Like I told the MPs who arrested me at the cafe, two weeks ago I received a Dear John letter from my wife. I guess you can say I went off my rocker and didn't give a shit about all the "what are we fighting for" crap that gets fed to us on a regular basis. I just spent thirty days straight on the line and was finally back in a rest camp, when my wife informed me that I might as well give her a divorce, because she moved in with some 4F asshole, who works in a defense plant."

Just because Sergeant Drilling was a prisoner facing disciplinary action didn't mean that Sam Carubba couldn't feel sorry for the guy. Prisoner or not, Sam proved that he had compassion for a fellow G.I., who received exceptionally bad news from home, when he said, "That's bad enough to deal with when you're stateside. I can't imagine how bad it is to have to deal with a Dear John letter when you've been knee deep in Germans for a solid month."

"Trust me, it stinks in plain English," remarked Sergeant Drilling, before he continued and said, "After reading her letter I was in a daze. When one of my buddies suggested that I speak to the Chaplain I decided to go for a walk. I managed to get past the MPs by jumping into the back of a truck that was on it's way to a Services of Supply depot. Once I got to Paris I met Private May. At the time he was selling packs of American cigarettes off the back of a truck that I later found out was stolen. To make a long story short, May took me in and introduced me to the other AWOL G.I.s that he was hiding out with."

In order to move things along Sam asked, "How many men were in May's gang?"

"Four including Everett May," responded AWOL Sergeant Drilling.

Since the prisoner was cooperating, Sam decided to cut to the chase and ask, "What caused the shootout?"

"When I told these guys that I was turning myself in, they sent May to convince me to stay," responded AWOL Sergeant Drilling, who paused when Sam offered him a cigarette and a light. After thanking the CID Agent for the smoke, the AWOL combat veteran went on to say, "According to Private May, the two that did the shooting at The Cafe La Dome were worried that I would spill the beans about their operation here in Paris. To tell you the truth, they had every reason to be worried, because I didn't care for some of the crap they were doing. Selling stolen Army cigarettes and gasoline was one thing, but committing armed robberies was more than I could stomach. Even May wanted out, but he was afraid of Sergeant Beaver and the section eight whose been following him around, ever since they arrived in the ETO as replacements back in November."

"Who shot you...Beaver or Nathan Gromley?" asked Sam.

Once again, Sergeant Drilling sounded like he was being completely honest and forthright when he answered Sam's question. "Beaver got me and Gromley shot May in the leg when they found us having a glass of wine at the Cafe La Dome. They gave us one chance to go back to their hangout. When we refused and we said we wouldn't say anything to the MPs about them, once we turned ourselves in, they pulled guns and started blasting."

"Did you know that Private May was armed?" asked Sam.

"Not when we first met at the cafe," responded Sergeant Drilling, before he added, "I found out he was packing a forty five when I was hit and I dove for cover under the table. That's when I saw May return fire. I knew he hit Sergeant Beaver in the leg when I saw that SOB limping as he ran away."

While Sergeant Drilling extinguished his cigarette in the ashtray that was next to his bed, Sam remarked, "According to witnesses at the cafe, the two shooters took off on foot, because their car didn't start. What was that all about?"

"When Gromley couldn't start their car he must'a panicked, because he took off running like a guy who was being chased by a pack of hungry dogs," responded Sergeant Drilling, before he continued and said, "By the time I was helped up off the floor by May, I lost sight of them. As soon as two MPs and pair of French gendarmes showed up, I told them who did the shooting and their direction of travel when they took off on foot. I also told the MPs that Sergeant Beaver must'a been wounded because he was limping when he ran away."

Under the circumstances, Sam decided to delve into a more serious subject matter when he looked at the prisoner and said, "Since you decided to cooperate, I might as well ask when you found out that the men you fell in with were committing robberies, in addition to selling stolen government property?"

"They kept things pretty close to the vest when it came to talking about their other ways of making money. In fact, I got the distinct impression, that the only guy who trusted me in this group was Everett May which was fine with me," responded Sergeant Drilling.

When Sam handed the prisoner a glass of water, AWOL Sergeant Drilling took a sip before he added, "It wasn't until a few days ago that I learned what these guys were up to. According to Everett, Sergeant Beaver, Private Gromley and another AWOL G.I. by the name of Steven Prescott, were making money hand over fist, by committing robberies and breaking into mansions on the other side of Paris. When they weren't robbing people and breaking into homes, they were stealing Army supplies." Then, after pausing for a split second, Sergeant Drilling added, "One thing more, Sarge. Even though he's not as crazy as Nathan Gromley, Steve Prescott is a gun crazy SOB who always carries two pistols. I'd keep that in mind when you go after him."

"Thanks for the tip," remarked Sam as he made a note of what the prisoner just said.

When the nurse entered the room and said that Sergeant Drilling needed to get some sleep, Sam Carubba asked if he could have one more minute with his prisoner before he left. As soon as the nurse left the room, Sam Carubba put his notebook in his coat pocket, while he addressed the prisoner in a cordial but businesslike tone of voice. "I'm gonna write this up just the way you told me. While I can't make you any promises, I can tell you that in addition to cooperating, the circumstances why you went AWOL and the fact that you have only been away from your unit for about three weeks should go in your favor. Once I check a few things out, I'll be back tomorrow with a few more questions. In the meantime, get some sleep." The moment Sergeant Drilling remarked, "I'll see you tomorrow, Sarge," the Army nurse entered the room carrying a tray containing a vial of medication and a syringe.

After smiling at the pretty redhead from Vermont, Sam remarked, "Perfect timing, Lieutenant," as he left the room.

When the joint American military and French Police raid was executed, Chief Inspector Dumont led one of his men, along with two U.S. Army MPs, through the crowd of Allied troops and prostitutes in search of Harry Moffett. Even though he knew that Pierre Mollet would not be found in this establishment, the Chief Inspector was certain, that he and his American colleagues would find Sergeant Harry Moffett, in the bedroom of the brothel's Madam.

The moment the Chief Inspector reached the top floor of the brothel, the Madam known as Miss Evette stepped out of her room and pointed to the closed door, to let the senior police official know, where he could find AWOL Sergeant Moffett. As Evette stepped aside, the raiding party entered her boudoir and found a panic stricken Harry Moffett in the process of frantically trying to get dressed.

While the two American military policemen took the prisoner in custody, the Chief Inspector stepped closer to Harry Moffett and presented his identification to the U.S. Army deserter and said, "Sergeant Moffett, I am Chief Inspector Dumont. I am working with CID and your American military police. I assure you, Sergeant, that you will make things much easier on yourself, if you cooperate and tell me and my American colleagues where we can find Pierre Mollet and his brother Antone."

While the overweight rear area slob stood partially dressed in the madam's bedroom, he acted like a belligerent tough guy, when he spit on the floor before he said, "Go to hell, Frenchie."

As the Chief Inspector faced the two MPs, he waved his left hand and spoke in his signature calm tone of voice when he said, "Take him away." A moment later, Major Savino, Sergeant Mike Mulligan and Sergeant Charlie Golovan arrived in time, to see AWOL Sergeant Harry Moffett being escorted out of the room by two military policemen and a French Police Inspector.

Immediately after Corporal Johnson apologized to the Negro Army Officer and the two enlisted men that he insulted, Al motioned his son to follow him so they could have some privacy. It had been some time since Al Parker and Jim Beauregard met Cal, when he shipped out of the New York Port of Embarkation to serve in the ETO. After all the time that passed since then, Al and his youngest son ended up meeting in a raid on a black market operation in Paris.

While Cal met privately with his father behind the warehouse, Al could tell by the look on the young man's face, that his youngest son was not the same person that he watched go off to war. When Al stepped closer to Cal, he smiled wide as he shook hands with his son and gripped his left shoulder and said, "It's good to see you, son."

"It's good to see you too, Pop," responded Cal, who quickly presented his father with a salute before he added, "Or should I say, Lieutenant."

After returning the salute, Al remarked, "I'm proud of you, son. You turned out to be one hell of an Army cop."

"Thanks, Pop," responded Cal, who didn't seem like his usual self when he went on to say, "I'm proud of you too, Dad. After Major Savino told me what happened, when you went after Ivan Larson and Shorty Mc Ghee, I was happy to hear the Army gave you the Silver Star and a commission."

Al could tell his son was troubled about something, but he initially wrote off the look on Cal's face, as a case of him coming back to normal after completing a dangerous assignment. Their private meeting was cut short, when Hank Blair stepped through the open back door to the warehouse that they just raided and said, "Excuse me, Lieutenant, but the Colonel asked me to tell you and Cal that we're getting ready to leave."

While two MPs and two French policemen transported nine of the prisoners to the booking station, Al and his son Cal walked back inside the warehouse. Once inside, they joined Hank Blair, Inspector Girard Dupray, Bill Hayes, Mike Butler and Joshua Fermi as they stood next to Benny Greene and the handcuffed prisoner AWOL Corporal Earl Johnson.

As soon as Jim Beauregard walked over to where everyone was standing, he handed an MP armband, a military police combat helmet and a pistol belt complete with a holster and a 1911 pistol to Benny Greene and said, "Put these on, Corporal. Thanks to the roomful of stolen Army weapons and equipment, that the soon to be convicted AWOL Sergeant Moffett has stored in this warehouse, you are now a fully equipped and deputized MP."

No man ever sounded more grateful than Benny Greene when he responded and said, "Yes, Sir," as he put the helmet on before he secured the pistol belt around his waist.

While Benny slipped the MP armband on his left arm, Jim Beauregard faced Al and the others and said, "While Sergeants Hayes, Butler and Fermi stay behind to inventory the contents of this warehouse, Corporal Johnson has decided to cooperate and will show us where Henri Duval lives. If we're lucky, we'll find Duval. If we find Duval, he might lead us to Pierre Mollett and his brother, Antone."

After pausing for a split second, Jim turned to Cal and said, "You and Benny can lead the way with Inspector Dupray, while we follow with Corporal Johnson."

By the time Cal responded and said, "Yes, Sir," Hank Blair was placing Corporal Johnson in the back seat of the CID staff car. While Jim held the front passenger side door open, he waited for Al to get into the back seat next to the prisoner, before he turned to Hank Blair and said, "OK, Hank. Let's get this show on the road." As the two vehicle convoy drove away, Agents Hayes, Butler and Fermi took a moment to admire the daunting task of having to inventory the warehouse, that was full of stolen U.S. Army vehicles and crates of stolen government property. After hearing Mike Butler comment on the volume of stolen property, that was stored in Moffet's warehouse, Bill Hayes remarked, "We might as well get started."

Once they arrived in the vicinity of Henri Duval's apartment building, additional MP and French Police units were called into the area. As soon as Chief Inspector Dumont and Major Tommy Savino arrived, Jim introduced them to AWOL Corporal Johnson.

When Al Parker and Inspector Girard Dupray returned from their scouting mission, they filed their report, while standing next to the open right rear passenger door of the staff car, where Corporal Johnson was sitting under guard. Without wasting any time, Al reported that they were able to look directly into the top floor apartment from the building across the street. Immediately after Al Parker paused to catch his breath, he patted Girard Dupray on the back and said, "Go ahead, Girard. Tell 'em what we saw."

While addressing the Chief Inspector, Jim Beauregard and Major Savino, Inspector Girard Dupray filed the rest of their scouting report. "The man that Lieutenant Parker and I observed, who was sitting inside the apartment, looks like Henri Duval. There was also a young woman with blonde hair in the apartment. After they had a drink they went into the bedroom and shut the light."

"The young blonde is Duval's girlfriend," remarked Johnson, who quickly added, "Her name is Marguerite. She used to be one of Mollet's prostitutes, before he started dealing on the black market."

"Is there anything else we should know about Duval?" asked Jim.

Without hesitating, the prisoner responded and said, "He always carries a gun, Colonel." After thanking Corporal Johnson, Jim Beauregard motioned his men away from the staff car to plan the raid on Duval's apartment. While facing the Chief Inspector, Jim said, "Duval is all yours, Francois. How do want to handle this?"

With Inspector Dupray standing by his side, the Chief Inspector responded and said, "Inspector Dupray and I will lead the raiding party." While facing his counterpart in CID, the Chief Inspector continued and said, "It is important for you and your men to know, Jim, that once we enter this apartment, you will find a large room off to the left, as well as a kitchen and a back bedroom that will be on the right. A narrow hallway will connect these rooms all the way to the kitchen."

"We'll be right behind you, Francois," responded Jim Beauregard.

After checking his watch, the Chief Inspector looked at Jim Beauregard and said, "We will execute the raid two minutes after we enter the building."

While the Chief Inspector relayed his orders to his men in French, Jim turned to his men and said, "Tom, Al and Cal will come with me." Jim then turned to Hank Blair and said, "Hank, I want you, Benny and the two MPs to stay with Corporal Johnson." After Hank and Benny acknowledged the order, Jim made eye contact with the men from CID who would be providing back up to their French police allies, "We go on the Chief Inspector's command."

Even though it was a very long day, no one seemed tired as long as there was police work to be performed. As the raiding party moved into position, six uniformed Paris Policemen, two U.S. Army MPs and several Paris Police Investigators surrounded Duval's apartment building.

After quietly making their way to the top floor, the Chief Inspector stopped for a second, before he motioned Inspector Dupray and the rest of the raiding party to follow him down the dimly lit hallway. Due to the lack of room on the top floor landing, Jim Beauregard, Tommy Savino, Al Parker and Cal Parker stood on the staircase, while the lead element of the raiding party took positions on both sides of the door to the apartment.

While the Chief Inspector gripped his .32 caliber French MAB Type 1 pistol in his right hand, he held up his left hand and whispered, "Un, deux, trois (One, two, three). Once the Chief Inspector said trois (three), Inspector Dupray kicked the door open. In a matter of seconds the entire raiding party was identifying themselves as they entered the dark apartment.

Just as a woman was heard screaming from the back bedroom, Duval appeared in the open doorway with a small caliber pistol in hand. While the men in the raiding party took the best cover available, Chief Inspector Dumont relayed the command in French for the collaborator turned criminal to drop the gun. The second Duval screamed, "Go to hell, you Gaullist pig," and he raised his pistol, the Chief Inspector and Inspector Dupray opened fire and wounded the subject.

As a uniformed French policeman restrained the naked young blonde and covered her with a blanket from the bed, Duval looked up from the floor, as the Chief Inspector retrieved the prisoner's pistol and said, "My men and I have been waiting a long time to say this. Henri Duval, you are under arrest for collaborating with the enemies of France and committing other serious crimes."

While Inspector Dupray used the bed sheet to apply pressure on Duval's more serious lower torso wound, the prisoner remarked, "How bad am I hit?"

"Don't worry, Duval," responded Dupray, "You will live long enough to tell us everything that we want to know."

As Jim Beauregard holstered his Ithaca Model 1911 pistol, he turned to Cal Parker and said, "We need an ambulance, Cal." Once Cal acknowledged the order, he left the apartment to get medical attention for the prisoner.

After offering a Lucky Strike cigarette to the Chief Inspector, Jim took one for himself, before he accepted a light from Francois Dumont. As soon as Jim took a drag on his cigarette, he looked at the Chief Inspector and said, "Tell me, Francois. Is it like this everyday?"

"No, my friend," responded the Chief Inspector, who took a drag on his cigarette, before he continued and said, "On Sunday, we get one hour off to thank God, for giving us a city full of criminals to pursue."

CHAPTER 7

AFTER MIDNIGHT

Despite the late hour and the fact that they were exhausted, Jim Beauregard, Al Parker and Chief Inspector Dumont entered the interrogation room where Harry Moffett was sitting under guard. After introducing himself and the other members of his interrogation team, Jim Beauregard tossed a pack of Lucky Strikes on the table as he remarked, "Help yourself."

While Jim leaned over and used his Zippo to light the prisoner's cigarette, he began the interrogation by saying, "It's late and we all want'a get some sleep, so I'll keep this short. As you can imagine, you're in a lot'a trouble. In fact, you're in so much trouble, it will be in your best interest to cooperate. If you act like a tough guy, or you try to bullshit us, you'll wish you never served in this man's army."

After taking a drag on his cigarette, Harry Moffett looked up at the new Commanding Officer of the CID Office in Paris, before he turned to face Al Parker and said, "I read about you and the Lieutenant in The Stars and Stripes Newspaper and Yank Magazine. You're the CID Agents who chased two fugitives who killed a cop and robbed a bank in New York, all the way to the damn Battle of the Bulge and shot it out with a Kraut SS unit in order to get your man."

As much as Jim and Al appreciated being remembered for their exploits, they were more interested in seeing if Moffett was willing to play ball and cooperate. After hearing what Moffett just said, Jim knew exactly how he needed to respond. While the Atlanta Police Captain of Detectives on military leave with Army CID leaned on the table, he looked down at their prisoner and remarked, "It took Lieutenant Parker and I over a year to find Ivan Larson and Francis Shorty Mc Ghee and take Larson's shot up sorry ass into custody, before we hauled Shorty McGhee's dead body to a makeshift morgue in Bastogne. The Lieutenant and I have been in Paris one day and we were able to shut your entire operation down and assist in your arrest. Naturally, we had help from Chief Inspector Dumont and his men, as well as from a number of CID Agents based in Paris." Then, as Jim stood up straight, he turned to face Al and said, "I think it's time we introduce our two secret weapons to the soon to be court marshaled AWOL Sergeant Harry Moffett."

"Yes, Sir," responded Al Parker as he walked to the other side of the room and opened the door. The moment Cal Parker and Benny Greene entered the room, the handcuffed shocked prisoner remarked, "Hey, what gives, Colonel?" and went to stand up, but was quickly shoved back down in his chair by Jim Beauregard.

"Sit down, stupid," responded Jim before he continued making the introductions. "I think it's time that you met Staff Sergeant Calvin Parker and Corporal Benny Greene. These men are the undercover agents who infiltrated your black market operation on behalf of Army CID."

As the pissed off prisoner remained silent, Jim Beauregard fudged the truth a bit and explained how once Corporal Benny Greene infiltrated Moffett's operation, they waited for the right time to introduce Agent Parker into his gang of thieves. When Jim continued, he sounded like a commander who was very proud of his men when he said, "While Corporal Greene and Staff Sergeant Parker infiltrated your organization from the inside, the rest of us in CID, along with our French Allies, have been following you and your men all over Paris. We even rounded up some of your French associates and customers. Needless to say, they are not very happy with you at the moment."

After regaining his composure, Moffett looked up at the new Commanding Officer of the CID Office in Paris and said, "If you and your men did such a good job, why are you talking to me, Colonel? Unless I'm missing something, CID should have enough to throw the book at me and put my ass in Leavenworth for a long time to come."

Once again, Jim leaned on the desk in the interrogation room and towered over the prisoner when he responded to his last remark. "That's an excellent question, so let me start off by saying, that you have one and only one card to play; one that can help get you a break of some kind, before we prosecute you to the fullest extent of the law. Unfortunately for you, that card has to be played right now or there is no deal."

"What card is that, Colonel?" asked Moffett. "We want Pierre Mollet, his brother Antone and everyone else they're associated with and we want 'em now," responded Jim Beauregard.

While Moffett paused to take one last drag on his cigarette, he responded as he stamped the butt out in the ashtray that was on the table in the interrogation room. "As far as a home address goes, I don't have one. They came to me with cash in hand and one thing led to another." Then, after pausing for a split second, the prisoner continued and said, "If I know Pierre Mollet, he already heard about the raids and is long gone. The same goes for his brother and the men they work with."

"Unfortunately for you, it doesn't sound like you can help us very much," remarked Jim Beauregard.

Harry Moffett perked up a bit when he remembered something else that might enable CID and the Paris Police to locate the Mollet brothers and their associates. "Hold on, Colonel. I got something else for you."

"I'm listening," remarked a bone tired Jim Beauregard.

While sounding a bit excited, Moffett continued and said, "One of Pierre Mollet's right hand men is a Frenchman by the name of Duval, Henri Duval. He lives with a whore who worked for Pierre Mollet before he got into the black market business. I can take you to his place. We can be there in a few minutes."

While Jim picked up his cigarettes, he turned to the MP who was guarding the prisoner and said, "Put this prisoner back in his cell, Corporal."

As soon as the MP grabbed Moffett by the arm, the prisoner blurted out, "What gives, Colonel? You wanted me to cooperate and I just did."

While Jim slipped his pack of cigarettes into his right hand pant's pocket, he looked at the prisoner who was being held onto by a rather large MP and said, "My men and I assisted Chief Inspector Dumont and his men raid Duval's apartment shortly after you were taken into custody. Duval was shot while resisting arrest, but he's alive and under guard, so you telling us where he lives will do you no good. As a result, I strongly suggest that you think of something else that will peak our interest, before you face the full weight of charges, that will be brought against you at your court martial."

The last person that Chief Inspector Dumont expected to meet, when he walked into his apartment building, after an exceptionally long day, was Marcel Badeau. The second the two men made eye contact, the Chief Inspector displayed his usual calm disposition, as he approached the man who once served as a policeman under his command. Since this meeting was Marcel's idea, he spoke first as he extended his hand and said, "It's good to see you, Francois."

As the observant Chief Inspector noticed a package wrapped in brown paper leaning up against the wall, he shook his friend's hand and said, "Even at this late hour it's good to see you as well, Marcel."

During the early days of the German occupation, Francois tried to convince Marcel not to leave the police department, so he could join a more aggressive resistance unit in the countryside. As far as Francois was concerned, there was plenty of work to be done at home in Paris.

Unlike Francois and the other policemen who remained in their police careers, Marcel was determined to kill the enemy and kill the enemy he did. While the resistance groups that operated in a major city like Paris, did their best to harass the Germans in more subtle ways, the French resistance units in the more rural areas, engaged the enemy in a more direct fashion, on a more regular basis. It was also no secret, that Marcel Badeau lost his wife and infant son, when Pierre Mollet led a Milice raid on one of his hideouts, while searching for the Paris policeman turned resistance leader.

The raid that was executed by Pierre Mollet's Milice unit, that caused the brutal death of Marcel's wife and infant son, did not go unanswered for and resulted in major reprisals by resistance fighters. Even though it took time to accomplish, five of the twelve members of this Vichy French paramilitary unit were hunted down and killed. Fortunately for Marcel and the other members of his resistance unit, by the time these collaborators were found hanging from the same tree, the German Army was too busy fighting the Allies, to focus their attention on the aggressive actions of one group of French "terrorists." The Germans became even less interested in looking for Marcel and his men, when their position in France became so untenable, the Nazis had no choice but to head east.

According to what Francois heard from his contacts in the resistance, immediately after two former members of the Milice were captured, they admitted that Pierre Mollet led the raid on Marcel's home and personally tossed three hand grenades inside. Worse yet, Pierre Mollet reportedly did so, after his men confirmed that the resistance leader was not inside. After promising to let the two prisoners live, the former members of this Milice unit told Marcel, that Pierre Mollet returned to Paris with a new identity and money provided by German intelligence, to conduct an operation against the Allied war effort. According to the two prisoners, Pierre Mollet would be conducting this covert operation with his younger brother Antone and four of his closest associates in the Milice, to include, Benard Allard, Jerome Paget, Edouard Tasse and Gregorie Petit.

It was also when Francois served with the French Police resistance group, known as The Gaullist Honneur de la Police, that he learned more about how Marcel and another former Paris policeman by the name of Charles Garnier, were serving in the Ain Department of France, in the region of Auvergne-Rhone-Alpes.[9] In one report, Francois learned that Marcel operated under the code name of Le Fossoyeur (The Grave Digger). Marcel was given this nickname, because he was responsible for sending more German soldiers and French collaborators to their grave, than anyone else in his resistance unit. These reports, along with the story about how Marcel's wife and infant son were murdered, were confirmed, when the Chief Inspector met with Charles Garnier's oldest son Rene, during the fighting to liberate Paris.

After hearing what Rene Garnier had to say, Francois asked the young resistance fighter to have his father relay his condolences to Marcel. Several weeks later, Francois found a hand written note on his desk that simply said, "Message received. Thank you, M."

While Marcel offered his former colleague a cigarette, he cut to the chase and said, "I know it's late and you had a long day, so I will say what needs to be said and let you consider my offer, after you get a good night's sleep." After offering Francois a light, Marcel used his lighter to light his own cigarette, before he looked directly at his former colleague and said, "I wish to trade many things of great value, for the life of an American deserter who surrendered to the American military police."

"The American's name?" asked Francois before he took a drag on his cigarette.

"Sergeant Charles Monacco," responded Marcel, who took a quick drag on his cigarette before he went on to say, "I give you my word, Francois, that even though Sergeant Monacco is as the Americans say, Absent Without Leave and he was involved in the black market, he is a man who is worth helping."

Despite the late hour and the fact that he was exhausted, did not prevent the Chief Inspector from asking a very pertinent question. "So am I to assume, that in addition to your outstanding service to France as a policeman and as a member of the resistance, that you have also joined the black market and have been working with this American deserter?"

When Marcel responded, the Chief Inspector was not prepared to hear what his former colleague had to say. "Do you know Colonel Andre Reynald?

"Of course," said the Chief Inspector.

While speaking in a matter of fact tone of voice, Marcel continued and said, "The Chief of French Army Intelligence in Paris will confirm, that I work for him and that I now hold a commission as a Captain in the Army of France. After serving out east in the Ain, I returned to Paris to command a special intelligence unit. My men and I were given two missions to perform. One was to infiltrate the black market and identify those involved in the theft of Allied military supplies. In order to complete this assignment, my men and I were given several truck loads of supplies and suitable facilities to work from in Paris. Our other mission was to locate an old adversary of ours, a collaborator who has eluded the Paris Police, various French resistance units and French Army Intelligence for some time. The man I speak of is Pierre Mollet. I can also confirm, that Pierre Mollet is being assisted by his brother Antone, three French thieves and four collaborators who served with Pierre Mollet in the Milice."

"I see you have been busy since you left the police department," remarked Francois.

"As busy as you, my friend," responded Marcel.

While Francois acknowledged the compliment, by bowing his head ever so slightly, Marcel took another drag on his cigarette before he continued.

"Before he surrendered to the military police, Sergeant Monacco left a number of stolen military vehicles and a large quantity of stolen government property in his warehouse, so it would be returned to the American Army. Sergeant Monacco also left a large amount of money in the safe for your friends in CID to find. In addition, Sergeant Monacco advised the men who worked with him to surrender as well."

When Marcel continued, he bent over and retrieved a package that was leaning up against the wall. "I also have something of great value to give you, that must be returned to France."

As soon as Marcel presented the square package, that was wrapped in heavy brown paper, to his former commanding officer, he went on to say, "Sergeant Monacco could have sold this for a great deal of money. Instead, he asked me to make sure that this was given back to the people of France. When he gave me this painting, I knew that he was a man worth helping. I hope you agree."

While the Chief Inspector tore enough of the paper back, to reveal that the package was a valuable piece of stolen French artwork, the policeman in him remarked, "I'm curious, Marcel. Where did an AWOL American soldier acquire such a valuable piece of French art?"

Marcel proved that this was one of those instances when the truth was stranger than fiction, when he looked his old friend and said, "While fighting in Normandy, Sergeant Monacco and his men raided a German supply depot. In addition to the usual German weapons, ammunition, rations and medical supplies, Sergeant Monacco and his men found this painting, along with truckloads of stolen French food, wine, cases of Cognac and champagne. Based on what I know, Sergeant Monacco and his men sold a plane load of captured German weapons and much of the liquor to a group of American Air Force personnel. A good portion of the food and all of the medical supplies that they recovered from the Germans, was distributed to the people in the towns that they passed through. I know this is true, because I had Charles Garnier visit these towns and confirm that Sergeant Monacco's unit was incredibly generous, in handing out such sought after items, when they passed through the area."

As Francois paid close attention to what was being said, he continued to smoke his cigarette while Marcel went on to say, "Sergeant Monacco kept the painting with the intentions of delivering it to the Louvre once he reached Paris. Rather than have the painting damaged in the fighting, Sergeant Monacco buried the painting on an abandoned farm, before he and his men entered the city. Unfortunately, he was wounded in combat and was sent to two different hospitals to recover."

After crushing the remains of his cigarette in the ashtray, that was located in the lobby of the building, Francois continued to hold onto the stolen artwork when he said, "I'm curious, Marcel? Why involve the Paris Police, when you and Colonel Reynald could easily handle this matter on your own?"

"First, I am here because my commanding officer knows that I am meeting with you," responded Marcel, who quickly added, "Colonel Reynald approved my request to handle this matter with your assistance for several reasons. One of the most important reasons, is because it is well known, that you have an excellent relationship with the American Army CID Agents in Paris. My commanding officer is also well aware of your service to France, including when you served as the deputy commander of the largest resistance unit in the Paris Police. He also knows that we served together for many years and that you have been hunting Pierre Mollet, ever since he betrayed France, by causing the death of several members of the resistance. It is also no secret, that Pierre Mollet and to a lesser extent his brother Antone, had a hand in helping the Germans arrest a number of Jews, including several French citizens. Because Colonel Reynald wants justice served as much as we do, he has agreed that we should work together, to bring this matter to a successful conclusion."

Then, after pausing for a split second, Marcel added, "I also know my limitations, Francois. I say this, because if you are not with me when we find Pierre Mollet, I will torture him slowly until he begs me to kill him. For this reason and because I was a good policeman for fifteen years, I need my friend Francois Dumont to be with me when Pierre Mollet is taken into custody."

After nodding his head ever so slightly in agreement, Francois remarked, "Pierre Mollet will never talk, because he knows that he must pay for his crimes with his life."

When Marcel responded he placed his cigarette butt in the nearby ashtray. "I agree, but all that matters to me, is that this traitor and his associates face the firing squad." As Marcel continued, he sounded like a man on a mission. "The fact that Pierre Mollet continues to serve his Nazi masters, by doing everything he can to prevent Allied supplies from reaching the men at the front, is another reason to see this man executed. Unfortunately, we can only execute Mollet once. The same is true for Antone Mollet and the men who served with his brother in the Milice."

As soon as Marcel stopped talking, the Chief Inspector remarked, "Before we see Pierre Mollet and his most trusted associates face the firing squad we will have to find them."

"And that is the reason why I came to see you at such a late hour," responded Marcel, who quickly added, "Pierre Mollet is in the process of preparing to leave Paris with his brother and his closest associates. The deserter Sergeant Moffett also has no idea, that Pierre Mollet and his men have been working with three other groups of Americans."

"And you know this because?" asked the Chief Inspector.

Without hesitating Marcel remarked, "Because I had a good teacher when I was a policeman and I was able to infiltrate Mollet's organization. In addition to the two people who are working for us on the inside of Pierre Mollet's organization, my men are watching the building where Antone Mollet and his men live. I also have men covering the garage where Pierre Mollet and his associates store delivery vehicles and a very large quantity of stolen American Army supplies. This particular location is the one that Pierre Mollet uses, when he conducts business with other groups of American soldiers, who are heavily involved in black market activities."

As Marcel continued, he handed a piece of paper to Francois. "Sergeant Monacco handed me this address before he surrendered to the American Military Police."

After he examined the information on the slip of paper, Francois looked at Marcel and said, "This address is in the Latin Quarter."

When Marcel responded, he did so, as if he was very proud of his American contacts. "Sergeant Monacco and a fellow deserter, a private by the name of George Zangolas, took it upon themselves, to do what the Paris Police and French Army Intelligence has been unable to do and used their black market contacts to locate Antone Mollet. They did so, because they know that I hate Pierre Mollet as much as they dislike his American partner, Sergeant Harry Moffett."

When the Chief Inspector asked if Marcel knew where Pierre Mollet was located at this time, the man who was now serving as a Captain in French Army Intelligence sounded like a police detective, who was filing a report to his superior when he said, "As of an hour ago, Pierre Mollet was in his garage, preparing to make his final delivery of stolen American military supplies to another group of American deserters. Since a critical part of our mission was to infiltrate certain black market activities, Colonel Reynald would like us to work together, to capture this group of AWOL Americans, when we take Pierre Mollet and the others into custody."

While Francois held up the piece of paper that Marcel just handed him, he remarked, "And this was the key to the puzzle, that was provided by Sergeant Monacco and the AWOL American Private?"

"Correct," responded Marcel who quickly added, "When Pierre Mollet's brother Antone and the three French thieves who serve as their drivers, are not making deliveries, they can be found at that address in the Latin Quarter. You also need to know, that Pierre Mollet, his brother Antone and the men who will be traveling with them, will be receiving new identify papers before they leave Paris. If everything goes according to plan, we will receive the new names they will be using, before they depart for Switzerland."

After hearing what Marcel had to say, the Chief Inspector asked, "Tell me, Marcel, how do you propose that we stop this from happening?"

Once again, Marcel responded in a very confident tone of voice and said, "We join forces with our American Allies and capture the Mollet brothers and their associates before the sun sets tomorrow. Every location and every individual that we are watching should be covered by a team consisting of my men, your men and some American CID Agents. All I ask in return, is that you do one favor for an old friend."

"What would that be?" asked the Chief Inspector.

While Marcel looked directly Francois Dumont he responded and said, "I would like you to ask the American Colonel in charge of CID to drop all charges against Sergeant Monacco, so he can rejoin his unit and continue to fight the Boche. I ask that you do the same for Private Zangolas as well."

After pausing to consider Marcel's offer, the Chief Inspector remarked, "Tell me, Marcel. What makes this AWOL American Sergeant so important to you?"

Under the circumstances, Marcel knew that his former police commander would be curious, why he would be so concerned about an American deserter who was facing serious charges. Once again, Marcel responded without delay. "Because my niece is in love with this American and they intend to get married, as soon as his charges for being a deserter are resolved. I have also come to know this man and I wish to help him and his friend."

"Is there anything else I should know about these men?" asked Francois.

When Marcel continued, he did his best to sound as convincing as possible. "I assure you, Francois, even though these men are Absent Without Leave, they are not cowards. After Sergeant Monacco was wounded in combat, he became impatient and left the hospital before the wounds in his leg healed. Private Zangolas also left the same hospital, when he recovered from his wounds and the American Army was slow to return him to his unit. After they arrived in Paris they met Raymond La Salle. As soon as Sergeant Monacco and the men he left the hospital with, started supplying Raymond with small quantities of stolen American gasoline, La Salle introduced me to his new black market contact."

"Let me guess. La Salle is one of your men?" remarked the Chief Inspector.

After nodding his head ever so slightly in agreement, Marcel responded and said, "That is correct, Francois," who quickly added, "It is also important for you to know, that last December, Sergeant Monacco became gravely ill and was unable to return to the fighting, during the German offensive in the Ardennes. If necessary, the French physician who cared for Sergeant Monacco, will be happy to provide the American Army with a statement, to confirm that this is the truth. As far as Private Zangolas is concerned, he did return to the fighting during the German offensive and was wounded again. Just as he did on a previous occasion, Private Zangolas left the hospital before he was discharged and went back to work with Sergeant Monacco."

In order to cut to the chase, Francois spoke in a matter of fact tone of voice when he remarked, "So you used this AWOL American Sergeant and his men to infiltrate the black market and locate Antone Mollet, his older brother Pierre Mollet and the criminals they are associated with."

"That is correct, Francois," responded Marcel, who quickly added, "Colonel Reynald and I can also provide the Americans with a full accounting of the supplies that were stolen by Sergeant Monacco and his men, that were "paid for" with French francs that came from French Army Intelligence. This accounting will prove, that only a portion of the stolen supplies actually ended up being sold on the black market. The bulk of what was taken was turned over to the French Army."

"What about the money that was paid to Sergeant Monacco and his men?" asked the Chief Inspector.

"That was, as the Americans like to say, the price of doing business," responded Marcel who quickly added, "And it was a small price to pay, because once my men and I began operating on the black market with Sergeant Monacco and his small group of fellow deserters, many doors were opened for us, that enabled us to complete our mission."

"How much time do we have to plan and execute such an operation?" asked Francois.

Without hesitating, Marcel responded and said, "Not much. I say that, because once some of Pierre Mollet's AWOL American contacts arrive late tomorrow afternoon, to deliver the payment for their last transaction, Pierre Mollet, Antone Mollet, Benard Allard, Jerome Paget, Edouard Tasse, Gregorie Petit and someone who is very valuable to them will leave France for Switzerland. Their plan is to depart Paris while dressed as Catholic priests."

After hearing what Marcel just said, Francois paid his former colleague a well deserved compliment. "I see you are just as good at being an intelligence officer, as you were at being a policeman."

After cracking a smile Marcel remarked, "You must be exhausted after such a long day, in such a long war. With your permission, we can continue this conversation in the morning at the American CID Office with Colonel Reynald. During this meeting I will also reveal to you and our American Allies, who we have working for us on the inside of Mollet's organization."

CHAPTER 8

CHANGING SIDES

After being fully briefed by Sam Carubba, Anthony Angelone and Sal Coppola, Lt. Colonel Jim Beauregard congratulated the three CID Agents for a job well done, before he instructed them to grab some breakfast. As soon as the three agents left the office, Jim met with Major Savino, Lieutenant Al Parker, Chief Inspector Dumont, Colonel Reynald and Captain Badeau in his office, to discuss other matters of importance. Based on what was said during this very informative meeting, Jim decided to honor Captain Badeau's request to speak to Sergeant Monacco, before the prisoner was brought to his office.

The moment Charlie Monacco saw the door to the interrogation room open, the last person that he expected to see was Marcel dressed in the uniform of a French Army Captain. Once the American military policeman closed the door and left them alone, Charlie couldn't resist and remarked, "If you stole a French Army Captain's uniform to break me outta this joint don't bother, because the two MPs who are my constant companions, are under orders to haul my ass before the Colonel in charge of CID in five minutes."

As soon as Marcel offered Charlie a Camel cigarette and a light, he wasted no time in saying, "Our time is short, my friend, so listen to me very carefully. Everything that I told you about myself is true except for one thing. When I fought with the resistance, the man I worked for was a French Army Intelligence Officer. When the Allies landed in Normandy, I was offered a commission in the Free French Forces and was assigned to work for Colonel Andre Reynald and his special intelligence unit. All of the men I served with in the resistance joined the French Army when I did. I was promoted to Captain after the liberation of Paris and was assigned two important missions. One mission was to infiltrate black market activities in France. The other was to locate several French collaborators who worked for Vichy and the Germans. As soon as you started dealing with Raymond La Salle, my men and I used you and your small group to accomplish our mission."

While Charlie smoked his cigarette in silence, Marcel went on to say, "Before I go any further, I want you to know, that the main reason I accepted this mission, was because I have a personal reason for wanting to find Pierre Mollet and the men who served with him in the Milice and see them executed." After pausing for a split second, Marcel continued and said, "You see, my friend, in addition to what I told you, Pierre Mollet murdered my wife and infant son when I served in the resistance. His brother Antone also worked for the Germans here in Paris and was a supporter of Vichy."

After lighting one of his own cigarettes, Marcel continued and said, "When I heard that you had no love for Pierre Mollet's AWOL American partner, I decided it was best if my men and I worked with you and your men. Naturally, I did not figure that we would become good friends, once we started to work together. I also did not think that you and my cousin Paulette would fall madly in love with each other, but you did."

After checking his watch, Marcel continued and said, "The man I served with before I left to join the Maqui is now the Chief Inspector of Police in Paris. Last night I told Chief Inspector Dumont that in addition to returning a warehouse full of stolen American vehicles and property, you gave me a very valuable French painting that you recovered from the enemy, before you were wounded in battle. I also told the Chief Inspector and my superior Colonel Reynald, that you and Private Zangolas located Antone Mollet and three French criminals who work with him, which enabled me and my men to locate Pierre Mollet and four of the collaborators that he commanded in the Milice. In return for all that you did for France, I asked the Chief Inspector and Colonel Reynald to intervene on your behalf, to have the charges against you dropped, so you could return to your unit. If you survive the war, which I expect you will, you and Paulette can marry. I made the same request for your friend Private Zangolas."

While Charlie Monacco stamped his cigarette butt out in the ashtray that was on the table, he looked up at Marcel and asked how Paulette was doing.

"Paulette sends her love and is waiting for you to return," responded Marcel who quickly added, "I moved her to her mother's farm, so know that she is safe and well cared for. Her brother Paul and one of my men are with them, to make sure that no harm comes to Paulette or her mother."

As soon as the door to the interrogation room opened, the MP Sergeant addressed Marcel in a respectful tone of voice when he said, "Excuse me, Captain, but the Colonel is waiting to meet the prisoner."

"One minute, Sergeant and we will be ready to leave," responded Captain Badeau.

"Yes, Sir," remarked the MP Sergeant as he closed the door again.

With no time to spare, Marcel had one more thing to say to his American friend as he stood up in preparation of being taken to meet Lt. Colonel James Beauregard. "Remember the American Lieutenant we did business with? The one who supplied us with fuel and trucks full of rations, cigarettes and clothing?"

"You mean Andy Armstrong?" said Charlie.

"Yes, the one who dresses like an American MP when he does his stealing," responded Marcel.

"What about him?" asked Charlie.

While speaking like a man who was giving good advice to a friend, Marcel looked at Charlie and said, "If you wish to impress Colonel Beauregard, I suggest you tell him about Armstrong and his men. I also asked Colonel Reynald, to allow you to be the one, to tell the American Colonel from CID about the Master Sergeant at the fuel dump, who has been supplying us with truckloads of stolen American Army gasoline. Last but not least, I also advise you to tell the American Colonel where Eddie Finch can be found, because it you don't, I will."

Even though Colonel Reynald was fully briefed about every black market contact that Marcel met, did business with, or became aware of through Charlie Monacco, Marcel and his commanding officer were giving this AWOL American an opportunity of a lifetime, to be the one to provide this information to Lt. Colonel James Beauregard. As far as Colonel Reynald was concerned, it was the least they could do to help the AWOL American, who unwittingly assisted them in completing their two pronged intelligence mission. The fact that Sergeant Monacco recovered and turned in such a valuable piece of French art work, also made it easy for French Army Intelligence to extend him an additional courtesy.

While the handcuffed prisoner stood before Marcel, he sounded a bit defiant when he remarked, "I'm no stool pigeon, Marcel."

For the first time in their relationship Marcel got upset with Charlie. As Marcel looked directly at the man who was destined to become a member of his family, he spoke in a firm tone of voice when he said, "You have two choices. You can either act like the decorated soldier that you really are, or you can act like a convict, who is willing to protect men who steal fuel, food and other critical supplies from the Allied soldiers who are fighting the Germans, as you once did. Either you are a changed man, or you are nothing but a fraud. When you consider your options you need to think about Paulette, because the man she fell in love with, is the Charles Monacco who is a highly decorated soldier in the American Army." Once he was finished, Marcel walked over to the door of the interrogation room, opened it and addressed the two military policemen. "The prisoner is ready to be taken to meet Colonel Beauregard."

As soon as Captain Badeau introduced Charlie Monacco to Lt. Colonel James Beauregard, Major Savino, Lieutenant Parker, Chief Inspector Francois Dumont and Colonel Reynald, the Commanding Officer of the Paris CID Office instructed the MP Sergeant to remove the prisoner's handcuffs. After telling the prisoner to take a seat, Jim turned to the pair of MPs who delivered the prisoner to his office and said, "Why don't you men grab some coffee and a smoke. We may be a while."

"Yes, Sir," responded the two MPs in unison, as they saluted the Colonel, turned smartly and left his office.

In order to kick things off, Jim Beauregard began the meeting by saying, "After speaking to Chief Inspector Dumont, Colonel Reynald and Captain Badeau, I took the time to review your service record. I also spoke to your former CO. Colonel Mc Kenner believes you developed a bit of a morale problem, after an intelligence officer in your unit, who couldn't cut it in the field, was bailed out of a jam by his general officer for a father. In fact, the way I heard the story, this intelligence officer got some good men killed and wounded, when he made some really bad calls in combat."

After Sergeant Monacco agreed with everything that was just said, Jim continued in a down to earth tone of voice when he remarked, "Unfortunately, the rules say we don't get to choose who we take orders from. We also don't have the right to adios amigo, when we're pissed off at the Army, even when we're justified to be pissed off at our Uncle Sam. That said, even though being AWOL under any circumstances is nothing to be proud of, the fact that you went AWOL while you were recovering from wounds sustained in combat, is a little easier to forgive, than deserting your post under other circumstances. Regardless, what's done is done. The question is where do we go from here?"

After pausing to remove a pack of Lucky Strikes from his right side pant's pocket, Jim offered the prisoner a cigarette and a light as he continued and said, "Chief Inspector Dumont, Colonel Reynald and Captain Badeau have intervened on your behalf and have asked the U.S. Army to make certain considerations in your case. The fact that your former commanding officer is willing to take you back, will also be taken into consideration when your case is adjudicated. It's also in your favor, that you turned over the keys to a warehouse full of stolen Army vehicles and supplies, when you voluntarily surrendered to the MPs."

While Jim retrieved a French Army Intelligence report from his desk, he continued as he flipped through several pages of the document. "I've also been told, that a good portion of the supplies that you and your men liberated from the United States Army, never made it to the streets of Paris and were turned over to the French Army." As Jim put the report back on his desk, he looked at the prisoner and said, "In addition, to receiving a full accounting of your nefarious activities, I also know that the lion's share of the money that you and your men received, that you thought came from the sale of stolen government property to a group of French thieves, actually came from French Army Intelligence. This is strictly my opinion, but the fact that you and your men unwittingly assisted our French Allies to accomplish a very sensitive mission, is a better boat to be in, than if you made a small fortune selling stolen government property on the black market."

As soon as Jim paused to light one of his own cigarettes, he went on to say, "Captain Badeau has also informed me, that you recovered a valuable piece of stolen French artwork and turned this over as well. In addition, I've been told that you left the 4th Convalescent Hospital before your wounds were fully healed and that you got so seriously ill, you were unable to voluntarily return to your unit during the German offensive last December. Captain Badeau has also provided CID with a sworn statement from the French doctor who cared for you."

While Charlie Monacco took another drag on his cigarette, he continued listening to every word that was spoken by the Commanding Officer of the Paris CID Office. After pausing to tap the ash from his cigarette in a nearby ashtray, Jim continued and said, "Before we go any further I want you to understand that you are under no obligation to make a statement at this time."

"I understand, Sir," responded Charlie Monacco who continued and said, "I also want you to know, Colonel, that I intend to cooperate with CID, regardless of what the Army decides to do with me." After taking another drag on his cigarette Charlie continued and said, "When I went AWOL I was tired of laying around that hospital while I waited for my leg to heal. I also admit, that back then I was pissed off at the Army for reasons that the Colonel is aware of. Even though that was the case, I knew the day would come when I would have to face the music. That day came yesterday, Sir. I also want you to know, Colonel, that I appreciate you seeing me. I'm also very grateful that Captain Badeau, the Chief Inspector, Colonel Reynald and my old CO have gone to bat for me."

Once again, Charlie took a drag on his cigarette before he continued. "I have two reasons to cooperate and repay my debt to the Army for screwing up, Sir. In addition to the fact that I've been in jail and I didn't like it, I met a French girl who I'd like to marry. If possible, I'd prefer to be wearing my uniform when I walk down the aisle. I also have no problem if the Army is willing to send me back into combat." After pausing to stamp his cigarette butt out, in the ashtray that was handed to him by the Commanding Officer of the Paris CID Office, Charlie added, "All I can do now, Sir, is hope that the Army will take my cooperation into consideration."

"I assure you it will, Sergeant," responded Jim before he got down to the business at hand and said, "My officers and I, as well as our counterparts in the Paris Police and French Army Intelligence, are particularly interested in hearing what you have to say about black market activities. That includes the involvement of Allied troops, AWOL personnel and French civilians." While Jim stamped his cigarette butt out in an ashtray, he concluded his remarks by saying, "As impressive as it is that you turned yourself in and surrendered a warehouse full of stolen government property and a pile of cash, you'll need to be thoroughly debriefed before a final determination can be made."

After looking over to Marcel, Charlie Monacco turned to face Colonel Beauregard as he spoke up and said, "Since I heard that you already arrested Harry Moffett and shut down his operation, I should probably begin by telling you, Sir, that Corporal Eddie Finch is hiding out in the cellar of a French cafe that is owned by Raymond La Salle. You and your men can find Finch in the room behind the false wall in the wine cellar. I can also help you make a case against a Master Sergeant by the name of Clyde C. Nelson. Sergeant Nelson is the NCO in charge of one of the local POL Dumps who supplied us with gasoline, as long as we cut him in for a piece of the action. Even though all of the men who worked for me had dealings with him, George Zangolas was the one who delivered Sergeant Nelson his cut, after we sold different amounts of stolen Army gasoline."

As Charlie continued, he looked directly at the CID Commanding Officer and said, "I'm also sure, Sir, that you and your men will also want to know about a group of AWOL G.I.s who are hijacking trucks right off the highway from transportation companies, as well as from supply depots, so they can sell the contents on the black market through their French contacts. These guys dress like MPs and drive around on a pair of motorcycles and a handful of Jeeps, that have the words military police stenciled under the windshield. I know about their operation, because some of the stuff in my warehouse, that I turned over after I surrendered, came from this group of AWOL G.I.s."[10]

As soon as Major Savino heard the prisoner mention a group of AWOL troops who were masquerading as military policemen, he spoke up and said,

"Excuse me, Colonel, but I have a question for Sergeant Monacco."

"Go ahead, Major," remarked Jim.

While Major Savino sat on the couch in the Colonel's office, he continued questioning the prisoner. "Tell us, Sergeant. Do you know who's in charge of this group of phony MPs and how they operate?"

Without hesitating, Charlie Monacco responded to the Major's questions in a respectful tone of voice. "Yes I do, Sir. Their leader is an AWOL First Lieutenant by the name of Andy Armstrong. Armstrong wears captain's bars when he operates with his men and a group of French crooks who dress up to look like French Army MPs. Once they pull trucks over on the highway, or they stop them at phony checkpoints, they arrest the drivers and seize their trucks as "evidence." The drivers are let go in the ass end of nowhere and are left to explain that some MPs took their trucks. Armstrong and his men have also driven right into the supply depots and truck stops, to steal everything from gasoline to cigarettes, rations, soap, medical supplies, clothing, blankets and shoes." Then, after pausing for a split second, Charlie continued while he faced Major Savino. "I'll be happy to show you and your men where Armstrong and his gang hang their hat, Sir."

After thanking the prisoner, Tom Savino looked at Jim Beauregard and said, "I'd say Sergeant Monacco is off to a good start, Colonel."

"Excellent," responded Jim Beauregard as he faced the prisoner.

Even though Jim was well aware that French Army Intelligence could provide the same information about subjects who were worth pursuing, having Charlie Monacco on board would make it a lot easier, to make rock solid cases against other U.S. Army personnel, who were violating the law and the Articles of War. As a result, Jim Beauregard extended his hand and said, "Welcome aboard, Sergeant. We need all the help we can get. However, I must tell you upfront that I have no idea how the Judge Advocate General's Office, or the members of your court martial will react, when they weigh the severity of your charges to the amount of cooperation that you provide. In other words, you could do the so called right thing and help us in a number of ways and not receive the break that you think you deserve."

When Charlie Monacco responded he sound like a man who knew exactly how the game was played. "With your permission, Sir, I'll take my chances and hope for the best."

After shaking the prisoner's hand, Jim remarked, "Lieutenant Parker, along with Sergeant Mulligan and one of the Chief Inspector's men will continue debriefing you. As soon as they're finished, I'll personally deliver a copy of your statement and our investigative report to the appropriate officials."

As soon as Lieutenant Al Parker left with Charlie Monacco, Jim picked up the phone on his desk and asked his secretary to send in Captain Barnes, Lieutenant Garnier, Sergeant Parker and Inspector Dupray. The moment the door to the Colonel's Office opened, Jim Beauregard called out, "Grab a chair and tell us what you think, Captain."

As the Agent from the Counter Intelligence Corps (CIC) sat down, he spoke up and said, "You and your men along with our French Allies have certainly been busy, Sir."

"Are you ready to help us catch some bad guys?" asked Jim

"Yes, Sir," responded Captain Barnes.

While turning to face the Commanding Officer of French Military Intelligence in Paris, Jim removed a cigarette from the pack on his desk and said, "Since your men are currently keeping an eye on several locations and individuals who are associated with Pierre Mollet, how do you recommend that we proceed, Colonel?"

Colonel Andre Reynald was one of the smartest and shrewdest men that Jim Beauregard ever met. The fact that this man survived effectively operating behind enemy lines in North Africa, as well as in France for several years, made him a legend among Allied intelligence officers. When the Commanding Officer of the U.S. Army CIC in the ETO was briefed about the efforts that were being made to find Pierre Mollet, he knew that it was just a question of time, before Colonel Reynald and his men located one of France's most wanted collaborators.

Even though it took some time to accomplish, the day finally came, when two AWOL American soldiers made it possible for Captain Marcel Badeau's special intelligence unit, to track the movements of Antone Mollet and some of his brother's closest known associates. After following Antone

Mollet, Bernard Allard, Charles Coti, Edouard Tasse and Gregoire Petit, Marcel and his men got their first glimpse of Pierre Mollet. Once Jim Beauregard was fully briefed by Colonel Renyald and Captain Badeau about Pierre Mollet's involvement with German intelligence, Captain Billy Barnes from CIC was immediately dispatched to lend a hand. Now that all of the appropriate Allied military and civilian authorities were on board, it was time to plan how they intended to apprehend Pierre Mollet and his associates, including his other AWOL American black market contacts.

When Al Parker, Agent Mulligan and French Police Inspector Maurice La Belle interviewed Sergeant Monacco, they found their prisoner to be very cooperative. After receiving additional information about the AWOL G.I.s and their French associates, who hijacked truckloads of U.S. Army supplies while impersonating MPs, Al Parker turned to Sergeant Mulligan and said, "Do me a favor, Mike and have Sergeant Monacco make a detailed drawing of the layout of Lieutenant Armstrong's hideout. I'll be back as soon as I brief the Major."

"You got it, Lieutenant," responded Sergeant Mulligan.

As Al Parker left the interrogation room, Mike Mulligan removed a pack of smokes from his pocket and offered one to Inspector La Belle, before he leaned across the table and offered one to the prisoner. "Help yourself, Sarge."

Even though Charlie Monacco never had much use for cops, he had to admit that the men from CID had their shit together. After thanking Agent Mulligan for the cigarette, Charlie remarked, "I have a feeling things are gonna get real interesting around here, once the Major and your CO get briefed by your Lieutenant."

"I got the same feeling," responded Mike Mulligan as he passed a pad of paper and a sharp pencil to the prisoner as he continued and said, "In the meantime, let's work on that drawing."

After getting nowhere with Henri Duval, Chief Inspector Dumont returned to Paris Police Headquarters to speak to Duval's girlfriend Marguerite. Even though he had no plans to prosecute her, the Chief Inspector was holding her in protective custody, for reasons that were explained to her when Duval was arrested. Once the former prostitute was shown the case file, that described in vivid detail, what happened to the girls who worked in Pierre Mollet's brothel and were murdered because they were members of the resistance, Marguerite became a river of information.

The moment her disposition changed and she began cooperating, the words that she used to describe Pierre Mollet were, "That pig." By the time she finished speaking, the Chief Inspector had some additional information to pass on to Marcel Badeau, Colonel Reynald and his American colleagues. This information included comments that Marguerite overheard Henri Duval make when he spoke to both Antone Mollet and Pierre Mollet on the phone. In fact, it was Henri Duval's idea to dress like Catholic Priests when they left Paris for Switzerland.

After being told that she should be ready to leave Paris at a moment's notice, Marguerite also overheard her boyfriend mention the border town of Annemasse, as the location where the Mollet brothers and their men intended to cross over into Switzerland. Having this information in hand enabled the Chief Inspector, Colonel Reynald and their American counterparts in CID and CIC to post men in this area of the border, to block the escape of the Mollet brothers and their associates, in the event that they were not apprehended in Paris.

Even though Charlie Monacco was unable to identify every member of Andy Armstrong's group of black market operators, he remembered the names of two AWOL U.S. Army soldiers and a French thief who were instrumental in helping the AWOL Lieutenant run his hijacking operation. This information could not have come at a better time, because two GMC CCKW deuce and a half cargo trucks filled with cigarettes, rations, blankets and medical supplies were just hijacked by men dressed as U.S. Army Military Policemen.

After speaking to the military police commander who filed the report, Major Savino stood up as he hung up the phone in his office and said, "Some men dressed as MPs just hijacked two trucks that were loaded with supplies that were headed to the troops who need this stuff the most."

Since Al just finished debriefing Charlie Monacco, he reacted to the news like the seasoned policeman that he was when he said. "If Charlie Monacco is telling the truth and I believe he is, we should be able to find those two stolen trucks and all of their contents, at the address that he gave us for AWOL Lieutenant Armstrong's hideout here in Paris."

As the Major walked around his desk, he sounded a bit excited when he responded to Al's last remark. "And I got an idea how we can pull that off. Come on, Al, I'll fill you in on the way to brief the Colonel."

When the door to the interrogation room opened, the MP on guard duty remained outside while Inspector La Belle, Agent Mulligan and Charlie Monacco stood up as the three Army Officers entered the room.

While Jim Beauregard approached the table, he held up his right hand and said, "As you were, men."

As everyone sat back down, Jim continued and said, "Did Sergeant Monacco come up with anything new while Lieutenant Parker was briefing me and the Major?"

While Sergeant Mulligan passed his two sheets of paper to his Commanding Officer, the former airborne military policeman who was now serving as a CID Agent responded and said, "Before Lieutenant Parker left the room, Sir, he asked Sergeant Monacco to draw the layout of Lieutenant Armstrong's hideout. Inspector La Belle also knows this section of Paris like the back of his hand and helped the prisoner with the sketch."

"This will definitely come in handy when we hit this place," remarked Jim Beauregard as he handed the two drawings to Major Savino and Lieutenant Parker.

While Jim stood next to the interrogation table, he looked down at the prisoner and said, "We just had two more trucks hijacked by men dressed as U.S. Army MPs, while their drivers were heading east to supply Allied units. Needless to say, we have to put an end to this crap."

"How can I help, Sir" responded Charlie Monacco.

Jim had been a cop long enough to know what needed to be done. He also knew that the U.S. Army was an organization that conducted every aspect of its mission according to certain rules. Since Sergeant Monacco was a prisoner who was facing serious charges, CID needed to do things the Army way. Even Benny Greene was no longer allowed to have his freedom, until his case was formally adjudicated.

While Jim offered the prisoner a cigarette and a light, he presented his plan in such a fashion as to give Charlie Monacco the opportunity to say yes or no to helping CID. "If I was back home in Atlanta, I'd have lunch with the DA and your case would be resolved in a matter of minutes. Since I'm on military leave from my duties as a Captain of Detectives and this isn't Atlanta, I have to conduct myself according to U.S. Army regulations. As a result, I need to know one thing before I start making calls on your behalf. Can I tell an Army prosecutor, an Army lawyer who will be your assigned counsel and an Army Judge, that you're willing to assist CID, the Paris Police and French Army Intelligence in making a rock solid case against the AWOL personnel and the French crooks that you identified to CID, even though no specific promises have been made to you in return for your cooperation?"

After quickly exhaling some cigarette smoke, Charlie wasted no time in saying, "Yes, Sir. Count me in, Sir." Then, after quickly pausing, Charlie added, "Like I said before, Sir. I'll be happy to take you and your men to Lieutenant Armstrong's hangout. I can also call him and see what he has for sale, before he gets wind of the fact that I surrendered. After that, we can visit Master Sergeant Clyde C. Nelson at his POL Dump."

"OK, sit tight while we see how we're gonna handle this," remarked Jim, before he turned to face Tommy Savino and Al Parker and said, "We need to talk."

After telling Al Parker and Tom Savino what he had in mind, Jim Beauregard looked directly at Al and said, "What'a you think, Al?"

Al Parker was well aware that the Commanding Officer of the Paris CID Office was not obligated to ask him, if he approved of his son Cal being asked to work undercover again. That said, Al appreciated the fact that his friend Jim Beauregard took the time to do so.

"I think it's a good plan, Sir," said Al, who quickly added, "Cal and Benny Greene are a good team. Besides, we certainly can't send Charlie Monacco and George Zangolas in by themselves. I also doubt that Lieutenant Armstrong, or any of his men will suspect that Cal and Benny are working for CID."

"I agree with, Al, Sir," remarked Tommy Savino.

After all they had been through together, Jim Beauregard felt uncomfortable with his subordinates standing on ceremony and referring to him as Colonel, or Sir when they addressed each other when they were alone. Since this was one of the few times when they met privately since they were reunited to work together in France, Jim decided to broach the topic and say, "Listen guys, I understand the need to be more formal with each other when we're in front of the men, but I see no reason why we can't be on a first name basis when we're alone, especially after all that we've been though together."

"You got it, Jim," responded Major Savino, before he turned to Al as he extended his hand and said, "That goes for you and me as well, Al." "My pleasure, Tom," said Al.

"Now that we got that outta the way, I need to make a few calls before I go over to the Judge Advocate General's Office," remarked Jim.

After facing his second in command, Jim went on to say, "Tom, I need you to get us ready to execute the raid on AWOL Lieutenant Armstrong's gang, as well as on Pierre Mollet's garage and every other location that Captain Badeau and his men are watching."

"I'll get right on it, Jim," responded the Army Officer who served as a cop in Providence, Rhode Island before the war.

When Jim continued he faced Al Parker and said, "Al, I need you to speak to Cal and see if he's willing to volunteer to work undercover again, either alone, or with Benny Greene, Charlie Monacco and George Zangolas. At the very least, we should be able to use Sergeant Monacco to call Lieutenant Armstrong and have Cal pick up some of the stolen government property, that this crook has in inventory. If we get real lucky, we'll be able to have Bennie Greene, Charlie Monacco and George Zangolas go with Cal, to make a purchase from Armstrong. In order to prepare for both possibilities, it's imperative that Cal, Benny, Charlie Monacco and George Zangolas get their story straight before they go operational. I'll leave it up to you to quarterback the strategy session between Cal and the others."

After pausing briefly to light a cigarette, Jim continued and said, "If for some reason the Army lawyers won't play ball, our fallback plan will be to use Charlie Monacco and Private Zangolas to identify anyone they know, who walks into, or out of, the location where Armstrong and his fellow crooks are operating. We also have to be prepared to keep an eye on any locations where Armstrong and his men eat, drink and live."

Once again, Al Parker proved that he was a veteran street cop when he remarked, "In the event that we can't use 'em, to meet face to face with Armstrong and his gang of phony MPs, I'll ask the Chief Inspector if he can get us a French delivery van to use, so Sergeant Monacco and Private Zangolas can make the IDs from a safe distance. We can also use this van, if we get the approval to use Charlie Monacco, Bennie Greene and George Zangolas to work undercover with Cal."

"Excellent idea," responded Jim, who checked his watch before he ended the meeting by saying, "Let's plan on meeting back here with the Chief Inspector, Captain Badeau, Colonel Reynald and Captain Barnes at 1045 hours. Cal and the others will also have to be ready to go undercover by then as well. Once we go over a few details, we'll brief the men before we head into the field."

CHAPTER 9

A FATHER AND SON CHAT BEFORE ALL HELL BREAKS LOSE

As soon as Al approached his son's desk, he wasted no time in saying, "We have an operation to plan and the Colonel asked if you'd be willing to work undercover again, possibly with Benny Greene, Sergeant Monacco and Private Zangolas?"

Even though Cal had no idea what he was being asked to do, he responded as if he had more important things on his mind when he said, "Sure, Pop. I'll do it. I'm sure Benny will too."

"Don't you want'a know what you and the others are being asked to do?" asked Al.

Cal proved that he had something more important to talk to his father about, than police work for the U.S. Army, when he looked up and said, "Do we have time to grab some lunch? There's something I need to talk to you about."

Al Parker had been a father long enough to know, when one of his sons had something important that they needed to talk to him about. After checking his watch, Al responded and said, "I'm sorry, son, but we have just enough time to grab some coffee, before we go over the game plan."

"Coffee's fine, Pop," responded Cal.

When Al said that he had one thing to do before he could leave the office, but he would meet his son at The Paris Cafe in a few minutes, Cal thanked his father as he cleared his desk."

While Cal Parker put his coat on and he left the CID office, Major Savino spotted Al with a puzzled look on his face.

"Are you OK, Al?" asked the Major.

Since no one was around, Al responded and said, "When I asked Cal if he was willing to work undercover again, he said yes right away and didn't even ask what the case was about. Then he asked if we could grab some lunch, because he had something important to talk to me about. When I told him we were short on time, he settled for meeting me for a cup of coffee at Gabby's place."

While sounding more like a friend than a superior officer, Major Savino limited his response to saying, "Go meet your son, Al."

"I know my son, Tom. Something is definitely bothering Cal," responded Al.

Once again, Major Savino sounded like a friend when he said, "I wish I could tell why you need to meet him, but I'm sworn to secrecy. Besides, this is stuff that a father and son need to talk about in private."

After hearing what Tommy Savino had to say, Al sounded like a typical concerned father when he asked, "Is Cal in trouble?"

"No, Al, he's not in trouble," responded Tom Savino, who quickly added, "But as soon as you two have a private talk, Cal will have a clear head and will be ready to get back to work on the Armstrong case."

"Will I have a clear head?" asked Al.

"Probably not," responded Tom Savino, before he went on to say, "After all, it's a father's job to worry. At least that's what my old man told me."

"You're father was right," responded Al, who continued as he headed for the door. "For a guy who isn't married and has no kids, you sure know a lot about being a father."

After cracking a smile, Tommy Savino remarked, "What can I tell you. I'm practicing."

As Al headed for his office, he turned toward the Major and said, "Thanks, Tom."

When Cal Parker saw his father coming his way, he stood up to greet him. "Thanks for coming, Pop."

"My pleasure, son," said Al, who quickly added, "Between all of the action at work we haven't been able to spend much time together."

As soon as Gabby saw Lieutenant Parker join his son, at a table along the back wall of the cafe, he welcomed Cal's father with a friendly embrace. "It is good to see you, my friend."

"The same here, Gabby," responded Al before he sat across from his son.

When Gabby said that the waiter would be right out with their coffee, Al figured that Cal already let the owner of The Paris Cafe know that they were short on time. Al's assumption was proven correctly, when their waiter delivered a shot glass filled with scotch in front of Al Parker and said, "Compliments of Gabby for your coffee sport, Lieutenant."

As soon as Al thanked the waiter and he returned to the kitchen, Al turned to his son and said, "It didn't take long for me to get Gabby, Francois and the Colonel hooked on putting a shot of scotch in their coffee."

Once their coffee was delivered and Al asked Cal if he wanted some scotch put in his cup, Cal waved his hand and said, "I've have something to tell you, Dad, and I'm not sure how you're gonna react."

Since this sounded serious and time was short, Al poured the entire shot in his cup and took a sip, while Cal looked across the table at his father and said, "Chief Inspector Dumont's daughter Michelle and I are in love. I plan to ask her to marry me. If she says yes and I expect that she will, I'll ask her father for his blessing. Before I do so, I'd like to get yours."

The second Cal stopped speaking, all Al could think about, was how much he wished his wife Mary was present. Initially, Al was speechless and didn't know what to say. As soon as Cal saw that his father wasn't responding, he remarked, "Let me guess. You don't approve?"

After taking another sip of the scotch laced coffee, Al made a concerted effort to use the right words when he responded and said, "Before we go any further, son, I want you to know that I have the highest respect for Michelle Dumont. In addition to being an incredibly brave young lady, she comes from one of the best families in Paris. In other words, I like that girl."

"But you don't approve of us getting married?" said Cal.

"I didn't say that," responded Al, who tried his best to sound like a down to earth father, when he continued and said, "You know, son, despite what you and your brother might think, there was a time when I was a young man too. I felt the same way about your mother as you feel about Michelle. In fact, my love for your mother has only gotten stronger over the years, so don't write me off, as someone who doesn't understand what you're going through, 'cause I've been there."

"Then what's the problem, Pop?" asked Cal.

Al could not believe that he was having this conversation with his youngest son. In fact, the only thing that would complicate this situation more, would be if Al received a letter from his son Jack, informing him that he intended to marry an Italian girl, who lived near Ramitelli Airfield, where he was stationed with the 332nd Fighter Squadron. While doing his best to have the patience of a saint, Al looked at Cal and said, "Do you know where Charlie Golovan is right now?"

"No, Sir, I don't," responded Cal.

"He's standing in the all colored section of a U.S. Army Hospital interviewing a Negro soldier who was found badly beaten in an alley in Paris. The reason he was attacked, was because he was observed walking down the street with his French girlfriend. When they took a shortcut to get to her apartment, they were followed by three white soldiers, who were by no means gentlemen from the south. Even though this Negro Sergeant had more decorations on his uniform than all of three of his attackers combined, they treated him as if he wasn't human."

While Cal took a sip from his coffee cup, his father went on to say, "After breaking a bottle over this colored sergeant's head and knocking him out, these three pieces of trash went to work on his French girlfriend. Even though she did her best to defend herself, she was no match for her three attackers. If it wasn't for an MP patrol, they probably would'a got away."

As Cal put his cup down, he responded and said, "I know how it is out there, Pop. I also know that there are good white folks in this world like the Colonel and the other men in the office."

While Al continued, he leaned closer to the table and said, "I had high hopes that this world would change for the better after the last war, but it didn't. I had even higher hopes that this world would change once we got into this war, but I'm sorry to report that it hasn't. This world is still full'a hate. I know, because just like you, I've seen this hatred up close. It's scary stuff to put it mildly."

While sounding a bit defensive, Cal remarked, "What'a you suggest I do, Dad? Walk away from the woman I love, because I'm colored and she's white?"

Deep down inside, Al Parker had absolutely no problem if either one, or both of his sons married girls with different color skin. Al proved he felt this way when he looked directly at Cal and said, "My one and only concern is how you and Michelle, as well as my future grandchildren, will be treated by the assholes in this world. I wouldn't feel this way, if the majority of the people back home were like some of the white cops I worked with in New York, or like the men we work with here in Paris. Heck, son, there's also plenty of colored folks who take a dim view of Negro men and women with white partners being together in public, let alone being married. Unless things have changed since we left the states, you can't even sit at the same table in a restaurant with Michelle and have a nice dinner together back home."

Cal knew that his father was 110% correct and wasted no time in saying, "You're right on all counts, Pop. That's why I decided to make a life for me and Michelle in Paris, once the war is over and I get discharged. I came to this decision, because as you well know, the French aren't like us. They're tolerant people and don't seem to have a problem with couples like me and Michelle being together. I also heard it's like that in Italy as well."

After taking another sip from his coffee cup, Cal added, "Did you know that our Army instructed the French 2nd Armored Division not to take their Colonial African troops with them when they liberated Paris.[11] According to Michelle's uncle, who's a Captain in this unit, our Army didn't want colored soldiers being photographed fighting alongside white troops while liberating this city, because the French Army isn't segregated like the U.S. Army is. Not for nothing, Pop, but these Colonial troops from Africa were fighting Krauts long before most of us got into this war."

From a father's perspective, Cal just dropped a second bomb in his lap, when he said that he planned to make a new life for himself in France after the war. Worse yet, everything Cal said was true and made perfect sense. While Al wished he had a glass full of scotch and soda to drink, instead of a small cup of whiskey laced coffee, he decided to press his son, for a better explanation of his plans to live in France after the war. "What about your plans to join the police department back home? I doubt the French will let an American become a cop in Paris. Do you have any idea how you'll support a wife and a family if you live in France?"

"I haven't worked out all of the details yet, but I have a few ideas," responded Cal.

Once again, Al did his best to watch the tone of voice that he used, when he spoke up and said, "For the sake of conversation, can you give me some idea of what you might be able to do for a living as a foreigner in France?"

Cal proved that he was in no mood to continue this conversation at this time when he remarked, "Can we do this some other time, Pop? Like you said, we have get back to work."

"OK, but this conversation isn't over," said Al who quickly added, "The coffee's on me, 'cause you gonna need every penny you have, to support that beautiful future wife of yours. In fact, I might have to buy a garage in Paris, so I can teach you how to fix cars. You could do worse things for a living you know."

After hearing what his father had to say, Cal felt the weight of the world lifted from his shoulders. As Cal smiled for the first time, since they spoke about such a serious matter, he looked at his softy for a father and said, "Thanks Pop."

CHAPTER 10

GOING OPERATIONAL

After going through the formalities of having their cases adjudicated on a contingency basis, Charlie Monacco and George Zangolas were technically free men, pending the outcome of their continued cooperation with CID and French authorities. The Army prosecutor also agreed to drop all charges against Corporal Benny Greene. Once that was done, Jim had Benny transferred to CID, at which time, the former Army truck driver was issued a CID Agent's badge and ID, along with a forty five caliber Model 1911 pistol.

In addition to the teams that were preparing to execute the raid on Pierre Mollet's garage, Major Tommy Savino and Al Parker, along with Cal Parker, Benny Greene, Mike Mulligan, Anthony Angelone and Sal Coppola were assigned to handle the case involving the AWOL Americans who were operating as military policemen. Because this group was working with French thieves, Chief Inspector Dumont assigned Inspector Maurice La Belle to provide assistance. Additional personnel from the 709th Military Police Battalion were placed on standby, to be called in when it came time to arrest AWOL Lieutenant Armstrong and the other members of his gang. As soon as this operation and the operation involving Pierre Mollet and his associates were completed, CID Agent Bill Hayes and Agent Hank Blair were assigned to arrest Master Sergeant Clyde C. Nelson.

Rather than leave, without knowing if the AWOL G.I.s who were masquerading as military policemen were in their garage, Major Savino had Agents Mulligan, Angelone and Coppola get into position to observe the location that they intended to raid. While the garage that was used by

AWOL Lieutenant Armstrong and his men was kept under surveillance, Major Savino, Al Parker and Inspector La Belle maintained a surveillance of the Cafe de la Rotonde in the Montparnasse section of Paris. The decision to do so, was made after Charlie Monacco called Lieutenant Armstrong to purchase some stolen merchandise and he was invited to meet the phony MP for a drink.

When Major Savino and Al Parker, along with the men under their command were preparing to leave the office, Jim stopped by to wish them well. "Good luck, men," said Jim, before he turned to Charlie Monacco, George Zangolas, Benny Greene and Cal Parker and remarked, "Do you men have your story straight?"

Without hesitating, the three freed prisoners and Cal Parker responded in unison and said, "Yes, Sir."

While Jim looked at Charlie Monacco, George Zangolas and Benny Greene, he continued and said, "Once you meet with AWOL Lieutenant Armstrong and any of his men, Sergeant Parker will be calling the shots." As Jim continued, he looked directly at Charlie Monacco and said, "As soon as your business with AWOL Lieutenant Armstrong is concluded, Sergeant Parker will remind you of the need to meet Marcel. That's the signal to break contact and leave. Do I make myself clear?"

Once again, Charlie Monacco sounded like a team player when he responded and said, "Yes, Sir. Agent Parker is calling the shots." The Colonel then turned to George Zangolas and said, "That's when you go to work, George." Private Zangolas sounded just as enthusiastic, when he acknowledged his orders and quickly added, "I won't let you down, Sir."

After nodding his head, Jim turned to face Tommy Savino and Al Parker and said, "Good hunting and be careful."

Once Major Savino and his team left the office, Jim held a briefing for the personnel who would be participating on the Mollet case. At the conclusion of this briefing session, Jim Beauregard presented two boxes containing items from the commissary and the post exchange to Sam Carubba and Lieutenant Garnier, before they left to man the observation platform. Sam was selected to work with Captain Badeau's second in command for two reasons. First, Agent Carubba spoke French like a native. Sam also made a big impression on the resident of the apartment that they approached with

Chief Inspector Dumont, when they needed to secure a suitable location to use as an observation post.

Once Mrs. Dubois eagerly agreed to assist the Allied agents, the decision was made to bring some very hard to get items along, as a way to repay the 60 year old woman for her assistance. It also made sense to provide the men working in the primary observation post with plenty of food and tobacco, because the average Parisian in early 1945 could barely afford to feed themselves, let alone two guests.

As soon as Sergeant Sam Carubba and Lieutenant Charles Garnier were invited into the fourth floor corner apartment, they presented Mrs. Dubois with the items that were difficult to impossible for the average Parisian to obtain during the war. While Lieutenant Garnier thanked Mrs. Dubois again, for allowing them to use her home as an observation post, the old lady's eyes opened wide when she saw the contents of the two boxes. Even though it had been years since Mrs Dubois had seen so many "luxury" items, her initial reaction as a proud Parisian was to remark, "I seek no reward for assisting my country and our American Allies."

While Agent Carubba continued to hold one of the boxes with both hands, he spoke fluent French when he responded and said, "This is not payment, Mrs. Dubois. These rations are from the American and French Army, to share with anyone who serves with us and you are serving with us in our moment of need."

As the older woman, who lost her husband and had three sons serving in the French Air Force and Army considered what the young American had to say, she smiled then said, "You may put our supplies on the kitchen table."

While Lieutenant Garnier and Agent Carubba assumed positions near the living room window, Mrs. Dubois emptied the two boxes that contained one pound of American coffee, a pound of sugar, six cans of evaporated milk, a carton of Pall Mall cigarettes, six C ration cans of meat, eggs and potatoes, and four chocolate D Bars. As Agent Carubba stood off to the side of the window and kept an eye on Mollet's garage/warehouse, Lieutenant Garnier checked his watch and said, "The other men should be in position by now."

The moment the phone rang in the apartment, Mrs. Dubois performed her duty as their assistant and took the call. After smiling and saying,

"Thank you, Chief Inspector. Yes, Sir, Lieutenant Garnier and Sergeant Carubba are in position. I will give you to Lieutenant Garnier."

As soon as Lieutenant Garnier arrived by her side, the 60 year old widow handed the phone to the French Army Intelligence Officer. While the Lieutenant listened, he wrote something in his notebook then said, "Yes, Sir. I have the number. We will do as you say, Sir," before he hung up the phone.

While Sam Carubba continued to keep an eye on Mollet's garage, he spoke up and said, "What's up, Lieutenant?"

After hanging up the phone, Lieutenant Garnier returned to where his American partner was standing and said, "Sergeant Blair and Inspector Dupray are in position to command the ground units that are covering the garage. Captain Barnes, Inspector Goulet and four men from my unit are in position to follow anyone who leaves the warehouse on foot. Agent Hayes and Inspector De La Fontaine are in position to follow any vehicles that leave the garage. Two other teams are also in position to follow vehicles if necessary. The rest of the men are covering Antone Mollet's apartment building."

When the French Intelligence Officer continued, he held up his notebook and said, "The Chief Inspector, Captain Badeau and Colonel Beauregard are positioned nearby, in the alley behind a shop that is owned by the family of a Paris policeman. Colonel Reynald is on his way to meet them. We are to call them at this number to report any movement."

With their cars parked three streets away from Pierre Mollet's garage, the Chief Inspector posted Inspector Philippe Leblanc inside the rear entrance of the shop to man the phone. While Chief Inspector Dumont stood next to his black 1939 Citroen Traction Avant sedan, he looked at his watch before he remarked, "All of our men are in position. Now we wait."

After lighting a cigarette, Jim Beauregard checked his watch as well then said, "So far, so good."

Once Captain Badeau finished checking the map of Paris, he looked at the Chief Inspector and Jim Beauregard and said, "Even if the men I told you about are unable to signal us, we have enough of our men in position to take action at the appropriate time."

After being fully briefed by Colonel Reynald and Captain Badeau, the American Agents from Army CID and the Counter Intelligence Corps, as well as Chief Inspector Dumont and his men, were very impressed that French Army Intelligence managed to infiltrate Pierre Mollet's organization from two different perspectives. Whether he was driven by his personal hatred of Pierre Mollet for killing his family, because he had no love for collaborators, or a combination of reasons, Marcel Badeau scored his first victory, when following Antone Mollet led the special French Intelligence unit to locate Gregorie Petit.

After discussing his plan with his commanding officer, Captain Badeau approached Gregorie Petit, when he was observed leaving his girlfriend's apartment in the Latin Quarter. Marcel played his hand well, when he made a late night visit on the one man in Mollet's former Milice unit, who had the least amount of French blood on his hands. In Gregorie Petit's case, his problems were twofold. In addition to being a wanted man for his involvement in Pierre Mollet's Milice unit, Petit's younger brother was in custody for the crimes that he committed against France. When Marcel offered to intervene and keep his younger brother from being executed, Petit asked what this favor would cost him.

Gregorie Petit changed sides, when he was assured by Captain Badeau and Colonel Reynald, that the crimes that he and his brother committed would be completely forgiven, in return for his full cooperation. The wanted collaborator began cooperating that night and provided additional details about Pierre Mollet's plan to disrupt Allied supply lines, by diverting additional stolen military supplies to the black market, before he and his men left for Switzerland. It was also through the cooperation of Gregorie Petit, that French Army Intelligence was able to plant a second undercover operative in Pierre Mollet's organization.

While Jim Beauregard leaned up against the side of the Chief Inspector's unmarked police car, he took a drag on his cigarette before he remarked, "Thanks to you, Marcel, we have two sets of eyes and ears on the inside."

After lighting a cigarette, Marcel pointed to Francois Dumont before he responded and said, "I owe my friend the Chief Inspector, for making it possible for me to get to know the one I call L'Artiste. I say that because Francois and I arrested this man several times, when we served together before the war. As Francois will confirm, L'Artiste is the best forger and counterfeiter in Paris."

After the nodding his head in agreement, Francois remarked, "Jacques Bayard is also a patriot."

"Correct," said Marcel, who went on to say, "Before I left the police department to join the resistance, I went to see L'Artiste. Once I told him what our plans were, L'Artiste eagerly offered to provide me and Charles Ganier with new identity cards and papers. When he refused to accept payment, all he asked was that we kill as many Germans as possible on his behalf. He also offered his services to the resistance and as Francois can confirm, he served well. The papers and documents that L'Artiste created were works of art and were never questioned. Many people, including me and Charles, owe our lives to Jacques Bayard."

Before he continued, Marcel paused to take a drag on his cigarette. "Once Petit proved himself to me, I had him recruit L'Artiste into Mollet's black market operation. This was easy to accomplish, after Colonel Reynald had French Military Police issue an order for the arrest of L'Artiste, for forging documents for the enemies of France. To insure that this would work, we arranged for two former collaborators who went to work for us, to vogue for L'Artiste. This enabled Petit to use their names as references. Doing so, helped to convince Pierre Mollet that L'Artiste was worth bringing into his organization."

After pausing to take another drag on his cigarette, Marcel continued and said, "Between Petit and L'Artiste we learned that Pierre Mollet decided to postpone his departure. The reason for this delay, is so Pierre Mollet can receive a sizable payment for the last delivery that he made, to the largest of the three groups of AWOL Americans that he has been doing business with. In order to motivate these AWOL Americans to bring him his money, Mollet informed his associates that he had an entire warehouse of stolen merchandise to turn over to them."

"The carrot on the stick," remarked the Chief Inspector.

"Correct," responded Marcel, who went on to say, "Even though Pierre Mollet will never receive payment, for all of the stolen merchandise that is stored in his garage, he will still be performing a valuable service for the Germans, by preventing these supplies from being used by Allied soldiers. Besides, by waiting to receive an additional payment for his last delivery, the Mollet brothers and their associates will be traveling to Switzerland with even more money in their pockets."

While the Chief Inspector leaned closer to his two colleagues, he spoke in a low tone of voice when he said, "Greed my friends, will be the downfall of Pierre Mollet and the men who follow him."

"If it wasn't for greed, we'd have a lot less work to do," added Jim Beauregard.

Immediately after hearing what the American Army Colonel had to say, Captain Badeau spoke as he raised his right hand in the air. "If I had a glass of wine in hand, I would propose a toast. To greed. It keeps policemen busy."

While Sam Carubba sipped a cup of freshly brewed American coffee, he continued to watch Mollet's warehouse that was located across the street. The moment a Citroen delivery van arrived in front of the warehouse, Sam remarked, "We have company, Lieutenant,"as he put his coffee cup down and picked up the binoculars that hung around his neck.

While standing off to the side and a step back from the window, Sam was joined by Lieutenant Garnier, just as the driver's assistant exited the passenger side of the cab and approached the large wooden doors to the garage. The second the doors were opened by a man wearing a leather jacket, Lieutenant Garnier remarked, "The one who opened the door is Edouard Tasse. He personally rounded up hundreds of French citizens, including Jews, for the Gestapo. In addition, Edouard Tasse took part in the torture and execution of six resistance members and was one of the men who participated in the Milice raid, that resulted in the death of Captain Badeau's wife and infant son. In fact, based on what we know, Tasse was the one who handed Pierre Mollet the grenades, that were used to kill the Captain's family."

Without taking his eyes off the subjects they had under surveillance, Sam Carubba remarked, "Maybe we'll get lucky, Lieutenant and Edouard

Tasse will resist arrest."

"That would be, how you say, a shame," responded the French Intelligence Officer, who began killing Germans as soon as he joined the Maqui in the early days of the war.

Once the vehicle was driven inside the garage, the wooden "barn" doors were immediately closed behind the van. Less than a minute later, another Frenchman emerged from the garage and used a box of matches to light a cigarette, before he looked up as if he was checking the weather. As soon as he did so, Lieutenant Garnier remarked, "The one you see smoking the cigarette is with us. Captain Badeau calls him L' Artiste. His real name is Jacques Bayard. He saved many lives with the documents that he forged for us when the Germans occupied France."

After walking over to the telephone, Lieutenant Garnier dialed the number that was passed to him earlier. As soon as Inspector Leblanc answered the phone, Lieutenant Garnier asked to speak to Captain Badeau. Once the Captain entered the shop, he took the phone from the police inspector and spoke into the receiver with a sense of urgency when he said, "Yes, Charles."

While Marcel held the phone next to his right ear, he listened as Charles Garnier filed his report. "A Citroen delivery van just arrived. Tasse was observed opening the doors to the garage. A minute later L' Artiste left the building and relayed the signal, that Pierre Mollet and the other members of his Milice unit are inside the warehouse. He also did as we instructed and looked up into the sky, to let us know that we should prepare to take action."

As soon as Marcel said, "Do as we planned and have the men in the concierge's residence pass the word to the others," before he quickly added, "Call as soon as anything changes."

"Yes, Sir," responded Marcel's second in command, before he hung up the phone on his end.

While Lieutenant Charles Garnier left the fourth floor apartment to alert the men stationed in the ground floor apartment, Marcel changed places with Inspector Leblanc and left the shop, to return to where the others were standing by their parked cars.

After walking over to where the Chief Inspector and Jim Beauregard were standing, Marcel was in exceptionally good spirits, when he faced the man that he served with in the Paris Police and said, "Charles Garnier and Sergeant Carubba just observed a Citroen delivery van return to the garage. Once Edouard Tasse opened the doors, the vehicle was driven inside. After the doors were closed, L' Artiste stood in front of the garage and relayed the signal that Pierre Mollet is inside with his men and that we should standby to take action." Then, after pausing for a spit second, Marcel reached out and gripped the Chief Inspector's left arm as he said, "The noose is tightening around their necks, Francois."

When Francois asked about the others, Marcel responded without hesitation. "The fact that we've heard nothing so far, means that the three French thieves who serve as drivers for Pierre Mollet are still in Antone Mollet's apartment. Based on the observations that have been made by our men and by the signal that we just received, we can be certain that Benard Allard, Jerome Paget, Edouard Tasse, Gregorie Petit and L' Artiste are with Pierre Mollet inside the garage."

"All we need now is for Pierre Mollet's brother Antone and their AWOL American contacts in the black market to arrive and we're in business," responded Jim Beauregard.

As soon as Charlie Monacco entered the Cafe de la Rotonde in the Montparnasse arrondissement of Paris, Major Savino spoke up from the back of the Citroen surveillance van and said, "Sergeant Monacco was right about Lieutenant Andy Armstrong. This AWOL son of a bitch has some pair of balls walking around Paris dressed like an MP Captain."

After checking his watch, Al responded and said, "The good news is, that by the time they finish their drinks and return to Armstrong's hideout, the rest of our men should have our trucks loaded with the supplies that these phony MPs just stole off the highway."

While Tommy Savino continued to crouch down in the back of the van, he looked at Al and said, "I can't wait to see the look on this AWOL Lieutenant's face, when he finds out that Charlie and his men are working for CID."

"Seeing that surprised look on a crook's face is always the best part next to saying, "You're under arrest," responded Al,

"You're right about that," said Tommy Savino.

As soon as Al spotted Charlie Monacco and Lieutenant Armstrong leave the Cafe de la Rotonde, he called out, "Here they come."

While Al started the engine, Major Savino watched from the back of van, as Charlie Monacco and Andy Armstrong walked to a Jeep, that was being driven by an AWOL G.I. masquerading as a military policeman. As soon as the Jeep, that was painted to look like a military police vehicle, drove away, Al put the Citroen delivery van in gear as he remarked, "There goes Inspector La Belle. He's hot on their tail."

While Major Savino stepped back into rear compartment of the French delivery van, Al Parker followed Inspector La Belle's Peugeot sedan back to the AWOL Lieutenant's storage facility and hideout. After extending the antenna, Major Savino used his portable HCR 536 handie talkie portable radio to contact Lieutenant Carl Miller of the 709th Military Police Battalion. As soon as MP Lieutenant Miller responded, he was instructed to position his men closer to the location that they were getting ready to raid. Immediately after MP Lieutenant Miller acknowledged the order, Major Savino leaned into the cab of the delivery van and said, "The cavalry is on the way, Al."

While Al wore a civilian leather jacket to conceal his Army uniform, he called out, "I heard."

As the Citroen van driven by Al Parker and Inspector La Belle's Peugeot followed the occupants of the phony MP Jeep at a safe distance, Major Savino spoke up again and said, "All we need now is the signal to move in and this gang of counterfeit MPs will be in for a big surprise."

As soon as Tommy Savino saw Al pull over to the curb behind Inspector Maurice La Belle's Peugeot, he new they were close enough to keep an eye on the location that they intended to raid. While Major Savino remained in the rear compartment of the delivery van, Al continued looking forward as he shut the engine off and said, "They just drove into the garage."

"I better let Lieutenant Miller know what's going on," remarked the

Major as he picked up his portable radio.

As soon as Charlie Monacco jumped out of the phony MP Jeep that was parked inside the closed garage, he did his best to appear impressed when he looked around and said, "I see you and your men have been busy since the last time we did business together."

While Lieutenant Armstrong offered Charlie a Chesterfield cigarette, before he took one for himself, he accepted a light from his guest and business associate and said, "I'm telling you, Charlie, you and your men ought'a come in with us. Parading around as MPs is the way to go."

Just as they had planned, Cal Parker walked over to Charlie Monacco when George Zangolas got into the cab on the lead GMC truck and Benny Greene got in behind the wheel of the second truck that was loaded with stolen U.S. Army property. "George wanted me to tell you that we're ready to go, Sarge. George also wanted me to remind you that we're supposed to meet Marcel and his men in thirty minutes."

"Thanks Cal," responded Charlie as he removed a rather large wad of French Francs from his pocket and he handed the pre-agreed upon amount to the AWOL Army Officer. "Here you go, Lieutenant, or should I say, Captain. I'll get the rest to you once Marcel and his men move this load for us."

As soon as AWOL Lieutenant Andy Armstrong slipped the money into his pant's pocket, he extended his hand and cracked a smile before he remarked, "Come by anytime. You and your men are always welcome."

While calling out to one of the fake MPs who was standing by the large wooden door to the warehouse, Lieutenant Armstrong said, "Open up, Steve. Charlie and his men are leaving."

Just as they planned, when George Zangolas started to drive the Army cargo truck out of the warehouse, he intentionally stalled the deuce and a half in such a fashion as the prevent the door from being closed. As soon as he did so, a group of heavily armed CID Agents and U.S. Army Military Policemen led by Major Tommy Savino, Lieutenant Al Parker and Lieutenant Miller raided the location.

"CID! Nobody Move!" yelled Al Parker.

As the raiding party filed into the garage, Cal Parker and Benny Greene jumped out of their truck with guns drawn and identified themselves as CID Agents. Once they did so, they were joined by Charlie Monacco and George Zangolas who were armed with M1 Carbines.

As tempted as they were to resist, the men who worked for the soon to be convicted Lieutenant Andy Armstrong, including several French thieves, submitted to arrest, once they saw that they were outnumbered and out-gunned. While Cal Parker and Benny Greene stood with Charlie Monacco and George Zangolas in between their two trucks, they watched as AWOL Lieutenant Armstrong was placed under arrest by Major Savino.

When Major Savino saw the way that Lieutenant Andy Armstrong was looking at Charlie Monacco and George Zangolas, the second in command of the CID Office in Paris remarked, "There's one thing I've been dying to do, ever since I heard about a group of G.I. Gangsters who like to commit crimes while dressed as MPs." The second he finished making his comment, Major Savino forcefully removed the prisoner's hat and the Captain's bars that he wore on his uniform jacket and said, "You're a disgrace to this uniform and don't deserve to be seen wearing the insignia of a commis-sioned officer of the United States Army, especially a rank that you never earned." While a pissed off Andy Armstrong continued to look at the two men who set him up, Major Savino turned to Sergeant Coppola and said, "Get this prisoner out of my sight, Sergeant."

"Yes, Sir," responded Sergeant Coppola as he yanked on Andy Armstrong's right arm and said, "You heard the Major. Let's go."

While the other prisoners were being disarmed, searched and hand-cuffed, Major Savino turned to Al Parker and said, "OK, Al, you know what to do."

"Yes, Sir," responded Lieutenant Parker, before he turned to CID Agent Anthony Angelone and said, "Come on, Ange. We have work to do."

As Al Parker and Agent Angelone headed toward the back of the ware-house to search the office, Al turned to his right and showed his approval for a job well done, by tossing his son Cal and Benny a casual salute. While Cal and Benny returned the salute, Al Parker and Agent Angelone vanished from sight, as they walked by crates of stolen property and entered the warehouse office.

While Benny tucked his pistol in his waistband under his Ike Jacket, he turned to face Cal Parker and said, "That's the first time an officer saluted me."

As Cal tucked his pistol in the small of his back under his Ike Jacket, he turned to face his undercover partner and remarked, "That's his way of letting us know that he's proud of the way we handled things today."

"I sure like being one of the good guys," remarked Benny.

After cracking a smile, Cal remarked, "Police work seems to agree with you, Benny. You ought'a think about becoming a cop in civilian life when this war ends and you get shipped home. I'm sure the Colonel, the Major and my dad will give you one hell of a recommendation. I know I will."

At first Benny didn't know what to say. When he did speak, he sounded about as sincere as a young man could be when he said, "I sure owe you and everyone else in CID an awful lot. No one's ever been this nice to me before. After going AWOL and working for Harry Moffett, the Army could'a thrown the book at me, but instead the Colonel went to bat for me. So did you, the Major and your father. I'm grateful, Cal, real grateful. All I hope is that I can stay in CID and work with you for the duration of this war." While Cal faced his undercover partner, he responded in a very confident tone of voice when he said, "Don't worry, Benny. You're not going anywhere."

Once the other prisoners were disarmed, searched, handcuffed and lined up, Inspector La Belle accompanied CID Agent Mike Mulligan when he walked over to Major Savino and said, "We're ready to go, Sir."

"OK, Mike, you and Maurice head back with the MPs and see what you can get from these prisoners. We'll meet back at the office later."

"Yes, Sir," responded Mike Mulligan, before he turned to the Paris Police Inspector and said, "Trying to get these guys to talk is the second best part of this job.

"I agree, Michel," remarked the Paris Police Inspector as he walked with the XXL size CID Agent back over to the line of American and French prisoners, who were being guarded by Lieutenant Carl Miller and his squad of Military Policemen.

"We're ready when you are, Lieutenant," said Mike Mulligan as he addressed the MP Officer in charge of the detail.

"OK, Sergeant. Move 'em out," remarked MP Lieutenant Carl Miller as he stood in the middle of the line of prisoners.

"OK, you heard the man," said MP Sergeant Rusty Morgan.

As MP Sergeant Rusty Morgan led the line of prisoners out of the garage, Lieutenant Carl Miller gave the second in command of the Paris CID Office a casual salute and called out, "It's always a pleasure doing business with you and your men, Major."

"Thanks, Carl," responded Major Savino as the MP Lieutenant left with the others.

As the prisoners were escorted under guard out of the warehouse, Major Savino walked over to where Cal Parker, Benny Greene, Charlie Monacco and George Zangolas were standing and said, "Good job, men."

After the four enlisted men responded to the Major's compliment, Major Savino looked around the warehouse that was jammed packed with stolen government property and said, "We'll need a complete inventory of everything in this place that belongs to Uncle Sam."

"We'll get right on it, Sir," responded Cal Parker.

After nodding his head, Major Savino sounded as if he was in good spirits when he said, "Carry on, men. You're in charge, Cal," before he walked toward the back of the warehouse to see how Al Parker and Agent Angelone were making out.

While the Major walked away, Cal Parker turned to the men in his detail and said, "OK guys you know what we have to do. As soon as George and Benny back these trucks up, Charlie and I will secure the doors so we can start our inventory."

Charlie Monacco had to admit that it felt good to be a soldier again. He proved it, when he sounded enthusiastic about the order that he was just given by a Negro CID Agent, when he clapped his hands and said, "You heard the Sergeant. Let's secure this place and get to work."

★ ★ ★

After entering the warehouse office, Major Savino found Al Parker placing ledger books, a telephone directory and a stack of papers in Agent Angelone's open arms. "I see you two found a few things to take back to the office," remarked the Major.

While Al retrieved a cash box from the top of the desk, he seemed to be in especially good spirits when he looked at the Major and said, "Between the testimony of Charlie Monacco and George Zangolas and what we found in this garage, I'd say a court marshal board will have no problem convicting AWOL Lieutenant Armstrong and his gang of deserters. There's even enough information in these ledger books for Chief Inspector Dumont and his men to convict every French crook who worked with this group of AWOL G.I.s."

"Outstanding," responded Major Savino.

CHAPTER 11

UNFINISHED BUSINESS

Ever since the Allied landings in Normandy and the subsequent landings in Southern France, Pierre Mollet proved that he was a loyal fascist, by working for the Germans and the Vichy government. After serving his German handlers in different ways when they occupied France, Pierre Mollet was asked to serve in another capacity, one that would make him rich, while also serving the Third Reich. In return for being given the funding to hire an army of thieves, purchase vehicles and establish locations to operate from in Paris, Pierre Mollet was instructed to do everything possible to prevent critical supplies from reaching Allied units. As an incentive, Mollet was told that he could keep every French Franc that he made and would not have to repay the expense money that he was given, to conduct successful black market operations behind enemy (Allied) lines. After six months of working in Allied occupied France, at great risk of being arrested, Pierre Mollet and his closest associates were ready to travel to Switzerland.

All Pierre Mollet had to do before he left for a neutral country, was collect a large sum of money from one of the largest groups of American black market operators that he was in business with. As soon as this last piece of business was concluded, Pierre Mollet would leave for Switzerland with his brother, four of his former Milice militiamen and the forger Jacques Bayard. Once they got settled in Geneva, Pierre Mollet and his associates would open a "legitimate" business, while continuing to serve the Third Reich, by having their forger provide expertly crafted counterfeit documents to their German clients.

As soon as Jerome Paget and Edouard Tasse finished loading a German submachine gun and a satchel filled with spare magazines into their vehicle, the two former members of Pierre Mollet's Milice unit reported to their commander that they were ready to go. After telling his men where they could meet their American customers, the two former Milice militiamen left the garage in a light gray 1938 Renault Juvaquatre Coupe.

Pierre Mollet then turned to Gregorie Petit and said, "You and I will go with our money in the BMW, while Allard and the others will follow in a Citroen delivery van. In fact, you might as well place everything that we're taking with us in the van, so we can leave as soon as we receive payment from the Americans. We can finish dressing like priests when we're ready to leave."

After acknowledging the order, Gregorie Petit called out to Bernard Allard to help load their luggage in the Citroen. The fact that Pierre Mollet and his men were wearing black suits was a clear indication that they were already partially dressed like priests.

While Petit and Allard loaded their luggage in the van, Pierre Mollet turned to Jacques Bayard and asked if he had their new documents ready. As the man know as L'Artiste sat at a nearby table, he responded while he used a handmade counterfeit stamp, to put the finishing touches to a travel document. "My work is done, patron."

"Excellent," remarked the man who Jacques Bayard knew would be arrested in a few short minutes and executed for his crimes against France. After pausing to light an American cigarette, Pierre Mollet picked up the phone in his garage and called his brother's apartment where the rest of their men were waiting. As soon as Antone answered the phone, Pierre said, "I just sent Paget and Tasse to meet our paying customers and escort them to the garage. Pay the others and tell them that they have the rest of the day off, then get over here as fast as you can."

After hearing Antone say, "I'll be right there," Pierre hung up the phone and took a drag on his cigarette, before he picked up his .32 ACP caliber Walther PP from the corner of his desk and slipped the German pistol into his right side pant's pocket. Pierre then retrieved four spare eight round magazines from a desk draw and placed them in his left side suit jacket pocket. With nothing else left to do but wait, Pierre poured himself a glass of wine, just as Jacques Bayard walked over carrying a handful of new documents.

As the man known as L'Artiste handed a stack of beautifully made forged documents to Pierre Mollet, he did his best to sound friendly when he remarked, "I hope your brother likes his new name."

While Pierre examined the documents, the man who rarely expressed a friendly emotion nodded his head and remarked, "You do good work, Jacques, which is why I am taking you with us to Switzerland. If things go as I expect, you will have more work than you can imagine."

"Now that I made the boss happy, I am going to stretch my legs and have a cigarette," said Jacques who quickly added, "Would you like anything from the bakery on the corner?"

Because everything seemed to be going according to plan, Pierre perked up a bit and said, "Bring us something to have with a cup of American coffee, but get back as soon as you can, because our guests should be arriving in a few minutes."

After nodding his head in agreement, Jacques walked by Gregorie Petit, as he helped Bernard Allard finish loading the clothing that would enable them look like Catholic Priests, into the back of the Citroen van. As the two men made eye contact, there was no need to speak or exchange nods, because Gregorie Petit knew exactly what Jacques Bayard was about to do once he left the garage.

As soon as Jerome Paget and Edouard Tasse left Mollet's garage in a light gray 1938 Renault Juvaquatre Coupe, one of the vehicles belonging to Chief Inspector Dumont's men followed Pierre Mollet's men through the streets of Paris. While maintaining a loose surveillance, Inspector Andre de la Fontaine and CID Agent Bill Hayes observed Paget and Tasse park their car near The Fontaine Saint Michel and remain in their vehicle.

"It looks like they're waiting for someone," said Agent Hayes, who quickly added, "Hopefully, it's the AWOL G.I.s they're planning to meet before they take off for Switzerland."

"Instead of using your radio, I better call this in from a phone in that cafe," remarked Inspector Fontaine, before he continued and said, "Our superiors will want to know what these two are up to."

After exiting his vehicle, Inspector Fontaine walked into a nearby cafe to use the phone, while Agent Hayes kept an eye on the men they followed from Pierre Mollet's garage.

Colonel Andre Reynald arrived just in time to hear that another critical message was relayed to the makeshift command post by Inspector Andre de la Fontaine. "Once the AWOL Americans are escorted to the garage and they conclude their business with Pierre Mollet, we can move in and make our arrests," remarked Marcel.

"A moment that we have been waiting for, ever since Pierre Mollet became a murderer and an enemy of France," responded the Chief Inspector.

"One thing is certain. Having Petit and The Artist working for us on the inside, is definitely making our job a lot easier," said Jim Beauregard.

"Correct, for without their assistance, we would be, how you say, shooting from the hip," responded Colonel Reynald.

After cracking a smile, Jim Beauregard remarked, "Well said, Colonel."

"He just entered the bakery on the corner, Lieutenant," remarked Sam Carubba while he used a pair of binoculars to keep an eye on L'Artiste.

While Sam continued, he quickly added, "Inspector Goulet and Captain Barnes are moving in to follow, L'Artiste, Sir."

"One of our men is in the back of the bakery as well," said Lieutenant Garnier as he picked up the telephone and dialed the number to the shop where Captain Badeau and the other superior officers were waiting.

As soon as Inspector Philippe Leblanc answered the phone, he relayed the message to Captain Badeau, the Chief Inspector, Colonel Reynald and

Lt. Colonel Beauregard, that L'Artiste just entered the bakery on the corner and was about to make contact with Inspector Goulet and Captain Barnes.

The second time the phone in the back of the shop rang, Captain Badeau faced the others and said, "That must be Inspector Goulet." Sure enough, the second call was from the Paris Police Inspector who made contact with Jacques Bayard in the corner bakery. The message was short and to the point. Paget and Tasse left in the light gray 1938 Renault Juvaquatre Coupe to escort the AWOL Americans to Pierre Mollet's garage. Antone Mollet is also on the way to join his brother and the others. A Citroen van and a black BMW will be used to make their escape. Everyone is armed.

After pausing for a split second, Inspector Leblanc relayed the last part of the conversation that he just had with his Inspector Goulet. "L'Artiste also gave our men a list of the names that are being used by Pierre Mollet and the others on their new forged documents."

As soon as Inspector Leblanc stepped back inside the shop to man the phone, Chief Inspector Dumont remarked, "Once the AWOL Americans arrive, we can put an end to Pierre Mollet's plans to escape to Switzerland with the others."

The moment Agent Bill Hayes and Inspector Fontaine observed Jerome Paget and Edouard Tasse meet with two American soldiers who drove up in a Jeep, they knew they had to be the AWOL G.I.s, who were expected to deliver a cash payment to Pierre Mollet. After a very brief verbal exchange, Paget and Tasse returned to their car and drove off with the two Americans following close behind. Rather than risk being spotted using a hand held portable radio, Inspector Fontaine held back a bit, while his American partner contacted Lt. Colonel Beauregard."

While Jim held the radio up to the right side of his face, he responded to the call and said, "Good work, Bill. We're on the way."

As Jim faced the others, he wasted no time in reporting that Mollet's men just met two American soldiers driving a Jeep." While Jim collapsed the radio antenna, he went on to say, "Bill Hayes and Andre Fontaine are keeping their distance, while they follow the two vehicles back to Mollet's garage.

"This is it. The moment we've been waiting for since 1940," remarked Marcel Badeau.

After taking a drag on his cigarette, Chief Inspector Dumont remarked, "As the American cowboys like to say in the western films, it is time for us to mount up." Then, as the Chief Inspector faced Jim Beauregard, he asked, "Did I say that correctly, Jim?"

While Jim faced the Chief Inspector, he responded and said, "That's close enough, Francois."

Just as they had planned, Jim Beauregard rode with the Chief Inspector and Inspector Leblanc, while Captain Marcel Badeau drove his commanding officer's car. As soon as Captain Badeau started the engine, Colonel Reynald turned to his left and said, "Remember, Marcel, we must make every effort to take Pierre Mollet and his men alive, so we can interrogate them, before we have them executed."

By the time Jacques Bayard returned to the garage with a loaf of bread, Pierre Mollet was pouring himself a cup of freshly brewed coffee and said, "Join me, Jacques. This may be the last cup of real coffee that we have until we reach Geneva."

"That coffee smells good, patron," remarked Jacques as he poured coffee into a cup, while he acted as if he wasn't concerned about the presence of a 9mm German MP 40 submachine gun, that was located on the other side of the large wooden desk. When Jacques spotted five additional 32 round MP40 magazines and four German M24 hand-grenades on stacks of cash in Pierre Mollet's open leather satchel, L' Artiste knew that the war criminal that he was helping to capture, would not be taken into custody without a fight.

Just as Pierre removed the knife from the ring of cheese that was on his desk, he cut the loaf of bread into several sections as he remarked, "The two things that I am going to miss about the Americans are their coffee and their cigarettes."

"I agree," responded Jacques, before he took another sip from his coffee cup.

Just as Pierre began to place a piece of cheese on a slice of bread, Gregorie Petit walked over and said, "The Citroen is ready to go, Pierre." Then, after checking his watch, the former Milice militiaman, who was now working for French Army Intelligence, continued as he helped himself to a piece of bread and some cheese from the tray on the table. "I'll get ready to open the doors for Paget and Tasse and our American customers."

After taking a sip from his coffee cup, Pierre Mollet remarked, "As usual, Gregorie, you are thinking ahead."

While Gregorie Petit walked toward the garage doors, Antone Mollet entered the garage carrying his luggage. "It's almost time to take our trip," remarked Antone as he passed the former Milice militiaman who was one of his brother's most trusted men.

In order to play along, Gregorie Petit responded and said, "I hope you brought some warm clothing along, because you'll need it where we're going."

After relaying critical information to his commanding officer, Bill Hayes put his radio on the floor of the unmarked Paris Police car and said, "Hit it, Andre." Now that it was safe to proceed, Inspector Fontaine picked up speed and followed the two vehicles back to Pierre Mollet's garage.

While Gregorie Petit stood in front of the garage, he tapped his French Gitanes twice to make it look as if he was removing the ash from his cigarette. Doing so, signaled the Allied surveillance team that the AWOL Americans were in route to Mollet's garage.

Now that this signal was given and the AWOL Americans were being followed back to Mollet's garage, Lieutenant Garnier turned to Sergeant Carubba and said, "Our job is finished here, Sam. It's time for us to join the others."

Immediately after Lieutenant Garnier and Sergeant Carubba thanked

Mrs. Dubois for her hospitality, they left the woman's apartment, to join the men who were stationed in the concierge's apartment on the ground floor.

As soon as Paget and Tasse, as well as the Jeep carrying two Americans, arrived in front of Mollet's garage, Gregorie Petit opened the wooden doors and stepped aside to let the vehicles proceed inside. While the two vehicles came to a stop, Petit casually looked for any signs of the raiding party as he closed the wooden doors to the garage.

After directing two French Military Policemen and a uniformed Paris cop to cover the rear of the garage, Colonel Reynald turned to Jim Beauregard and said, "Whenever you are ready, Colonel."

Once again, Jim used his handie-talkie portable radio to communicate with is men. This time Jim contacted the MP Sergeant, who would pick up other members of the raiding party, who were stationed in the apartment building across from Mollet's garage. "It's time to pickup Sam Carubba and the others, Sergeant. Good luck."

Immediately after MP Sergeant Steve Dalton acknowledged the order, Jim faced Colonel Reynald, Captain Badeau, Chief Inspector Dumont and Police Inspector Philippe Leblanc and said, "We're ready."

CHAPTER 12

THE MOLLET RAID

As soon as the Army cargo truck arrived on the corner, Sam Carubba and Lieutenant Garnier along with Lieutenant Dan Kelly and Sergeant Fred Janowski from CIC jumped into the back and retrieved the M1 Carbines that were placed inside the vehicle by MP Sergeant Dalton. To make sure that these members of the raiding party had an ample supply of ammunition, the M1 Carbines that were placed in the back of the truck were equipped with extra ammunition. In addition to being loaded with a fifteen round magazine, each M1 Carbine had a magazine pouch attached to the wooden stock, that contained two additional fifteen round magazines.

Once MP Sergeant Dalton observed the rest of the raiding party make their way across the street and down the block toward Mollet's garage, he called out, "Standby in the back. Any second now!"

As soon as MP Sergeant Dalton observed Lt. Colonel Beauregard and the others line up near the entrance to Mollet's garage, he engaged the clutch and put the truck in gear. "Hold on in the back. We're going in," called out Sergeant Dalton, just before he drove the cargo truck toward the location that they intended to raid.

After shaking hands with his American business associates, Pierre offered AWOL Sergeant Martin Baldwin and AWOL Sergeant Jesse Taylor a glass of wine, while he made them an offer they would be foolish to refuse. "I told you that I had a surprise for you after we concluded our business." As soon as Sergeant Baldwin handed Pierre Mollet an envelope that was filled with cash, the French collaborator quickly inspected the contents, before he

looked at the two Americans and said, "My men and I are moving our operation to Marseille. Before I contact the other Americans that we do business
with, I would like to offer you and your men the opportunity to sell the contents of this garage."

When Pierre continued, he handed Sergeant Baldwin a list of the stolen
supplies that were available for sale. "This is a complete inventory of this
garage down to the last carton of American cigarettes, the last box of rations
and the last gallon of gasoline. All of the vehicles are loaded and can be
moved whenever you are ready to make a delivery."

While Pierre put on his overcoat and the two AWOL American soldiers
examined the list, a loud crash was heard, when a U.S. Army cargo truck
broke through the wooden doors of the warehouse. A split second later,
Sergeant Sam Carubba jumped out of the truck and yelled, "Army CID!
You're under arrest." At the same time, two different sections of the Allied
raiding party entered Mollet's warehouse with guns drawn. While the group
led by Colonel James Beauregard took cover behind several wooden crates
and the truck that crashed through the front doors, the second group led
by Colonel Reynald, advanced deeper into the warehouse and took cover
behind other wooden crates and a line of parked cargo trucks.

The first to react to the raid were Jerome Paget and Edouard Tasse.
While Paget drew his .32 caliber Sauer 38H pistol and opened fire,
Edouard Tasse removed a German MP40 submachine gun from the cab of
the 1938 Renault Juvaquatre Coupe and emptied the entire 32 round mag-
azine at the Allied personnel. At the same time, AWOL Sergeant Martin
Baldwin and AWOL Sergeant Jessie Taylor drew their forty fives and began
firing, as they took cover behind the black BMW, that was parked near
Pierre Mollet's desk.

As the exchange of gunfire intensified, Pierre Mollet grabbed the MP40
and the stack of forged documents and took cover behind his desk, along
with Gregorie Petit, Jacques Bayard, his brother Antone and Bernard
Allard. While Bernard Allard and Antone Mollet returned fire at the
raiding party, Gregorie Petit held the satchel open, as Pierre placed the
forged documents in with the stacks of cash, spare MP40 magazines and
grenades.

After loading the chamber of the MP40, Pierre Mollet patted his brother and Allard on their backs to get their attention. While facing Gregorie Petit and Bernard Allard. Pierre pointed to the back of the warehouse and said, "Cover us while we make our way to the back of the warehouse....then we'll cover you." Pierre then turned to his brother Antone and Jacques Bayard and said, "Let's go."

As soon as Pierre and the others began to crawl away, Bernard Allard reloaded his 9mm Walther P38 pistol and continued to provide covering fire. When Bernard Allard noticed that Gregorie Petit wasn't firing he called out, "Why aren't you firing?"

"My gun is in the BMW," responded Petit.

"Check the desk drawers," said Bernard Allard, who quickly added, "You know Pierre. He has guns hidden all over this place."

Even though Petit was carrying a Walther PPK .32 caliber pistol in his pant's pocket, Petit acted as if he was unarmed, while he opened desk drawers, to locate a handgun that he could use. Since Petit had no intentions of shooting at the men who would pardon him and his brother, he delayed his efforts to locate a firearm, by taking cover, when bullets fired by the Allied raiding party struck Mollet's desk. Petit even went as far as grabbing Allard and pulling him down when bullets struck nearby. As soon as Allard thanked his friend, Petit remarked, "We need more than pistols to cover Pierre and the others."

While Allard got back up into a kneeling position, he opened the bottom draw on his side of the desk and removed a Fabrique Nationale (FN) Model 1935 9mm (P35) pistol with two spare 13 round magazines. When Allard remarked, "This will have to do," he handed the pistol to Petit and placed the two spare magazines on the floor next to his position."

As long as Colonel Reynald and Captain Badeau believed that he did everything possible, to help them capture Pierre Mollet and his associates, Gregorie Petit and his younger brother would receive clemency from the French government. However, in order to do more to impress French Intelligence, Petit would have to get away from Bernard Allard. With limited options at his disposal, Gregorie Petit decided to strike Allard on the head, so he could break free and do something to prevent the escape of the Mollet brothers. Petit made his move, when he saw Allard turn to his right, while he reloaded his P38 from a kneeling position. Unfortunately, the second Petit went to do so, Allard looked up to see why his friend wasn't firing.

As surprised as he was by Petit's actions, Allard reacted instinctively and grabbed his attacker's right hand, to prevent from being pistol whipped. At the same time, Allard used his right thumb to depress the slide lever, which loaded a round of ammunition into the chamber of his P38. Once that was done, Allard pulled the trigger and killed the man he served with in the Milice Francaise (French Militia).

With no time to wonder what motivated Gregorie Petit to take such action, Bernard Allard continued firing at the Allied raiding party. While Allard emptied his Walther pistol, his ability to oppose the Allied raiding party ended, when he was shot and killed, in an exchange of gunfire with Colonel Reynald and the men in his section.

After getting into a low crouch, Pierre Mollet, his brother Antone and L' Artist moved without being seen, until they reached one of the Citroen delivery vans, that was parked toward the back of the warehouse. As soon as they stopped, Pierre Mollet removed two hand-grenades from the leather satchel that he was carrying. After placing the two German stick grenades in his left and right side coat pockets, Pierre handed the satchel to his brother to carry. As soon as Pierre did so, Antone asked Jacques Bayard to carry his suitcase.

"We'll use the vehicles for cover until we reach the back of the warehouse," said Pierre, who quickly added, "Before we turn left and make our way to the far end of the garage, I'll signal the others to join us."

Immediately after the Mollet brothers and Jacques Bayard reached the far end of the garage, Pierre looked back and saw Bernard Allard and Gregorie Petit's bodies lying next to each other, on the floor behind his desk. As soon he spotted the two dead men, Pierre Mollet faced his brother and Jacques Bayard and said, "Allard and Petit won't be joining us."

After hanging the leather sling that was attached to the MP40 around his neck, Pierre continued as he removed one of the German stick grenades from his coat pocket. "I suspect Paget and Tasse won't last very long either. As a result, we need to move fast. In order to make our escape, we'll use the wooden crates for cover. When we get to the last crate, I'll throw this grenade into the back of the stolen American truck, that's parked on the other side of the garage. Once that truck explodes and we make our way to the other side of the warehouse, I'll toss another grenade on the drums of gasoline, that are stacked up by the back door. To further cover our escape, I'll throw a third grenade into another truck that's loaded with cans of gasoline. Doing so, should make it impossible for anyone to follow us."

The moment Marcel spotted the Mollet brothers and L'Artiste moving in a slight crouch along a row of wooden crates in the back of the warehouse, he fired three rounds from his 9mm FN P35 pistol that just missed the two fugitives. When the slide locked back because the pistol was empty, a pissed off Marcel cursed out load and said "Fils de pute," (son of a bitch) as he reloaded the P35 with another thirteen round magazine. As soon as Marcel racked the slide and loaded the chamber, he turned to his commanding officer and said, "The Mollet brothers have The Artist with them and are moving along the line of wooden crates in the back of the warehouse. We must get the American deserters to stop shooting at us, so we can go after the Mollet brothers and rescue L'Artiste."

After hearing what Marcel had to say, Colonel Reynald spoke fast when he turned to the men in his section and said, "The Mollet brothers are on the move! We have to eliminate the threat from the American deserters in order to advance any further! Everyone reload and prepare to open fire at the same time!"

As soon as Colonel Reynald and the men in his section concentrated their fire on the two American black market operators, AWOL Sergeant Baldwin was wounded in his right arm and AWOL Sergeant Taylor was hit in his left hand and shoulder. After dropping their guns, AWOL Sergeant Baldwin stood up as they called out, "We surrender, don't shoot!"

Once the two Americans surrendered, Captain Barnes turned to Sergeant Hayes and said, "As soon as you and Inspector Fontaine take the two AWOLs into custody, you can help the other section engage the two collaborators, who have taken cover behind the gray car."

After acknowledging their orders, Agent Hayes and Inspector Fontaine advanced to where the two wounded AWOL Americans were waiting to be arrested. Once the wounded deserters were disarmed and placed faced down on the floor of the garage, Sergeant Hayes and his French partner began firing at Jerome Paget and Edouard Tasse. Doing so, placed Paget and Tasse in an effective cross fire, that enabled the rest of Colonel Reynald's section of the raiding party, to focus on advancing behind the available cover toward the back of the warehouse.

While Jerome Paget reloaded his pistol behind a wooden crate, that was positioned near the 1938 Renault Coupe and Edouard Tasse fired one last burst of ammunition that emptied his MP40, James Beauregard, Chief Inspector Dumont, Sergeant Sam Carubba, MP Sergeant Steve Dalton, Inspector Leblanc, Lieutenant Charles Garnier, Lieutenant Dan Kelly, Sergeant Fred Janowski and two enlisted men from French Army Intelligence stood up from behind positions of cover and opened fire. At the same time, Bill Hayes and Inspector Fontaine continued firing as well. In addition to shooting up the otherwise well maintained 1938 Renault Juvaquatre Coupe, Jerome Paget and Edouard Tasse were riddled with a fuselage of bullets.

As the lifeless bodies of Jerome Paget and Edouard Tasse collapsed on the warehouse floor, Jim Beauregard holstered his almost empty 1911 pistol and drew his 1903 Colt backup gun, as he called out, "Cover me!"

While Jim Beauregard, Sam Carubba and Chief Inspector Dumont advanced with guns drawn, Inspector Leblanc, Lieutenant Charles Garnier, Lieutenant Dan Kelly, Sergeant Fred Janowski, MP Sergeant Dalton and two enlisted men from French Army Intelligence remained standing and prepared to open fire if necessary.

As soon as Sam Carubba checked on the two collaborators, he looked up at Lt. Colonel Beauregard and Chief Inspector Dumont and said, "They're dead, Sir."

"Get their IDs, Sam," responded Jim who quickly added, "And while you're at it, pickup any weapons and spare ammunition that you find."

Jim then turned toward the Chief Inspector and said, "Let's check on the others, Francois."

While a gun battle ensued on the other side of the warehouse, the two wounded AWOL Americans were escorted out of the garage by Sergeant Hayes and Inspector Fontaine. As the men in Jim's section of the raiding party advanced in a slight crouch, toward the shot up BMW and Pierre Mollet's desk, Jim called out, "Take cover and reload your weapons before we go any further!"

As soon as Jim and Francois took cover behind the desk, Jim removed a 50 round box of .45 ACP ammunition from his left side pant's pocket and placed it on the floor as he called out, "I don't know about you, Francois, but I need to reload my forty five, or I'll be throwing spit balls at Mollet and his brother."

"I am almost out of ammunition as well," responded Francois, as he ignored the empty Walther P38, that was next to Bernard Allard's dead body and he retrieved the 9mm P35 that was next to Gregorie Petit's dead body.

While Jim quickly reloaded two seven round 1911 magazines, Francois removed the magazine from the P35 and retracted the slide to see if a round of ammunition was in the chamber. Once he confirmed that the chamber was empty, Francois inserted the loaded magazine into the pistol and racked the slide. Now that the pistol was loaded, Francois manually lowered the hammer and tucked the captured P35 in his waistband.

While Jim slipped the two reloaded 1911 magazines into the double magazine pouch on his pistol belt, Francois retrieved the pair of fully loaded 13 round magazines, that were on the floor next to Gregorie Petit's dead body. As Francois placed the two spare magazines in his coat pocket, Jim removed the partially loaded magazine from his Ithaca Model 1911 .45

caliber pistol and topped it off with a few rounds of ammunition. Once Jim loaded his service pistol, he turned toward Francois and remarked, "I'm ready if you are, Francois?"

"I have nothing else planned for the rest of the day," joked Francois, who continued as he checked on the men in their section, who had their weapons reloaded and were taking cover all around their position. "The men are ready as well."

As Jim, Francois and their men stood up, Jim slipped the box of .45 ACP ammunition into his left side pant's pocket. The moment they began to cautiously advance toward the back of the garage, they took cover again, when a burst from a German submachine gun was fired in their direction, as well as at the men in Colonel Reynald's section of the Allied raiding party.

"We seem to have lost the momentum of our surprise attack," remarked Francois as he drew the captured P35 from his waistband while he knelt next to Jim, behind the back of a parked French delivery van.

As Jim held his 1911 pistol in his right hand, he agreed with Francois as he carefully looked toward the back of the garage. While Jim continued to size up the situation at hand, he looked around the interior of the large garage, that was jammed packed with stolen U.S. military vehicles, a long line of parked French Citroen delivery vans and crates of stolen Allied supplies, that were stacked up the ceiling. After turning to his left, Jim addressed Francois in another low tone of voice. "Now that Mollet has our section and Colonel Reynald's section pinned down, what'a you say we use this line of parked vehicles as cover, as we make our way to the back of the garage."

"I will pass the word to the men," responded Francois before he left to alert the others.

On the other side of the building, Colonel Reynald, Captain Badeau, Captain Barnes from CIC, Inspector Goulet and two men from French Army Intelligence also took cover, when they were shot at, while advancing toward the back of the warehouse. As soon as the men in Colonel Reynald's section of the raiding party took cover behind a stolen U.S. Army cargo truck, Marcel spotted a hand-grenade coming their way.

Because he was no stranger to close quarters combat, Marcel reacted quickly, as he turned to the men who were positioned behind him and called out, "Grenade! Everyone down!" Two seconds later, a loud explosion was heard, when the truck next to their position exploded. A few seconds later, another explosion was heard and another fireball was observed engulfing the back of the warehouse, where the rear door was located. When a third grenade exploded in the back of another truck filled with cans of stolen gasoline, the fire that engulfed the back of the warehouse became even more intense.

Colonel Reynald was another soldier who knew exactly how to react to such threats. "Follow me," said the French Army Colonel as he led the men in his section of the raiding party toward the other side of the large warehouse. In a matter of seconds, the teams led by Colonel Reynald and Jim Beauregard met by Pierre Mollet's desk; with most of the men providing security, while taking cover behind parked vehicles and wooden crates filled with stolen supplies.

Now that a raging fire prevented the Allied personnel from continuing their pursuit, Chief Inspector Dumont used the phone on Pierre Mollet's desk, to request that additional police and fire department personnel respond to their location. Despite the worsening operating conditions, Marcel Badeau was more determined than ever, to capture the Mollet brothers and insure the safety of Jacques Bayard. While Marcel pointed toward the back of the warehouse, he described how he spotted the Mollet brothers and The Artist making their way along the line of wooden crates in the back of the garage. When Marcel finished his remarks, Colonel Reynald added, "Mollet planned his escape well, by starting three fires that prevent us from pursuing him any further in this garage."

"Thank God we told the men covering the back door not to enter, unless we instructed them to do so," remarked the Chief Inspector as he hung up the phone.

Jim Beauregard instinctively knew that something was wrong and proved when he spoke up and said, "The bad news for us, is that the Mollet brothers must have another way outta this place, that doesn't include going out the back door."

"I agree," remarked Chief Inspector Dumont."

The next time Jim spoke he looked directly at Colonel Reynald. "With your permission, Colonel, I think we should send some men outside, to cordon off the area until more help arrives. We also need to tell the men covering the back of this garage, that the Mollet brothers are on the run and have another way out'a here. And that includes using the roof, or a tunnel system, that will take them to a nearby building."

Colonel Reynald knew when he received good advice from a respected colleague. It took less than a second for Colonel Reynald to agree and dispatch everyone except Captain Badeau, Lt. Colonel Beauregard, Chief Inspector Dumont, Lieutenant Garnier and Captain Barnes from CIC, to get men up on the roofs of nearby buildings and cover as much of the immediate area as possible.

Once the men started to leave, Jim turned to Sergeant Carubba and said, "Get on that phone, Sam and get some additional MPs over here. Once you make that call, go out front and give the others a hand."

Immediately after Sergeant Carubba acknowledged the order, the CID Agent coughed from the smell of smoke as he picked up the phone and dialed the number to the 709th MP Battalion Headquarters. While Sam identified himself and requested additional assistance from the military police, Colonel Reynald spoke up and said, "Unfortunately, there is nothing else that we can do, until the firemen arrive and it is safe to continue the search of this building."

Before he left to carry out the rest of his orders, Sam Carubba handed the M1 Carbine that he was carrying to his commanding officer and said, "You better take this with you, Sir. The chamber's empty, but all three mags are topped off and ready to go."

"Thanks Sam," said Jim as he racked the slide, loaded the chamber and applied the safety on the M1 Carbine that Agent Carubba just handed him. While Agent Carubba left to join the others, the Paris firefighters who entered the garage began to fight the fire.

As soon as they made their way into the back of the smoke filled garage,

Pierre Mollet knelt down in front of a large wooden crate that was positioned up against the wall. After using a key to open the lock that was secured to the crate on a metal plate, Pierre opened the outer panel that was attached to the crate by a pair of metal hinges. While Pierre held the hinged door open, he pointed inside and whispered, "You first, Antone."

As soon as Antone Mollet got on his hands and knees and entered the crate, Jacques Bayard whispered, "Where does this go, Patron?"

"There's a hole in the wall that leads into the building next door. We placed a large picture frame over the hole, so no one would know about our secret passage way to freedom," responded Pierre as he placed his leather satchel and the suitcase inside the opened crate.

As soon as Pierre heard Antone say, "I'm in," and he pushed the satchel and the piece of luggage toward his brother, Jacques knew that he had to do something to stop Pierre Mollet from escaping. Because the man known as L'Artiste never carried a gun, he was unable to use a firearm to hold Pierre Mollet at gunpoint until help arrived. Instead, the man who volunteered to help French Army Intelligence capture the Mollet brothers and their associates used the only weapon he had.

Even with the fire spreading, Jacques Bayard knew that it was just a question of time, before the raiding party headed his way. The man known as L' Artist decided to make his move, when Antone Mollet called out in a voice that was just above whisper and said, "OK, Jacques. It's your turn."

After getting down on his right knee and hearing Pierre Mollet remark, "Hurry up, Jacques," the man known as L' Artist called out, "Revenez ici! Revenez ici! Venez vite! Venez Vite!" as he tackled the collaborator who was wanted for murder, war crimes and other criminal activity. Jacques Bayard didn't take the action that he did, because he was promised a full pardon for his work with the resistance and for helping to capture Pierre Mollet and his associates. Instead, Jacques Bayard took the action he did for France.

The second a single gunshot was heard being fired, the Allied raiding party was still helpless to advance any further, because the fire was by no means contained. "That's Jacques Bayard calling out that they're in the back and to come quickly," remarked Marcel.

Marcel then turned to his commanding officer and asked if he could try and see if there was a path that they could take through the fire. Even though it was obvious, that no one was getting through the inferno, that engulfed a large section of the warehouse, Colonel Reynald pointed at the parked Citroen delivery vans, that were lined up between Pierre Mollet's desk and the back of the warehouse and said, "We will do this together and take up a position at the end of these parked vehicles. Once the firemen clear a path for us, we will proceed, but not before."

As much as he wanted things to be different, Marcel knew that the fire was far too intense, to allow them to advance beyond the position that was selected by his commanding officer. Despite the fact that the warehouse was filling with smoke, Marcel led the way, with Colonel Reynald, Lt. Colonel Beauregard, Chief Inspector Dumont, Lieutenant Garnier and Captain Barnes following close behind.

As soon as they reached their new position, another stolen U.S. Army truck exploded as the fire spread even further. A split second later, several flaming five gallon cans of stolen U.S. Army gasoline exploded and were hurled through the air in front of their position. Once this happened, Marcel and the others were forced to pull back from the raging inferno, that blocked their way to the other side of the warehouse. The raiding party's situation was made even worse, when the fire that blocked the back door of the warehouse, began to spread and several wooden crates of stolen U.S. Army supplies became engulfed in flames.

To his credit, Police Inspector Philippe Leblanc saw their dilemma and came to the rescue with two additional squads of Paris firefighters. Once they arrived in the back of the garage, the firemen manning the hoses began to put water on the burning trucks and the crates that were filled with stolen U.S. Army property. While the firemen began to make some headway fighting the raging inferno, Chief Inspector Dumont patted the Paris Police Inspector on the back and said, "Excellent work, Philippe."

"Merci Chef," responded Inspector Leblanc, as the Paris firemen continued fighting the fire, that prevented the raiding party from gaining access to the opposite end of the warehouse.

Two weeks before Pierre Mollet and his men moved into this location, so they could expand their business dealings with other AWOL Americans, the Mollet brothers purchased the shop next door, from the elderly owner who was looking to retire. The Mollet brothers kept the ownership of this shop from their associates, because Pierre wanted to secure an additional escape route, if the day ever came when the authorities raided this particular warehouse.

After crawling through the open crate and entering the empty shop next door, Pierre Mollet and his brother made their way to the storage area. Once Pierre locked the door to the back room, the Mollet brothers worked quickly to position a heavy wooden table against the door. To make it more difficult for anyone to pursue them, they placed several chairs and wooden crates filled with used books on top of the table.

As soon as the makeshift barricade was completed, the Mollet brothers walked over to the back door and prepared to make their escape. While Pierre stood off to the side, he slowly pulled the dusty curtain away from the window, just enough to see a Paris policeman and two French Army MPs standing guard near the back door of their garage.

As Pierre slowly let the curtain fall back to its regular position, he reported what he observed to his brother. While Pierre continued, he looked directly at Antone and said, "If you're willing to chance it, we can try and go out the back, as soon as the Flique (slang for police) who is looking this way turns around."

"How about the roof?" asked Antone.

"We have no time for that. Besides, that's the first place the Americans and their French allies will look for us," responded Pierre who quickly added, "It's the back door, or nothing and we better make our move in a matter of seconds, because we're running out of time."

Rather than leave the 9mm MP40 behind, Pierre Mollet dumped the contents of Antone's luggage on the floor, before he replaced his brother's possession with the contents of his leather satchel. While Pierre remarked, "I'll buy you more clothes when we get to Geneva," he handed his brother two stacks of cash. "Hold onto this money in case we get separated."

After removing the last of the German stick grenades from the satchel and securing it in his belt, Pierre removed the 32 round magazine from the MP40, before placing the German submachine gun with the folded metal stock, on top of stacks of cash and his supply of spare magazines.

"You also better carry the luggage," said Pierre as he handed his younger brother his suitcase. Pierre then grabbed the long scarf, the black beret and the wooden cane that was left behind by the previous owner. As soon as Pierre wrapped the long scarf around his neck, he put the beret on his head as he continued and said, "When we walk through this door, I'm going to act like the old man who once owned this shop and you are going to hold onto me, as if you are helping me to walk. If for any reason they look this way, there's a good chance that the police will never suspect us, especially if we look like we have no reason to be in a hurry."

As soon as Antone swallowed the lump in his throat and said, "That might work," Pierre remarked, "If it doesn't...start shooting and run like hell."

Once the Paris firemen cleared a narrow path through the fire, Jim Beauregard turned to the Chief Inspector and said, "Just to be on the safe side, we should have these firemen hose us down as we make our way to the other side."

"Good idea, Jim. I will give the order," responded Francois Dumont, before he tapped a senior fireman on the shoulder and relayed the command to have his men turn their hoses on him and the others, when they ran through the narrow path that snaked through the fire. As soon as the order was relayed, Marcel led the way, as he and the others were soaked with water, while they ran through the path in the fire, that was in the process of being contained. Once the soaking wet raiding party arrived by the back wall, they found Jacques Bayard lying on the ground with a bullet hole in his chest.

While Marcel knelt by the wounded man's side, Jacques Bayard pointed to the open crate as he spoke just above a whisper and said, "In there, mon Capitaine, it leads to the shop next door, but be careful. Pierre Mollet is armed with a pistol and a submachine gun. He also has one grenade left."

After instructing Captain Barnes to get an ambulance for Mr. Bayard and meet him inside the shop next door with some additional help, Jim Beauregard remarked, "Let's get these bastards before anyone else gets hurt," as he flicked off the safety and entered the crate with his M1 Carbine in hand."

CHAPTER 13

THE GREAT ESCAPE

The moment Antone Mollet opened the back door to the empty shop, he stepped out of the building backwards, while he slowly helped his brother out of the store. As tempted as they were to look toward the military and civilian policemen, who were guarding the back of the warehouse, the Mollet brothers kept their act going, as Antone called out, "Attends Papa. J'ai besoin de verrouiller la porte (Wait, Papa. I need to lock the door.)"

Just as they hoped, when one of the French MPs spotted the old man being helped out of the shop next door, he pointed at the elderly man and his helper and said, "Thank God that old man got out of the building next door, before this whole street goes up in flames."

Even when several firemen approached the hunched over old man and his younger helper, no one became suspicious when a senior fireman asked if the fire spread into their shop. While Pierre Mollet continued to act like a hunched over old man, Antone sounded as if he appreciated their concern when he said, "Our shop if fine. Thank you for asking."

While the Mollet brothers walked away from the commotion of the fire and the raiding party that was determined to capture them, Antone leaned even closer to his brother Pierre and whispered, "It's working."

"Let's proceed, but do so like we discussed," whispered Pierre, while he continued to walk with the aid of a cane, while being assisted by his brother, as he pretended to be an elderly man who had difficulty walking on his own.

Once Captain Barnes directed two Army medics to go to the aid of L'Artist, he continued as he faced Sam Carubba, Lieutenant Kelly,

Lieutenant Miller and Sergeant Janowski. "The Mollet brothers entered this shop through a hole in the wall. I want Sergeant Carubba and Lieutenant Kelly to come with me to give Colonel Beauregard and the others a hand." Captain Barnes then instructed MP Lieutenant Carl Miller and Sergeant Fred Janowski to get some men on the roofs of the nearby buildings. Doing so, he explained, just might cut off their escape, if the Mollet brothers have already gotten up on the roof above the shop where they were standing.

As soon as MP Lieutenant Miller and Sergeant Janowski acknowledged the order, Captain Barnes remarked, "Let's go," as he kicked the door open, to the shop that was located next to Pierre Mollet's warehouse.

The second Captain Barnes, Lieutenant Kelly and Sam Carubba entered the empty shop, they found Lt. Colonel James Beauregard and Chief Inspector Dumont trying to forcibly open the back door of the storage area. "Sam, you're with us! The rest of you get up on the roof and give Lieutenant Garnier and Inspector Leblanc a hand looking around!" called out Jim.

"Yes, Sir," responded Captain Barnes as he motioned Lieutenant Kelly to follow him, while Sam Carubba went to assist his commanding officer and the Chief Inspector.

After the three men tried in vain to push open the back door and it wouldn't budge, Jim turned to Sam Carubba and Francois and remarked, "We're gonna have to do this the hard way." While Jim pointed the barrel of the M1 Carbine at the lock on the door he fired two shots. Once the lock was destroyed, Jim, Francois and Sam pushed the heavy table that was positioned as a barricade aside and opened the door.

The moment they entered the back room and they spotted the clothes on the floor by the door, Jim called out, "This way! Everyone back here!" Jim then turned to Agent Carubba and said, "See if any of the men covering the back of the garage observed anyone leave this shop. If they did, I want'a know why they weren't stopped."

"Yes, Sir," responded Sam as he quickly left the shop through the back door.

Just as Sam Carubba left the shop, Jim and Francois were joined by

Colonel Reynald and Captain Badeau. When Jim asked who was with L' Artist, Marcel responded in a somber tone and said, "I am sorry to report, Colonel, that Jacques Bayard is dead."

Immediately after Jim expressed his regrets, that their undercover operative was killed in action, Captain Barnes, Lieutenant Kelly, Lieutenant Garnier and Inspector Leblanc entered the back room and reported that there was no one on the roof. A split second later, Sergeant Carubba opened the back door and reported that the men covering the rear exit to the garage, just observed an old man, who was hunched over and barely able to walk with a cane, being helped out of the back of this building by a younger man. Even some firemen stopped to see if their shop was affected by the fire."

"And they weren't stopped?" asked Jim.

"No, Sir," responded Sam Carubba.

"That must be them," remarked Chief Inspector Dumont.

While Marcel quickly walked over to the door that was being held open by Sergeant Carubba, the former Paris Police Inspector, who fought in the resistance before becoming a Captain in French Army Intelligence, looked at the others and said, "We still have a chance to catch the Mollet brothers, as long as they pretend to be an old man who is being assisted by a companion."

"I agree, Marcel, but we have to do it the right way," responded Jim Beauregard.

After hearing what the American Colonel from CID just said, Colonel Reynald remarked, "I am open to suggestions, gentlemen, on the best way to handle this search."

"From both ends at the same time," responded the Chief Inspector.

While facing Colonel Reynald, the Commanding Officer of Army CID in Paris continued and said, "The Chief Inspector is right. We need to conduct this search from both ends, with some of us going forward as fast as possible to screen the crowd, while the rest of us canvass both sides of the street, to see if anyone resembling a hunched over old man and his companion veered off course and went in another direction."

"That is a sound strategy. I concur," responded the Colonel from French Army Intelligence.

Without wasting any time Jim turned to Agent Carubba and added,

"Take point, Sam and be careful. Get through the crowd as fast as you can, while we check every cafe and shop along the way to see if the Mollet brothers veered off to the right or the left."

"Will do, Sir," responded Agent Carubba.

Rather than have the CID Agent proceed alone, Captain Billy Barnes turned to Lieutenant Dan Kelly and said, "You better go with Sergeant Carubba."

"Yes, Sir," responded Lieutenant Kelly as he jogged off with Sam Carubba.

As soon as the two Americans left, Chief Inspector Dumont turned to Inspector Leblanc and said, "Keep Sergeant Carubba and Lieutenant Kelly company, Philippe."

Immediately after he acknowledged the order, Inspector Leblanc ran off to catch up with the two uniformed American Army Agents, as they screened the crowd and made their way past a number of cafes and shops. While Inspector Leblanc did so, Jim faced Colonel Reynald and made the following suggestion. "With your permission, Colonel, I'll cover the right side of the street with the Chief Inspector and Lieutenant Garnier, while you, Captain Badeau and Captain Barnes cover the left."

As soon as Colonel Reynald remarked, "We will do as you say, Colonel," the rest of the Allied search team fanned out and began talking to people who were shopping, walking by, or sitting in cafes.

After walking a fair distance away from the shop that was next to the garage, Pierre Mollet turned toward his brother and said, "There is a cafe with a red awning coming up on the right, That cafe has a back door that leads to an ally. Once we reach that ally, I can lose this disguise and we can move more quickly."

"I see it," responded Antone.

As much as Pierre wanted to drop his cane, stand up straight and walk as fast as possible, he knew that he would draw more attention to himself if he did so. "Stick to the plan," was all that Pierre Mollet kept saying to himself, while he walked like a crippled old man, who was being assisted by a younger companion.

While Antone played his role perfectly, he helped his brother along, as they made their way to the cafe that was coming up on their right. "I can't believe that we got away," said Antone.

"We're not out of danger yet, but we're close," remarked Pierre as his brother helped him enter the cafe.

After just missing the Mollet brothers, when they veered off course and entered one of the cafes, that were situated on the right, Sam Carubba spoke up and said, "There isn't a hunched over old man in France who could walk fast enough to beat us to the end of this street. That means that they entered one of the shops or cafes that we passed, to try and make their way to another side street in this neighborhood. Since the street in front of the garage is filled with MPs and Paris cops, I'm willing to bet that the Mollet brothers went in the opposite direction."

"What do you suggest, Sergeant?" asked Lieutenant Kelly.

"We need to go left and right, Lieutenant and start searching the streets on either side of this block," responded Sergeant Carubba, before he went on to say, "We also need to get the men covering the front of Mollet's garage to start looking for a hunched over old man and his traveling companion, who might be hiding out in one of the shops, or the cafes on their side of the street."

Inspector Leblanc agreed, then added, "Whoever goes to the left, can get help from the small army of MPs and Paris policemen, who were called in cordon off the area in front of Mollet's garage"

Once again Sam turned to Lieutenant Kelly and said, "If you go left, Lieutenant, Inspector Leblanc and I will go right." Then, after pausing for a split second, Sam added, "If we come up empty, we'll need all the help you can get us, to expand this search in different directions."

"Don't worry, Sergeant. I'll get you that help. You two be careful," responded Lieutenant Kelly before he jogged off."

"Let's go, Philippe. Who knows maybe we'll get lucky," said Sam.

As soon as they entered the cafe, Pierre Mollet turned to his brother and whispered, "Once we make our way out the back door of this cafe, we need to get as far away from here as possible, as quickly as possible."

When a waiter asked if they wished to be seated at a nearby empty table, Antone spoke up and said, "My father is going to be sick. Where is your back door."

"This way," responded the waiter as he led the way into the back of the cafe.

Once they reached the back door, Antone thanked the waiter for showing them the way, as he continued the act and said, "Père facile. (Easy father.)"

As soon as the waiter returned to his duties, Antone guided his brother through the back door. Immediately after they were clear of the cafe, Pierre looked around to make sure that there were no military or civilian police in sight. Once he was satisfied that the coast was clear, Pierre stood up straight and leaned the cane that he was using up against the back wall of the cafe, before he faced his brother and said, "Let's go."

The second Inspector Leblanc spotted two men, who looked like they fit the description of the Mollet brothers, approaching from a distance, he turned to his American partner and said, "I think that's them, Sam." In order to avoid being spotted by the two wanted collaborators, Sam Carubba ducked into a doorway at the far end of the alley. While Sam hid from view, he drew his .45 caliber Model 1911 pistol and racked the slide to chamber a round.

In an effort to look less obvious, Inspector Leblanc intentionally stood sideways, while he used a box of matches to light a cigarette. While the Paris Police Inspector acted like he was more interested in the two attractive girls who were passing by, he whispered, "Standby, Sam. They are almost halfway to our position." Inspector Leblanc then relayed to his American partner, that with the exception of a wooden cart, a parked delivery truck and a few doorways, there weren't that many places for the Mollet brothers to take cover, once they challenged the two wanted collaborators.

After being told by several pedestrians that a hunched over old man and his companion entered the next cafe on the right side of the street, Francois translated what he was just told, before he remarked, "That has to be them."

The second Jim and the members of his team entered the cafe, the Chief Inspector identified himself and said, "We are looking for two enemies of France who were observed entering this cafe. One of these traitors is pretending to be a hunched over old man who walks with a cane. The other traitor is acting as the old man's companion."

"The ones you want just walked out the back door," called out the waiter, who quickly added, "The one who was helping the old man said his father was going to be sick."

After turning to the Lieutenant from French Army Intelligence, Jim instructed Charles Garnier to get Colonel Reynald and the members of his search team, while he and the Chief Inspector continued on. As Lieutenant Garnier left the cafe in an obvious hurry, Jim turned to the Chief Inspector and said, "We're gonna get these guys yet, Francois."

Just as Jim Beauregard and the Chief Inspector entered the alley behind the cafe, Sam Carubba and Philippe Leblanc began exchanging gunfire with the Mollet brothers. Once the shooting started, the few innocent civilians who were in the alley, took the best cover available to avoid being hit. Fortunately, the only casualty during the initial exchange was Antone Mollet, who was shot in the right leg and the right side of his torso, just before he and his brother fell back and took cover in between the wooden cart and the parked delivery truck.

By the time Marcel Badeau, Colonel Reynald, Lieutenant Garnier and Captain Barnes entered the alley, Jim and Francois were firing at the two wanted collaborators from a kneeling position, behind stacks of wooden crates. While Jim and Francois continued firing, Colonel Reynald led the rest of the men to positions of cover on the other side of the alley. Doing so, enabled the Allied personnel to engage the Mollet brothers from three different firing positions.

While Pierre Mollet removed the German submachine gun from the suitcase, Jim Beauregard reloaded his M1 Carbine and continued returning fire. At the same time that Jim began firing, the Chief Inspector reloaded the captured P35. While Jim, Francois and the other members of the Allied raiding party continued firing, Antone Mollet was shot in his left hand and fell back behind cover.

"Antone Mollet is hit," called out the Chief Inspector.

"He's wounded but not dead," responded Jim.

As the Commanding Officer of U.S Army CID in Paris and the Chief Inspector continued to exchange gunfire with the two wanted collaborators, Jim put the empty M1 Carbine down and drew his .45 caliber pistol as he called out, "We better end this gunfight soon, or we'll have to start throwing rocks at the Mollet brothers."

"Let's hope it does not come to that," responded Francois as he reloaded his last spare magazine into the captured P35 and he considered that the other members of the raiding party also had to be concerned about running low or out of ammunition.

While his brother Antone dropped his empty P38 and he finished wrapping a handkerchief around his badly wounded hand, Pierre reloaded the MP40 as he called out and said, "We have to move!"

As different caliber bullets whizzed overhead and struck the truck and the cart, that they took cover behind, Antone Mollet remarked, "I can't. I'm hit too bad. You go." While the bullets continued to whiz overhead and strike nearby, Pierre continued firing a succession of short bursts at the Allied personnel. When his younger brother crawled closer to him and said, "Give me that thing and whatever ammunition you have left. As soon as I open fire, take off and don't look back."

After nodding his head ever so slightly in agreement, Pierre handed the submachine gun and the remaining supply of ammunition to his younger brother. As Antone grimaced in pain, he got up on his good knee and did his best to force a smile, before he remarked, "Goodbye, Pierre."

Rather than say anything, Pierre merely nodded his head as he grabbed the suitcase that contained stacks of cash and his newly forged documents. Once Antone started providing covering fire, Pierre Mollet tossed the last of his grenades, at the Allied personnel who were positioned on the other side of the alley. The second the grenade exploded, Pierre Mollet ran in slight crouch into a nearby open doorway. While Jim and the others remained behind the best cover available and continued to return fire, they just missed hitting Pierre Mollet. Antone Mollet wasn't so lucky and was hit several times, when he stopped to reload the submachine gun.

After seeing his mortally wounded brother collapse on the ground, Pierre Mollet became enraged and began firing at the Allied personnel with his Walther PP. When the pistol ran empty, Pierre stepped back into the hallway and removed one of the spare magazines that he carried in his suit jacket pocket. As soon as Pierre had the pistol reloaded, he stepped closer to the open doorway and fired three rounds into the alley, to keep the Allied raiding party at bay.

Despite the fact that he was an experienced policeman, resistance fighter and French Intelligence Army Officer, Marcel Badeau allowed his personal hatred for Pierre Mollet to cloud his judgment. Instead, of using the proper tactics, Marcel called out, "He's getting away!" as he stood up and ran across the alley toward Pierre Mollet's last known position.

At the same time that Francois Dumont stood up with an empty P35 in his hand and called out, "Take cover, Marcel," Pierre Mollet took one last look at his brother. As soon as he did so, Pierre spotted his arch enemy running toward his position.

While Jim called out, "Let's go," he loaded his last magazine into his

Ithaca Model 1911 pistol before he said, "Here, Francois. Take this. It's loaded but the safety's on," and he handed his 1903 Model .32 caliber backup gun to the Chief Inspector. As Jim, Francois and the other members of the Allied raiding party ran toward Pierre Mollet's last known position, Francois lowered the safety lever on Jim's backup pistol, in preparation of using it.

After waiting for the right time to make his move, Pierre stepped closer to the open doorway, just as Marcel Badeau reached his position. The second the two adversaries made eye contact, Pierre Mollet opened fire and sent three .32 ACP caliber bullets into the French Intelligence Officer's chest at point blank range. While Marcel grabbed his chest with his left hand and he dropped to one knee, he raised his 9mm P35 pistol and fired two rounds, just as Pierre Mollet turned and started to run into the building.

As Marcel collapsed on the cold ground, Jim Beauregard and Francois Dumont reached the doorway and opened fire. After being riddled with a stream of .45 ACP and .32 ACP caliber bullets, the already badly wounded Pierre Mollet stumbled, then fell over and died before he hit the floor.

While Sam Carubba and Inspector Leblanc made sure Pierre Mollet was dead and recovered his weapon, Jim stood nearby as the Chief Inspector and Colonel Reynald knelt by Marcel's side. As Francois held Marcel's head off the cold ground, the mortally wounded French Army Captain spoke up and said, "Pierre Mollet...Did we get Mollet?"

"Yes, Marcel. Pierre Mollet is dead. So is his brother," responded the Chief Inspector.

As Lieutenant Kelly, Sergeant Bill Hayes, MP Staff Sergeant Steve Dalton and a squad of military policemen arrived on scene, Colonel Reynald gripped his subordinates left shoulder and said, "Hold on, Marcel. An ambulance is on the way."

After coughing up blood, Marcel appeared to be in a peaceful state when he said, "I can see my wife and infant son. With your permission, Colonel, I must go and join them."

As tears streamed down Francois's face, even a hardened combat veteran like Colonel Reynald found it difficult to speak when he remarked, "You can take leave for as long as you like, Captain Badeau."

"Thank you, Sir," responded Marcel.

Even though his time on this earth was short, Marcel looked up at Jim Beauregard and spoke just above a whisper when he said, "It was an honor to serve with you and your men, Colonel."

"The honor was ours, Captain," responded Jim.

After coughing again, Marcel looked up at his friend Charles Garnier and said, "Take command of the men, Charles."

After all they had been through, Lieutenant Charles Garnier also found it hard to speak, as he saluted his commanding officer and limited his response to a simple, "Oui, Capitaine."

Marcel then looked up and made eye contact with the Chief Inspector and said, "Goodbye, Francois." A split second later, Marcel closed his eyes and passed away.

As soon as a U.S. Army ambulance arrived, Sam Carubba, Bill Hayes and one of the medics passed out woolen army blankets to the men in the Allied raiding party, who were still wet and cold, after being hosed down, when they ran through the raging garage fire. As Francois Dumont wiped tears from his eyes as he stood up, Jim Beauregard placed an Army blanket around the Chief Inspector's shoulders, while Sam Carubba covered Colonel Reynald.

While an Army medic gave the Colonel from CID a blanket, Jim spoke in a soft tone of voice and said, "I'm sorry about Marcel. The Captain was a good man. He'll be missed by everyone who served with him and knew him."

Instead of responding, Francois reacted by nodding his head ever so slightly in agreement.

After being sentenced to thirty years of hard labor and a dishonorable discharge, Harry Moffett was transported to the U.S. Army Disciplinary Training Center in Loire, France to begin serving his sentence, before being shipped to a federal prison in the United States. Because he cooperated with CID and the French Police, Corporal Earl Johnson had his sentence reduced to fifteen years with a dishonorable discharge.

The fact that Corporal Eddie Finch was AWOL for several months and was actively involved in black market operations was the least of his legal troubles with the U.S. Army. In a unanimous decision, the members of his court martial sentenced Corporal Finch to be hanged until dead for his willful disregard for human life, when he shot at CID Agents, MPs and a Paris Policeman, before he used a hand-grenade to blow up a stolen Army ambulance, that was filled with stolen U.S. Army gasoline.

Sergeant Martin Baldwin and Sergeant Jessie Taylor received sentences of life in prison and a dishonorable discharge for being armed and using firearms to resist arrest, while being AWOL and involved in black market activities with French criminals who also collaborated with the enemy.

For his involvement in the assault and rape of Marie Marchand, Sergeant Wilbur Carlton was charged with several violations of the Articles of War, to include conduct unbecoming a non commissioned officer, assault and resisting arrest. The court also included in its finding that Sergeant Wilbur Carlton exercised complete influence over Private Shelby Wilmont and was responsible for encouraging his subordinate to commit rape. As a result, in a unanimous decision, Sergeant Wilbur Carlton was sentenced to life in prison with a dishonorable discharge. Shelby Wilmont was sentenced to death by hanging for raping Marie Marchand.

For being AWOL, illegally armed and involved in black market operations, as well as a number of armed robberies and assaults with firearms, Sergeant Beaver, Private Nathan Gromley and Private Steven Prescott were sentenced to life in federal prison. For his cooperation in helping to convict Beaver, Gromley and Prescott, Private Everett May received a reduced sentence of 20 years hard labor after being found guilty of being AWOL, carrying an unauthorized firearm, being involved in black market activities and assault with a deadly weapon.

For his cooperation and in light of the fact that he was AWOL for less than three weeks due to severe emotional stress, Sergeant Thomas Drilling was demoted in rank to Private First Class, ordered to forfeit two thirds of his pay for three months and be returned to his combat unit.

After hearing testimony from the CID Case Agents, as well as from

Private Charles Monacco and Private George Zangolas, Master Sergeant Clyde C. Nelson was found guilty and sentenced to 25 years in federal prison and a dishonorable discharge, for participating in black market operations, that limited the amount of gasoline that was available to Allied combat units in time of war.

After hearing testimony from Major Thomas Savino, Lieutenant Al Parker, Sergeant Cal Parker, Corporal Benny Greene, Private Charles Monacco and Private George Zangolas, the court found Lieutenant Andrew Armstrong guilty as charged on all counts and sentenced him to life in federal prison, a dishonorable discharge and the loss of all pay and benefits for violating a number of sections of the Articles of War to include, being AWOL, conduct unbecoming a commissioned officer of the United States Army, committing robberies while armed, being involved in black market activities and impersonating a military policeman. Even a charge of kidnapping was filed against Lieutenant Armstrong, for illegally detaining and holding hijacked U.S. Army Services of Supply truck drivers against their will, in order to facilitate the commission of a crime.

All AWOL U.S. Army personnel who engaged in criminal activity with and for Lieutenant Armstrong received sentences ranging from 15 to 25 years, depending on their level of cooperation and culpability, as well as a dishonorable discharge, loss of rank and a loss of all pay and benefits. The French criminals who were arrested as a result of this investigation were turned over to French authorities for prosecution.

After escorting Private Charlie Monacco and Private George Zangolas to the Replacement Depot, Al Parker waited with the two soldiers next to the CID staff car, while Major Savino entered the military police office. As soon as Major Savino returned, he stood by the side of the vehicle and said, "This is it. They're waiting for you in the MP Office. You'll be leaving in about an hour for the front."

After looking directly at Private Zangolas, the Major added, "Since you make such a good team together, I pulled a few strings and got you assigned to Charlie's old unit."

George Zangolas was one lucky soldier and he knew it. Had things not worked out the way they did, he and Charlie would be heading for the stockade, before being taken back to the states to serve long jail sentences in federal prison. To show his appreciation Private Zangolas presented Major Savino with a snappy salute as he said, "Thank you, Sir."

After turning to face Private Monacco, Major Savino said, "You did good work for us and that earned you both a free pass. Good luck."

Just like his buddy, Charlie presented the Major from CID with an equally snappy salute as he said, "Thank you, Sir."

"I know we told this before, but we're sorry about what happened to Captain Badeau," remarked the Major from CID. Then, after pausing for a split second, Major Savino added, "I hope you survive this miserable war and marry that French girl."

"That's the plan, Sir," responded Private Monacco.

Rather than walk away and enter the MP Office without addressing Lieutenant Parker, the two men who were once prisoners of CID until they cooperated, turned to the Negro Commissioned Officer and saluted him as well, before they spoke almost in unison and said, "Thanks, Lieutenant."

"It was a pleasure working with you and your men, Sir," added Charlie Monacco.

After returning the salute, Al responded and said, "Like the Major said, good luck."

As Private Monacco and Private Zangolas walked into the MP Office, Major Savino spoke as he headed over to the front passenger side door of the staff car. "I have good news, Al. Our commanding officer has invited us to join him for an early supper at Gabbys, as soon as we get back to Paris."

"You know what they say, Tom. You gotta take it when you can get it," responded Al as he sat behind the wheel and started the staff car.

CHAPTER 14

DUTY CALLS

AWOL Private Jack Fishman knew that he was about to get ambushed, the second he left the La Mere Catherine Restaurant and he spotted three armed men in civilian clothes with scarves covering their faces, open fire in his direction. As soon as the seriously wounded Jack Fishman collapsed on the cold ground, he knew who was leading his assailants when he heard a familiar voice call out, "This is for being a traitor, you Jew bastard!" just before another shot was fired into the AWOL Private's body. A few seconds later, Jack Fishman heard the sound of men running away and a car leaving the scene of the crime.

After meeting their commanding officer at The Paris Cafe, Major Savino and Al Parker sat at a table along the back wall and enjoyed some French wine, while Jim Beauregard returned to his seat after calling the office to check in with the duty agent.

"I can't believe it," said Jim, who continued as he sat down. "We might actually be able to enjoy the rest of the night without having to go back to work."

"The night is young and this is Paris," remarked Tommy Savino.

"You're right, Tom, but we can still hope for the best," responded Jim. While Al puffed on a White Owl cigar and seemed lost in thought, Jim looked across the table and said, "Are you OK, Al?"

Before Al responded he removed the cigar from his mouth. "I was just thinking about Cal. He's supposed to be meeting Michelle tonight."

"That's what young people do, Al," responded Jim.

If Al Parker ever needed a friend it was now. As Al looked at Tom, then at Jim, he spoke up and said, "Cal said he plans to make a life with Michelle in Paris after the war."

"Have you written Mary about Cal's plans?" asked Jim.

After shaking his head from left to right Al said, "Not yet."

"Don't you think you should?" asked Jim.

While Al seemed as if he was at a loss for words, Tommy Savino spoke up and said, "Jim's right, Al. It might help if you wrote your wife."

After taking two quick puffs on his cigar, Al continued and said, "I can't tell you how many times I wrote a letter to Mary in my head, about Cal's plan to marry Michelle and live in Paris after the war. The problem is he's right. Cal and Michelle are better off making a life for themselves in France. Nothing's changed back home. Heck, even here in Europe, our own army still treats us like were second class citizens."

"You, Cal and Benny Greene aren't second class citizens as far as we're concerned," responded Jim.

While Jim and Tom remained silent, Al apologized for putting a damper on their first real night off before he went on to say, "If everyone was like you, Tom and the other men we work with, this world would be a much better place. Unfortunately, that's not the case."

Even though the conversation they were having touched on a very sensitive subject in 1945, Jim wanted to say something to make Al feel better. As soon as Jim asked Al about his oldest son, Al perked right up and said, "According to his last letter, Jack wants to make a career in the Air Force."

"I bet he makes general before he retires," responded Jim.

"That would be something," responded Al, who sounded like a very proud father when he continued and said, "General John Jack Parker. I like the way that sounds."

"What's his count up to now, Al" asked Tom, who was referring to the number of German planes that Jack Parker was credited with shooting down.

"Three so far," responded Al.

When Al looked across the table and asked Jim how his sons were doing, Jim seemed to be in exceptionally good spirits when he responded and said, "According to Bea, Michael came home on leave after being discharged from the hospital. By now he should be on his way to become an instructor at Ft.

Bragg. I also received a letter from our son Peter, who wrote to tell me that his request to transfer to destroyer duty just got approved."

As Al raised his glass of wine, he proposed a toast that was befitting their conversation. "To all the boys. May they come home safe and sound."

"I'll drink to that," said Jim as he raised his glass.

"Me too," remarked Tommy Savino.

After the three men who had become Army buddies finished the toast, Jim looked across the table at Al and said, "Cal is a fine young man, Al. He'll figure this out. In the meantime, write Mary a nice long letter and let her know everything. She has a right to know."

Jim's advice hit a cord and made Al feel better. As Al tapped the ash off his cigar in the ashtray on the table, he spoke from his heart and said, "I give you my word. I'll write that letter to Mary tonight before I hit the sack."

"How 'bout we order something to eat," said Jim.

As soon as Al and Tom agreed that they should chow down while they had the chance, Gabby came over with a serious look on his face and said, "Excuse me for interrupting, my friends, but Sergeant Blair is on the phone. He asked me to tell you that it is most important."

"Duty calls, gentlemen," remarked Jim as he, along with Al Parker and Tom Savino, stood up and walked over to the phone that was on the bar, to hear what the duty agent had to say.

After leaving The Paris Cafe, Tommy Savino and Al Parker followed their commanding officer in another staff car, as they responded to meet the duty agent at the crime scene. The arrival of the recently promoted Captain Don Lorenz to the Paris CID Office, meant that Jim Beauregard had another experienced criminal investigator on his team. The fact that Jim and Al worked with the New Haven, Connecticut Policeman turned CID Agent back in New York, also meant that they would be serving with a colleague, who participated in the Ivan Larson/Shorty Mc Ghee manhunt.

As soon as Al spotted Captain Lorenz interviewing a witness at the crime scene, he turned to Tommy Savino and said, "Look at Don. He just got here and he's already on the job."

"You and Jim went to work as soon as you stepped off the plane as well," responded Major Savino.

"What a night that was," remarked Al as he parked the CID staff car near the Restaurant a La Mere Catherine, behind the car that was being driven by Jim Beauregard.

As Al shut the engine off, he turned to Tommy Savino and remarked, "This could'a been a lot worse if whoever did the shooting opened fire inside this place."

While Tommy Savino opened the driver's side door, he paused before he got out of the car and remarked, "I don't know if you know this, Al, but La Mere Catherine is the oldest restaurant in this section of Paris. In fact, it dates back to the late 1700s."[12]

"That's when I was born," joked Al as he stepped out of the car.

As Major Savino cracked a smile, he walked around the front of the staff car and met Al on the sidewalk. After patting Al on the back, the Major added, "Come on, old timer. It's time to do what we do best."

After being greeted with hearty handshakes from Jim Beauregard and Al Parker, Jim introduced Captain Don Lorenz to his second in command.

"Welcome to the Paris CID Office, said Tommy Savino.

"Thanks, Major," responded Captain Lorenz who went on to say, "The second I walked in the office, I met Sergeant Blair as he was on his way out the door to respond to this mess. When I asked him what happened and he told me about this shooting, I figured I might as well tag along and give him a hand."

While Jim looked around at the crime scene, he spoke up and said, "Do we know who did this?"

"When Sergeant Blair and I arrived we found two MPs kneeling next to an AWOL G.I. wearing civilian clothes who was shot up pretty bad. The MPs found a .32 caliber automatic in his pant's pocket, but the AWOL G.I. never had time to draw his gun and return fire. Even though Private Fishman refused to talk, several witnesses reported that he was gunned down by three masked men wearing civilian clothes, as he walked out of the restaurant. These same witnesses also said that the gunmen were armed with American weapons and fled the scene in a civilian car, that was parked nearby. Two of the witnesses also heard the taller of the three gunmen call out something about the victim being a traitor and referred to him as a "Jew bastard." As Captain Lorenz finished his briefing, he added, "I sent Sergeant Blair to the hospital with the wounded prisoner and took over the crime scene knowing that you were on the way, Sir."

"Good work, Don. We'll fan out and give you a hand," said Jim, before he turned to Al Parker and said, "Al, why don't you give Don a hand interviewing these witnesses, while Tom and I start canvassing the area.

As soon as Al acknowledged the order, Jim added, "When you get a chance call the Chief Inspector to let him know what's going on."

While Al responded and said, "Will do," he and Don Lorenz walked over to the small group of witnesses who were being guarded by a U.S. Army Military Policeman and a uniformed Paris cop.

When an MP Jeep pulled up carrying Sergeant's Butler and Fermi, Agent Butler spoke up as he and his partner jumped out of the Jeep and approached their CO. "We hitched a ride with the MPs when we heard about this shooting, Sir. How can we help?"

"Mike, you come with me. Josh, you go with the Major," responded Jim, before he continued and said, "We have a neighborhood to canvass."

As soon as they returned to their hideout, the four AWOL G.I.s who attacked their former business associate celebrated by filling four glasses with Cognac. While his men sipped their drinks, AWOL Sergeant Kevin Donnelly tossed his .45 caliber pistol on the kitchen table in his girlfriend's apartment and said, "Now that we settled that score, we can get back to making money without that Jew bastard getting in our way."

After hearing what the leader of their gang had to say, AWOL Corporal Jessie Peterson spoke as he admired the stack of French money that was on the table. "Look at all that, jack. With Fishman out'a the way we can go back to making even more dough. The problem is, we can't find enough stuff to spend our money on."

AWOL Private Vincent Chiperelli from Chicago proved that he was the sharpest member of their gang next to Sergeant Donnely, when he spoke up and said, "We'll need every penny we can make, to set ourselves up with a new life in Europe, 'cause we're never going home unless we do so under arrest."

"Vinny's right. This is the last stop for us," remarked AWOL Sergeant Donnely, who paused to light a cigarette before he continued and said, "We're deserters remember. After what we've done, we'd be lucky to get life in prison. In fact, if the Jew lives and he talks, we better hope the MPs and CID never get their hands on us, 'cause if they do, every one of us we'll get hung by the neck until dead. That means we're in this together."

"That makes us the four Musketeers, Sarge," remarked, Private Stanislaus "Stan" Balinski.

After pausing again to take a drag on his cigarette, AWOL Sergeant Donnely added, "Once this war is over, we can live real good anywhere in Europe with the lettuce that we got stashed. In fact, if we're smart, we'll move to a neutral country, where the U.S. Army isn't allowed to hang out in force. In the meantime, I say we divvy up this pile of cash and celebrate as soon as the girls get back from their shopping spree."

While Sergeant Donnely picked up a stack of money, Vinny Chiperelli remarked, "Can't we wait to find out if Fishman is dead, before we start moving all our stuff? After all, Sarge, I doubt he's alive after we drilled the shit out'a him and even if he is, he might not live long enough to give any of us up."

As Donnely began to equally distribute the pile of money, he stopped what he was doing and said, "I know it's a pain in the ass to move again, but we have no choice. Even though we hit Fishman pretty hard, we can't risk him living long enough to spill the beans about us. Besides, it's never good to get too comfortable in one place when you're on the run. Fortunately, he's never been to our new storage facility. He also has no idea where we moved the gambling operation."

When Stan Balanski asked if Donnely was worried, that Fishman might remember enough about their girlfriends, to help the Army cops track them down, Donnely responded and said, "As long as the girls move with us we should be alright."

While Donnely continued dividing the money into equal shares, Jessie Peterson sounded concerned when he spoke up and said, "What about Tommy Callaghan? Do you think Fishman remembers him?"

Once again, Donnely stopped divvying up the cash while he answered Jessie's question. "Fishman knows that Callaghan owed me money, but I'm pretty sure he doesn't know, that our young friend from the Services of Supply, is helping to send cash home to our closest relatives. The bad news is, that even though Fishman doesn't know the whole set up, I sent a grand back to the states for him, before he turned traitor and went into business for himself. However, at the time, I told our Jew accountant, that this was a one shot deal, that he could take advantage of, because none of us wanted to send a Postal Money Order, or a War Bond to any of our relatives back in the states."

As soon as Cal met Michelle near the Prefecture of Police on the Ile de Cite, the couple walked down to the Rue de la Cite and stood by Petit Pont to have a private chat. Despite the fact that it was after sunset in early 1945 in Paris, Michelle didn't seem to mind having this conversation while standing by a bridge that overlooked the Seine.

Being the considerate young man that he was, Cal wasted no time in saying, "Are you sure you don't want to sit in a cafe while we talk?"

"I'm fine," responded Michelle, before she went on to say, "Whenever I visited my father and my grand-père at work, this is the place where they would take me for a walk before I went home. We would stand on this very spot and talk about all the things that we love about living in Paris."

As Michelle pointed to the other side of the bridge, she continued and said, "My grand-père Maurice, that is my mother's father, or as we say in French her père, would take me fishing on the other side of this bridge. In fact, that is how my parents met. My mother's father and my father's father worked together in the Sûre·té. Since both men loved to fish on their days off, they invited my mother and father to join them. The moment my parents met, they fell in love and were married within two months."

"Regardless of the weather, that makes this a special place," remarked

Cal.

"Very special," responded Michelle.

"I also have a special place where I spent time with my father and my grandfather back in New York," said Cal, who leaned close to Michelle when he continued and said, "It was cold there too in the winter, but I didn't mind, because being with them, when they worked on cars and trucks, taught me more about life than all the time that I spent in school."

After hearing what Cal just said, Michelle was even more determined to say what was on her mind. "I'm sorry, Cal, but I cannot allow you to leave your family and your country just to marry me."

Cal Parker wasn't giving in and said, "If my father understands, so will my mother. As far as leaving my country goes, what am I leaving behind; a place where I have less rights than white folks, even when I wear this uniform. Even German Prisoners of War are treated better than Negroes in the land of free and the home of the brave."

While tears streamed down her face, Michelle remained quiet as Cal gently took her right hand and kissed it before he said, "I didn't come here to fall in love with a French girl. I came here to fight the Germans. After I was transferred to CID, I came to Paris to chase deserters and G.I.s who were committing all kinds of crimes. In the process, I met you and once that happened I knew that we were destined to be together."

As Michelle turned to face the love of her life, she looked directly at Cal and said, "Then I will go to America."

After shaking his head ever so slightly from left to right, Cal responded and said, "No, Michelle. Once we get married we'll make a new life for ourselves here in Paris. I already spoke to your father and Gabby and they said they would help me open a cafe. With your permission, I'm gonna call the place Michelle's Cafe Americain."

After having their discussion by the bridge, Cal and his future wife decided to have supper at The Paris Café. Being the trained observer that he was, Cal noticed that he and Michelle were drawing a few angry stares, from two American soldiers who were sitting at table near the dance floor.

By the way they were looking at Cal and Michelle and talking among them-selves, it seemed obvious, that these two American soldiers were disturbed to see an American Negro soldier with a white French girl. Michelle proved to be equally as observant, a skill that she developed when she served in the resistance. After leaning closer to the edge of the table, Michelle reached out and patted Cal's right hand, while she spoke loud enough to be heard over the soft music that the band was playing. "I see them too. They must be new to Paris and have no idea that The Paris Café is the favorite hangout for CID Agents, MPs and French policemen like my father and his men. Please ignore them, Cal, so we can go back to enjoying our time together."

After doing his best to calm down, Cal returned his attentions to Michelle just as the band members returned to their positions on the bandstand. While Cal continued to casually keep an eye on the two G.I.s, the radio was turned off, while the band began warming up to play some popular American music.

Being the outgoing person that she was, Michelle smiled wide as she stood up and extended her hand and said, "You promised that you would dance with me after we had supper. Now is your chance."

Cal had been a military policeman and a CID Agent long enough, to develop the instincts that all good cops needed to possess in order to predict trouble. As tempted as Cal was to tell Michelle that they needed to sit this one out, the young man who was tired of being treated differently, stood up and escorted Michelle to the dance floor.

Sure enough, just like Cal expected, the shorter of the two enlisted men grabbed the off duty CID Agent by the arm as he walked by and remarked, "What kind of a joint is this? Where I'm from they'd hang a nigger for being with a white girl." When his friend acted as if he was trying to calm things down and said, "Forgive my buddy, Sarge, and let me buy you a drink," the situation was made worse when the taller G.I. stood up and threw his drink in Cal's face.

The second Cal knocked the taller of the two troublemakers on his ass and the band stopped playing, Gabby Allaire, Anthony Angelone and Sal Coppola left the bar to come to the rescue. As soon as the shorter soldier reached into his right hand pant's pocket, Sergeants Angelone and Coppola arrived just as Cal went to draw the Model 1903 Colt pistol, that he carried concealed under his Ike Jacket.

"CID!" was all Sergeant Angelone had to say, to stop the shorter G.I. from drawing the switchblade that he carried while on leave in Paris. As Cal released the grip on his pistol and removed his hand from under his jacket, Sergeant Coppola was picking the taller soldier with the bloody nose off the floor, while Gabby instructed the band to get back to work.

While Sergeant Angelone recovered the switchblade from the shorter soldier's pocket, he sounded like a pissed off cop when he said, "You two just picked a fight with an off duty CID Agent in the official hangout of Army CID, the MPs and the Paris Police and you were stupid enough to do so in front of witnesses. As a result, you're both under arrest." When two MPs who were on patrol in the area entered the bar, Sergeant Angelone produced his CID Badge and called out, "Thanks for stopping by, but we'll handle this." While the taller of the two MPs waved his right hand, before he and his partner left The Paris Café, Sergeant Angelone continued as he held onto his prisoner's arm, "Excuse us, Michelle, but we have some official business to attend to." Sergeant Angelone then turned to Cal and said, "You're welcome to join me and Sal when we have a friendly chat with these two assholes out back."

When the soldier with the bloody nose remarked, "That's fine with me. I'm not gonna get sucker punched by some nigger," Michelle grabbed Cal by the arm and said, "I would rather have you spend your time off dancing with me than fighting with these men."

Even though his blood was still boiling, Cal looked at Sergeant Angelone and said, "Forget it, Ange. Let 'em go."

"Are you sure?" asked Sergeant Angelone, who quickly added, "Cause me and Sal don't mind bouncing these two off the walls out back, before we take 'em to the stockade."

"I appreciate that, Ange, but as long as they're not AWOL, you and Sal can let 'em go," remarked Cal, while he wiped his face with his Army issue handkerchief.

"Whatever you say, Cal," responded Sergeant Angelone as he let go of his prisoner and asked for his ID, dog tags and pass.

"You too, pal," added Sal Coppola as he held out his right hand and asked for the other soldier's identification and written authorization to be on leave.

While the two G.I.s produced their passes and identification, Cal addressed the two troublemakers in a dead serious tone of voice. "If either one of you come anywhere near me or my girl again, I'm gonna assume that you mean us harm and I will kill you both."

"That goes double for us and every other agent assigned to CID," remarked Sergeant Angelone, while Cal escorted Michelle to the dance floor.

While Cal and Michelle danced to the Glenn Miller song Moonlight Serenade, Sergeants Angelone and Coppola finished inspecting the 48 hour passes and identification of the two enlisted men, before the troublemakers were escorted out of The Paris Café. Once outside, Gabby approached the two soldiers to issue them a warning of his own.

"The couple you just insulted are members of my family. If you ever go near them again, you will wish you were captured by the Gestapo."

"Consider yourselves warned," remarked Sal Coppola.

As the two troublemakers walked away, Gabby turned to Sergeants Angelone and Coppola and said, "Now that this unpleasant business has been concluded, I would be honored if you gentlemen would join me for drinks at the bar. After all, the night is young."

Just as Gabby, Anthony Angelone and Sal Coppola entered the café and Cal received a friendly nod from his fellow CID Agents, he stepped back from Michelle while they continued to dance and said, "Now you know why we can't live in America when the war is over."

As soon as Private Jack Fishman opened his eyes after being operated on, he found himself under guard by a rather large military policeman who was reading a recent copy of The Stars and Stripes Newspaper. "You're alive," said the MP, who quickly added, "Now the Army can toss your AWOL ass in the federal pen and throw away the key for decades to come."

"You got a cigarette, pal," asked the prisoner who was still in a bit of a daze, after coming out of surgery.

"I'm not your pal," remarked the MP as he removed a pack of smokes from his shirt pocket and tossed them on the bed along with a Ronson lighter.

"Thanks anyway," responded Private Fishman as he spoke just above a whisper.

By the time the prisoner took his first drag on his cigarette, Captain Don Lorenz and Sergeant Hank Blair entered his room to check on their prisoner.

"Private Fishman just woke up, Sir," remarked the MP as he stood up and greeted the Army Officer from CID.

As Captain Lorenz and Sergeant Blair stood by the side of the bed, the Captain from CID addressed the MP Sergeant in a friendly tone of voice and said, "Grab yourself some coffee, Sergeant, while we talk to the prisoner."

"Yes, Sir," responded the MP Sergeant as he scooped up his pack of cigarettes and his lighter off the bed before he left the room.

While the MP Sergeant left the room, Captain Lorenz introduced himself and Sergeant Blair to Private Fishman. Just as Captain Lorenz was about to continue, an Army doctor and a nurse entered to check on their patient.

"Prisoner or not, Captain. This man just got out of surgery," said the Army doctor, who quickly added, "You can come back tomorrow and interrogate the crap out'a him, but right now Private Fishman needs his rest. Besides, after I administer this injection, he'll be lights out before you can say the Pledge of Allegiance."

Because of the severity of the case at hand, Captain Lorenz did his best to sound as polite as possible, when he asked if the doctor could give him and his partner five minutes alone with their prisoner. The second the doctor stopped filling the syringe and he appeared to be considering the CID Agent's request, Don Lorenz quickly added, "This isn't just about being AWOL, Sir. Private Fishman was shot by three masked gunmen as he left a Paris cafe. Five minutes is all I ask and we'll come back tomorrow."

"OK, Captain, but I'll be back in five minutes to throw you and your partner out'a here," responded the Army doctor, who was bone tired after a long day and night on his feet.

"Thank you, Sir," said Don Lorenz who checked his watch, while the doctor and the nurse left the room. As soon as they did so, Captain Lorenz wasted no time in saying, "I only have one question for you, Private, before that doctor comes back and knocks you out for the rest of the night."

"What's that, Sir?" asked the AWOL Private, before he took one last drag on his cigarette and crushed it in an ashtray.

"You're under no obligation to talk to us, until you get an Army lawyer and we file formal charges against you," said Captain Lorenz, who paused for a split second before he continued and said, "But if you do cooperate, CID will make your cooperation known to the Judge Advocate General's Office."

Under the circumstances Private Fishman knew that he had plenty to say, providing that he received the right deal from the Army cops. Even though AWOL Private Fishman was still a bit groggy after being operated on, he was anxious to make the best deal possible, now that he was under arrest. "I'll cooperate, Captain," responded Fishman, who paused to catch his breath before he said, "But I want a deal, Sir. A real deal, not just a general promise that CID will repeat what I say at my court martial."

"You're the one in big trouble, not us," responded Captain Lorenz.

Despite the fact that he was in pain after being operated on, Private Fishman did his best to suck it up, so he could try and get the best deal possible from CID. "You're right, Captain. I'm the one who is behind the proverbial eight ball," remarked the AWOL G.I. who quickly added, "And to prove to you that I know how the game is played, I'll give you a taste of what I know, that goes way beyond telling you who the masked gunmen were who filled me full'a lead."

"I'm listening," responded Captain Lorenz.

Immediately after Sergeant Blair handed Private Fishman a glass of water, the wounded prisoner responded and said, "I don't know if you were stationed in France at the time, Captain, but after we landed in Normandy, the Army had a big problem with supplies being stolen in transit to front line units. This included by truck and by train. I know about this problem, because I was in one of the infantry units that was taken off the line and sent to Paris to serve as guards and prevent some of these thefts.[13] It took some doing, but CID was eventually able to nail a group of Army Officers and enlisted men, who were very successful train robbers until they got caught."

After pausing to take another sip of water, Private Fishman continued making his preliminary statement. "One gang of AWOL G.I.s, that was heavily involved in stealing Army supplies from trains that never got caught, is the gang that I ended up working with when I went AWOL. Even though I didn't see their faces, I also know that the key members of that gang, were the ones who made Swiss cheese out'a me when I left La Mire Catherine."

After pausing to take a sip of water, Private Fishman continued and said, "To prove to you that I know enough to get some serious consideration, I'll also tell you, Captain, that the ring leader of this gang found a way to send money back to the states. Even though he told me at the time that his ability to send War Bonds and Postal Money Orders home was a one shot deal, I wouldn't be surprised to find out that this group of black market operators, who also run a gambling operation on the side, still have a way to get money home to the states. To prove that I know what I'm talking about, all you have to do is check the records for the Postal Money Order that ended up being delivered to my folks. The paperwork for that transaction will show that I never signed for that money. Whoever did so, was, or still is involved with the people that I'm talking about."

Just when their conversation was getting interesting, the Army doctor and the nurse came back into the room. Rather than push the issue and piss off the doctor, Captain Lorenz thanked the surgeon for the extra five minutes, before he turned to the prisoner and said, "Get some rest, Private. We'll see you tomorrow."

It didn't take long for Al Parker, Jim Beauregard and Francois Dumont to hear about the incident at The Paris Café that involved Cal, Michelle and two trouble making soldiers on leave. While the three men enjoyed a late night drink of scotch in the CID Office, Al remarked, "You'd think this world would change for the better, after the way the Germans and the Japs have been carrying on."

"You're right, Al," responded Jim, who paused to take a sip of scotch before he went on to say, "Sometimes I wonder what it's gonna take, for some of our people to realize, that they're not much different than the bastards we're fighting."

After taking a sip from his glass of scotch, the Chief Inspector joined the conversation and said, "Unfortunately, no matter how many wars we fight, there will always be hatred in the world."

As Jim leaned over and refilled Al's glass with a healthy splash of scotch, he looked at the man that he had the pleasure to serve with and said, "I know one thing. The three of us, along with Gabby, are gonna give those kids a wedding that Paris will never forget."

Even though it was customary for the father of the bride to pay for his daughter's wedding, Francois was deeply moved when he was approached by Jim and asked if he and his men could do something as friends of the girl's family and colleagues of the groom, to help make their wedding a special occasion. "It's all settled, Al. You and me are providing all the liquor, Tommy Savino has that Army cook that he gave a break too making the wedding cake, Gabby and Francois are providing the food, the band and the use of The Paris Café. Gabby and Francois are also providing the happy couple with a car and a trunk full of groceries and champagne, so they can spend the weekend on the Dumont family farm for their honeymoon. Last but not least, our favorite C47 pilot, Major Billy Davis, has made arrangements for the U.S. Army Air Corps to donate the silk from a "damaged" parachute, so Francois's wife Annette can make Michelle's wedding gown."

Al Parker was deeply moved after hearing what was just said. As he raised his glass into the air, the father of the young man who was deeply in love with the Chief Inspector's daughter, smiled then said, "To Cal and Michelle. With a sendoff like that, they should be truly blessed for the rest of their lives."

"Here, here," said Jim as he and Francois joined Al in the toast.

When Al remarked, "I wish Mary could be here for the wedding," Jim reached into his jacket pocket and removed a cable. After presenting the cable to his good friend, Jim gave Al a few seconds to read the message, before he spoke up and said, "Since Cal can't walk down the aisle without a best man, I got the best man I could find to serve in that capacity."

As troubled as he was after hearing what happened to Cal and Michelle in Gabby's café, Al was all smiles when he read the cable that Jim just handed him. "I don't believe it. You arranged for Cal's brother Jack to come to the wedding? I can't wait to hear how you pulled that off?"

"Francois and I came up with the idea after we heard what happened at Gabby's place," said Jim, who quickly added, "When Gabby said that it was a shame that your wife Mary wouldn't be able to travel to Paris to attend the wedding, we figured the least we could do, was have your son Jack be given a few days off, so he could be his brother's best man."

As soon as Al remarked, "You still haven't told me how you managed to get Jack flown to Paris." "It took a few phone calls and a few German pistols, but thanks to Billy Davis and a buddy of his, who's flying a desk in Air Force Headquarters, the recently promoted Captain John Jack Parker will be escorting his brother down the aisle," responded Jim.

After hearing the news, Al was a very happy man. Then it hit him. He had no idea that his oldest son was recently promoted to captain. "Captain Parker? When did that happen?" asked Al.

"I'm not sure," responded Jim, who went on to say, "It must'a happened after you received his last letter."

Al proved that he still had a sense a humor when he remarked, "Superior officer or not, I'm still giving Captain Jack Parker a big hug from me and his mother after I salute him."

While the three men had a good laugh, the Armed Forces Radio Network broadcasted a report that described how the Allied armies continued to engage the Axis Forces on all fronts. Even though the war was by no means over, the tide of the war had turned in favor of the Allies. The bad news was, that the fighting was just as savage and destructive as the war went on. In the Pacific, the Allies were pressing their attacks ever closer to Japan. The raising of the flag on Mount Suribachi on Iwo Jima by U.S. Marines, let the Japanese know that the Americans were prepared to invade the home islands, if that's what it took to force the enemy to capitulate. To further drive this point home, U.S. led Allied Forces, that included Philippine personnel, eliminated the Japanese hold on the Philippine Islands and liberated Manila on March 3, 1945. Elsewhere in the Pacific, the U.S. Navy was preventing badly needed supplies from reaching Japan, while squadrons of U.S. Army Air Force B29s firebombed Japanese cities. In Europe, the Allies were pressing attacks on all fronts. Once the Germans were forced from the Colmar Pocket, Allied forces in the west prepared to execute the crossing of the Rhine River. Meanwhile, the Red Army continued to engage the enemy on a broad front and make the drive to Berlin. Unless the Axis Forces were able to deploy so called "wonder weapons," that were powerful enough to stop the Allied advance, it was just a question of time before the enemy would be forced to accept the terms of an unconditional surrender.

When Corporal Tommy Callighan met AWOL Sergeant Kevin Donnely at a cafe in the Montmartre arrondissement of Paris, he looked up at the young G.I. who helped him transfer some of his money home and said, "She's waiting upstairs."

"Thanks, Sarge," said the degenerate gambler, who was beholding to Kevin Donnely for putting him to work, to pay back the money that he borrowed to cover his losses at the card table. As an added benefit, for helping Donnely send postal money orders and war bonds home to his family, the AWOL Sergeant, who also ran a successful black market operation, provided the young corporal with the services of French prostitutes. "Have fun, kid. You deserve it," responded Donnely.

As the young corporal from the Paris based COMZ Services of Supply Command removed two receipts from his right side pant's pocket, he handed the documents to Donnely and said. "I almost forgot, Sarge. These receipts are for you."

"Good work, Tommy," remarked Donnely as he examined the amounts that were sent to New York, before he motioned the young man to be on his way and said, "Nail her once for me, but don't get lost, because in a few days, I'll need you to send another pile of cash home to my brother, that I don't want our Uncle Sam to know came from me."

"Sure thing, Sarge," responded Corporal Callaghan as he walked away from the corner table in the cafe.

By using Corporal Tommy Callaghan to help him send postal money orders and war bonds home, Kevin Donnely and his core group of fellow G.I. Gangsters were able to launder some of the money they made, from their black market and gambling operations. Donnely and his three main associates accomplished this, by giving American soldiers who were not AWOL a ten percent commission, for sending money through U.S. Army channels to various addresses back in the states. This enabled Kevin Donnely, Jessie Peterson, Vinny Chiperelli and Stanislaus "Stan" Balinski to periodically send money to relatives back home, that they would never be able to get out of France on their own, because they were deserters.

Running a gambling parlor, in addition to a thriving black market operation, also made it possible for Kevin Donnely to use Corporal Tommy Callaghan, to recruit other gamblers, who had no problem accepting a generous commission, for sending War Bonds and Postal Money Orders to the states, as a favor for another G.I. The fact that different soldiers were used to pull off this scam, meant that no one would ever be suspected of breaking the rules. This was the case, because every soldier was allowed to convert government script and local currency, including money made from gambling profits, into War Bonds and Postal Money Orders.[14]

Because Donnely and his men weren't greedy and they used this method sparingly, no one ever caught on until now. The fact that their Postal Money Orders and the War Bonds were sent to a number of different addresses in New York, Connecticut, New Jersey and Chicago, also prevented Army officials from getting suspicious. It also helped, that the men who agreed to perform this service for a fee, did so by swearing to the terms of the transaction. This meant, that every soldier who participated in this scam, was compromising their integrity and was just as guilty of committing a fraudulent act, as the actual provider of the money. It was even safer to use soldiers who were on leave in Paris, because once they returned to a frontline unit, they could end up anywhere, including in a hospital, in a grave, or in a prison camp.

The last American soldier, who lost a pile of cash at Donnely's gambling house, took all of two seconds to agree to do a fellow soldier a favor and send his gambling winnings home for a 10% "handling" fee. This enabled Kevin Donnely to use another compromised surrogate to send a $1000 dollar Postal Money Order and a $1000 dollar War Bond to an address in Brooklyn. Stan Balasnki was also able to send $1000 dollars home to his younger brother in Jersey City, New Jersey, while Vinny Chiperelli had one of their gambling customers send a $1000 War Bond to his grandfather in Chicago.

As soon as Al Parker arrived at The Paris Cafe, he headed straight for the kitchen to meet with Gabby. "I got here as soon as I got your message, Gabby," said Al.

"Thank you for coming, Lieutenant Al. I am sure you will like to hear what I have to say," responded Gabby, as he gestured his guest to have a seat at a private table in the back of the cafe near the bar.

While Al sat down across from Gabby, the former resistance fighter turned cafe owner continued as he filled two glasses with wine. "Allow me to begin while we wait for Francois to join us."

After taking a sip of wine, Gabby began briefing Al Parker. "As soon as I heard about the shooting at the Restaurant a La Mere Catherine, I met with some of the men I served with in the resistance and asked them to help me find the ones responsible for this terrible crime. All of my former colleagues know that Francois is working with CID, to find the Americans deserters who act like gangsters in Paris."

While Al took a sip of wine and continued to listen, Gabby went on to say, "According to my associates, the American deserter who was seriously wounded and taken prisoner is known as The Broker. He was once a member of a gang of AWOL American black market operators, that is led by an American Sergeant by the name of Kevin Donnely."

Al Parker had been a cop long enough to know when it was necessary to take notes and when it was more important to listen. While Al removed a cigar from his inside uniform jacket pocket, Gabby produced a box of matches and offered his guest a light as he said, "The one called The Broker left Donnely's gang to go into business for himself. He operates no trucks and commits no thefts on his own. He simply sits in an office and makes, how you say, deals, by connecting the Americans who are doing the stealing, with the French thieves who are in a position to sell stolen U.S. Army merchandise."

While Gabby took a sip of wine, Al remarked, "I can see why they call this guy The Broker. It sounds like he has some racket."

"He is how you say, the one in the middle," remarked Gabby.

"The middle man," responded Al.

"Yes, the middle man," said Gabby, who went on to say, "But this middle man put himself at great risk, by leaving the gang run by the AWOL American Sergeant Donnely. This happened because The Broker took some of Donnely's customers with him, when he went into business for himself. Unfortunately, for the one called The Broker, this crazy Irishman from your New York City is one to hold a grudge."

As soon as Francois arrived, he shook hands with Al Parker and sat at the table while Gabby filled another glass with wine. While the Chief Inspector sipped some wine, Gabby informed his brother-in-law that he just finished briefing Lieutenant Al, about the wounded American known as The Broker and the AWOL American Sergeant Donnely.

Once Gabby was finished talking, the Chief Inspector looked at Al and said, "Gabby's contacts are correct. The deserter you have in custody has much he can tell us. The one we must be most concerned about is the AWOL American Sergeant Donnely, for he is, by all accounts, a very dangerous man."

"Do we have any idea where Donnely hangs his hat?" asked Al, who quickly added, "I mean where we can find him?"

"I like that American saying as well, "hangs his hat." I will have to remember to use that the next time I wish to know where someone can be found," remarked Gabby.

As Al cracked a smile, the Chief Inspector finished lighting a cigarette, before he continued with his end of the briefing. "When Gabby told me what he uncovered, I had Inspectors Goulet and La Belle come with me when I met with his friend Emil. Emil is an ambulance driver who helped Gabby rescue a number of French soldiers, Allied airmen and Jews and get them to safety in England. This former member of the resistance has proven to be very helpful in the past and introduced us to a man who has no love for the American deserter Sergeant Donnely. This Frenchman has no love for your AWOL Sergeant Donnely, because his girlfriend left him to go live with this American deserter. In fact, three of her girlfriends left with her and are now with the men who are closest to Donnely. Once we locate these girls, we will find Donnely and the deserters who are working with him."

Al was impressed. Paris was their town and they proved it, when Gabby and the Chief Inspector developed some very promising leads on such short notice. After tapping the ash from his cigar in the ashtray that was on the table, Al looked at the Chief Inspector and said, "How many of our men should we send to assist Inspectors Goulet and La Belle?"

As soon as Chief Inspector Dumont checked his watch, he responded and said, "I told Inspectors Goulet and La Belle to call us here if anything changes. Once we leave, Gabby will tell them to contact us at your office, until we meet them in the field with more men. Naturally, more of our men will be needed to watch for the American deserters once we locate these four girls. In the meantime we can brief Jim, Tom and Captain Lorenz back at your office."

While Al stood up, he quickly added, "This is perfect timing, Francois, because Captain Lorenz and Hank Blair are scheduled to return to the hospital later this afternoon to question Private Fishman."

"Excellent," responded Francois, who continued as he faced his brother-in-law, "Will you stay by the phone and call us at the CID Office if you hear anything from your contacts?"

As usual, Gabby played his part well, when he saluted his brother in law and remarked, "Yes Francois. I will remain at my post and will report directly to you if I hear anything."

"Thanks, Gabby," said Al as he reached out and shook hands with the owner of The Paris Cafe.

"You are most welcome, Lieutenant Al," responded the former French resistance fighter.

Before he left the back room of the cafe, Al faced Gabby and said, "Since we're gonna be part of the same family, I'd prefer it if you called me Al."

Gabby Allaire never sounded more serious when he responded and said, "I call you Lieutenant Al, because I wish to show respect for your rank, as a commissioned officer of the American Army and because you are my friend."

Immediately after Al nodded his head to signal that he understood, he continued and said, "I look forward to the day when this war is over, so I can be known as plain old Al."

"Me too, my friend," responded Gabby.

CHAPTER 15

FROM BOTH SIDES OF THE ATLANTIC

While Jim Beauregard, Captain Don Lorenz and Hank Blair were being briefed by Al Parker and Chief Inspector Dumont, Inspector Patrice Goulet called in from the field with some good news. After taking the call, the Chief Inspector removed his notebook and fountain pen from his suit jacket pocket and made a few notes, while he listened to one of his most experienced men file his report. "Excellent work, Patrice. You and Maurice have done well."

After jotting down some additional information, the Chief Inspector continued and said, "I agree. That could be the same car that was used in the shooting at the cafe." As the Chief Inspector handed his notebook to Al Parker, he spoke into the phone and said, "I'll be along with some of the CID men in a few minutes. If you and Maurice have to move from that location, call the CID duty agent and let him know where we can find you. In the meantime, I want you and Maurice to be careful."

While the Chief Inspector hung up the phone, he looked at Jim Beauregard and the others and said, "Inspectors Goulet and La Belle found one of the girls. If our information is correct, she will lead us to the others. There is also a car parked in front of the building, that matches the description of the vehicle that was used in the shooting at the Restaurant a La Mere Catherine."

"Thank God for jealous boyfriends," remarked Al.

When the door to the Colonel's spacious corner office opened, Major Savino entered carrying a file folder in hand. As he presented his commanding officer with the file, Tommy Savino remarked, "I had Chris Jacko pull AWOL Sergeant Kevin Donnely's personnel file, so we could show our men and the Chief Inspector's men what this character looks like."

"Let's see who we're dealing with," said Jim as he opened the file.

The next to speak was Captain Lorenz. "With your permission, Sir, Hank and I will get over to the hospital to have a talk with Private Fishman. It might also help if we can show the prisoner a copy of Donnely's photograph. Doing so should have a humbling effect on Private Fishman and make him less likely to think that he has us over a barrel."

"Good idea, Don," responded Jim as he handed Donnely's official photograph to Captain Lorenz.

As Captain Lorenz and Sergeant Blair started to leave the Colonel's office, Jim called out, "Take care of the Captain, Hank. He's new in Paris. We can't afford to lose him on any of the side streets."

Immediately after Sergeant Blair cracked a smile and said, "Will do, Sir," Don Lorenz smiled as well and tossed the Colonel a casual salute as he left the office with his partner.

As soon as Captain Lorenz and Sergeant Blair left the room, Jim looked at Al Parker and said, "Al, I want you to give Don and Hank a hand on this. Once we learn more about AWOL Sergeant Donnely, I need you to draft a cable to our office in New York and request assistance from Colonel Richmond and Captain Murphy. If Donnely is from our old stomping grounds, we'll need Colonel Richmond, Captain Murphy and some of our buddies back in New York, to work a piece'a this case from their end."

"If anyone can help us work this case from the other side of the Atlantic, it's Colonel Richmond and the men we worked with in the CID Task Force," responded Al.

"My sentiments exactly," remarked Jim who leaned back in his chair as he continued and said, "I like this case and I like the way it's moving along. I also think we need to do something special for Gabby for helping us out the way he did." While Jim leaned forward, he continued as he looked directly at the Chief Inspector. "You were right about Gabby, Francois. He's a good man."

"My brother-in-law misses the action of resistance work," responded the Chief Inspector, before he went on to say, "If it wasn't for the fact that he was badly wounded in the leg during the fighting to liberate Paris, Gabby would have been recruited by the Prefecture of Police here in Paris."

★ ★ ★

When Private Fishman got a bit cocky and tried to hold out for a better deal, Captain Lorenz dropped AWOL Sergeant Kevin Donnely's photograph on the prisoner's hospital bed and said, "Nice try, Private, but as you can see, we know a lot more than you think about your old pal."

As important as his cooperation was, Private Fishman wasn't happy to hear, that CID and their French Allies were well on their way to identifying and locating AWOL Sergeant Kevin Donnely. In his favor, Private Fishman had a good sense of humor and remarked, "I hope you and the Sergeant don't hold it against me, Sir, for trying to get the best deal possible."

When Captain Lorenz responded he sounded like a regular guy when he said, "Na, we would'a done the same thing if we were in your shoes."

"The Captain's right, Private," said Hank Blair, who quickly added, "As long as you help us make a case against these guys, the significance of your cooperation will be made known to the Judge Advocate General. However, understand that you're gonna have to impress the hell out of a courts martial board, for them to give you anything close to the deal that you expect."

"I understand," said the prisoner, who seemed resigned to do everything he could to help CID, which in turn would hopefully help his case in some way.

For the next five minutes Private Fishman gave the two CID Agents an overview of AWOL Sergeant Kevin Donnely and his black market activities. Fishman also explained how he knew Donnely's voice well enough to identify him as the gunman, who called him a traitor and a Jew bastard, before he put another bullet into his body.

When Hank Blair asked Private Fishman if Donnely was prone to violence, their prisoner wasted no time in saying, "Kevin Donnely is like a grenade with the pin pulled, because you never know when he's gonna go off." After pausing for a split second, Fishman continued and said, "Even when Donnely was making more money than he could spend, he was never happy with what he had. I also think it bothers him to no end, that he'll never be able to return home, unless he's on his way to a federal prison."

When Captain Lorenz asked Private Fishman to identify everyone who was associated with Donnely, he proceeded to name every deserter who was affiliated in any way with the AWOL Sergeant. As soon as Private Fishman was finished answering the question, Hank Blair handed a glass of water to the prisoner, while he asked a followup question about Donnely's temperament. Once again, Private Fishman sounded like he was being fully cooperative when he responded and said, "Based on what Vinny Chiperelli said, Kevin Donnely was one tough son of a bitch. In fact, everything I know about Donnely's past came from Chiperelli. Chiperelli was also responsible for helping Donnely make his way to Paris in a stolen Jeep."

"This sounds like a story that we need to hear more about," remarked Captain Lorenz.

After taking a sip of water, Private Fishman remarked, "According to Chiperelli, Donnely was one hell of a soldier who killed his fair share of Krauts. I was also told, that Donnely saved Chiperelli's life, not once, but twice, Sir."

While the prisoner continued, he placed the glass of water back on the table next to his bed. "You and Sergeant Blair also need to know, Sir, that Donnely's anger wasn't always directed against the enemy. Based on what Chiperelli said, Donnely became know as Crazy Kevin, because he had one too many fights with other G.I.s and was told that he would lose his stripes if it ever happened again. I don't know if this is true, but the last time Donnely lost his temper, he beat a replacement bad enough to put him in the hospital. Apparently, this kid froze in combat and caused one of Donnely's men to get badly wounded. Donnely was even more pissed off, when he learned that his buddy Vinny Chiperelli was slightly wounded, as a result of this replacement's failure to follow orders. Even though Vinny only had a scratch on his left leg, Donnely beat this replacement so bad, the medics had to carry him away from the front line on a stretcher."

When Private Fishman removed a cigarette from the pack that was handed to him by Sergeant Blair, Captain Lorenz offered the prisoner a light as he remarked, "You're doing fine, Private. Please continue."

After taking a second quick drag on his cigarette, Private Fishman picked up where he left off and said, "Shortly after Donnely was arrested and confined to camp, Vinny Chiperelli filled two duffel bags with cigarettes and rations and drove Donnely to Paris in a stolen Jeep. Instead of dropping him off and returning to their unit, Chiperelli decided to stay with Donnely. If you ask me, Donnely was Chiperelli's hero and could do no wrong."

Once again, Fishman took a quick drag on his cigarette before he finished his comment. "From what I heard, once they sold the contents of the two duffel bags, Donnely and his young sidekick were on their way to becoming two of the most successful black market operators in Paris. Their operation really expanded, when they hooked up with some Frenchmen, who were involved in the black market long before we landed in Normandy."

As soon as Captain Lorenz remarked, "We'll also need to know as much as you can tell us about Donnely's French contacts," Fishman tapped the ash from his cigarette into the ashtray that Sergeant Blair handed him.

"I figured you would, Sir," responded Fishman, who continued while he held the ashtray in his left hand. "The best way for me to answer your question, Captain, is to say that we did business with two different groups of Frenchmen. One group consisted of a few local French crooks and a number of businessmen. We also sold tons of smokes and rations to people on the street, but once we started making the right contacts, we made larger deliveries directly to our best customers. If you give me some paper and a pencil, Sir, I can write down as much as I remember about this group, including the businesses that we made deliveries too."

After pausing to take one last drag on his cigarette, Fishman added, "The second group was a gang of French crooks from Marseille. Donnely loved these guys, because when they bought stuff from us, they bought truckloads at a time. There was nothing nickel and dime about these guys."

As Fishman continued, he stamped his cigarette butt out in the ashtray that he held in is hand. "The only ones I ever met from group two were the workers, you know, truck driver types. In fact, one of the main reasons I decided to go off on my own, was because I figured if Donnely didn't trust me enough, to introduce me to the number one French crook that he was dealing with, why should I remain loyal to him? Donnely was so tight lipped about identifying the Frenchman in charge of group two, he used a code name when he referred to a sale that we made to the big shot from Marseille. All Donnely ever said to me was, Mr. M's drivers are on the way to pick up 100 cartons of smokes, 300 Chocolate D Bars and 50 Jerry cans of gasoline. I'm convinced, the only reason he told me as much as he did, was because I was keeping his books and Donnely liked to go over what we sold and what we had in inventory."

This time it was Sergeant Hank Blair who asked the appropriate follow-up question. "Can you tell us anything about this big shot French crook?"

After handing the ashtray back to Hank Blair, the prisoner answered the question in a matter of fact tone of voice. "All I know, Sarge, is that this Frenchman from Marseille returned to a life of crime after serving in the resistance."

The next question came from Captain Lorenz. "Do know how Donnely met this guy?"

Once again, Private Fishman responded in a tone of voice that made his interrogators believe that he was telling the truth. "According to a conversation I overheard between Jessie Peterson and Stan Balinski, the Frenchman called Mr. M for Marseille, got more heavily involved in the black market in Paris after he met Donnely at his gambling den. The only reason they talked about this guy, was because he turned out to be one hell of a card player. Based on what I overheard, one night this Frenchman won so much money, that Donnely offered to pay him off in smokes and gasoline. From that point on, the Frenchman from Marseille became one of our biggest and best customers."

"I'm curious about something, Private?" asked Captain Lorenz.

"What's that, Sir," said Private Fishman.

After hearing the Captain from CID ask if he was ever a trusted member of Donnely's gang, the prisoner responded without hesitation and said, "The best way for me to answer your question, Sir, is to say that Donnely and I tolerated each other."

"Can you give us more detail than that?" asked Hank Blair.

"Sure thing,' Sarge," responded the prisoner, who went on to say, "The day I met Donnely I was delivering a van loaded with fresh bread, that was made with stolen Army flour to one of his customers. Once we were introduced, he offered to buy me a drink. When Donnely heard that I was a bookkeeper back in the states, he asked if I would give him a hand with his bookkeeping, because none of his guys could count, unless it involved playing cards or rolling dice. I agreed. When Donnely asked if he could come in with me in my bakery racket, I did my best to let him down easy, by telling him that it wasn't a big enough money maker for me to take on a partner. The truth was, that he needed my services to handle his bookkeeping, a lot more than

I needed to take on a partner, who would get paid for doing nothing."

After pausing for a split second, Private Fishman continued answering the question. "In an effort to show Donnely that I wasn't being a prick, I offered to go 50/50 with him on whatever other supplies of value that I managed to get my hands on, when I picked up stolen Army flour. After we did a few small deals together, he pressed me again about coming in with me on my bakery racket. Once again I turned him down, only this time I explained, that if he could have his gambling operation on the side, why couldn't I keep my bread racket for myself, without taking him in as a partner? Even though he said that I was right, I know for a fact that he was pissed."

"How do you know that?" asked Sergeant Blair.

After taking a quick sip of water, Private Fishman continued and said. "Because from that moment on Donnely referred to me as his Jew accountant. I also knew I had to move on, when one of the other AWOL G.I.s who worked for Donnely warned me that I better watch my back. According to this guy, Donnely told him and his other pals to give me the cold shoulder, because my days were numbered."

When Captain Lorenz said that they would need to talk to this AWOL soldier, Private Fishman wasted no time in saying, "As far as I know, Sir, Private Jimmy Burns turned himself in during the Kraut breakthrough in the Ardennes. Burnsy decided to do so, when he heard the Army was dropping desertion charges on any personnel who volunteered to return to a combat unit. The last time I saw Burnsy, was the day he turned himself into the MPs. If he's still alive, I'm sure he'll be happy to talk to you, Sir."

Once again the prisoner took a sip of water before he continued and said, "I can also tell you that Crazy Kevin wasn't very happy, when he read the note that Burnsy left, that thanked Donnely for taking him in and explained why he was leaving. You also need to know, Sir, that it was Private Burns, who told me that Donnely and his men were heavily involved in stealing Army supplies from the train shipments that traveled through Paris."

When Captain Lorenz asked if Burns knew about those thefts, because he was involved in those crimes, Private Fishman sounded like he was defending a friend when he said, "No, Sir. Burnsy came to work for Donnely after I did, which was after Donnely, Chiperelli, Peterson and Baliniski stopped robbing supply trains. In fact, if it wasn't for Burnsy, I would'a never found out about this."

"You have me sitting at the edge of my seat, Private," remarked Captain Lorenz, who went on to ask their prisoner how Private Burns came to know this information.

The more he talked, the more that Private Fishman proved his usefulness as a witness, especially when he answered the Captain's question and added some personal insight to his response. "Chiperelli told him, Sir. According to Burnsy, Chiperelli was drunk at the time and was bragging how thanks to the way his idol Kevin Donnely operated, they were the only gang of G.I.s who were never arrested for stealing tons of cigarettes, rations and other government property from the supply trains that passed through Paris. Later on that night, a very nervous Stan Balinski told Burnsy to forget what he heard and never let Donnely know that Chiperelli slipped up and mentioned their escapades in the rail yards. Burnsy was also told not to say anything about this to me."

Then, after pausing for a split second, Fishman added, "You and Sergeant Blair are the experts, Sir, but if you ask me, Stan Baliniski is the weak link in the chain so to speak. He's the one you and the sergeant want'a put the squeeze on, because he's Donnely's lacky and knows everything. Even though he's like the rest of them and carries a gun, it's all an act, because deep down inside Balliniski is a nervous wreck."

While Hank Blair continued to take notes, Captain Lorenz said, "It would help a great deal, if you could tell us everything that you know about Private Burns, because the more we know, the faster we can track him down.

"I'll tell you everything I know, Sir," responded Private Fishman, who went on to say, "Private Jimmy Burns is a 20 year old combat engineer from Idaho. Based on what he told me, he went AWOL after his best friend stepped on one of those Kraut mines made of wood, on a road that Jimmy and his buddy just cleared. After his buddy had his left foot blown off, Burnsy blamed himself for what happened to his friend and was sent to an aid station in the rear for a few days. As soon as they cleaned him up, gave him a new uniform, some hot chow, he stole a Jeep and headed to Paris. Burnsy used the money he made from selling the five gallons of gas in the fuel can that came with the Jeep, to survive for a few days in Paris.

Rather than get into any more trouble than he was already in, he asked a Chaplain that he met on the streets of Paris, to return the stolen Jeep to his unit for him. Burnsy got recruited to join Donnely's gang, when he ran into Vinny Chiperelli, while he was making a delivery to one of their French customers."

"We covered a lot today. Is there anything else you can add, before we let you get some rest?" asked Captain Lorenz.

"Yes, Sir, there is," responded Private Fishman, who continued without prompting and said, "One of Donnely's best customers at his gambling operation was a Corporal by the name of Tommy Callaghan. Callaghan is stationed right here in Paris and is assigned to COMZ Services of Supply. I don't know the whole story, but after Callaghan lost his shirt gambling at Donnely's place, he went to work for Donnely as a way to pay him back. I also know that Donnely was planning to move his gambling operation to a new location. It used to be in an apartment in the Latin Quarter. I wish I could tell you where it is now, but we parted company before Donnely found a new place to move his gambling den. They also moved their black market operation as well."

"When Hank Blair refilled the prisoner's glass with water, AWOL Private Fishman paused to take a sip before he looked at Captain Lorenz and said, "Like I said, before, Sir. Donnely and his men are always armed. This is strictly my opinion, Captain, but the ones that I would be the most concerned about are Donnely and Chiperelli. Even though Jessie Peterson has more balls than Baliniski, he's a follower, not a fighter."

As soon as Captain Lorenz picked up his Army Officer's Trench Coat and put it over his left arm, he looked at the prisoner and said, "You did good, Private. We'll see you tomorrow. Get some rest."

Immediately after Captain Lorenz passed Hank Blair his coat, the Sergeant from CID tossed a pack of Camel cigarettes on the bed and said, "Can I bring you anything else besides more smokes?"

As Private Fishman retrieved the pack of premium brand cigarettes, he joked, "How 'bout a full pardon?"

While Hank Blair held the door to the hospital room open, Captain Lorenz cracked a smile then said, "We'll see you tomorrow, Private."

As soon as they returned to the office, Captain Lorenz and Sergeant Blair briefed their Commanding Officer and Lieutenant Al Parker about the information that was provided by Private Fishman. Because Jim knew that his men were experienced criminal investigators, he had no intentions of dictating how they should proceed. Instead, he turned to Captain Lorenz and said, "How do you and Hank want to handle this, now that we know more about AWOL Sergeant Donnely and his fellow deserters?"

Captain Lorenz didn't need time to think in order to respond and make sense at the same time. He proved that he was an accomplished CID Agent, when he responded in a very confident tone of voice and said, "With your permission, Sir, I'd like to have Ange and Sal work with me and Hank, along with Al and some of the Chief Inspector's men, to locate and follow Donnely and his fellow deserters. Once we find Donnely's black market operation and his gambling den, we can bring in more men as required."

"If need help don't hesitate to call, The Major and I are always available," said Jim.

Immediately after Captain Lorenz thanked his commanding officer, Jim remarked, "We also need to find Private Burns and learn more about the supply clerk who is indebted to AWOL Sergeant Donnely."

"Once we locate Private Burns, we'll pick up Corporal Callaghan and have a long talk with the young man from the Services of Supply," responded the Captain.

As soon as Captain Lorenz finished speaking, Jim added, "After hearing what Private Fishman had to say about Donnely's ability to send money home, we'll definitely need to work this case from both sides of the Atlantic." After turning to face Al Parker, Jim seemed to be in exceptionally good spirits when he added, "Now that we have some worthwhile leads to follow, our distinguished representative from the New York City Police Department, who is serving our country in time of war as a CID Agent, can pass this new information on to Colonel Richmond."

After Al grinned, he offered Jim a casual salute and said, "I'll have that cable ready to go out within the hour."

"Thanks, Al," responded Jim.

With nothing else left to discuss at this time, Captain Lorenz and Hank Blair stood up in preparation of getting back to work. As soon as they did so, Captain Lorenz addressed their commanding officer one more time before they left his office. "Hank and I will get back out in the field, Sir, as soon as we locate the personnel file for Private Burns and update the case file."

While Jim remained seated, he responded as he removed a cigarette from the pack that was on his desk, "Good work, men. Carry on."

As soon Captain Lorenz and Hank Blair left the Colonel's spacious office, Al Parker spoke as he stood up and faced Jim. "I'd give a months pay to see the look on everyone's face back in New York, when they receive our request for assistance, especially when Frank Angelone and Joe Coppola hear that their sons are working on this investigation."

After lighting his Lucky Strike cigarette, Jim looked at Al then said, "I miss those guys, Al. We did good work together."

"Yes we did," responded Al Parker, who continued as he walked out of the Colonel's corner office. "I'll call Francois and let him know what's new on our end."

"Thanks, Al," said Jim, before he took a drag on his cigarette and exhaled, while he thought about the time he spent working with the CID Task Force in New York City. Thanks to the combined efforts of a number of talented criminal investigators, Jim and Al were able to pursue Ivan Larson and Francis Shorty Mc Ghee all the way to the front lines, during the now famous Battle of the Bulge. After taking another drag on his Lucky Strike, Jim remarked, "Those were the days."

It took one phone call for Hank Blair to confirm that Private James Burns from Boise, Idaho was killed in action in early January of 1945. Despite this setback, it took less than three days for teams of U.S. Army CID Agents and Paris Police Investigators to locate AWOL Sergeant Kevin Donnely, AWOL Corporal Jessie Peterson, AWOL Private Vincent Chiperelli and AWOL Private Stanislaus Balinski. This was accomplished by locating and following the four French women who were living with the four American deserters. Once again, Chief Inspector Dumont and his men proved to a most capable group of criminal investigators, when they assisted CID in locating these young women, even though they recently moved from their previous known addresses. The first break in this aspect of the case was achieved, when Donnely's Parisian girlfriend was followed, after she was observed visiting her parents. Having her jealous ex boyfriend agree to work with Army CID and the Chief Inspector's men, insured the success of this surveillance effort.

Once Donnely and the four men who were closest to him were finally located, they were followed to the commercial building, that was used to house their black market operation. Later that night, Al Parker and his team that consisted of Sergeant Angelone, Sergeant Coppola and two French Police Inspectors followed AWOL Sergeant Donnely and his girlfriend to an apartment building in the Les Halles District of the 1st Arrondisement of Paris. A few minutes later, AWOL Corporal Jessie Peterson and AWOL Private Vincent Chiperelli were followed by other CID Agents and Paris Police Investigators to the same apartment building. Once a number of American soldiers began entering the same building, Lieutenant Parker and his men were convinced that they located Donnely's gambling operation.

After observing this building for several hours, Al Parker directed a team of CID Agents to follow some of the American servicemen who were observed leaving the apartment building. This was done, to determine where these men were billeted, so they could be identified. Al also instructed these agents to use their discretion and have some of the soldiers who left Donnely's gambling den stopped for a routine check by the military police. When Al Parker relayed these instructions to his men, he emphasized the need to wait until these troops got some distance away from the location that was under surveillance. Doing so, enabled Al and his men to fully identify some of the American servicemen who were associated with Kevin Donnely, without making anyone suspicious.

When Hank Blair entered the Paris CID Office he made a bee line for Lieutenant Al Parker's office. Just as he arrived, Lieutenant Parker received a phone call from Chief Inspector Dumont. While Al listened to the Chief Inspector, he motioned Hank to come in. As soon as the young CID Agent did so, he seemed to be in exceptionally good spirits, when he pointed to the file that he had in his right hand, before he handed the file to the Lieutenant.

The moment Al opened the file and read the contents, he looked up at Hank and smiled before he turned his attention to the phone call that he was having with the Chief Inspector. After waiting for the Chief Inspector to brief him about what was happening in the field, Al spoke up and said, "Hank just brought us some good news, Francois."

While Al continued, he reviewed the copy of the affidavit and said, "It looks like Private Fishman is telling the truth, about Donnely making it possible for him to send a Postal Money Order to his folks. According to the paperwork that Hank found, a Sergeant by the name of Lawrence Gaddison signed the affidavit on Monday January 15th, 1945." This proves that Sergeant Gaddison was the soldier that Donnely used to send money home to Fishman's folks."

After listening to the Chief Inspector, Al responded and said, "You're right, Francois. Not only does this corroborate Fishman's story and makes him a more credible witness, but it gives us another lead to follow, to learn how a deserter like Donnely was able to send money back to home."

As Al handed the file back to Hank, he continued speaking into the phone and said, "That's correct, Francois. Once we find out where this G.I. is stationed, we'll meet you in the field."

After reviewing the file that Hank Blair located, Jim Beauregard remarked, "Excellent work, Hank."

As soon as Hank thanked the Colonel, Jim tapped the ash from his cigarette into the ashtray on his desk, as he continued addressing Major Savino, Captain Lorenz, Al Parker and Hank Blair. "Once we locate Sergeant Gaddison, I want Hank and Chris to pick him up and bring him back here, no matter how important he is to the war effort. As it stands right now, this soldier is under investigation for being part of a scheme to send money home for a deserter. Even if Sergeant Gaddison thinks he was doing a fellow soldier a favor, he's still in trouble and will have to face the music."

When Jim continued, he looked directly at Al Parker. "While Hank and Chris go after Sergeant Gaddison, Ange and Sal will continue to serve as co case agents, to help you keep an eye on Donnely and his gambling operation."

Jim then faced Captain Lorenz and said, "I'll also assign Mike Mulligan to give you and Sam a hand, while you keep an eye on Donnely's black market operation."

After taking a drag on his cigarette, Jim finished laying out his investigative strategy by saying, "Private Fishman also has to give us a lot more details about any AWOL Army personnel and local thieves that he's been doing business with. I know we've been swamped with work, but we need to send some of our agents over to Fishman's office to pick up any books, notes, or records that can help us make a case against his customers. Bill Hayes and Joshua Fermi can handle that assignment, along with one of the Chief Inspector's men."

Without hesitating Captain Lorenz remarked, "I'll tell Bill and Josh to tear Fishman's apartment and his office apart today, Sir. I also ask the Chief Inspector to send one of his men with our agents."

"Excellent," responded Jim Beauregard, before he looked directly at Al Parker and said, "You better draft another cable to New York, Al and let Colonel Richmond and Captain Murphy know about this new lead."

As soon as Al responded and said, "I'll get on it right away, Sir," Jim looked up at his subordinates and added, "This is one hell of an interesting case."

CHAPTER 16

WE GO WHERE THE LEADS TAKE US

W hile the surveillance teams were busy keeping an eye on Kevin Donnely and his associates in Paris, Hank Blair and Chris Jacko were flown to an improvised landing strip in a forward area, where the 9th Armored Division and the 27th Armored Infantry Battalion were staging, before these units advanced further into Germany. After disembarking the aircraft, the two CID Agents were transported in a Military Police Jeep to the 9th Armored Division Headquarters in Meckenheim, Germany at 1415 hours on Wednesday, March 7, 1945.[15]

After meeting with the commanding officer of military police at the 9th Armored Division Headquarters, Sergeants Blair and Jacko were told that Sergeant Lawrence Gaddison was part of the advance column, that left at 0820 hours earlier that day, to scout the bridge crossing at Remagen.[16] (*17) In an effort to catch up with this column, Sergeant Blair and Sergeant Jacko were given a Jeep and pointed in the right direction.

As they drove away from the temporary headquarters of the 9th Armored Division, Sergeant Blair checked his watch, before he turned to his partner and said, "If we don't get Gaddison before he crosses that bridge, we'll be the first CID Agents to cross the Rhine."

"I always wanted to make history," responded Chris as he drove the borrowed Jeep at flank speed toward the town of Remagen.

By the time Sergeant Lawrence Gaddison jumped out of the truck, that transported him and the other members of his squad to the assembly area, a handful of M26 Pershing Tanks and a dozen M4 Sherman tanks were getting into position along the Rhine River. While Sergeant Gaddison and his men made their way through Remagen, their armored support from the 9th Armored Division began bombarding the German troops, who were defending the Ludendorff Bridge Rhine River crossing.[17]

When the German attempt to destroy the bridge failed, for reasons that were credited to faulty explosives and the possibility that demolition equipment was damaged by enemy fire, a lead element from Company A of the 27th Armored Infantry Battalion (AIB) advanced onto the bridge. Even though they came under under intense enemy fire, from the German positions on the other side of the Rhine, the American troops made a mad dash across the bridge. In between returning fire, the American troops did their best to destroy as much of the demolition equipment that they could find, while they made their way to the other side of the bridge.[18]

After parking the borrowed Jeep with a detail of MPs from the 9th Armored Division, Hank Blair and Chris Jacko were told that three platoons of men from the 27th Armored Infantry Battalion were in the process of crossing the Ludendorff Bridge. By the time the two CID Agents made their way to the entrance of the bridge, they met a Lieutenant who was leading men from the 3rd platoon over the bridge. According to this Lieutenant, Sergeant Lawrence Gaddison was in A Company's 2nd Platoon. [19] Once they confirmed that the soldier they needed to take into custody was in front of their position, the two CID Agents knew exactly what needed to be done to complete their assignment.

"You ready to make history?" asked Hank.

While Chris Jacko racked a round into the chamber of his M1 Carbine, the CID Agent who served with Hank Blair during the pursuit of Ivan Larson and Shorty Mc Ghee remarked, "Absolutely."

After making their way across the Ludendorff Bridgem with A Company's 3rd platoon, Hank Blair and Chris Jacko asked to meet with the ranking officer in charge of the lead elements of the 27th Armored Infantry Battalion. As soon as the two CID Agents met this commissioned officer, they produced their CID badges and identification and explained the purpose of their mission.

Immediately after Hank Blair slipped his credentials into his right side pant's pocket, he handed a copy of their orders to the Lieutenant, while he provided some additional details to the commissioned officer. "As you can see, Sir, we have orders to take Sergeant Lawrence Gaddison into custody and transport him back to Paris. He's being charged with the illegal transfer of money to the states, for an AWOL Non Commissioned Officer. In addition to being involved in the black market, the deserter who Sergeant Gaddison assisted, is also wanted for the unauthorized possession of firearms and attempted murder."

"These are serious charges," remarked the Army Officer.

"Yes, Sir, they are," responded Hank Blair, who quickly added, "Even if Sergeant Gaddison thought he was doing a fellow soldier a favor and he had no idea that he was helping a deserter, who was involved in all kinds of criminal activity, he's still in trouble, Sir."

After handing their orders back to the two men from CID, the Lieutenant in charge of the three platoons from the 27th Armored Infantry Battalion spoke up and said, "My problem, is that my men and I, are the only American troops holding a position on the east side of the Ludendorf Bridge, which happens to be the only bridge that's still standing on the Rhine River. The fact that we're shorthanded, means I can't afford to lose anyone, especially an experienced soldier like Sergeant Gaddison." Then, after pausing for a split second, the Lieutenant continued and said, "If you can wait a bit to make your arrest, the situation should improve, once the 9th Armored Division can get some of their Shermans across the Ludendorff Bridge."

"I'm sorry, Sir, but we have orders to arrest Sergeant Gaddison," responded Hank Blair.

While the Lieutenant from the 27th AIB paused to light a cigarette, Chris Jacko spoke up and said, "If you're shorthanded, Sir, I'll take Sergeant Gaddison's place on the line."

As soon as the Army Officer looked at Chris Jacko and asked if he had any combat experience, the former MP, who was recruited into CID by Jim Beauregard, responded with confidence and said, "Yes, Sir, I do."

"Count me in as well, Sir," added Hank Blair.

After hearing the two CID Agents offer to take their prisoner's place on the frontline, the surprised Army Officer remarked, "So what you're telling me, is that if I take Sergeant Gaddison off the line and place him under arrest, the two of you will give us a hand until reinforcements arrive?"

"Yes, Sir," responded the two CID Agents in unison.

"And you both have combat experience?" asked the Army Officer.

Once again, the two CID Agents responded in the affirmative.

"OK, you got a deal," said the Army Officer, who quickly added, "I'll have Sergeant Gaddison disarmed and put in the safest place possible on this side of the Rhine, while you gentlemen will be put to good use killing Germans."

As soon as Hank Blair and Chris Jacko thanked the commissioned officer, the young Lieutenant removed the M1 Carbine from his shoulder and said, "Follow me,"

Even though over two months had passed since Hank Blair and Chris Jacko were in combat, they had no trouble adjusting to the sights, sounds and smells that were associated with being in a close quarters battle situation. The only difference was, this time they would be involved in a night action.

After being assigned to a rifle squad, that was holding a position on the south side of the thinly held American perimeter, Chris Jacko and Hank Blair wished they brought more ammunition and a few hand-grenades along. Regardless, the two former military policemen who were now serving as CID Agents, settled into their fighting position, next to a seasoned veteran who was no stranger to ground combat in the ETO.

"I didn't know they were bringing replacements up to the line," remarked the 28 year old squad leader from Kansas as he placed two grenades on top of their fighting position.

While doing his best to sound as friendly as possible, Chris Jacko responded and said, "We're not replacements, Sarge."

After hearing Chris Jacko's response, the seasoned squad leader looked at the two strangers and said, "If you're not replacements and you're not engineers, who the hell are you?"

"We're CID Agents from Paris," said Hank Blair.

"CID! What the hell are you guys doing up on the line?," asked the squad leader, before he added, "Didn't anyone tell you that we're in the middle of a battle?"

"What can I tell you, Sarge. We go where the leads take us," responded Chris Jacko.

A split second later, the Germans opened fire and began aggressively advancing toward the positions that were being held by the two CID Agents and the soldiers from the 27th Armored Infantry Battalion. After firing fifteen rounds of .30 caliber ammunition at the enemy, Chris Jacko handed his reloaded M1 Carbine to Hank Blair and said, "Use this while I get something a little bigger to shoot with."

No sooner did Hank call out, "Where the hell are you going, Chris?," Sergeant Jacko was scurrying off in a low crouch with his .45 caliber pistol in hand, as he left their fighting position in search of a more powerful weapon. While Hank Blair and the Squad Leader that he was fighting next to, continued to engage the enemy, Chris Jacko stopped to help a wounded G.I. who was hit in the right hand. After telling the young private that he would be OK and that he got himself a "million dollar" wound, Chris used his teeth to rip open a packet of sulfur powder, so he could sprinkle the medication on the soldier's wounded hand. After calling for a medic, Chris placed a clean bandage on the private's wound while he said, "You mind if I borrow your M1?"

"Be my guest," responded the G.I. as a medic arrived to take care of the wounded soldier.

Once Chris relieved the wounded soldier of his rifle and two bandoleers of ammunition, he made his way back to where Hank Blair was located. As soon as Chris arrived, he loaded a fresh eight round clip into the M1 Garand while he called out, "Sorry I'm late, but I had to patch up a wounded G.I., who had no use for his rifle and ammo after he got shot in the hand."

"Better late than never," responded Hank, while he reloaded one of the M1 Carbines and Chris began picking off German Army Engineers who were trying to overrun their position. The second Chris got up in a slight crouch and emptied his rifle into a German soldier, who was about to toss a grenade at another group of American soldiers, an enemy bullet grazed his right arm above the elbow.

The second the bullet scraped along the outer layer of skin on his right arm, Chris felt as if he was stung by a giant Wasp. While Chris called out, "Son of a bitch," and he fell back down behind cover to examine his wound, Hank stopped shooting and called out, "Are you alright?"

"I'm fine. It's just a scratch," responded Chris as he ignored the pain and inserted another eight round clip of ammunition into the M1 Garand Rifle that he borrowed from a wounded G.I.

Just about the time that Chris, Hank and the squad leader they were fighting alongside were halfway through their supply of ammunition, the surviving Germans stopped counter attacking the well entrenched Americans, who were determined to hold onto their positions on the east side of the Luderdorff Bridge, in the village of Erpel, Germany.[20]

Once the coast was clear, Chris and Hank said goodbye to the soldiers they were fighting with, before they returned to their original mission. As soon as they met the Lieutenant from the 27th AIB, and this Army Officer saw Chris Jacko holding his bandaged right arm across his chest, the Lieutenant remarked, "I see you got clipped."

"It's just a scratch, Sir," responded Chris.

After nodding his head ever so slightly, the Lieutenant called a medic over to examine Sergeant Jacko's wounded arm before he went on to say, "Once you get patched up, I'll call the engineers and have them take you, your partner and your prisoner to the other side of the Rhine by boat."

While the Army medic removed the bloody bandage from Chris Jacko's arm, the two CID Agents thanked the Lieutenant as he walked away to check on the rest of his men.

One of the best presents that Captain Pat Murphy Sr. received on his birthday, was a letter from Al Parker and a copy of the cable from the Paris CID Office, that was forwarded to him from Colonel Richmond. After reading Al's letter, Captain Murphy reviewed the official request to provide investigative support to the Paris CID Office, on an investigation that involved the shooting of an AWOL soldier, by a group of AWOL G.I.s who were competitors on the black market. Included in this cable was a message, that notified Detective Frank Angelone and U.S. Customs Agent Joe Coppola that Sergeant Anthony Angelone and Sergeant Sal Coppola were co-case agents on this investigation.

As soon as Captain Murphy left his office in the Chief of Detectives Office, he walked over to the two desks that were facing each other in the back of the squad room. While Captain Murphy held the cable traffic up in front of his chest, he called out, "The boys in Paris need our help."

"What's up, Captain," asked Detective Johnny Mc Donald.

While standing in between the two desks, Captain Murphy wasted no time in briefing his two favorite detectives on the job. "Jim and Al are looking for an AWOL Irish Mic from Brooklyn by the name of Kevin Donnely. Sergeant Donnely is a deserter who likes to fight and shoot his own people. After he went AWOL last year, Donnely started stealing Army supplies and got involved in the black market. This character also runs a gambling operation in Paris. Jim and his men are also investigating this AWOL Sergeant for sending money home to his family through nefarious means. Needless to say, deserters don't get to send money back to the states and that includes deserters who are making money on the black market."

Before he walked away, Captain Murphy handed the cable traffic to Frank Angelone and said, "Oh, there's one more thing. It seems that a young Army Sergeant by the name of Anthony Angelone, is one of the co-case agents assigned to this investigation, along with another young lad by the name of Sergeant Salvatore Coppola."

As Detective Frank Angelone held up the cable traffic, the proud father smiled wide as he looked at his partner and said, "Check it out, Johnny. Little Anthony is working this case with Joe Coppola's kid."

After shaking his head, Johnny remarked, "Just think. I used to bounce Anthony on my knee and now he's running around Paris chasing deserters and crooks for the Army, while armed with a forty five."

When Frank handed the cable traffic back to his boss, Captain Murphy said, "Call our favorite Customs Agent and see if he wants to tag along. Tell him I said that we always have room in the Chief of Detectives Office for another proud father. You might also give our favorite FBI Agent a call as well. In fact, let's make this a real reunion and tell Jack Donovan that we need the services of a Post Office Inspector, to check the mail that's going to

Sergeant Donnely's family members."

By the time the Captain started to walk away, an anxious Frank Angelone had the phone in his left hand and was dialing a number while he remarked, "Why don't you call Andy and Jack, while I call Joe Coppola. Then, I'll call the wife to give her the good news."

"Lord help, me. I'm working with two proud fathers," remarked Johnny, who paused for a second before he added, "This should be fun."

After fighting alongside the men from the 27th AIB, to repel a counter-attack by several hundred German Army Engineers and Luftwaffe troops, Hank Blair, Chris Jacko and Sergeant Lawrence Gaddison had some hot coffee, while they waited to be taken across the Rhine. The decision to cross the river by boat was made, because the Ludendorff Bridge was still being repaired. While the American engineers worked on the bridge, nine Sherman tanks crossed the Rhine to reinforce the newly established bridge-head in Germany.[21]

Once a small boat that was operated by a U.S. Army Combat Engineer arrived to pick up his passengers, the Lieutenant from the 27th Armored Infantry Battalion thanked the two CID Agents, for lending a hand during the German counterattack. As soon as the Lieutenant saw Chris Jacko winch in pain, as he stepped into the small boat, the young Army Officer remarked, "Take care of that arm, Sergeant."

While Chris Jacko held onto his bandaged arm, the CID Agent who sustained a grazing wound while fighting alongside the Lieutenant's men responded and said, "I will, Lieutenant."

The Lieutenant then turned to Sergeant Gaddison and spoke as he extended his hand, "Good luck, Larry. And don't worry. The CO's a man of his word. If he said he'll do what he can to help you out, I guarantee he'll do just that."

While it didn't seem like a big deal at the time, once Sergeant Gaddison was confronted by the pair of CID Agents, he knew that he screwed up, by helping an Army Sergeant by the name of Kevin Donnely send money home to the states. The fact that Sergeant Gaddison helped someone who turned out to be a deserter, who was heavily involved in the black market, made the him feel twice as bad and equally as guilty.

While shaking the Lieutenant's hand, Sergeant Gaddison sounded like a man who appreciated any support that he received from his command staff when he said, "Thanks, Lieutenant and thank the CO again for me, 'cause I'm gonna need all the help I can get."

As soon as Hank Blair remarked, "Good luck, Lieutenant," the two CID Agents and their prisoner were transported across the Rhine River, at a little after midnight on March 8, 1945. After being transported to the west side of the river, the two CID Agents and their prisoner were taken to a nearby open pasture, where they camped out with the staff from a field hospital, until they boarded a C47 that took them to Paris in the morning.

At 1350 hours Hank Blair, Chris Jacko and Sergeant Gaddison returned to Paris. The moment the three men entered the CID office, it was easy to see by their appearance that they were just back from the frontlines. As soon as Major Savino approached the two agents and their prisoner, Chris Jacko grimaced in pain when he joined Hank and Sergeant Gaddison in saluting the superior officer.

While Major Savino returned the salute, Hank Blair remarked, "Mission accomplished, Sir," before he turned their prisoner and said, "Sergeant Gaddison, this is Major Savino, our executive officer at CID."

As the Major faced the prisoner, he sounded sincere when he said, "Welcome to Paris, Sergeant. I wish it was other under circumstances."

"Me too, Sir," responded Sergeant Gaddison.

While Major Savino sized up his men, he continued and said, "You boys look like you've been though the mill, especially you, Chris. Where'd you get the Purple Heart?"

"On the other side of the Rhine River, Sir," responded the young CID Agent.

Just as they expected, Major Savino sounded surprised to hear that two of his men went deeper into Germany than expected to locate Sergeant Gaddison. "You crossed the Rhine River in the middle of a battle in order to make an arrest?"

This time Hank Blair responded to the Major's comment. "We had no choice, Sir. By the time we got to Meckenheim, three platoons from the 27th

Armored Infantry Battalion had already left for the town of Remagen to scout the area along the Rhine River. Once we got to Remagen, Sergeant Gaddison and his men were already across the Ludendorff Bridge. In fact, Sir, thanks to Sergeant Gaddison and the other men from the 27th Armored Infantry Battalion and the 9th Armored Division, we now have a foothold on the other side of the Rhine."

As soon as Hank finished briefing the Major, Chris Jacko spoke up and said, "Sergeant Gaddison has been fully cooperative, Sir and he's willing to help us make a case against AWOL Sergeant Donnely."

"I'm glad to hear that," said Major Savino before he added, "After you get yourselves cleaned up and grab some chow, we'll talk about how we're gonna make a case against AWOL Sergeant Kevin Donnely and his associates." The Major then turned to Agent Jacko and said, "But not before Chris gets his arm checked out at the hospital."

After several days of working around the clock, teams of CID Agents and Paris Police Investigators were following every move that was made by AWOL Sergeant Donnely, his band of deserters and their French girlfriends. This included observing every delivery that was made into and out of the commercial property, that was used by Donnely's black market operation. Once again, it paid to have investigators from the Paris Police along, when teams of CID agents followed Donnely's fleet of delivery vehicles to various locations in the Montaparnesse arrondisement of Paris.

At this point of the investigation, the decision was made to have Captain Lorenz and Hank Blair pick up Corporal Thomas Callaghan, after the young supply clerk got off duty and was on his way to have supper. As soon as Captain Lorenz and Sergeant Blair identified themselves, they advised the young supply clerk that he was being taken into custody for questioning, in regards to an investigation that CID was conducting.

When Corporal Callaghan's initial reaction, was to deny that he had any involvement in any criminal activity and he was told that the matter involved the illegal transfer of money to the United States, Callaghan reacted by saying, "But I was only doing a favor for a fellow G.I., Sir." Between this admission of guilt and the sworn statements that were made by Private Fishman and Sergeant Gaddison, Captain Lorenz turned to Agent Blair and said, "Standby to handcuff Corporal Callaghan."

While Agent Blair removed the handcuffs from his belt, it was clear by the expression on Corporal Callaghan's face, that he understood the seriousness of the situation. Because CID was anxious to gain the Corporal's cooperation, the decision was made to offer the supply clerk the option of becoming a cooperating witness, instead of an incarcerated defendant.

As soon as Jim Beauregard entered the interrogation room, he displayed the official demeanor of a Lieutenant Colonel in charge of CID. While playing his part as the lead case agent, Captain Lorenz wasted no time in reporting, that Corporal Callaghan is one of the soldiers who was involved in the illegal transfer of money to the states, for a Sergeant by the name of Kevin Donnely.

While Jim looked down at the supply clerk, who was two seconds away from being formally charged, he addressed the corporal in a businesslike tone of voice. "You're in a lotta trouble, Corporal. In fact, this is your time to come to Jesus, or forever hold your peace. However, bear in mind that you're under no obligation to give us a statement until you are formally charged. If you wish to be formally charged, Captain Lorenz will be happy to do so at this time. If you elect to cooperate and you corroborate some of the things that we already know and if you assist us further in our investigation, CID will consider you a valuable witness. However, even if you cooperate, you will still have to face disciplinary action, for any misdeeds that you've done. That said, cooperating with CID will certainly mitigate whatever comes your way, in the way of disciplinary action. Do I make myself clear?"

Both Jim Beauregard and Don Lorenz had been cops long enough to know, when someone they were interrogating was uncomfortable about being questioned. When Corporal Callaghan asked what it would take for him to "get off the hook," Jim Beauregard spoke up and said, "Let me put it to you this way, Corporal. Once we arrest Sergeant Donnely and the other members of his gang, whoever is smart enough to cooperate first, will likely get the best deal." Then, after pausing for a split second, Jim added, "I should also let you know, that we already have two soldiers in custody who are cooperating, so if you choose to help us, now would be a good time to do so. Your other option is to ask for an Army lawyer and take your chances in court. It's your call."

After hearing what the Colonel from CID had to say, Corporal Callaghan got a bit excited and did his best to sound as convincing as possible when he said, "When it comes to Donnely's gambling operation no one knows more than I do, Sir."

"Can you prove that?" asked Captain Lorenz.

"Ask away, Sir, and I'll tell you the whole set up," responded the Corporal from the Services of Supply.

As Captain Lorenz opened his note book and prepared to take notes, he began by asking some basic questions. While answering these questions, Corporal Callaghan identified everyone involved in Donnely's gambling operation and explained how he helped Donnely recruit customers. He also identified the prostitutes who work for Donnely and entertain some of his best customers."

After asking a few more questions and getting what sounded like honest answers, Captain Lorenz asked the Corporal if he knew what unit Kevin Donnely was assigned to. Without hesitating, Corporal Callaghan responded and said, "Sergeant Donnely said that he and his men are assigned to a maintenance unit for one of the transportation companies."

Because Captain Lorenz and his Commanding Officer wanted to know everything possible about AWOL Sergeant Donnely and the other members of his gang, the Captain encouraged the young supply clerk to continue when he said, "Go on, Corporal?"

Once again, Corporal Callaghan sounded like he was telling the truth, as he knew it, when he said, "Sergeant Donnely and his men sounded like they were kept real busy keeping Army cargo trucks on the road, Sir."

"What makes you say that?" asked Captain Lorenz.

"Because they knew the locations of every supply dump and POL dump in and around Paris, Sir" responded the supply clerk who quickly added, "Donnely and his men were also very familiar with the routes that were used by the Red Ball Express and every other transportation outfit that hauls supplies through France. Whenever they were off duty, they'd show up and move back in with their French girlfriends. Two of Sergeant Donnely's men even stopped by a cafe where we were having a drink, with a truck that they fixed that broke down on the road. Donnely even told me stories about how he and his men had to recover Army trucks that were loaded with ammo and gasoline, while they were being shelled by the Krauts, after they landed in Normandy."

When Jim walked around to the other side of the table, he looked at Captain Lorenz and said, "Excuse me, Captain, but I have a few questions that I'd like to ask the Corporal."

As soon as Don Lorenz said, "The Corporal is all yours, Colonel," Jim sat next to the Captain and removed a pack of cigarettes and a lighter from his pocket. After offering a cigarette to the Corporal, who respectfully declined and said, "Thank you, Sir, but I don't smoke," Jim used his Zippo to light a Lucky Strike.

As Jim snapped the lighter closed, he looked directly at Corporal Callaghan and said, "I was wondering if you knew how much Sergeant Donnely and his men made from running a gambling operation in Paris?"

Once again the Corporal responded to a question like someone who was telling the truth. "They seem to be doing pretty good, Sir."

"How so," asked Jim.

"Like I said before, Sir. They live with these real pretty French girls and are always picking up the tab," said the Corporal, who quickly added, "They even had real expensive suits made and told me that they're all thinking of living in Paris after the war."

While Jim took a drag on his cigarette, he figured it was time to move this conversation along after he exhaled and said, "I'm still curious about the money that Donnely and his men must be making, given the popularity of his gambling operation. After all, even CID has better things to do than go after soldiers who gamble. If we did, half the Army would be in the stockade, including some of my own men."

"I know what you mean, Sir," said Callaghan, who went on to say, "And you're right about the Army not caring about men who make money gambling. As you know, Sir, a soldier can even send money home to his family, that he made from playing cards or shooting craps. That's why I didn't think it was a big deal, to help Sergeant Donnely and some of his men send their winnings back to the states."

There came a time in every interrogation, when the investigators involved asked the right question at the right time, knowing that there could only be one truthful response. After taking another drag on his cigarette, Jim looked at the subject under investigation and said, "Tell me, Corporal, if the Army has no problem with men gambling and if the Army allows men to send the money they earn from gambling back home, why would Sergeant Donnely, or any of his fellow soldiers, need help from you or anyone else, to sign the affidavit that goes with the transfer of funds, for a Postal Money Order or a War Bond?"

Whether Corporal Callaghan was a naïve kid, he wasn't all that bright, or he failed to see the implications of his actions, until this question was posed to him, he sounded like he was being truthful when he responded and said, "I never thought I was doing anything wrong, Sir. I just thought I was doing Sergeant Donnely a favor, because he was worried that the Army might not like the idea, that he was winning so much. The same went for some of the men in his unit."

In order to get Corporal Callaghan to be more specific, Jim looked across the table and said, "Is this something that you thought was the case, or is something that Donnely told you?"

"That's exactly what Donnely told me, Colonel. Stan Balinski and Vinny Chiperelli told me the same thing and were real appreciative that I helped them send some of their winnings back to the states," responded the Corporal.

After turning to Don Lorenz, the Commanding Officer of the Paris CID Office said, "Why don't you take it from here, Captain."

"Yes, Sir," responded Captain Lorenz, who continued questioning the Corporal by asking exactly how he helped Sergeant Donnely and any of his men send money home, if they weren't the ones who converted government script, or French Francs into dollars, that could then be transferred to the states in the form of a Postal Money Order or a War Bond.[22]

Now that Corporal Callaghan was committed to fully cooperating with CID, he wasted no time in saying, "The way it works, Sir, it this. Sergeant Donnely pays G.I.s who lose at cards or craps, a ten percent fee to send some of his money home for him. Since Donnely usually sends a grand home at a time, that means whoever signs for a Postal Money Order, or a War Bond can make a hundred bucks for doing him a favor. Stan Balinski and Vinny Chiperelli also paid the same percentage to send money home to the states." Then, after pausing for a split second, the Corporal continued and said, "To tell you the truth, Sir, I haven't met a guy yet who lost his shirt gambling, who refused a hundred bucks to send some cash home for another soldier. The same system was also used to send War Bonds home."

"I'm curious, Corporal, but why did you do this and what did you get out'a this?" asked the Captain.

"To tell you the truth, Sir, I ran up a bit of a gambling debt with Sergeant Donnely," responded the Corporal, who quickly added, "When I sent a money transfer back to the state for the sarge, I earned the same 10% as anyone else. In my case, the Sarge subtracted whatever I earned from what I owed him. When someone else sent money back to the states for Sergeant Donnely, my job was to make sure the deed was done. Once the transfer was made and the money was on its way to the states, I'd bring the receipt back to the Sarge. I also got paid a small commission for bringing customers to his card games and dice games."

After looking at his commanding officer, Captain Lorenz remarked, "Would you like to wrap this up, Sir?"

As soon as Jim said, "Thank you, Captain," he stamped his cigarette butt out in an ashtray as he looked at the young man they were questioning and said, "I have some really bad news for you, Corporal. Sergeant Kevin Donnely and his men are not assigned to a transportation company maintenance unit. They're deserters, who are wanted by CID for a lot more than being involved in the illegal transfer of money to the United States. AWOL Sergeant Kevin Donnely and his men are also wanted for being actively involved in the theft of government property and for selling stolen government property on the black market."

While Corporal Callaghan reacted as if he was genuinely surprised to hear what the Colonel from CID had to say, Jim continued as he stood up and towered over the prisoner. "To make matters worse, your friend Sergeant Donnely and his fellow deserters are also wanted, for attempting to murder an AWOL Private by the name of Jack Fishman. Does that name ring a bell?"

After swallowing the lump in his throat, Corporal Callaghan remarked, "I read that Fishman got shot, Sir, but I never thought that Sergeant Donnely or any of his men were involved. You got'a believe me, Colonel. As far as I knew, Donnley and his men were in a maintenance unit and ran a successful gambling racket on the side in their off duty hours. I swear on a stack of bibles, Sir, I didn't know anything about this other stuff."

When Jim continued, he sounded a lot more official when he remarked, "Be specific, Corporal. How many times did you or anyone else send money home for AWOL Sergeant Kevin Donnely or any of his associates?"

"I did it twice, Sir," responded the Corporal, who quickly added, "On three other occasions, I went with the G.I.s who got paid a hundred bucks to send Postal Money Orders and War Bonds home for Donnely, Chiperelli and Ballinski. I swear, Sir. That's all I know." Then, after pausing, the panic stricken Corporal went on to say, "I also have to tell you, Sir, that Donnely wants me to be available this week, to help him send some more cash home to his brother Shaun."

Immediately after Jim used his Zippo to light another cigarette, he remarked, "Sit tight, Corporal, while I discuss your situation with the Captain."

After making arrangements for Corporal Callaghan to be given some leave, Jim Beauregard had one of his agents stay with the young man on a 24 hour basis until his services were required. In the meantime, Jim sent a cable to New York with an update and asked Lt. Colonel Fred Richmond and Captain Patrick Murphy Sr. to stand by to raid any location where Donnely's next fraudulent payment is sent. While Jim was sending an updated report to the New York CID Office, Major Savino, Captain Lorenz, Lieutenant Al Parker and Chief Inspector Dumont had teams of men keeping an eye on every subject and location that was identified to date.

While Corporal Tommy Callaghan was in protective custody, he was being instructed how to act, when he met AWOL Sergeant Donnely and any of his men. After coaching Callaghan for several hours, the Corporal was ready to serve as an undercover operative for CID, if for no other reason than to save his own skin.

CHAPTER 17

THE WEDDING

After considering his options, Bill Hayes asked to speak to Major Savino. As uncomfortable as it was to have this conversation, Bill felt that he had no choice in the matter. "Thanks for seeing me, Sir," said Bill, after being invited to have a seat in front of the Major's desk.

"What can I do for you, Bill," asked Major Savino.

Rather than beat around the bush, Bill responded and explained how he volunteered to cover the duty for Hank Blair, so he could attend the wedding, but he was told that the Major arranged for MP Sergeant Steve Dalton to answer the phones in the office that night."

"That's correct," said Major Savino who quickly added, "If anything serious comes up, Sergeant Dalton will call The Paris Cafe, so we can dispatch the right number of agents into the field."

After pausing for a second before he continued, Bill did his best to sound as if he found no pleasure in having this discussion when he said, "I know Lieutenant Parker and his son Cal are very brave men, Sir. I also have the highest regard for Chief Inspector Dumont. That said, Sir, I just don't feel comfortable going to Cal's wedding. I also want you to know, Sir, that I don't want'a hurt anyone's feelings." Then, after pausing for a second, Bill Hayes added, "I also respectfully request that you keep this conversation between us, Sir."

As much as Tommy Savino wished that things were different, he knew that it was quite common for Caucasian Americans to object to Negroes being seen in public with white women, let alone married to one. Even though Bill Hayes never explained his personal feelings in detail, it wasn't hard for the Major to figure out, why one of his best agents had no desire to attend Cal Parker's wedding to Michelle Dumont.

After considering the Sergeant's request and agreeing that there was no need to make this an issue that went any further, Major Savino made a command decision and said, "Since you're willing to serve as the duty agent, why don't we have you work with Sergeant Dalton on the night of the wedding. This way, the men who are attending the wedding won't have to be called into the field, unless you and Sergeant Dalton need help."

"Thank you, Sir," responded Bill, before he stood up and saluted the Major.

Based on the few comments that were being made by the other men, Major Savino came to conclusion that Cal's plans to marry Michelle seemed more acceptable, because they had plans to make a life for themselves in Paris after the war. Since everyone was aware that the French were more open minded when he came to race relations, the general attitude among the men in the office was to accept this union, because it wasn't taking place back home. The fact that Bill Hayes was an outstanding CID Agent, also made it easy for Major Savino to accommodate his request.

"Don't worry, Bill," said Major Savino, "This stays between us," added the Major as he walked the Dallas cop who was serving as a CID Agent during the war to the door of his office.

"Thank you, Sir," responded Bill before he left the Major's office.

The day Captain Jack Parker arrived in Paris was one of the happiest days in his father's life. In addition to the fact that it had been some time since Al saw his oldest son, it meant a great deal to all parties involved, to have Jack Parker come to Paris to attend his brother's wedding. Even Mary Parker was elated, when she heard that Jim Beauregard made it possible for Jack to serve as his brother's best man.

As soon as Jack Parker stepped off the plane and he spotted his father, the young man who was now a decorated fighter pilot, smiled wide when he saw his dad waiting by an Army staff car. After saluting his oldest son, Al couldn't resist and gave Jack a hearty hug, that included patting him on the back as he remarked, "God, it's good to see you, son."

While father and son ignored the other officers and enlisted men who walked by, Al grabbed his son's bag and said, "Let's go. We have a lot to talk about," as he led the way to the staff car that was parked in a restricted area on the tarmac.

Once they got settled inside the khaki colored Ford sedan, Al did the driving while they headed back into the city. While Al shifted through the gears, he glanced to his right and said, "I can't wait to write your mother and tell her that you made it to Paris in time for Cal's wedding."

"I just heard from Mom before I left Ramatelli," remarked Jack, who quickly added, "She's worried about all of us and asked a lotta questions." Then, after pausing for a split second, Jack continued looking at the sights when he said, "As worried as Mom is about me and Cal, she's twice as worried about you, Pop."

"Why is your mother worried about me? All I'm doing is chasing crooks in Paris. I'm nowhere near where the real fighting is taking place," responded Al.

John "Jack" Parker proved that he agreed with his mother, when he turned to face his father and said, "Because Mom knows that you and Colonel Beauregard will go to hell and back, if that's what it takes to make an arrest."

"I can't fool your Mother," responded Al, who quickly added, "I've been trying for a long time but it doesn't work."

After pausing to change lanes, Al continued and said, "I'm curious what you think about your brother getting married and his decision to make a life for him and Michelle in Paris after the war?"

Jack knew that he would end up addressing this issue with both his father and his younger brother before the wedding. In fact, Jack already told Cal how he felt in a recent letter, after his brother sent him a picture of him and Michelle and he explained their plans for the future.

After lighting a cigarette, Jack cracked the window while he turned to his left and said, "I'll tell you the same thing I told Cal, in the letter that I sent him after he told me what his plans were. First, there's no doubt about it, Pop. If Michelle is half as pretty in real life, as she is in the picture that Cal sent me, he's a lucky man. I also have to tell you, Pop, that I am actually happy that they decided to live in France after the war. I feel this way, because not a damn thing has changed as far as how white folks treat us back home. No matter how many Germans we kill, no matter how many medals we get, we're still riding in the back of the bus and serving in segregated Army units."

Even though Al agreed, he let his oldest son continue, without interjecting any of his own thoughts on the subject of race relations in the United States. "To tell you the truth, Pop, I'm getting tired of hoping that things will change in the future," said Jack, who went on to say, "It's true that some white folks treat us like human beings, but not enough to make a difference, at least not yet."

"We can only do what we can do, son," responded Al, who quickly added, "Who knows what the future will bring."

After taking a drag on his cigarette, Jack flicked the ash out of the partially opened window as he continued and said, "Right now I'm more concerned about how this world is gonna treat Cal and Michelle."

"That's my concern as well," responded Al.

"So much for Cal's plans to join the police department after the war," remarked Jack.

While Al continued to drive the staff car to the CID Office in Paris, he glanced to his right and said, "All your mother and I want is for you and your brother to be happy. If Cal and Michelle have to live in Paris in order to have a better life, then so be it."

While Al watched Francois give his only daughter away to his son Cal, he was just as happy as he was concerned. Despite the fact that his youngest son was a decorated soldier, the sad truth was, that Cal and Michelle were better off living in France after the war, because the people back home did not approve of interracial marriages. Even the U.S. Army was still supporting a policy of segregation, with one exception. The powerful United States Army could not stop Negro soldiers from being killed, wounded and captured on the same battlefield as white troops. American Negro fighter pilots like Al's son Jack, were also allowed to risk their lives, to protect all white U.S. Army Air Corps bomber crews in the same sky over Germany. However, after flying these perilous combat missions, the American Negro fighter pilots were forced to return to a segregated air base in Italy.

Although it didn't seem like much at the time, there were those who took notice of the contribution that was made by Negro troops and by doing so, Al believed that additional seeds of progress were planted during World War II. Al felt this way, because of the relationship that he was able to develop with the Murphy family, as well as with Jim Beauregard and the other members of the New York City based CID Task Force. Even though it wasn't easy for Al and Jim to travel together, they made the most of their adventure and were generally assisted in every way possible, during their pursuit of Ivan Larson and Francis Shorty Mc Ghee.

Having a man like General Nathan Tremble endorse the recommendation, to decorate Al Parker with the Silver Star and recommend that he be offered a commission, was another act that moved the ball forward a bit, as far as race relations were concerned. Al Parker and his youngest son Cal were also treated with respect, by the men they worked with in the Paris CID Office. The same was true for Benny Greene. The fact that every CID Agent in their office, except for the man who volunteered to serve as the duty agent, was attending Cal's wedding, also meant that progress was being made. All Al hoped, was that more change would come sooner than later.

When Al watched as Cal repeated his vows, all he could think about, was how much he wished his wife Mary was standing by his side, to witness this moment. While Al imagined Mary wiping tears of joy from her eyes, a few tears of joy trickled down his face as well, when a lifetime of memories flashed through his mind. Once Michelle repeated her vows and the smiling French Priest looked at the happy couple and said, "You may now kiss the bride," Al felt Jim Beauregard patting him on the back as he whispered, "Congratulations, Al."

After traveling to The Paris Cafe with a police escort, Cal and Michelle were given a wonderful reception, that lasted into the early hours of the morning. Once the couple finished dancing to the 1941 Harry James song, You Made Me Love You, Gabby had the band pick up the beat and play some other American favorites. This selection of popular big band music included, Glenn Miller's In The Mood, The American Patrol, I've Got A Girl In Kalamazoo, Don't Sit Under The Apple Tree With Anyone Else But Me, as well as Artie Shaw's, Begin the Beguine and Benny Goodman's Sing, Sing, Sing and Roll 'Em.

As soon as the band picked up the beat, the unattached men from CID, along with some MPs and Paris cops, paired off with Michelle's single girl-friends and cousins who attended the reception. Even Al Parker surprised the younger men, including his two sons, when he danced up a storm with his new daughter-in-law to some popular swing music. Jim Beauregard, Tommy Savino and Captain Don Lorenz also danced with the bride.

When the band switched to something softer, the bride and groom danced to Tommy Dorsey's song, I'm Getting Sentimental Over You. Al Parker also ended back on the dance floor when the bride's mother, Annette Dumont, walked over to the father of the groom and said, "Would your wife Mary mind if I stood in for her for one dance?"

Just as the band started to play the 1939 hit song, We'll Meet Again, that was made famous by the British singer Vera Lynn, Al faced the Chief Inspector's wife and said, "Perfect timing, Annette, 'cause this is one of Mary's favorites."

As soon as Bill Hayes entered The Paris Cafe, Major Savino automatically assumed that the man who volunteered to serve as the Duty Agent, was called out on a case that needed the attention of a CID Agent. After making his way past the crowded dance floor, Major Savino spoke loud enough to be heard over the music as he leaned closer to Sergeant Hayes and said, "What's up, Bill?"

Even though Bill Hayes struggled with his personal feelings about Negroes marrying white women, he had to admit that Lieutenant Parker and his two sons were incredibly brave American soldiers, who deserved to be given the same level of respect, that he gave the brave white troops that he served with. As a result, Bill felt obligated to at least stop by and pay his respects to the happy couple and their family members.

After explaining his reasons for stopping by, Major Savino smiled and said, "After you pay your respects, get yourself something to eat and join me at the bar for a drink."

"I'll see you at the bar, Sir," responded Bill as he walked over to Cal and Michelle.

Even though Major Savino never shared any of the details from his private conversation with Bill Hayes to anyone, it didn't take much for the other men in the office, to figure out why the cop from Texas was serving as the duty agent, when arrangements were made to a have military policeman cover the phones in the office. As soon as Bill made his way to where Cal and his wife were sitting with their family members, the other men from the office welcomed him to the party as if nothing was wrong.

The bride and groom were also very gracious when they stood up and greeted Bill, "Michelle and I are glad you could make it, Bill," remarked Cal.

"Hopefully, it will be quiet tonight, so there will be no reason for you to leave," added Michelle.

Just as Bill finished paying his respects to Michelle's parents, Gabby came over and grabbed the Duty Agent by the arm and said, "I am under orders from Major Savino to make you a plate of food and have you join us at the bar."

A second later, a smiling Lieutenant Al Parker walked over and extended his hand in friendship before he handed Bill Hayes a glass of champagne and said, "Welcome to the party, Bill."

As soon as Bill Hayes thanked the only Negro Army Officer that he ever met or served with, he faced everyone at the table as he raised his glass and said, "To Cal and Michelle."

Once the toast was over, Gabby tugged on the duty agent's arm and said, "Now it is time for you to have something to eat."

While Gabby escorted Bill Hayes over to a table that was filled with food, Al turned to his son Cal and limited his comment to a simple, "I'm glad he came."

"Me too, Pop," responded Cal, before he turned to Michelle and invited his wife to join him for another dance. Of all the people who attended the wedding, Captain John Jack Parker made a friend for life out of Major Billy Davis; a fellow Army aviator, who was familiar with the outstanding record of the African American fighter pilots who were serving in Europe. While Billy Davis stood at the bar with Jack Parker, Al Parker, Jim Beauregard, Tommy Savino, Francois Dumont and Gabby Allaire, he described the very impressive record that Jack's squadron had, when it came to air to air engagements and escorting our bombers on missions into Germany. When Billy Davis finished his remarks, he turned to Al Parker and said, "You're a lucky man, Al. You have two fine sons."

While the proud father smiled and thanked Billy Davis for his kind words, Francois Dumont raised his glass in the air as he proposed a toast. "To Cal and his brother John. My wife and I welcome you both into our family. Now you have a home in Paris, as well as in New York."

After the toast, Al and Francois embraced each other like best friends and close relatives do. "Thanks Francois," remarked Al.

"You are welcome, my friend," responded Francois.

While Al admired the happy couple as they danced to big band music with their guests, he leaned closer to Francois and said, "Life won't be easy for them, but somehow I feel they'll do just fine."

After nodding his head in agreement, Francois leaned closer to Al as he responded and said, "You know what they say. Love conquers all."

After spending forty eight hours in Paris, Captain Jack Parker was ready to return to Italy to rejoin his fighter squadron. While Jack stood on the tarmac and waited to board a C47, he faced his father and said, "I'll see you, Pop."

When his oldest son extended his right hand, Al shook Jack's hand, before he gave him a hearty embrace and a pat on the back as he said, "Always remember that your mother and I are very proud of you. Just do us both a favor and be as careful as you can be up there in the wild blue yonder."

While Jack felt his father's bear like hug squeeze him one last time, the veteran fighter pilot did his best to reassure his dad, that he would do his best to comply with his request. "I promise, Pop."

As Al stepped back and faced Jack, he didn't want to think about the fact that this could be the last time that he saw his oldest son. Both Al and his oldest son knew that far too many good people had already died in this war and would continue to be killed and seriously wounded until it was over. When the engines on the C47 began to turn over, Al spoke in a raised tone of voice at a fast pace as he faced his oldest son and said, "When you were a little boy I used to tell you all the time how much I loved you."

"I know, Pop. I remember," remarked Jack.

When Al continued he did his best to hold it together. "I'm glad you remember, cause I love you more now than ever."

"I love you too, Pop," responded Jack, before he added, "I better go, or I'll be AWOL."

While Jack picked up his bag and began walking over to the C47, Al called out, "Don't forget to write your mother!"

As soon as Jack Parker reached the cargo door of the C47, he turned and saluted his father before he boarded the plane. When Al returned the salute, he did his best to fight back the tears, while his mind filled with thoughts of days gone by, when both of his sons were little boys growing up in New York City. Now they were young men serving in a world war, one that had claimed millions of lives and would claim a lot more before the hostilities came to an end.

CHAPTER 18

NEW ORDERS

T he day Jim Beauregard received a call from General Nathan Tremble, he assured the recently promoted Major General, that he and Al Parker would be happy to pick him up when his plane landed and join him for dinner. When General Tremble explained the reason for this meeting, he limited his remarks to saying, "A unit I just inspected has a problem that needs to be resolved and I need my favorite Army cops to solve this case, before we advance any further into Germany. I also have another mission for you and your men to handle, that we need to discuss in person."

After enthusiastically agreeing to help the General in any way necessary, General Tremble ended the call by saying, "If my plans change, I'll have my aide call you. Otherwise, my plane is expected to land at Le Bourget Airport at 1800 hours tonight."

"Lieutenant Parker and I will be on the tarmac waiting for you to arrive, Sir," responded Jim.

"Thank you, Colonel," remarked General Tremble, before he ended the call to the CID Office in Paris.

While Jim and Al sat in their staff car on the tarmac, Jim cracked the passenger side window before he used his Zippo to light a Lucky Strike cigarette. After taking another drag on his cigarette, Jim turned to Al and said, "I can't wait to hear what the General wants to talk to us about."

"It must be pretty important for him to fly to Paris, just to speak to us in person," responded Al.

"You're right," said Jim, who quickly added, "He could have easily sent for

us and we'd have to go to Reims, France where he hangs his hat at SHAFE."
Then, after pausing for a split second, Jim added, "I'm really curious about
this other matter that he wants us to handle."

"I guess we'll find out soon enough," remarked Al.

"We sure will," said Jim.

The sound of a C47 taxing their way was a clear indication that General
Tremble's plane was on time. While Al looked at his watch, he confirmed
this when he remarked, "1800 hours right on the nose."

As Al put the staff car in gear, he looked to his right and remarked,
"Knowing General Tremble the way we do, the pilot flying that C47 would
be in the infantry if he landed one minute late."

While the two men who had become very close friends had a good laugh
at the general's expense, the plane came to a stop and was marshaled into a
parking space near the terminal building by a ground crewman. By the time
the crew chief opened the large cargo hatch, the CID staff car came to a
stop on the pilot's side of the plane, near the tip of the left wing.

Just as he expected, Major General Nathan Tremble found his two
favorite Army cops standing at a comfortable attention by their vehicle,
while they waited for his arrival. After saluting the General and having their
salute returned, General Tremble extended his hand and said, "It's good to
see you boys again."

"The same here, Sir" responded Jim Beauregard as he shook hands with
the General.

When the General shook hands with Al Parker, he seemed to be in very
good spirits when he said, "I was happy to hear that you accepted the commission, Lieutenant. I also want'a thank you for the cigars. Cubans no less.
It wasn't necessary, but I appreciate it."

"It was the least I could do, Sir." responded Al.

When the general's luggage was delivered to the staff car, Al spoke up
and said, "Excuse me, Sir, while I take care of your luggage." As Al addressed
the Army Air Forces enlisted man and said, "This way, Sergeant," he walked
around to the back of the car and opened the trunk, while Jim opened the

rear door for the general."

Once Al got in behind the wheel, General Tremble spoke up from the back seat and said, "Dinner's on me, gentlemen. We have a lot to discuss."

While Jim Beauregard and Al Parker were meeting with General Tremble, Major Savino met with Captain Don Lorenz, Sergeant Hank Blair, Corporal Tommy Callaghan and Sergeant Lawrence Gaddison, to plan the next phase of their investigation, into AWOL Sergeant Kevin Donnely's black market and gambling operation. After discussing the operational plan with his subordinates, Major Savino addressed the two soldiers who were facing formal charges for helping deserters to commit fraud.

"This is the deal," said Major Savino as he sat behind Jim Beauregard's desk, while he addressed the two soldiers who agreed to help CID, in order to minimize their legal problems with the U.S. Army. "In addition to having you testify against Donnely and his associates, you can help us by agreeing to return to his gambling operation, to act as if you are still willing to send some of his money back to the states. If you agree to serve in this capacity, my men and I will be close by at all times and will cover you as best as possible."

Without hesitating, Sergeant Gaddison spoke up and said, "Count me in, Sir."

After having some time to think about his options, Corporal Callaghan remarked, "Me too, Sir."

As glad as he was that they volunteered to help, Major Savino had no intention of sending Corporal Callaghan and Sergeant Gaddison in harm's way, until he reminded them that they were going up against a group of deserters, who were wanted for more than just being involved in black market activities and the fraudulent transfer of money to the states. "Before you men agree to assist us, I want'a remind you that AWOL Sergeant Donnely, AWOL Corporal Jessie Peterson, AWOL Private Vincent Chiperelli and AWOL Private Stanislaus Balinski are also prime suspects in the attempt to kill Private Fishman. The reason why we need to go through with this, is to make an iron clad case against Donnely, for fraudulently sending money home to the states. Our case against Donnely and his fellow deserters, for their involvement in the black market, is also coming along nicely. In fact, we're hoping to make such a rock solid case against these deserters, some of them will likely cooperate and give us what we need to prove, that Donnely led the attempt to kill Private Fishman."

While Corporal Callaghan still looked a bit concerned, Sergeant Gaddison showed no concern at all, after being reminded that the men they were going up against had committed an act of violence against another G.I. As a result, it was obvious to Major Savino, that a combat veteran like Sergeant Gaddison wasn't the slightest bit worried, about helping CID make a case against a group of deserters, who were considered armed and dangerous. In contrast, Corporal Callaghan was a rear area soldier, who never heard a shot fired in anger, let alone in his direction.

After seeing the expression on Corporal Callaghan's face, Sergeant Gaddison spoke up and said, "I'm not worried about Donnely, Sir. He has no reason to suspect me or the Corporal. I guess what I'm trying to say, Sir, is that we'll be fine."

While the Major faced the Corporal and he asked if he would be able to handle this assignment, Tommy Callaghan seemed a bit more composed when he responded and said, "Like I told the Colonel and Captain Lorenz, Sir. I knew Donnely was a tough guy, but I had no idea that he carried a gun and liked to use one." After pausing for a split second to look at his under-cover partner, Corporal Callaghan faced Major Savino and said, "Knowing that I'll be working with Sergeant Gaddison will help me get through this, Sir. I also think the plan that your men briefed us on will work just fine."

"OK, then, we're in business," responded the Major, who went on to say, "As soon as we get Sergeant Gaddison over to the hospital to get that cast put on his arm, you can stop by Donnely's gambling den to help us wrap this case up." When the Major continued he looked directly at Corporal Callaghan when he said, "If Donnely still wants you to make a money transfer to his family, we'll have you and Sergeant Gaddison send his money back to New York as planned. Once that's done, we'll have agents in New York, along with Post Office Inspectors, visit Donnely's family to recover the dough and have a talk with them about previous transfers. We're also looking into the other transfers that have been made for the rest of Donnely's crew, all of which will be used as evidence when they're court martialed."

While Captain Lorenz and Sergeant Blair stood next to the two men who were facing formal charges, Sergeant Gaddison and Corporal Callaghan both said they understood their instructions.

After hearing their response, Major Savino limited his response to saying, "Let's get this done."

Immediately after Corporal Callaghan and Sergeant Gaddison saluted Major Savino and said "Yes, Sir," the two CID Agents escorted the two cooperating individuals out of the office. As soon as they left, Major Savino picked up the phone on his desk and called the 709th Military Police Battalion Headquarters. "Sergeant, this is Major Savino from CID. Let me speak to your CO."

After briefing everyone who was involved in this investigation, Major Savino directed Corporal Callaghan to take Sergeant Gaddison to AWOL Sergeant Donnely's gambling den. While carrying funds provided by Major Savino, the two cooperating soldiers entered the apartment building, under the watchful eyes of a number of American CID Agents and Paris Police Inspectors.

After observing the two cooperating individuals enter the building where Donnely's gambling den was located, Chief Inspector Dumont remarked, "Now we wait."

Major Savino proved that he had been in Paris long enough to know his way around the city, when he faced the Chief Inspector and said, "A window seat in La Pointe St. Eustache will give us an excellent view of the building that we need to keep an eye on."

"An excellent choice," responded the Chief Inspector.

As soon as the two investigators entered the café located at 1 Rue Montorgeuil, the Chief Inspector turned Major Savino and said, "We're in luck, Tom. There is a table right by the window that will suit our needs perfectly."

"Once they sat at the table and the waiter took their order, Major Savino and Chief Inspector Dumont continued to observe the location that they had under surveillance. As soon as the waiter filled two glasses with wine and left, Tommy Savino raised his glass a bit and said, "Cheers, Francois. Let's hope we get lucky today."

Immediately after Francois sipped some wine, he looked at Tommy Savino as the young Major from CID was performing his surveillance duties and said, "According to Jim and Al, American policemen have a saying that a good cop makes his own luck."

While Francois kept an eye on the location that they were watching, Tommy Savino turned to face the Chief Inspector when he responded and said, "Jim and Al are right. In fact, my father told me the same thing, when I joined the police department back home in Rhode Island. My dad was a detective sergeant back then. He made Lieutenant after I joined the Army and got assigned to CID."

"Your father must be very proud of you," responded the Chief Inspector.

After taking a sip of wine, Tommy Savino responded while he continued to observe the building they had under surveillance. "I have a way to go be half as good as my father. That man knows every crook in the State of Rhode Island, as well as in other parts of New England. He's one hell of a cop. In fact, you and my father are a lot alike. The same goes for Jim Beauregard and Al Parker. You're all in the same league and I for one am getting one hell of an education in police work, by working with you guys."

Francois Dumont proved that he was a humble man, when he responded to the compliment by saying, "The simple truth, Tom, is that policemen like your father and I, along with Jim and Al have been around long enough to learn how to be successful in our profession. Besides, it's the younger men who work with us, who are devoted to their duties, who make us older gendarmes look as good as we do. You are one of those men, as are the men who work under your command."

"Thanks, Chief," responded Tommy Savino.

"You are most welcome, my friend," said the Chief Inspector, before he took a sip from his wine glass, while he continued to watch the building where AWOL Sergeant Donnely's gambling den was located.

★ ★ ★

After enjoying a sumptuous meal, Major General Tremble sipped his after dinner drink before he remarked, "Now that we ate, we can get down to business."

"How can we help, Sir," asked Jim.

As General Tremble leaned closer to the table, he looked at the two men from CID, who had a well deserved reputation for being extremely capable criminal investigators and said, "In addition to fighting the damn Germans, we also have to deal with the politics of fighting a war with our Allies. What I have to say is top secret, so keep it in your barracks bag as the saying goes."

After hearing Jim and Al respond almost in unison and say, "Yes, Sir," General Tremble spoke in a low tone of voice when he continued. "Army Intelligence believes that the Krauts are dead serious about mounting a guerrilla war, once we push deeper into Germany and we finish off The Third Reich. This Nazi resistance movement is expected to consist of SS men, die hard regular troops who refuse to surrender, as well as civilian fighters, including women and young kids. In other words, based on what we know so far, the Germans intend to fight on. Whether this movement proves to be an actual threat or not is yet to be determined. The fact that Southern Germany includes a number of caves, mines, large forested areas and alpine passes, will provide these guerrilla fighters, who are called Werewolves, with ample locations to hide supplies and evade Allied search teams. This type of terrain is also ideal for launching attacks on our troops. Even though the so called headquarters for this resistance movement is based in Southern Germany, other parts of Germany are expected to face similar threats from these Nazi guerrilla fighters. That includes big cities and small towns."

Once again, General Tremble paused to sip his drink. As soon as he put his glass down, the two star general casually looked around, to make sure that no one was paying attention to their conversation, before he faced his dinner guests and said, "Even though our British Allies don't see this Werwolf movement as a serious threat, SHAFE does. Between you and me, I'm not sure the Krauts will pose enough of a threat to change the outcome of the war, even if some variation of this Werwolf operation is activated. Unfortunately, the threat of being subjected to attacks by well armed Nazi fanatics, who may or may not be wearing uniforms, is too serious to ignore.

The fact that we've lost enough men in this war, is another reason to be prepared to crush any attempt by any group of Nazi resistance fighters to prolong hostilities. Should that happen, we could end up having to maintain a much larger number of troops in an occupation force, instead of sending the additional personnel to the Pacific to fight the Japs."[23]

While General Tremble paused to remove a lighter from his jacket pocket, Jim spoke up and said, "We have enough trouble dealing with the theft of critical supplies from our own soldiers. The last thing we need, is to have these Werwolf resistance fighters attacking supply depots and ambushing Allied troops."

"Correct on all counts," responded the General before he used his Zippo to light his cigar. As the General snapped his lighter closed and put it on the table, he continued with his briefing. "Even after we win this war, we'll be keeping an occupation force in Germany that will need to be properly supplied and protected. That means, that until we can use ports in Germany, we'll need to maintain supply lines that extend from France and Belgium, all the way to where the fighting is taking place. Right now we have three Army Groups in the field, that are beginning to make the drive toward the Rhine. Once we cross the Rhine in force on a wider front, we'll be going all out to put an end to this war as fast as possible."

After pausing to take a quick puff on his cigar, General Tremble picked up where he left off and said, "Our problem, is that we're currently dealing with a fifteen to twenty percent shortfall in the amount of supplies that are being delivered to front line units. This shortage of supplies is due to theft. As a result, we can't afford to have acts of sabotage from Nazi holdouts, or a thriving black market take more from the supply chain, when we're already forced to fight with less than we need."[24]

Once again, General Tremble paused to sip his drink. As soon as he put his glass down, the two star general continued briefing his dinner guests. "I have three assignments for you and your men. One is to investigate the theft of supplies from our Quarter Master depot in Liege, Belgium. Officially this depot is designated Q179.[25] The MP Commander in this area is a Major by the name of Jason Brickel. By tomorrow morning you'll be receiving a detailed report from Major Brickel about this matter. I recently met the Major and two of his MPs on an inspection tour of the area. They're good soldiers and they seem to have two suspects who are worth watching. The Major's problem is his unit is shorthanded and can't devote the time to conduct investigations like you and your men can. Do what you can to clean up this problem up and do it fast. If there's a black market operation at Q179, we need it shut down as soon as possible. Doing so, will insure that every drop of gasoline and everything else that a soldier needs will get to the troops who are doing the fighting."

Both Jim and Al could tell by the General's demeanor that he had more to say. General Tremble proved their suspicions were correct, when he leaned closer to the table again as he continued and said, "Mission number two involves the threat to Allied supply lines and our occupation forces, once we cross the Rhine on a much wider front and drive deeper into Germany. This particular mission involves the need to investigate and address any threats, or attacks, that involve the Nazi Werwolf resistance movement. Included in this mission, is the need to be prepared to react to any efforts by the SS to organize, train and direct stragglers from regular German military units, as well as by civilian militia fighters, to make some last ditch effort to defend the Fatherland."

Before he continued, General Tremble took another quick puff on his cigar. As he held his smoldering cigar in his right hand, the General went on to say, "Mission number three will be to have you and some of your agents in position to establish the first CID Office in Germany, as soon as we occupy the American sector in Berlin. Once you get settled, I'll have Major Savino flown to Berlin to serve as your XO. Until he gets there, you and Al will have to run the show. You'll also get all he help you need, as far as additional CID Agents are concerned."

After pausing again to sip his drink, the General continued as he looked directly at Jim and said, "In order to accomplish your three fold mission, SHAFE wants you to put a composite unit together that consists of CID and CIC Agents, along with a few experienced MPs. I want you and your men to be ready to cross the Rhine at Speyer, Germany bright and early on March 31st. I'm assigning you to the First French Army, because a French Colonel by the name of Andre Reynald, requested that the American Liaison Unit, that will be traveling with our French Allies, should consist of you and your men."

While the General continued to look at Jim, he took a quick puff on his cigar before he continued and said, "Part of mission number three involves making a stop in the Town of Remagen, on your way to meet up with the French Army." After turning to face Al Parker, the General went on to say, "Since your cigar smoking partner speaks fluent German, I want Al to work with your contingent of CIC Agents and interrogate German POWs, who are being held in open air encampments along the Rhine River."

After turning to face Jim, the General quickly added, "The purpose of these interrogations will be to pick up whatever intelligence you can squeeze from enemy POWs, before you head into Southern Germany. Once you cross the Rhine, I want you and your men to work with CIC, to search for contraband and locate troublemakers in every city and town that is captured and occupied along your line of march."

After pausing briefly to re-light his cigar, General Tremble went on to say, "One of the problems that we envision involves the need to properly administer occupied territory. SHAFE intends to handle this mission, by sending special teams from the Psychological Warfare Division consisting of three to four commissioned officers and five enlisted men. These teams will be responsible to help establish working civilian governments in every German city and town that we secure and occupy. This mission will include appointing the right Germans to serve as public servants, to include mayors and policemen. In order to enhance the capabilities of your liaison unit, a small army of CIC Agents will also be aggressively looking for SS men, members of the Gestapo and any of their recently recruited fanatics, who pose a threat to Allied personnel, Allied supply lines and Germans who cooperate with our occupation forces. We also have plans to send other teams into Germany to locate scientists, advanced weapons, stolen artwork and anything else of value, that the Krauts plundered when they invaded and occupied Europe."[26]

"When Jim asked how many men he would be authorized to take along on this mission, General Tremble paused to take two quick puffs on his cigar before he responded. "I'll leave that up to you, Jim. Just make sure you leave enough men behind to police Paris, because we fully expect Paris to remain a busy outpost for CID and the MPs for some time to come."

While he continued, General Tremble refilled all three of their glasses with more Cognac. "One thing is certain. If you think the black market problem in Paris is bad, wait until this war is over and we end up camping out in Germany for Lord knows how long." As the General put the bottle down, he continued and said, "According to Army Intelligence, food, fuel, medicine, soap, coal and everything else that people need to live like human beings is either non existent, or in very short supply in Germany and will be even harder to find by the time the fighting stops. Until the situation changes, the U.S. Army will possess the largest stockpile of supplies in the ETO. We're also gonna have every Allied Army, including the damn Russians, occupying Germany at the same time. As a result, we expect to have plenty of work for CID, CIC and our MPs. This is why I want a composite unit of Army cops and Counter Intelligence Corps personnel serving as my eyes and ears in Southern Germany, before you swing north and make your way to Berlin."

Both Jim and Al knew all about the impact that the black market had on the U.S. Army's ability to supply front line combat units. Even the theft of cigarettes had a negative impact on the morale of troops operating in forward areas. Having a fanatical group of Nazis mount acts of sabotage and other attacks, before or after the regular German Armed Forces surrendered, would also negatively impact the ability of the Allies to stabilize Europe and focus their attention on the Pacific.

After taking a sip of his after dinner drink, Jim looked across the table and said, "I'll send two of our agents to Liege in the morning, Sir. Al and I will also get to work preparing for mission number two and three."

As soon as Jim finished speaking, General Tremble asked his two favorite Army cops if they had any contacts in CIC who they would like to work with?"

While Jim removed a pack of cigarettes from his pant's pocket, he responded without hesitation and said, "Yes, Sir, we do. We just finished working a case with Captain Billy Barnes, Lieutenant Dan Kelly and Sergeant Fred Janowski. They're good men, Sir. We worked together when we assisted Colonel Reynald and his special French intelligence team go after the Mollet brothers and their associates."

"I heard about that one," remarked the General, who sipped his drink before he went on to say, "You and your men, along with the boys from

CIC, scored some big points with SHAFE and our French Allies, when you worked your magic and put those Nazi collaborating black market operators in their graves. Unfortunately, it cost the life of a French Intelligence Officer to make that case."

"Captain Badeau was a good man, Sir," responded Jim, who quickly added, "I wish he was going into Germany with us."

"Colonel Reynald said the same thing," remarked the General, who returned to the issue at hand and said, "I'm sure you and your crime fighting partner also know a few top notch MPs as well?"

"Yes we do, Sir," responded Jim.

"I knew I could count on you boys," said the General, who quickly added, "Put an operational plan together for my signature and have it ready for me when we meet for lunch tomorrow. I also want you to draft a letter for my signature, that will serve as written orders for your liaison mission with the French Army."

As soon as Jim acknowledged his orders, General Tremble raised his glass in a toast and remarked, "Cops in a combat zone. What's this war coming to?"

As soon as AWOL Sergeant Donnely saw Tommy Callaghan enter his gambling den with an old customer, he walked right over to greet them. While facing Sergeant Gaddison, the AWOL G.I. Gangster remarked, "I didn't think I'd ever see you again, now that the big push is on into Germany."

"That makes two of us," responded Sergeant Gaddison.

When Kevin Donnely continued, he pointed to the cast on the injured GI's arm and said, "What happened to you?"

Sergeant Lawrence Gaddison proved that he was well suited for undercover work when he responded and said, "I was tossing crates of explosives over the Remagen Bridge into the Rhine River, to keep the Germans from blowing it up, when a Kraut bullet ricocheted off a steel girder and hit my arm. They flew me back to Paris the next day with the rest of the injured and wounded. Once I got tired of laying in bed and hanging out in the Day

Room, I scrounged a pass from a friendly doctor and went to see Tommy. You're our first stop on a well deserved night out on the town."

Kevin Donnely was by no means suspicious and appeared to be in good spirits when he invited Tommy Callighan and Sergeant Gaddison to join him for a drink. On the way over to the bar, Donnely looked at the supply clerk and said, "I got that money I need you to send to the states for me."

"No problem, Sarge," responded Corporal Callaghan.

Once they made their way to the makeshift bar that was set up in the kitchen, Donnely poured a liberal amount of Johnny Walker Red Label scotch whiskey into three glasses. After handing the drinks to his two guests, Donnely raised his glass and said, "Down the hatch." As soon as the toast was over, Donnely addressed Sergeant Gaddison and said, "You want'a sit in on a card game, or throw some dice with your good arm?"

While Donnely refilled his glass with scotch, Sergeant Gaddison responded and said, "I think I'll play cards," before he turned to Corporal Callaghan and asked, "You want'a join me?

"Maybe later," remarked the Corporal, who quickly added, "I got'a take care of some business with the Sarge."

After motioning one of the more attractive French hostesses over to the makeshift bar area, AWOL Sergeant Donnely asked the young woman to take his friend Sergeant Gaddison to the table in the corner, where the high rollers were known to play.

When Agent Sam Carubba entered La Pointe St. Eustache Cafe, he headed directly over to the table where Major Savino and the Chief Inspector were seated. As Agent Carubba stood by the side of the table, he spoke in a low tone of voice when he addressed Major Savino. "Excuse me, Sir, but I have a message from Captain Lorenz."

"Have a seat, Sam and fill us in," responded the Major.

When the Chief Inspector asked if Sam would like something to drink, the cop from Baltimore who was serving as a CID Agent in Paris said, "No thank you, Sir," as he sat down and relayed the message from Captain Lorenz. "The Captain wants you and the Chief Inspector to know, that fifteen minutes after an Army truck arrived at our friend's warehouse, two French Citroen delivery vans showed up. The other good news, Sir, is that Inspector Goulet identified one of the Frenchmen who arrived in one of the vans, as a crook by the name of Jardan Moreau. Patrice said that the Chief Inspector is very familiar with Moreau and can tell you everything there is to know about him and his men."

As soon as Agent Carubba finished relaying the message, the Chief Inspector faced Major Savino and said, "Jardan Moreau is one of the most successful smugglers in France. Even though he is known to do business here in Paris, he is based in Marseille. To his credit, Jardan put his talents as an accomplished smuggler to work for the resistance and was responsible for getting a number of shot down Allied airmen back to Allied lines, during the German occupation of France. I also know from Marcel, that Jardan and his men killed their fair share of Germans and provided the Allies with a great deal of assistance, when they invaded North Africa and Southern France. Jardan was able to be of such distinguished service, because his smuggling operation extends throughout France and the Mediterranean."

"This guy sounds like some character," remarked Major Savino.

While speaking in his signature calm tone of voice, the Chief Inspector responded and said, "Yes, Tom, Jardan Moreau is how you say, some character."

After checking his watch, Major Savino looked at the Chief Inspector and said, "Jim and Al should be back from their dinner engagement with General Tremble. I better give 'em a call and fill them in on what's going on. If they're not back, I'll leave a message with the duty agent." After pausing for a split second, Major Savino continued looking at Chief Inspector Dumont when he went on to say, "How 'bout this for a plan, Francois? Once we hear from Sergeant Gaddison and Corporal Callaghan, I'll lead the raid on Donnely's gambling den, while you give Jim, Al and Don a hand when they move against his black market operation."

As soon as he finished taking a sip of wine, the Chief Inspector responded and said, "An excellent plan, Tom."

When Major Savino stood up, so did Sergeant Carubba. While the Major grabbed his trench coat off the back of an empty chair, he looked at the Chief Inspector and said, "I'll be back as soon as I call the office,

Francois."

"I will keep an eye on things while you are gone," responded the Chief Inspector as he sat by the window and continued observing the location they had under surveillance.

While the Major stood up, he faced Agent Carubba and said, "While I call the duty agent, I have a message that I need you to relay to Captain Lorenz."

After doing fairly well playing cards, Sergeant Gaddison decided to take his winnings into the back bedroom, that was converted into the place where Donnely held his dice games. It was in this room that Sergeant Gaddison intentionally lost whatever he won and then some while playing cards. After calling it quits, Sergeant Gaddison joined Donnely and Corporal Callaghan at the bar.

When Donnely asked how he did, Gaddison took the last cigarette from the pack in his shirt pocket and responded as he tossed the crumpled empty pack into a nearby trash can. "The good news is I won a few bucks playing cards, but I lost it all plus a few sheckles shooting craps. To make a bad situation worse, I'm even out'a smokes."

After opening a nearby cabinet that was filled with expensive liquor and cartons of American cigarettes, Donelly remarked, "Compliments of the house" as he handed two packs of hard to get Camels to the sergeant, who he believed was wounded while serving in combat.

As soon as Sergeant Gaddison thanked him for the free smokes, Donnely made his guest an offer he couldn't refuse when he said, "Like I told you the last time you did me a favor. I made some good dough running my side business after duty hours here in Paris. In fact, I've done so well, I can't send anymore money home, because if I do, the Army cops might come sniffing around. Since one hand washes the other, I'll make you the same offer I did the last time you helped me out. I'll give you a ten percent fee, if you go with Tommy and take care of the paperwork to send a grand home to my older brother."

Just like he was instructed by the CID case agents, Sergeant Gaddison acted as if what he was just asked to do was no big deal. "You're right, Sarge, one hand does wash the other, because that'll cover what I lost tonight and put a few bucks in my pocket."

After removing a wad of money from his pant's pocket, Kevin Connely continued as he handed the cash to Corporal Callaghan. "Tommy will go with you in the morning to send a Postal Money Order for a thousand bucks to my brother Shaun in the states." When Donnely continued he handed a slip of paper to Callaghan. "This is the address in Brooklyn where the money order needs to go. Once you take care of business, Tommy will give you a C Note for services rendered."

While continuing to act as if what he was asked to do was no big deal, Sergeant Gaddison remarked, "Sounds good to me." As he continued to keep up his act, Gaddison turned to his undercover partner for the night and said, "I don't know about you, Tommy, but I'm starving. Why don't we get something to eat, before we finish making the rounds? Thanks to Sergeant Donnely I'm buying."

"The name's Kevin," said Donnely as he extended his hand.

"My friends call me, Larry," responded Gaddison as he shook hands with the subject of the CID investigation that he was helping to convict.

Just as he was instructed, Corporal Callaghan checked the time on his watch before he looked at Sergeant Donnely and said, "Two guys from the Third Army were supposed to meet us here, to get in on a game, before they returned to their unit in the morning. Do me a favor, Sarge and tell 'em we went to get some chow if they show up. We'll be at the Stage Door Canteen if they want'a meet us later on."

When Donnely asked Callaghan what their names were, the supply clerk responded and said, "Tony and Sal. They're good guys, Sarge, so do me a favor and show them a good time."

"Don't worry, Tommy. I'll take care of them," responded Donnely.

As soon as Sergeant Gaddison and Corporal Callaghan left Donnely's gambling den, Gaddison relayed the signal that they were successful. Once this was done, Francois Dumont and Major Savino left the café and followed the two cooperating G.I.s out of the immediate area.

After receiving a message from the duty agent, Jim Beauregard and Al Parker left the office to meet Major Savino and the Chief Inspector in the field, while they debriefed Sergeant Gaddison and Corporal Callaghan. During this debriefing session, Corporal Callaghan gave Major Savino the cash that Donnely gave him, to make the money transfer and pay Sergeant Gaddison. The Corporal also turned over the slip of paper, that indicated the address in Brooklyn where Donnely wanted the money transfer sent. It was also during this debriefing session, that Corporal Callaghan and Sergeant Gaddison reported, that while Sergeant Kevin Donnely and Private Vincent Chiperelli were running the gambling operation inside the apartment, Corporal Jessie Peterson was pulling guard duty on the front door. While this debriefing was taking place, Captain Lorenz and the men in his team had AWOL Private Stanislaus Balinksi and several French subjects under surveillance, at the storage facility that was used by Donnely and his men to run their black market operation.

Now that they had the additional evidence that they were hoping to get their hands on, Jim Beauregard agreed with his case agents, that it was a good time to arrest Donnely and all of his known associates. While Major Savino would lead the raiding party that would take Donnely, Peterson and Chiperelli into custody, Jim Beauregard, Al Parker and Chief Inspector Dumont would assist Captain Lorenz and his mixed contingent of CID Agents, MPs and Paris Police Inspectors, when they raided Donnely's storage facility. Once the first two raids were executed, the private quarters where Donnely and his men lived would also be searched.

Before Major Savino left to lead the raid on Donnely's gambling den, Al Parker handed him the well worn metal flask that he carried throughout his police career. When Al did so, he suggested that Sergeants Angelone and Coppola would look more like typical G.I.s on leave, if they had his flask in hand when they approached Donnely and his men. It was a good idea, one that the Major promised to pass along.

When Al continued he added, "Wish them well for me, Tom. And tell those crazy kids not to drink all of my scotch."

After cracking a smile, the Major responded and said, "Will do, Al."

While meeting in the empty lobby of a nearby building, Mike Butler, Bill Hayes, Inspector La Belle and five uniformed MPs stood by, as Major Savino addressed the two agents who would be going in first. "We'll move in as soon as you pin the AWOL G.I. who is posted outside the door to Donnely's gambling den."

"One more thing," remarked Major Savino, who continued while he handed Sergeant Angelone a metal flask. "Lieutenant Parker thought it might be a good idea if you carry his flask when you approach Donnely and any of his men."

As usual, Sergeant Angelone proved to be just as much of a joker as his father, when he turned to his partner as he held up the flask and said, "Look, Sal, we get to drink on duty."

"Free booze. What a deal," remarked Sergeant Coppola.

After listening to the two sergeants joke around, Major Savino remarked, "Oh, I almost forgot. Lieutenant Parker wanted me to tell you not to drink all of his scotch."

As soon as the two undercover agents reluctantly acknowledged the order, the CID Agent from Brooklyn, who was known to have a sarcastically irreverent sense of humor, turned to his partner and remarked, "There's always a catch, Sal."

After checking his watch, Major Savino looked at Sergeants Angelone and Coppola and said, "You two be careful and that's an order."

As soon as Sergeant Angelone remarked, "We'll see you upstairs, Sir," Sal Coppola patted his partner on the back and said, "Let's go, Ange."

While pretending to be soldiers looking for a card game, Sergeants Angelone and Coppola approached Corporal Peterson, while the AWOL G.I. sat on a chair outside of Donnely's gambling den. After passing the flask back to his partner, Sergeant Coppola addressed the AWOL Private and said, "Corporal Tommy Callaghan said we could play some cards, if we stopped by this apartment before we headed back to our unit."

"Tommy left about an hour ago, but he said two guys from the 3rd Army were coming by," responded the young deserter, who continued as he glanced at the shoulder patch on their uniforms. "How's old blood and guts treating you?"

While Sergeant Angelone leaned closer to Corporal Peterson, he spoke just above a whisper when he said, "We're not with the Third Army. We're with CID, asshole."

The second the deserter on guard duty reeled back in his chair and looked both scared and surprised, Agent Coppola grabbed Peterson by the throat and put his left hand over the lookout's face, while his partner searched the prisoner for weapons. Just as Agent Angelone removed a stolen U.S. Army .45 caliber pistol from the prisoner's waistband, Major Savino and the rest of the raiding party arrived on the top floor landing.

"Good work, men," whispered the Major, before he turned to Agent Hayes and said, "Turn the prisoner over to one of the MPs on the stairs and pass the word that we move in two minutes." Once AWOL Corporal Peterson was taken away by an MP, Major Savino faced Sergeants Angelone and Coppola and whispered, "You know what to do. You have ninety seconds to locate Donnely and Chiperelli and pin them down, to prevent any gun play from taking place once we move in."

"We understand, Sir," whispered Agent Angelone as he handed Peterson's pistol over to Major Savino.

As soon as Major Savino wished his men good luck, the two CID Agents from New York City checked their watches before entering the gambling den. Once inside, the two agents removed a wad of cash from their pockets and admired the set up, while they acted like soldiers who were looking for a game of chance.

The second they were approached by an attractive French hostess, Sal Coppola explained that they were friends of Corporal Tommy Callaghan, but the Corporal who was watching the door said that he already left. When Vinny Chiperelli approached the two undercover agents and the English speaking French hostess explained that they were friends of Tommy

Callaghan, the AWOL G.I. Gangster asked if they would like a drink before they sat in on a game? After being escorted to the makeshift bar, Chiperelli introduced the two sergeants from Patton's Third Army to his boss. By the time Kevin Donnely finished asking his two new customers what they would like to drink, the door to the apartment was kicked open by the CID raiding party. The second Donnely and Chiperelli reached for the pistols they carried under their jackets, Sergeant Angelone and his partner punched the two G.I. Gangsters in the face and flipped them to the floor. After drawing their forty fives, the two undercover agents held the two prisoners at gunpoint, while Major Savino approached with two MPs.

While Donnely and Chiperelli remained on the floor, with forty fives pressed up against their chests, Sergeant Coppola disarmed the two prisoners, while his partner looked up at Major Savino and said, "Would you like to do the honors, Sir?"

"Thank you, Sergeant. Don't mind if I do," responded the Major, before he leaned over and looked down at Donnely and Chiperelli and said, "My name is Major Savino. I with CID. You're both under arrest."

Once the two prisoners were helped up off the floor and handcuffed, Major Savino addressed the two military policemen who were holding onto the two prisoners and said, "Take 'em away." Major Savino then turned to Sergeants Angelone and Coppola and cracked a smile before he remarked, "Well done...very well done."

Just as they planned, the CID Agents and MPs who were members of the raiding party had every customer lined up against the walls of the apartment. While the CID Agents and MPs were searching and questioning the military customers, Inspector La Belle was questioning the two French girls, who were employed as hostesses at Donnely's gambling operation. After seeing that everything was under control, Major Savino used the telephone in the apartment, to notify the CID duty agent that their mission was a success.

In another section of Paris, Jim Beauregard, Don Lorenz, Al Parker, Chief Inspector Dumont, Hank Blair, Chris Jacko, Cal Parker, Benny

Greene, three Paris Police Inspectors and a squad of military policemen prepared to raid Donnely's storage facility. Knowing that Jardan Moreau and his band of French thieves were still inside, motivated the Chief Inspector to tell Jim, Al and the others, what he relayed to Major Savino about the famous French smuggler.

After pausing to light a cigarette, Jim looked at the Chief Inspector and said, "What do you suggest, Francois?"

Without hesitating, Francois Dumont remarked, "Jardan Moreau is no fool. He knows that what he and his men are facing in the way of charges, are by no means as harsh as what your AWOL soldiers will face for being involved in the black market. As a result, I suggest that we simply knock on the door and advise everyone inside, that it is in their best interest to surrender, because the building is completely surrounded. Besides, if I know Jardan, he already knows that we are here and he is waiting to see how we approach the situation. Telling him that Donnely and the others are already in custody, should also help to convince Jardan and his men that it would be foolish to resist arrest."

Jim Beauregard respected Francois Dumont enough by now to know, that he was an outstanding criminal investigator with impeccable instincts. If the Chief Inspector recommended that they offer the occupants of Donnely's black market storage facility the opportunity to surrender, they had nothing to lose by doing so. "OK, Francois, we'll play it your way," said Jim.

When one of Jardan Moreau's men answered the door to the storage facility, he reacted just as Jim Beauregard and Francois Dumont expected, when he saw a rather impressive number of heavily armed military policemen, CID Agents and Paris cops, standing behind the well known Chief Inspector and three U.S. Army Officers. While speaking in a matter of fact tone of voice, the Chief Inspector spoke in French when he addressed the underling and said, "Tell Jardan that Chief Inspector Francois Dumont, along with Colonel James Beauregard and two of his officers from the American Army CID Office in Paris wish to speak to him."

After the French thief closed the door to the storage facility, only a few seconds passed before the door was opened, by a rugged looking Frenchman, who had a long scar on his face. As soon as Jardan Moreau stepped outside to meet the members of the raiding party, he proved that he was as charming, as he was dangerous, when he greeted the famous Chief Inspector of Police in a respectful, but friendly tone of voice. "Hello, Francois. You are looking well."

While responding in English, Francois introduced Lt. Colonel James Beauregard, Captain Don Lorenz and Lieutenant Al Parker to the famous French smuggler and resistance fighter. After being properly introduced, Jarden nodded his head in a respectful fashion, as he looked directly at Jim Beauregard and said, "What can I do for you and your men, Colonel?"

Jim Beauregard proved that he was another veteran policeman, who could be just as charming and professional as the man that he was facing, when he responded and said, "After hearing about your wartime service to France and the Allies, we decided that it served everyone's best interest, to handle this matter in a more peaceful fashion. Doing so, will enable us to recover stolen U.S. government property and arrest Private Stanislaus Balinski, a U.S. Army deserter who is wanted for attempted murder and other serious crimes."

Even though Jardan was a well known criminal, he appreciated the way the American Colonel from CID recognized his service in the resistance. Jardan became even more impressed with the American Colonel from CID, when Jim offered him a cigarette and a said, "As far as my men and I are concerned, Chief Inspector Dumont can determine the fate of you and your men. Naturally, as Allies we welcome any assistance that you and your men can provide."

After leaning over a bit, to accept a light from the American Colonel, Jardan turned to one of his men and said, "Bring the American deserter to the door, as well as the weapon that we took from him."

As soon as one of his men left to follow his instructions, Jardan faced Jim Beauregard and said, "Once we saw you and your men arrive and surround this building, I took the liberty of disarming your Private Balinski and having him guarded by two of my men. I assure you, Colonel, that my men and I did not know, that Sergeant Donnely and his men were wanted for trying to kill another American soldier. We learned of this crime, when your men surrounded the building and the Private decided to tell us what he and the others did at A La Mere Catherine."

As soon as Private Balinski was brought to the front door, Jardan turned the American deserter over to the Colonel from CID and said, "I will have my men open the doors, so you can recover the supplies and the American Army vehicles, that were stolen by Donnely and the other deserters."

Under the circumstances, the Chief Inspector played along, as he faced the Commanding Officer of the U.S. Army CID Office in Paris and said, "With your permission, Colonel, I will release Monsieur Moreau's men, while he and I have a conversation over a glass of wine."

While Jim Beauregard turned toward the Chief Inspector and said, "As you wish, Francois," one of Jardan's men handed the Negro Lieutenant from CID the stolen American Army pistol that AWOL Private Balinski was carrying. As Al Parker held the stolen pistol in his left hand, he instructed Sergeant Blair to take custody of the prisoner.

While the prisoner was taken away, Jim looked at Jardan and said, "I'm sure you won't mind giving us a witness statement, that documents Private Baliniski's confession, about the attempt on an American soldier's life at La Mire Catherine?"

After bowing his head in a respectful fashion, the career criminal and former resistance fighter made a friendly hand gesture while he responded and said, "As you wish, mon Colonel."

While one of Jardan's men opened the large wooden door to the warehouse, Jim Beauregard turned to Captain Lorenz and said, "Captain, release all of the MPs except for two men to guard the entrance, while the rest of us have a look inside."

While Jardan addressed his men in French and instructed them to meet him later on in his apartment, Captain Lorenz relayed the Colonel's instructions to MP Lieutenant Carl Miller, before he turned to Al Parker and the other men from CID and said, "Let's go."

As the small group of French thieves walked past the contingent of American CID Agents, MPs and Paris Policemen, the Chief Inspector extended his hand toward a nearby café and said, "Shall we go?"

Clearly, the way that this situation was handled, impressed Jardan to no end and made it easy for him to cooperate with the combined American military and Paris Police raiding party. While Jardan and the Chief Inspector walked over to a local café, the famous smuggler and black market operator wondered what he would have to do, to repay Francois Dumont, for the courtesy that was extended to him and his men. After all, the Chief Inspector could still arrange for Jardan Moreau and his men to be prosecuted, for dealing in stolen U.S. Army property. Fortunately, the two men knew each other for many years. Even more important, they respected each other, for they were both top men in their respective professions. Last but not least, Francois Dumont and Jardan Moreau both fought for France, when their country needed their help more than ever.

When Francois Dumont called to say that he was on his way to the CID Office with some important information, Jim told the Chief Inspector that he and Al weren't going anywhere, because they had plenty of work to do. As soon as Francois arrived, Jim handed the Chief Inspector a mug of hot American coffee, before he picked up the phone on his desk and called Al. "Francois just arrived. Bring your favorite mug along, because it's time for some coffee sport."

After putting the phone back on the receiver, Jim picked up the bottle of Dewar's White Label that was on his desk and poured a shot of blended scotch whiskey into the Chief Inspector's mug. While Al was on the way, Francois gave Jim a quick run down of the information that Jardan Moreau just provided.

When Al arrived with his coffee mug in hand and he said hello to Francois, Jim was on the phone speaking to Major Savino. "That's good news, Tom, but get back to the office as soon as you can, because Jardan Moreau gave Francois some information that is definitely worth pursuing."

As soon as Jim hung up the phone, he spoke while he stood up and poured a splash of scotch into Al's coffee mug. "Once Tom got Private Balinski to sign his confession, we put the final nail in AWOL Sergeant Donnely's coffin. Balinski also gave us enough to send his other buddies to prison for decades to come."

After taking a sip of his whiskey laced coffee, Al asked, "What made him cooperate?"

When Jim responded he looked at Al and said, "According to Baliniski, all he did was drive the getaway car when Donnely and the others shot Private Fishman. He also gave Tom and Don enough to hang Donnely and his men for stealing Army supplies from the trains that passed through Paris." As Jim picked up his coffee mug, he went on to say, "That kid's been AWOL for so long, he knows he needs all the help he can get, now that he has to face the music for what he's done."

"That wraps that case up," said Al.

As soon as Jim finished taking a sip from his coffee mug, he looked at Al and said, "Thanks to Francois and the chat that he had with Jardan Moreau we have another case to work."

"What'a you got for us, Francois?" asked Al.

"As I told Jim, this is a case that you and all of your CID men will enjoy," responded the Chief Inspector, who paused to take a sip of his whiskey laced coffee before he continued. "According to Jardan, there is a group of American deserters who have a reputation for being heavily armed at all times. As my fellow policemen from America would say, this gang has served as "the muscle" for several black market operations here in Paris. Jardan also believes, that there is a chance, that this gang might be responsible for the commission of several armed robberies of Paris cafes."

When Jim asked the Chief Inspector why Jardan Moreau believes that this gang of AWOL G.I.s committed these robberies, Francois responded and said, "Because the witness statements and the newspaper articles about these robberies reported, that the gunmen who committed these crimes always drove stolen U.S. Army staff cars. According to Jardan, the gang of American deserters that he did business with, also always drove around Paris in stolen staff cars, unless they were using a stolen army truck, to make a delivery to their black market customers."

Once again, Francois paused to take a quick sip from his coffee mug before he went on to say, "I became convinced that Jardan might be passing along a lead that is worth pursuing, when he explained that this gang of American deserters stopped driving around Paris in stolen staff cars, immediately after the newspaper and radio reports referred to this gang of armed robbers as The Staff Car Bandits."

"We heard about those stick ups," said Jim, who quickly added, "They happened before Al and I returned to Paris."

"Can Jardan identify any of these characters?" asked Al."

When the Chief Inspector responded, he did so in his usual calm and matter of fact tone of voice. "If the deserters who committed these cafe robberies are the same men who Jardan is aware of, then their leader is an AWOL American Corporal by the name of Frank Durkin. According to Jardan, Durkin and his men have served in combat and have a reputation for being very dangerous."

After lighting a cigarette, Jim wasted no time in saying, "Can Jardan help us find Durkin and the other members of his gang, before they commit any more crimes?"

When the Chief Inspector responded to Jim's question, he removed a notebook from his suit jacket pocket. "While Jardan has no idea where we can find Durkin, he gave me an address where one of his fellow deserters was living as of a few weeks ago. This AWOL American soldier's name is Thomas Walton."

After leaning closer to Jim's desk and showing him the page in his note-book where he documented this information, Francois continued his brief-ing, while Jim copied the address on a piece of paper. "Because Jardan never liked or trusted Durkin, he had Walton followed after he delivered a truck loaded with stolen American cigarettes and gasoline to him and his men. Once Walton was followed to this address, Jardan's men continued to watch this building. While doing so, they observed Walton in the company of an attractive French woman. Both Walton and this woman were observed walking to the third floor, where they were heard entering one of the apart-ments. Even though this information is several weeks old, it should not be difficult for us to determine if Private Walton continues to reside in this building."

Al Parker proved that he was a first class detective, when he turned toward Francois and said, "Let me guess. Jardan wanted to know where he could get his hands on one of Durkin's men, so he could find Durkin, if he every had the need to do so?"

"That is correct, Al," responded Francois, who never doubted that his

American Allies would figure out Jardan's motive for having one of Durkin's men followed.

"Even if Durkin and his men haven't committed any armed robberies, we can at least pick them up for being deserters," responded Jim, who quickly added, "With Jardan's help we should also be able to make a case against them for dealing in the black market. If we get real lucky, we'll be able to connect Durkin and his men in one or more armed robberies."

While Jim handed the notebook back to the Chief Inspector, Francois continued and said, "As soon as I received this information, I took the liberty of having Inspectors Goulet and La Belle observe the entrance to this apartment building. However, in order to be successful, we need to get a copy of AWOL Private Walton's photograph to the men who will be watching this location. Once we have this photograph in hand, our men can show Walton's picture to some of the local residents. In fact, if we show his picture to anyone, it should be the concierge who is responsible for managing this apartment building."

After being fully briefed by the Chief Inspector, Jim turned to Al and said, "We need to get two of our men into the field with a copy of the photograph from Walton's personnel file. While we're at it, we should also get a copy of Corporal Durkin's photograph. If we can't wrap this up before we leave for Remagen, Tom and Francois will have to handle this case without us."

As Al stood up, he spoke with a sense of urgency when he responded and said, "I'll get Chris Jacko and Charlie Golovan on this right away."

"Thanks, Al," responded Jim.

"See you later, Francois," remarked Al.

"I am looking forward to it, my friend," responded Francois.

As Al faced Jim, he held up his mug and said, "In addition to being my commanding officer, you also serve the best coffee sport in Paris."

"A bad habit that I picked up from you," joked Jim.

"Guilty as charged," responded Al, as he cracked a smile and left the spacious corner office.

After taking one last drag on his Lucky Strike, Jim stamped the cigarette butt out in the ashtray that was on his desk as he looked at Francois and said, "I'm telling you, Francois. No one is gonna believe, that we worked a non stop steady stream of major criminal investigations in Paris, when I publish my book about working in CID during the war."

After taking a sip from his coffee mug, Francois looked at Jim and remarked, "And what a story it will be."

At 0900 hours on the following morning, Captain Don Lorenz and Sergeant Bill Hayes were flown to Liege, Belgium in a twine engine C47. When they arrived, the two CID Agents were picked up by a military policeman and transported to a location in the city to meet MP Major Jason Brickel.

After taking General Tremble to The Paris Cafe and introducing him to Gabby, Jim, Al and the visiting superior officer from SHAFE were escorted to a private table in the corner of the restaurant. As soon as Jim presented the General with a file folder containing an operational plan and two envelopes, he reported that Captain Don Lorenz and Sergeant Bill Hayes were flown to Liege at 0900 and were working with Major Brickel and his MPs on the Q179 investigation."

As Jim continued briefing the General, he added, "If you approve, Sir, we plan on stopping at Q179 to pick up supplies and check on the status of the investigation that our men are conducting in Liege, before we rendezvous with the French Army. If our men are finished we'll take 'em with us. If not, they'll remain in Liege for as long as it takes to get the job done."

After responding to Jim's additional comments by saying, "Killing two birds with one stone. I like that," the General finished reading the operational plan. As General Tremble closed the file folder, he looked across the table at Jim and Al and said, "This is excellent, Jim. You and Al covered all the bases. If you need any additional authorizations for personnel or supplies, contact my aide and he'll move whatever mountains need to be moved, to get you what you want."

While Jim responded and said, "Thank you, Sir," General Tremble opened the first envelope that contained the letter that would serve as their written orders for their mission into German held territory. This letter contained a synopsis of the information that was listed in more detail in the operational plan. After the General read the letter, he removed the fountain pen from his pocket and remarked, "This makes it official," as he signed the order that authorized Jim and his men to serve with the French Army during the Invasion of Southern Germany.

The moment the General picked up the second letter, Jim spoke up and said, "Excuse me, Sir, but before you read the letter in the second envelope, I'd like to brief you on an idea that we had when we drafted the operational plan."

While the General put the second envelope down, Jim explained that they wanted to expand on his order to interrogate German POWs to gather intelligence, by trying to recruit one or two German POWs, who would be willing to serve as guides and extra interpreters on their mission. As Jim continued, he went on to say, "If you approve, Sir, we'd like to have whoever we recruit discharged from the German Army, so they can serve as civilian German policemen. Doing so, complies with the plan to recruit friendly Germans who can help Allied Forces stabilize occupied territory."

While the General took a sip of wine, Jim continued and said, "You see, Sir, we believe it wouldn't hurt to take a regular German Army MP or two with us who are familiar with Southern Germany. No SS men, just regular German Army or Air Force personnel, preferably an MP, or possibly an intelligence officer who knows our area of operation."

While the General removed the letter from the envelope and he read the contents, Jim continued and said, "If he's still alive and he's been taken prisoner, one of the Germans we'd like to take with us, is Master Sergeant Hans Sigmann, the German MP who turned Ivan Larson over to us and let us complete our mission, without taking any of us prisoner last December. The fact that Sergeant Sigmann was a cop in Munich before the war, also means that he's familiar with Southern Germany."

Even though he didn't have a problem with their proposal, the General sounded justifiably curious, when he looked at his two favorite Army cops and said, "Do you and Al actually believe that you can find this German MP in an overcrowded POW compound along the Rhine River?"

While sounding as confident as ever, Jim wasted no tome in responding to the General's comment. "We did some checking, Sir, and according to Captain Barnes from CIC, a large number of German troops from the 26th Volksgrenadier Division who were captured, were taken to one of the open air encampments near Remagen."

As the General used his fountain pen to sign the order, he remarked, "Even though the odds of finding your friendly German are at least a million to one, I learned a long time ago, that you and your partner have a tendency to pull off the impossible."

While the General placed the signed order in the envelope, Jim and Al thanked him for doing so. Once the General returned the file containing the operational plan and the signed orders to Jim, General Nathan Tremble remarked, "As soon as I get back to SHAFE, I'm gonna start a pool and bet fifty bucks that you boys find your German."

Immediately after they parked next to the General's plane and exited the CID staff car, General Tremble remarked, "I have one more piece of official business to conduct before I head back to SHAFE." After removing a small box from his trench coat pocket, the General handed the box to Al Parker and said, "I can't have you running around Germany as a Lieutenant. These used to belong to me. Wear 'em in good health, Captain."

Both Al Parker and Jim Beauregard were initially speechless and taken off guard by the impromptu promotion ceremony that was taking place by General Tremble's C47. As a shocked Al Parker admired the pair of Captain's bars, he swallowed the lump in his throat then said, "Thank you, Sir. This means a lot to me."

"You're welcome," responded the General.

While Al faced the man that he had no love for when they first met, he snapped to attention and presented General Tremble with a snappy salute as he continued and said, "It will be an honor to wear your Captain bars, Sir. I won't let you down."

After returning the salute, General Tremble continued as he faced Al Parker and Jim Beauregard. "Just make sure that you two come back in one piece and that goes for your men as well."

As soon as Al and Jim responded in unison and said, "Yes Sir," the General remarked, "God invented radios for a reason, so stay in touch. I especially want'a hear from you boys on a regular basis once you cross the Rhine. I also want'a know if you find that Kraut MP so I can collect on my bet."

Once Jim and Al acknowledged the order, General Tremble looked as if he was reluctant to send them off on such a potentially dangerous mission. The General proved that he was genuinely concerned about their safety when he said, "It's not easy being a general, any more than it's easy being a colonel, a captain, or a sergeant in charge of a rifle squad. Like it or not, someone has to call the shots and we're it."

After pausing briefly, General Tremble remarked, "Carry on," as he exchanged salutes with the two CID Agents, before he turned and walked toward the open cargo door of his plane. While General Tremble climbed into the aircraft, the crew chief carried the General's luggage from the CID staff car into the C47. Once the crew chief secured the cargo door, the pilot started the starboard engine.

As the General's plane taxied toward the active runway, Jim waited for the C47 to get far enough away so he could be heard, before he turned to Al and said, "That man is full of surprises."

"He sure is," said Al.

After extending his hand, Jim said, "Congratulations, Al."

While they shook hands, Al continued to seem a bit dazed by what just transpired and proved it when he looked at Jim and said, "I still don't believe that what just happened, really happened."

As Jim smiled, he responded as he walked around to the driver's side of the staff car, "I better drive us back to the office, while you recover from the shock of being promoted." Then, after opening the driver's side door of the staff car, Jim called out, "Let's go, Al. We have a promotion party to plan and an operation to prepare for."

CHAPTER 19

MORE WORK AND A PARTY BEFORE GOING OFF TO WAR

While Frank Durkin stood by the window of his apartment and smoked a cigarette, he waited for his girlfriend to return with some groceries. Between operating on the black market, providing security for different gangs of G.I. Gangsters and committing five armed robberies, Durkin and his men were some of the wealthiest deserters in Paris. Even though this was the case, they decided to get back to work as black market operators, after they committed their last robbery.

The problem that Durkin and his men had, was that they had as many enemies as they had so called friends among the ranks of their fellow deserters. As a result, they had to be concerned about someone giving them up to the authorities. In their favor, Durkin and his men had excellent forged documents and had been AWOL long enough to be very familiar with Paris. The fact that Durkin and his five men were also combat veterans of the North African Campaign and the D Day landings in Normandy meant that they didn't scare easily.

Once again, it proved to be incredibly helpful for U.S. Army CID Agents to be assisted by such a skilled group of investigators from the Paris Police. Now that the joint surveillance team of CID Agents and Paris Police Investigators had copies of AWOL Private Walton's photograph and AWOL Corporal Durkin's official photograph, Inspector Goulet was directed by the Chief Inspector to show these photos to the concierge, who was responsible for the apartment building that was under surveillance.

As soon as Inspector Goulet returned to the Citroen delivery van, that he and his American partner were using as a surveillance platform, an anxious Charlie Golovan remarked, "The suspense is killing me, Patrice. Are we in business, or what?"

As someone who had worked with U.S. Army CID Agents ever since they arrived in Paris, Patrice Goulet had become very familiar with how the Americans spoke under different circumstances. This included, how they used slang, sarcasm and a sense of humor when they communicated.

"Yes, Charles. We are, as you say, in business," responded Inspector Goulet as he removed a cigarette from the pack that he carried in his coat pocket and his American partner offered him a light.

After thanking Charlie Golovan for the light, Patrice continued his briefing. "Mrs. Le Clair was very helpful and confirmed that an American soldier, who she believes is stationed in Paris, is living in an apartment on the third floor. According to Mrs. Le Clair, this soldier is reportedly engaged to the French woman who visits him on a regular basis. When I showed her Private Walton's photograph, she immediately identified him as the soldier who has been a resident of this building for several months. When I showed her Corporal Durkin's photograph, she gave no reaction and said that she has never seen this American."

"You do good work, Patrice," remarked Charlie Golovan as he kept an eye on the apartment building from the back of the delivery van.

"Thank you, my friend," responded the veteran Paris Police Inspector before he took a drag on his cigarette and said, "When I told Mrs. Le Clair that she needed to keep our interest in this American confidential, she agreed to do so. She also invited us to use her apartment, if doing so helped us to observe Walton and his fiance."

While Sergeant Golovan continued to keep and eye on the entrance to the apartment building, he asked his partner from the Paris Police if he trusted Mrs. Le Clair. After taking another drag on his Gauloises cigarette, Patrice Goulet responded and said, "Yes, Charles, I do. Mrs. Le Clair is a patriot who has sacrificed a great deal in this war. Her oldest son was killed protecting the evacuation at Dunkirk, one of her other sons is a military policeman and her youngest is with the First French Armored Division. Even her husband is serving on a French merchant vessel and has survived

being strafed and torpedoed." Then, after taking another drag on his cigarette, Patrice added, "Her offer to assist us is genuine."

While Sergeant Golovan continued to observe the entrance of the apartment house, he took his eyes off the target location long enough to look at
Patrice Goulet and say, "We better call this in."

"I agree," said Inspector Goulet, who quickly added, "While you continue
watching for Private Walton, I will let Chris and Maurice know what we
have uncovered. Once they have been briefed, we can call our superiors."

As Inspector Goulet got out of the delivery van, that gave him and his
American partner an excellent view of the location under surveillance, he
spoke in a low tone of voice and said, "Just like your General Douglas Mc
Arthur, I promise to return."

In typical Charlie Golovan fashion, the American CID Agent joked
around with the veteran investigator from the Paris Police when he
responded and said, "Just don't make any side trips to the Philippines. We're
short handed enough as it is here in Paris. Besides, to lose you would have a
negative impact on the war effort."

Seeing the Paris Police Inspector grin, as he walked away to brief the
other surveillance team, was a clear indication that he understood the compliment that his American partner just relayed to him.

After taking General Tremble to the airport, Jim and Al returned to the
CID Office to prepare for their upcoming mission. As the two men who
had become very close friends entered the office, Jim turned to Al and said,
"Just to be on the safe side we should bring a medic on this trip. What'a you
think about drafting Doc Keller to go with us?"

Al not only agreed that it wouldn't hurt to have a medic on their mission,
but he liked the idea of bringing Doc Keller along. After all, Doc Keller was
the medic who volunteered to serve with them, when they flew to Bastgone
in a Waco Glider to pursue Ivan Larson and Francis Shorty Mc Ghee.

While Al stood next to Jim, he wasted no time in agreeing with the suggestion. "As soon as I get to my desk, I'll use the authority from our new
orders to get Doc Keller assigned to our liaison unit. I'll also draft the cable

to Colonel Richmond, to let him know that the Postal Money Order to Donnely's older brother is on its way to New York."

"That sounds like a plan, Al," said Jim, who quickly added, "As soon as you're finished, let's meet in my office."

As soon as Al delivered a copy of the cable that needed to be sent to New York, Jim reviewed the message and signed it, before he looked at Al and said, "The boys back in New York are gonna have a field day, when they deliver that Postal Money Order to Shaun Donnely and they have a chat with him and his father, about all the money they've been receiving from their AWOL relative."

"Too bad we can't hop on a plane and join them," remarked Al.

While Jim put the cable on top of the case file, he looked at Al and said, "Unfortunately, we can't be in two places at once. Besides, we're gonna need every day we have left, to get ready for our trip."

"You're right. I just thought it would be fun to be back in action with Captain Murphy and the old gang from the CID Task Force," responded Al.

After nodding his head ever so slightly, Jim remarked, "Yes, it would be."

It didn't take long for Captain Don Lorenz and Sergeant Bill Hayes to put a game plan together with Major Brickel and his squad of military policemen. With the Germans nowhere in sight, the threat to this particular Quarter Master Supply Depot was from U.S. military personnel and local thieves who were involved in black market activities. Even the theft of supplies by U.S. Army personnel could not be tolerated, when everything that was kept in inventory at Q179 was desperately needed by the Allied troops, who were advancing deeper into Germany.

Based on the report that was sent to the CID Office in Paris, the main suspect in the Liege investigation was a Senior Non Commissioned Officer by the name of First Sergeant Steven Ross. According to Major Brickel and two of his MPs, First Sergeant Ross was first suspected of being involved in black market activities, when MP Sergeant David Coulter spotted Ross having a heated discussion with a Negro Sergeant behind his truck. The fact that this vehicle was parked across the street from The Cafe Liege and that this heated discussion took place at night, made this encounter even more suspicious. This was the case, because this Negro truck driver should have returned directly to his company area, to secure his vehicle after making his run.

As soon as this heated discussion was over, MP Sergeant Coulter continued to observe First Sergeant Ross when he crossed the street and entered The Cafe Liege. Meanwhile, his partner, MP Corporal John Parks, followed the Army supply truck when it drove away.

Once the truck was a safe distance away from The Cafe Liege, MP Corporal Parks pulled the vehicle over and conducted a "routine" stop in order to identify the driver. When the MP Corporal asked the truck driver why he seemed nervous, when everything appeared to be in order, Sergeant Louis Davies stated that he was exhausted, after putting in some long days delivering supplies to front line units. While acting as if he accepted his explanation, MP Corporal Parks told Sergeant Davies that he hoped he got some sleep soon, before he waved him on and returned to meet Sergeant Coulter back in Liege.

After two days of conducting a surveillance operation, Captain Lorenz and Agent Hayes were convinced that First Sergeant Ross was up to no good. The two CID Agents came to this conclusion, when they the observed the supply sergeant from Q179 spending all of his off duty time with the widow who owned The Cafe Liege. While it wasn't uncommon for soldiers to cultivate relationships with local women, Sergeant Ross acted like he owned this cafe, especially when he was observed working behind the bar and buying drinks for fellow G.I.s. The two CID Agents became even more suspicious of Ross, when the supply sergeant was observed spending long periods of time in the back room, that served as the office for the cafe.

After meeting with Bill Hayes down the street from The Cafe Liege, Captain Lorenz spoke while he pulled up the collar on his Army Officer's trench coat. "Well, Bill, what'a you think?"

As the two experienced civilian cops, who were now serving in CID faced each other, Bill Hayes responded and said, "There's no doubt about it, Sir. Sergeant Ross is defiantly up to no good. In addition to spending all of his free time with the lady that owns The Cafe Liege, Ross has free reign in this joint and acts like he owns the place. I also noticed that some of the locals are chain smoking American cigarettes. Ross is also always buying drinks for some of the colored truck drivers and Quarter Master Company personnel who work for him at Q179. I also think he's running a brothel in this place, because Ross has pushed a few ladies of the evening off on some of these G.Is."

"I got the same impression," said Captain Lorenz.

"The question, Sir, is how do we prove it?" responded Agent Hayes.

After looking down the street at The Cafe Liege, Captain Lorenz remarked, "I think it's time to bring in some special help."

As soon as Jim Beauregard consulted with Tommy Savino and Al Parker, the decision was made to ask Cal Parker and Benny Greene to go undercover as transportation company truck drivers. Doing so, would enable CID to conduct a portion of the black market investigation at Q179 from the inside. The plan was to have Cal and Benny assigned to work for Sergeant Louis Davies, the NCO who was observed having a heated discussion with First Sergeant Steven Ross in Liege.

Just as Jim, Al and Major Savino expected, Cal and Benny agreed to work undercover as truck drivers assigned to the transportation company where Sergeant Davies was stationed. While Al Parker handed his son a copy of the case file, Jim Beauregard continued with his briefing. "Once you and Benny become familiar with this investigation, we'll fix you up with new IDs and get you flown up to an LZ near Liege in the morning. Captain Lorenz and Bill Hayes will pick you up and make sure you get into position."

After pausing to light a cigarette, the CO of the CID Office in Paris sounded more like a concerned father than a superior officer when he added, "In addition to looking out for each other, I want you men to be very careful, because we don't know who else may be involved with First Sergeant Ross. According to Captain Lorenz and Bill Hayes, this supply sergeant appears to be up to no good. What he's up to and who he may be involved with is yet to be determined. One thing is certain, two experienced MPs based in Liege spotted First Sergeant Ross having a very heated discussion with Sergeant Davies across the street from the cafe, where this supply sergeant hangs his hat on a regular basis. Both Captain Lorenz and Bill Hayes have also observed Ross behaving like he owns this joint. It also seems plain as day, that Ross is involved with the widow who took over running The Café Liege, after her husband was killed in the war. We also know from speaking to General Tremble and Major Brickel, that the theft problem at Q179 is bad enough to be noticed."

As soon as Jim paused long enough to take a drag on his cigarette, he looked at Cal before he looked at Corporal Greene and said, "While you and Benny work this case from the Quarter Master Truck Company side of this investigation, Captain Lorenz and Bill Hayes will keep an eye on First Sergeant Ross and The Café Liege. Captain Lorenz and Bill Hayes will also do their best to keep an eye on you and Benny." Then, after pausing to take another drag on his cigarette, Jim quickly added, "Hopefully, between the four of you, we'll be able to wrap this case up before the Army pushes deeper into Germany."

Once Cal responded and said, "Understood, Sir," Benny added, "Don't worry, Colonel, you can count on me and Cal."

"I know I can. That's why I'm sending my best undercover agents to help Captain Lorenz and Bill Hayes," remarked Jim, who sounded dead serious when he quickly added, "Just remember. This case takes a back seat to your personal safety. If at any time you feel like you need to pull out, I'm ordering you to do so."

After acknowledging the order, Cal and Benny left the Colonel's Office to prepare for their new undercover assignment. As soon as they left, Al faced Jim and said, "Both Cal and Benny are hoping to go with us when we crossed the Rhine with the French."

"I know," said Jim.

"You sound like you don't want'a take them with us," responded Al.

Once Jim stamped his cigarette butt out in the ashtray on his desk, he spoke like a friend and not a superior officer when he said, "I can't explain it, but I have a feeling in the pit of my stomach that something bad's gonna happen when we make the trip into Germany." Then, after pausing for a split second, Jim added, "This is worse than the feeling I had, when I told you that we needed to advance deeper behind enemy lines on foot, rather than use our vehicles to search for Ivan Larson and Shorty Mc Ghee."

"That bad uh?" said Al.

After nodding his head, Jim continued as if he was deeply troubled about their upcoming mission. "Cal just got married and needs to spend some time with his bride. As far as I'm concerned, two days on the Dumont family farm doesn't count for much of a honeymoon. When this case is over, he's taking a week off to spend time with Michelle."

"He's not gonna like that," said Al.

"He'll get over it," responded Jim.

When Tommy Savino joined the conversation and asked about Benny Greene, Jim stood up behind his desk and said, "He needs a break too. That kid's done everything we asked him to do and more since he started working with us. Cal and Benny are taking a vacation when this one is over. In fact, I want every man who's left behind to be given some time off." As Jim continued, he looked directly at Major Savino and said, "And that goes for you too, Tom. Once the Liege case is wrapped up, Don Lorenz can run the shop while you take some time to see the sights."

It was blatantly obvious to Al Parker and Tommy Savino that their Commanding Officer was worried about the upcoming mission into Germany. Rather than push the issue any further, Al and Tom excused themselves to get back to work. By the time the two officers made it to the door, Jim called out and said, "Don't forget, Tom. Pass the word to the men that I'm hosting a promotion party for Captain Parker at Gabby's tonight. We deserve a night off before we hit the road."

As Al and Tom stood by the door to the Colonel's office, Major Savino responded and said, "Will do, Sir."

"Thanks," remarked Jim as he sat back down behind his desk, while his two subordinates left his corner office. Once outside the Colonel's office, Tommy Savino faced Al and said, "I've never seen Jim this concerned before."

As soon as Al agreed, he quickly added, "Unfortunately, Jim is under orders from a two star general, to command the American Liaison Unit that will follow the French Army into Germany. Bad feelings or not, someone has to go with him. The question that Jim is wrestling with, is who should go and should stay behind."

"If it was up to Jim, he'd go by himself," responded Tom Savino.

"Ain't that the truth," remarked Al, as the two Army Officers who were assigned to the Paris CID Office walked down the hallway.

While Lt. Colonel Fred Richmond stood in front of the squad room and began the briefing, Captain Patrick Murphy Sr. finished passing out copies of Shaun Donnely's booking photograph. "As you all know by now, we received a request to provide assistance to our CID Office in Paris. The case they need help on, involves the fraudulent transfer of Postal Money Orders by an AWOL soldier to his family members here in New York. Based on what we received from our office in France, in addition to being involved in black market activities, AWOL Sergeant Kevin Donnely is the prime suspect in the shooting of another AWOL soldier. Until he was recently arrested by our agents in Paris, Donnely was also running a gambling operation in the City of Light."

As Colonel Richmond continued, he removed his favorite smoking pipe from his suit jacket pocket. "Our original plan was to execute a search warrant on Donnely's Bar, immediately after Inspector Jack Donovan delivers the Postal Money Order, that AWOL Sergeant Donnely had another G.I. send to his brother Shaun. As a result of some new information that was developed by detectives from the local precinct, Army CID was asked to assist the police department, by having one of our agents become a patron at Donnely's Bar. The reason this request was made, is because Shaun Donnely is running an illegal gambling operation, that caters to servicemen and some of the most trusted civilian customers from his father's gin mill."

After turning to Captain Patrick Murphy Sr., the Colonel in command of the CID Office in New continued and said, "I'll let Captain Murphy take it from here."

While Colonel Richmond used a wooden match to light his pipe, Captain Murphy walked to the front of the squad room and addressed the men who were assigned to work on this collateral investigation. "The booking photograph that I just passed around, was taken when AWOL Sergeant Kevin Donnely's older brother Shaun was arrested for assault and possession of a deadly weapon. I passed that photograph around for several reasons. First and foremost, the Colonel and I want every man who is assigned to work this joint investigation, to be fully aware that Shaun Donnely is a convicted felon, who has a well earned reputation for being as violent as they come. Shaun Donnely is also the person who will be receiving the Postal Money Order, that was recently sent from Paris by his AWOL brother Kevin. The fact that deserters can't transfer money to the states, means that someone else signed the affidavit for the Postal Money Order on behalf of AWOL Sergeant Donnely. Since doing so isn't kosher, we can't allow that money to end up in anyone's hands."

After pausing to take a sip from his coffee mug, Captain Murphy continued his briefing. "Third, according to Lieutenant Moore from the precinct where Donnely's Bar is located, detectives from the local squad are about as convinced as cops can be, that Shaun Donnely recently beat a customer half to death and left his body in the alley behind his father's bar. As Colonel Richmond just mentioned, these same detectives also recently heard that Shaun Donnely is running an illegal gambling operation in the apartment above the bar. And like the Colonel said, this fits with the information that we received from Jim and Al, because in addition to being involved in the black market and the shooting of another AWOL soldier, AWOL Sergeant Kevin Donnely was also running a gambling operation in Paris."

After placing his coffee mug on the corner of a nearby desk, Captain Murphy went on to say, "Since Donnely's Bar is frequented by a large number of servicemen and Brooklyn Navy Yard workers, Colonel Richmond agreed to have Sergeant Pike from CID go undercover for us and see if he could learn more about the subjects of our investigation and their illegal activities. Sure enough, it didn't take long for Sergeant Pike to get in on a card game in the apartment upstairs. Now that we confirmed that Shaun Donnely is running an illegal gambling operation, we intend to have Inspector Jack Donovan deliver the Postal Money Order to the bar later today. If Shaun Donnely, or anyone for that matter, leaves that bar to make a run to the bank, we'll move in, recover the money order and have a talk with the Donnelys. If that doesn't happen, we'll wait for Sergeant Pike to spend some time gambling, before we execute our search warrant. Either way, Shaun Donnely is going back to prison and his father will have some explaining to do."

"That means we're gonna give the Donnely family the double whammy," remarked Detective Frank Angelone, as he sat in the CID Office squad room next to his partner Detective Johnny Mc Donald.

"That's correct, Ange," responded Captain Murphy, who sounded like a man who was in very good spirits when he joked, "And there isn't a cop on the job who enjoys giving crooks the double whammy more than you and your partner."

While everyone present had a good laugh, Captain Murphy held up his right hand to get everyone's attention. Once the collection of law enforcement officers from various agencies quieted down, the Captain from the Chief of Detectives Office continued with his briefing. "Once we leave the office, Colonel Richmond and I will meet Lieutenant Moore, while the rest of you take your assigned positions. As soon as we're ready, we'll give our resident Post Office Inspector the signal and Jack will deliver the Postal Money Order with the rest of the mail to Donnely's Bar. Once Shaun Donnely takes possession of his brother's money order, we'll sit tight and wait for him to make the next move. If nothing happens by twenty hundred hours tonight, Sergeant Pike will enter the bar and act like a serviceman who's looking to do some gambling before he leaves for the ETO."

As Captain Murphy looked around the room, he continued and said, "Lieutenant Toland from Army CID, along with Andy Dubrowsky and Jack Donovan are in charge of this investigation and will be looking for evidence that connects AWOL Sergeant Kevin Donnely to his family here in New York. Because this is a federal matter, Andy Dubrowsky, Jack Donovan and Lieutenant Toland will lead the raid on Donnely's gambling den. Johnny Mc Donald, Frank Angelone and Joe Coppola will provide back up on the raid, while one of Lieutenant Moore's detectives and two uniformed patrolmen will cover the fire escape, that leads into the alley behind the apartment building. The raid will be executed ten minutes after Sergeant Pike goes upstairs to gamble. Once all hell breaks loose, we'll have four additional uniformed patrolmen from the local station house on hand, to keep the peace and transport prisoners. The rest of us will assist as needed."

At the conclusion of his end of the briefing, Captain Murphy turned to Colonel Richmond and said, "Now some parting words from Colonel Richmond."

While the Colonel from CID removed the pipe from the corner of his mouth, he walked back up to the front of the room and said, "Captain Murphy and I can't emphasis this enough. Shaun Donnely has a violent streak in him that appears to be a mile wide and then some. Keep this in mind when we execute the raid on the bar and on the apartment above the bar." Then, after pausing for a split second, Colonel Richmond remarked, "OK gentlemen. You all know what to do."

By 1900 hours The Paris Cafe was packed with off duty CID Agents, military policemen and Paris Police Inspectors who were celebrating the promotion of Al Parker to the rank of Captain. Colonel Reynald also joined the party to congratulate Al Parker and present decorations to someone who had no idea that he was going to be recognized for heroism.

Despite the concerns that Jim had about the upcoming mission, he had every intention of enjoying the evening, as he led the effort to honor Al Parker and someone who he and his men had become close to while working in Paris. After getting everyone's attention, Jim stood in front of the bandstand while he addressed the crowd. "We're here tonight to celebrate Lieutenant Al Parker's promotion to the rank of Captain." As the room that was filled with off duty CID Agents, Army MPs, Army lawyers, Michelle Dumont, her parents and all of the Chief Inspectors men applauded and cheered, Jim pinned a set of Captain's bars on Al's uniform to make his promotion official. While the two men smiled and shook hands, Sergeants Angelone and Coppola got the crowd all revved up when they started calling out, "Speech! Speech!"

As Jim faced the enthusiastic crowd, he extended his hand and said, "Go ahead, Captain, say a few words."

While Al stood in front of the roomful of guests, he remembered the day when Jim Beauregard asked him to brief the men assigned to the Provost Marshal's Task Force, after they interviewed Sister O'Rourke and they learned more about the fugitive identified as Ivan Larson. Clearly, a lot had transpired since then.

As Al addressed the crowd, he looked around the room as he spoke from the heart and said, "I want'a thank each and everyone of you for coming tonight. It means a lot to me to share this moment with my son Cal and his wife Michelle and the men I serve with. If I seem a little dazed, it's because I still can't believe, that the army made an old buck private like me a staff sergeant, let alone a lieutenant and a captain." After the guests laughed at Al's last remark, the newly promoted Captain continued and said, "In summation let me say, that the drinks are on the Colonel, because he's throwing this shindig."

While the roomful of guests applauded and cheered, Al and Jim smiled wide as they shook hands the way good friends do.

As soon as Jim remarked, "Now for round two," Al quickly added, "This should be fun."

While Jim held up his right hand to get everyone's attention, he spoke up and said, "When we planned this promotion party, we decided to make it a double header. I ask everyone to remain standing while Colonel Reynald and I make the next presentation. As soon as Jim finished speaking, Colonel Reynald joined him in front of the bandstand. With Colonel Reynald by his side, Jim asked Gabby to step forward. As the surprised café owner and former resistance fighter wondered why he was being summoned, Major Savino handed Jim Beauregard a framed certificate.

While Gabby stood in between the American CID Commander and Colonel Reynald, Jim Beauregard began his presentation. "In addition to taking the time to honor Captain Parker on his recent promotion, Colonel Reynald and I would like to take this opportunity to recognize someone, who has served France and her Allies in more ways than one. Many of you know Gabriel Allaire as the owner of The Paris Café, a place that has become a home away from home for those of us who are stationed in Paris. What some of you may not know, is that in addition to serving with great distinction as a member of the French resistance, Gabby has also gathered valuable intelligence information for Army CID and the Paris Police. As a result, it is my pleasure to present Gabriel Allaire with this certificate of appreciation from the Provost Marshal General's Office."

When Gabby accepted the award, the man who never had difficulty engaging his customers in conversation was initially speechless. Once he regained his composure, Gabby was visibly moved when he thanked his friends in the American Army for all they have done to help liberate France.

As soon as Gabby finished speaking, Jim continued with the presentation and said, "Also with us tonight, is a man who many of us recently had the opportunity to serve with, on one of the most important investigations conducted to date in Paris. It is my honor to introduce Colonel Andre Reynald of the French Army."

After being warmly received by the roomful of Americans and Frenchmen, Colonel Reynald spoke in English as he addressed the roomful of guests. "Tonight, I have the honor to decorate a true patriot, who served in the organized French resistance during the German occupation of our great nation. During four years of service, Gabriel Allaire routinely risked his life, while directing and participating in a succession of highly dangerous missions. In the early days of the occupation, Gabriel Allaire organized one of the most successful resistance newspapers, that gave hope to the citizens of France and encouraged others to resist. Gabriel Allaire also worked with a resistance unit that was responsible for destroying French railroad equipment that was being used by the Germans. These missions alone will one day be the stories of legend. On a number of other occasions, Gabriel Allaire participated in the rescue of Allied personnel and a number of French citizens who were being hunted by the Nazis. His outstanding service to France. as a member of the organized resistance ended, when he was wounded, while heroically fighting during the liberation of Paris in August of 1944."

While Colonel Reynald continued with the presentation, he pinned two medals on Gabby's dark blue suit jacket. "By the authority of General Charles De Gaulle, I award Gabriel Allaire The French Resistance Medal and The Order of the Liberation." Once the Colonel finished pinning the second medal on Gabby's dark blue suit, he kissed Gabby on both cheeks, before he took one step back and saluted the recipient of the two decorations.

While tears streamed down Gabby's face and he returned the salute, everyone remained standing while Lt. Colonel James Beauregard spoke in a very respectful tone of voice when he said, "Ladies and gentlemen, I give you La Marseille."

Even the most red blooded Americans had to admit, that the French National Anthem was one of the most moving and inspiring patriotic songs every written. This became evident, when the 1942 movie Casablanca (released in January of 1943 staring Humphrey Bogart, Ingrid Bergman, Claude Rains, Paul Henreid, Conrad Veidt, Dooley Wilson and other outstanding actors) included a riveting scene, when the freedom loving patrons of Rick's Café Americain sang La Marseille louder than the German soldiers, who were singing one of their songs. Even though the Germans and the other Axis Forces were winning the war in 1942, this scene inspired audiences around the world, to do whatever they could to help the war effort.

While Gabby and every other French citizen in The Paris Café, along with CID Agent Sam Carubba, sang the French National Anthem with tremendous enthusiasm, the non French speaking American soldiers who were present stood at attention and saluted the French tri-color flag and the American flag, that hung side by side over the bandstand. Even people who were passing by The Paris Café stopped and joined in, when they heard the band playing and a roomful of French citizens singing La Marseille. This was without a doubt, a moment that would be remembered by everyone who was present that night.

Later that night, while Gabby and his staff cleaned up after the party, Jim Beauregard and Al Parker had a private drink at the empty bar and used the time alone to discuss their upcoming mission. When Al asked Jim if he gave any more thought to allowing Cal and Benny to go along, on their mission into Germany, Jim spoke from his heart when he responded and said, "Whenever I think about leaving them behind, I tell myself that there's no difference between Cal and Benny and anyone else who we would take with us." After pausing to tap the ash from his cigarette into a nearby ashtray, Jim went on to say, "Every man in this unit has a family back home, who would be heartbroken if anything happened to them. Since we can't take everyone with us, the question is who should go and who should remain behind."

While sounding like the close personal friend that he had become, Al remarked, "It's a tough call, Jim and I for one don't envy you for having to choose who goes with us."

After taking a drag on his cigarette, Jim looked at Al and said, "Tell me, Al, who do you think we should take on this mission into the unknown?"

While Al Parker placed his cigar in the ashtray, that was in front of his place at the bar, he responded and said, "The reason it's a tough call is because they're all good men. In fact, as far as I'm concerned, I'd invade hell with any of the men in our command."

After pausing to take a sip of his drink, Al finished his response by saying, "I could also never allow another man to go with us, just so my son Cal can stay behind. I guess what I'm trying to say, is that I agree with you, Jim. Every man in our office has someone who cares about 'em, including my son Cal. The same goes for Bennie Greene."

"I knew we felt the same way about this," said Jim, who continued as he stamped his cigarette out in a nearby ashtray, "How's this for a starting lineup? Hank Blair, Mike Mulligan, Anthony Angelone, Sal Coppola, Sam Carubba, Cal and Bennie."

"And Doc Keller," added Al.

"Correct," said Jim, who went on to say, "That leaves Bill Hayes, Chris Jacko, Mike Butler, Charlie Golovan, Joshua Fermi and the seven new agents who are arriving in a week, to help Don Lorenz and Tommy Savino run the office while we're gone. If the case in Liege hasn't been wrapped up by the time we get resupplied, we'll go without Cal and Bennie. As far as MPs go, I made arrangements for Lieutenant Carl Miller, Sergeant Rusty Morgan, Sergeant Steve Dalton and Corporal Tommy Baines to go with us, on our trip into the crumbling Third Reich. Nothing's changed as far as the three men we're taking with us from CIC."

"You picked a good group of men to go to war with," responded Al.

"It better be, because our lives just might depend on how well we take care of each other," said Jim, who continued as he removed a folded piece of paper from his jacket and handed it to Al. "Take a look at this list of supplies and equipment and let me know if you think we need to bring anything else with us. I also want you to know, that when I put that list together, I did so with the idea of taking Cal and Bennie along, providing they're no longer needed to work undercover in Liege."

As soon as Al put on his reading glasses, he began calling off the items that Jim wanted to requisition from the Quarter Master. "Two M3 Half Tracks with trailers, one canvass top two and a half ton six by six cargo truck, five Jeeps, including two with trailers, six Thompson sub machine guns, one M3 Grease gun for me, two more Grease Guns for Cal and Bennie, three M1 Garand rifles, three M1 Carbines, one M1A1 Paratrooper Model Carbine for you, one M2 belt fed .50 caliber machine gun for the lead M3, one M2 .50 cal for the number two Half Track, ten 30 round magazines for each Grease Gun, ten 30 round magazines for each Thompson, a dozen 15 round magazines for each M1 Carbine, assorted ammunition pouches for the spare carbine and submachine gun magazines, a case of fragmentation grenades, one case of white phosphorous grenades, one case of smoke grenades, sixteen belt knives, three bayonets for the M1 Garands, entrenching tools, shovels and hand axes for every vehicle, enough rations for us to operate in the field for three weeks, four coffee pots, mess tins for every man plus three spares, one hundred gallons of water, one extra fuel can for each Jeep, four extra fuel cans for the Half Tracks and the truck, two dozen blankets, rain ponchos for every enlisted man, trench coats for the officers, two command post tents and additional canvass tent quarters, four foot lockers, three field stoves, two stretchers and what looks like plenty of smokes and coffee, a ton of medical supplies and enough ammunition to win World War III."

As Al put the list on the bar, he joked, "The only thing we're not bringing with us is the kitchen sink."

"I thought about bringing one along but there's no room," responded Jim.

After thinking about other items that might be needed, Al spoke up and said, "I know we're gonna be loaded down with supplies and equipment, but how about bringing some extra uniforms and boots along, for any friendly Germans who agree to work with us. We certainly can't have them looking like the enemy, when they travel with us into Germany."

"Good idea, Al. Put it on the list," responded Jim as he removed another Lucky Strike cigarette from the pack that was on the bar. After quickly lighting the unfiltered cigarette, Jim went on to say, "We also need to make sure, that everyone who goes with us takes extra uniforms along, including some heavy clothing, because it looks like we'll be staying in Germany for a while."

While Al used his pen to make some notes on the list, he spoke up and said, "I'll also make sure to bring extra uniforms along for Cal and Benny. If they can't make the trip, I'll leave their extra uniforms with Don Lorenz."

"Good idea," said Jim who quickly added, "I almost forgot. We need to make sure that everyone who goes along has a sidearm." After taking a quick drag on his cigarette, Jim continued and said, "I know all our men and the three CIC Agents have issued forty fives. The two of us also have issued 1911s and personal weapons that we carry. If the MPs who are making this trip can't take the sidearms that they normally carry on duty, we'll have to provide them with forty fives. I'll also take a few of the captured pistols and spare magazines that we have in the safe with us, so we can issue a sidearm to any friendly Germans who are willing to go along."

While Al added another note on the list, Jim continued and said, "You'll also be happy to know, that I used our orders from General Tremble, to have Billy Davis and a C47 crew put on standby, in case we need to be resupplied once we cross the Rhine." Then, after pausing for a split second, Jim added, "Let's hope it won't be necessary, but we can also use Billy to fly our wounded back to a hospital, if God forbid we sustain any casualties along the way."

"I'll be happy if all Billy brings us is the mail," remarked Al before he used a wooden match to light his cigar.

"I agree," responded Jim.

When Al asked when he and some of the men should start picking everything up from the Quarter Master, Jim took a drag on his Lucky Strike before he responded and said, "I'll call our contact at COMZ to put a rush on our request. Having orders signed by SHAFE will insure that we'll get everything we want in time for us to leave on schedule."

As Jim stamped his cigarette butt out in the ashtray on his bar, he sounded like a man who was no stranger to sadness when he said, "You know, Al, I was just thinking about Chester Wright. He was a fine officer and one hell of an MP. I wish he was going with us."

Al knew that the loss of MP Lieutenant Chester Wright had a profound effect on everyone who participated in the pursuit of Ivan Larson and Francis Shorty Mc Ghee, especially Jim. As Al faced the man who was his friend, his partner and his commanding officer, he spoke in a soft tone of voice when he said, "Lieutenant Wright will always be with us in spirit, Jim."

After nodding his head in agreement, Jim remarked, "So will Patrolman Patrick Murphy Jr."

In an effort to brighten up the moment, Jim raised his glass and quickly added, "What'a you say we have one more to celebrate your promotion before we call it a night?" "That sounds like a plan. Cheers," said Al, as he raised his glass to join in the toast.

As the two men who had become very close personal friends tapped their glasses together, Jim said, "Congratulations, Al." "Thanks, Jim," responded Al, who finished his drink in one shot and refilled their glasses with Cognac as he remarked, "This stuff isn't Irish Whiskey, but it's not bad once you get used to it."

After switching places with the postman who normally delivered mail in this section of Brooklyn, U.S. Post Office Inspector Jack Donovan acted like an experienced mailman, when he delivered mail on the street where Donnely's Bar was located. While carrying a leather sack full of mail, Jack entered the bar and acted as if he had no idea who the subject of their investigation was. After taking a quick look around, Jack approached the bartender and said, "The only mail I have today is a Postal Money Order for a Shaun Donnely."

As Shaun Donnely pushed his lunch aside, he came off his bar stool and said, "I'll take that." Once again, the veteran federal law enforcement officer, who began his career as a Prohibition Agent, remarked, "I'm just filling in for Harry who's out sick. Are you Shaun Donnely?"

In his usual abrupt demeanor, Shaun Donnely ripped the envelope out of Jack's hand and said, "I said, I'll take that," before he turned to the bartender and quickly added, "Give him a drink on me."

While Shaun ripped open the envelope as he walked toward the back room, Jack acted like a man who didn't want any trouble when he remarked,

"Thanks for the drink." Jack then faced the bartender and said, "How 'bout a short beer."

The only time Shaun Donnely was observed leaving his father's bar, was when he walked to a local grocery store, before returning to the apartment that was located above the family business. Later on in the day, the local grocer delivered enough food to feed a large number of people to the apartment above the bar.

At 2012 hours Shaun Donnely was observed by members of the surveillance team leaving the apartment and entering his father's bar. As the bar became crowded with civilians and off duty military customers, Sergeant Pike went to work and ordered a drink at the bar. Joe Coppola from the U.S. Customs Service, Detective Frank Angelone and his partner Detective Johnny Mc Donald from the PDNY, followed the undercover CID Agent into the bar at different intervals.

Since Donnely's Bar was located in the vicinity of the Brooklyn Navy Yard, it was common for this particular licensed premise to do a bristling business with dock workers and military personnel. This made it possible for Joe Coppola, Johnny Mc Donald and Frank Angelone to dress like blue collar workers and blend in with the crowd of bar patrons.

Once Sergeant Pike left the bar with two other servicemen and an attractive woman, who was a known associate of Shaun Donnely, Customs Agent Joe Coppola checked his watch before making eye contact with Frank Angelone and Johnny Mc Donald. As experienced law enforcement officers, no words needed to be spoken, because the two city police detectives and their counterpart from U.S. Customs knew exactly what needed to be done next.

After several days and nights of observing the 3rd Floor apartment, Sergeant Chris Jacko turned to Inspector La Belle and said, "Guess who just came home, Maurice?"

As soon as Inspector La Belle joined his American partner in looking across the street, the Paris Police Investigator remarked, "That's him."

Now that the two men on surveillance duty spotted AWOL Private Walton, CID Agent Chris Jacko told his French partner to sit tight, while he called the office to get some help. Twenty minutes later, Lt. Colonel Beauregard arrived with Chief Inspector Dumont, Major Savino, Captain Parker, Sergeant Golovan, Sergeant Fermi and Inspector Patrice Goulet.

In order to execute this arrest with the least amount of fanfare, the decision was made to have the three CID Agents and their Paris Police counterparts filter into the building at different intervals and stage from Mrs. Le Clair's apartment. This enabled Lt. Colonel Beauregard, Chief Inspector Dumont, Major Savino and Captain Parker to casually position themselves near the entrance to the building. In order to add another layer of security to the arrest team, two U.S. Army MPs and two uniformed Paris policemen were positioned on the corner.

After checking his watch and seeing that it was just about time for their men to raid the apartment, Major Savino turned to Jim and said, "It's time," before they moved quickly up the stairs, just as they heard the arrest team make their way past Walton's irate French girlfriend.

As soon as the door was pushed open and Walton's girlfriend was detained by Inspector La Belle, the rest of the raiding party secured the apartment and took the AWOL Private into custody as he scrambled to get out of bed. When Major Savino entered the bedroom, he played his part to the hilt, when he looked at the prisoner with disgust and said, "Get some clothes on this deserter, while the rest of us rip this place apart."

As soon as Sergeants Jacko and Fermi handed the prisoner some clothes and he got dressed, AWOL Private Walton was handcuffed and instructed to sit down and keep quiet, while the apartment was being searched. While Sergeant Joshua Fermi guarded the prisoner, Major Savino and Sergeant Jacko searched the bedroom and found a stolen U.S. Army .45 caliber Model 1911 pistol and a large stack of French currency.

Just as Major Savino held up the pistol and remarked, "I'll bet a months pay this forty five is stolen," Jim Beauregard, Al Parker and Chief Inspector Dumont entered the bedroom.

While Major Savino handed the recovered pistol to Agent Jacko, he introduced the other superior officers and the Chief Inspector to the prisoner. As the prisoner sat in silence, Jim Beauregard addressed Private Walton in a no nonsense tone of voice. "Understand this, Private. We know a lot more about you than you think, so whatever you do, don't try to bullshit me, or any of my men, or our allies in the Paris Police. I also suggest you pay close attention to what Captain Parker has to say."

While Al Parker stood over the seated prisoner, he picked up where Jim left off and said, "You're not just a deserter who's facing a dishonorable discharge. You're also a thief, who's been involved in black market activities. To top all that off, a reliable witness recently came forward and informed us, that you and your pals are the gunmen we've been looking for, who held up several cafes in Paris. If you doubt that we know what we're talking about, consider this. We found you because you were followed to this apartment, after you delivered a truckload of stolen U.S. Army cigarettes and gasoline to a very famous French smuggler, who is well known to the Paris Police. I think you know who I'm talking about, but if you need me to refresh your memory, I'll be happy to do so. In fact, Chief Inspector Dumont can tell you a lot more about this famous French smuggler than I can." Then, after turning to face Francios, Al remarked, "Isn't that so, Chief Inspector?"

It was obvious that Jim Beauregard, Tommy Savino, Al Parker and Francois Dumont were highly skilled criminal investigators, who choreographed every move they made with tremendous precision, when the Chief Inspector looked down at the prisoner and said, "By the expression on Private Walton's face, it appears that it will not be necessary for me to refresh his memory."

Once again, it was Major Savino's turn to address the prisoner. While the Major pointed his right index finger at Private Walton, he kept the act going when he said, "You and your other AWOL buddies also brought a great deal of attention to yourselves, when you stopped driving around in stolen U.S. Army staff cars, after you used these vehicles when you robbed several cafes in Paris. The day you clowns became known as The Staff Car Bandits, was the day you signed your own arrest warrants."

Just like his superiors, Agent Jacko proved that he knew exactly how to handle a prisoner who was in a tight spot. After removing a pack of Camels from his shirt pocket, Agent Jacko remarked, "You look like you could use a smoke."

As soon as Agent Jacko offered the prisoner, who was purposely hand-cuffed in front of his body and not behind his back, a cigarette and a light, Private Walton thanked the Army cop, before he looked up at the Colonel from CID and said, "Tell me, Colonel. What am I looking at if I cooperate?"

Without hesitating, Jim Beauregard responded and said, "A lot better deal than you're gonna get if you don't and for that to happen, you're gonna have to impress the hell out'a me, every member of my command who is assigned to this case, as well as Chief Inspector Dumont and the U.S. Army Judge Advocate General."

While standing with their mess tins in hand, Cal Parker aka Private Andy Carter and Benny Greene aka Private Benjamin Redman waited in line with Sergeant Davies to grab some chow, before making their first delivery of the day. So far everything was working out as planned, now that Captain Lorenz and Major Brickel met privately with the commanding officer of the transportation company where Sergeant Davies was assigned.

After being assigned to serve as truck drivers, the two undercover CID Agents let the Army rumor mill be responsible for letting Sergeant Davies know, that Private Andy Carter and Private Benjamin Redman were recent-ly demoted non-commissioned officers, who went AWOL in Paris after they recovered from a stint in the hospital. While standing in line with his two new men, Cal and Benny knew that Sergeant Davies took the bait when he said, "I heard you boys had some trouble with the MPs in Paris."

Once again Cal Parker and Benny Greene proved to be an outstanding team of undercover agents, when Cal leaned closer to Sergeant Davies and said, "Let's just say we got away cheap by only losing our stripes."

"Andy's right. We were sure lucky," responded Benny Greene who was using the name Benjamin Redman while working undercover on this assignment.

After hearing what the man he knew as Private Andy Carter had to say, Sergeant Davies got the distinct impression that his new drivers were guilty of a lot more than just being Absent Without Leave. As the three truck drivers reached the front of the line, one soldier filled Sergeant Davies mess tin with a ladle full of powdered eggs, while a second soldier filled his canteen cup with hot black coffee. With two slices of white bread topping off his mess tin, Sergeant Davies moved away from the line just as Cal and Benny received their food.

While eating by the tailgate of a parked supply truck, Benny Greene played his part just like he and Cal rehearsed. After Benny looked around, to make sure that no one was close enough to hear what he was about to say, he leaned closer to Sergeant Davies and said, "One thing me and Andy learned during our time in the stockade, was that the white man's Army has no love for colored folks."

After hearing what Benny had to say, Sergeant Louis Davies didn't have much of a poker face and reacted like a man who was deeply troubled. As Sergeant Davies faced Cal Parker aka Andy Carter, he sounded like a man who was desperate to know more when he said, "I ain't never been in jail. Is is as bad as they say it is?"

After swallowing a spoonful of powdered eggs, Cal took a sip of coffee, before he responded like a young man who knew what he was talking about. "Well, Sarge, let me put it to you this way. While an army stockade is no fun for white G.I.s who get into trouble, being behind bars is a lot worse for us colored boys."

After hearing hearing Cal Parker's last comment, Sergeant Davies wanted to hear more about the conditions in an Army jail and wasted no time in asking, "Why's that?"

While continuing to play his part to the hilt, Cal looked directly at Sergeant Davies and said, "Cause most of the guards in an Army stockade are rednecks from down south and you know how much they hate colored folks."

The second his undercover partner finished speaking, Benny Greene drove Cal's point home by saying, "Andy's right, Sarge, those redneck MPs can beat you to death in an Army prison and all they have to say, is you tried to assault them. We know, 'cause we saw how those MPs put the sticks they carry to work, on colored prisoners in the stockade."

As soon as Benny finished scaring the crap out of Sergeant Davies, Cal spoke up and said, "Me and Benny were real lucky, Sarge, 'cause if the Army didn't need truck drivers and riflemen, we'd still be in the stockade and would probably be going home in handcuffs."

Cal and Benny knew that Sergeant Davies was worried about something, when he checked his watch, before he spoke in a low tone of voice and said, "Once you finish your chow and you clean your mess kits, we'll get loaded and make our first run. We leave in ten minutes."

"OK, Sarge," remarked Cal, as the subject of their undercover operation looked like a man who had the weight of the world on his shoulders when he walked away.

Once Sergeant Davies was far enough away from the back of the truck where they were standing, Benny leaned closer to Cal and whispered, "That man is definitely worried about something and it ain't the Germans."

After waiting the prescribed ten minutes for Sergeant Pike to get settled in a game of cards, the members of the raiding party finished their drinks and left the bar. Once outside, Johnny Mc Donald, Frank Angelone, Joe Coppola entered the apartment building next door, just as Captain Murphy, Colonel Richmond, Andy Dubrowsky, Jack Donovan, Lieutenant Toland and Detective Fitzgerald arrived on scene with six uniformed patrolmen.

While Detective Fitzgerald took two uniformed patrolman to cover the alley behind the building, FBI Agent Andy Dubrowsky and Post Office Inspector Jack Donovan led the raiding party up the stairs to the second floor apartment. Unfortunately, Shaun Donnely heard the commotion outside, as a car door slammed shut and the raiding party made their way to the second floor apartment.

The second the door to the apartment was kicked open and Agent Andy Dubrowsky called out, "FBI!...Nobody move!," Shaun drew the six shot Colt Detective Special that he carried in his waistband and fired three shots at the raiding party. Between the shots fired by Post Office Inspector Jack Donovan, FBI Agent Andy Dubrowsky and Sergeant Pike, Shaun Donnely was hit several times, as he made his way into the back bedroom. Once inside the room, Shaun Donnely slammed the door and headed for the fire escape. The moment Donnely went to step out of the bedroom window and onto the fire escape, several shots fired by Detective Fitzgerald and two uniformed patrolmen forced him back inside.

While the last of the gamblers were ushered out of the apartment, a badly wounded and pissed off Shaun Donnely emptied his revolver at the city cops covering the alley behind the building. After tossing the empty revolver on the edge of the bed, Donnely opened a dresser draw and removed another Colt Detective Special with a two inch barrel. While Shaun knelt down by the foot of the bed, he heard the same G Man call out, "This is the FBI! You haven't got a chance. You're completely surrounded. Open the door nice and slow and throw your gun out. Then come out with your hands up!"

Under the circumstances, Shaun Donnely had no intention of ending up in a prison hospital, just so he could get patched up and spend more time behind bars. Besides, between his belabored breathing and the amount of blood that he was losing, Shaun Donnely had good reason to believe that his time on this earth was limited.

After hearing the FBI Agent outside his room try one more time to get him to surrender, Shaun Donnely decided to have the law enforcement officers who had him surrounded, send him on his way. "OK, I'm throwing my gun out!" said Donnely, who coughed up a mouthful of blood, as he opened the bedroom door and added, "Here it comes!"

As soon as the empty revolver was thrown out of the room, Agent Dubrowsky called out, "Now come out with your hands up!....Nice and slow, Donnely."

While doing his best to sound as convincing as possible, Donnely moved closer to the open door and called out, "I'm coming out! But I'm hit pretty bad and I'm moving slow! I can only hold up my left hand, so don't shoot!"

To their credit, the men who made up the raiding party were veteran law enforcement officers, who knew that it never paid to trust a criminal, especially one like Shaun Donnely. As a result, the moment Shaun Donnely began to step out of the bedroom, the members of the raiding party remained behind overturned gambling tables, with their guns aimed in and ready to fire.

The second Donnely stepped all the way out of the bedroom with a revolver in his right hand, every member of the raiding party opened fire. While Shaun Donnely's body was riddled with bullets, he got off one shot that hit an overturned gambling table. By the time, Donnely's body hit the floor, he was dead. After drawing his back up gun, Detective Frank Angelone stood up and remarked, "I hope nobody thought that this was gonna end any other way."

As Andy Dubrowsk stood up while he reloaded his service revolver, the veteran FBI Agent responded and said. "You're right, Ange. This outcome was pretty predictable with a hot head like Shaun Donnely."

While Johnny Mc Donald checked the body and retrieved the two Colt revolvers, Post Office Inspector Jack Donovan searched Shaun Donnely's pockets, until he found what he was looking for. As the U.S. Post Office Inspector stood up with the Postal Money Order in hand, he turned to the other members of the raiding party and said, "We have Exhibit A in our possession."

"Now we can have a talk with Mr. Donnely about his two sons," remarked Andy Dubrowsly.

From their position behind a long line of parked trucks, Captain Don Lorenz and Sergeant Bill Hayes were able to observe First Sergeant Ross, as he stood by, while the three trucks that were driven by Sergeant Davies and his two new drivers were being loaded with supplies. Their surveillance really paid off, when they observed Sergeant Ross point to Cal and Bennie, as they helped load their trucks, while Ross had a private conversation with Sergeant Davies.

"What's the story with those two?" asked Ross.

"They're OK, Top," responded Sergeant Davies, who quickly added, "They used to be sergeants like me, but they got in a little trouble in Paris and lost their stripes. The way I heard it, they were lucky they didn't get sent home in chains. One thing is certain, Top. Andy Carter and Benny Redman don't like MPs."

After hearing what Sergeant Davies had to say, First Sergeant Ross patted the Negro NCO on the back and said, "When you get back from your run bring 'em by The Café Liege for a drink. I'm buy'in," before he walked away.

The night before Jim, Al and the members of their composite unit left for Remagen, they assisted Major Savino, Chief Inspector Dumont and their men round up AWOL Corporal Frank Durkin and his fellow G.I. Gangsters. Between the detailed confession that was made by AWOL Private Walton and the cooperation of Jardan Moreau, the arrest of AWOL Corporal and his men went down without incident.

As the Chief Inspector and the famous smuggler watched Corporal Durkin being escorted out of a nearby apartment building in handcuffs, Jardan remarked, "You may not believe me, Francois, but this war has motivated me to think about making some changes in my life."

"I am not surprised to hear you say that," said the Chief Inspector, who quickly added, "After all, we both know from experience that serving in a war can affect a person in many ways."

While Jardan faced the famous Chief Inspector of the Paris Police, he surprised Francois when he said, "If you need to contact me in the future, you can find me in the Foreign Legion. I leave in the morning. If I survive this adventure, in five years I will have a new identify and a new life, with all of my sins forgiven by the French Government."

On one hand Francois was surprised, but on the other, he wasn't. Jardan's service in the French Resistance was just as legendary as his reputation as a smuggler. In fact, it was his capabilities as a smuggler, that enabled Jardan to serve France and her Allies in a very special way. As a result, Francois was happy to hear that Jardan had changed sides once again, only this time, it appeared that he was making a more permanent change in the right direction.

"Bonn chance, mon amie," responded Francois as he shook hands with Jardan. After pausing to offer Francois a black market American cigarette and taking one for himself, Jardan accepted a light from the Chief Inspector, before he added, "Give our American Allies my regards and tell them for me that they still make the best cigarettes."

As Francois cracked a smile, Jardan smiled as well, as he nodded his head ever so slightly, before he turned and walked away. Just like Jardan was a legend among smugglers and resistance fighters, so would he become a legend of sorts in the French Foreign Legion.

Once the Military Police took custody of AWOL Corporal Durkin and the rest of his associates, Jim and Al said goodbye to Major Savino, the Chief Inspector and the men from CID who would not be going with them in the morning. Because it was late and they planned to get an early start, there was no time for a night cap at The Paris Cafe.

After Tommy Savino wished them well, Francois Dumont seemed equally as concerned when he shook their hands and said, "Please be careful, my friends. I will pray for the safe return of you and all of your men."

As soon as Jim and Al thanked Francois, they got into their Jeep and drove off. In a few hours, Jim, Al and their men would be on their way to Allied occupied territory along the Rhine River near Remagen, Germany.

TO BE CONTINUED....

ENDNOTES

CHAPTER 1

1   *Death Traps-The Survival of an American Armored Division in World War II*, Belton Y. Cooper. See Page 283-283 for comments on tank repair after killed crew members were recovered. See Page 210-211 for comments on combat expedient training for tank replacement crews.

2   *4ᵗʰ Convalescent Hospital Unit History*, WW2 U.S. Medical Research Centre.

CHAPTER 3.

3   *Resistance France 1940-1945*, Blake Ehrlich, page 22.

CHAPTER 4

4   *The Road To Victory*, David P. Colley, page 160.

5   *The Deserters*, Charles Glass. SeePages 199 and 280 re: black market prices.

6   *The Guns At Late August, The War In Western Europe 1944-1945*, Rick Atkinson. Also discusses the exorbitant prices paid for certain items on the black market in Paris.

7   *The Guns At Last August, The War In Western Europe 1944-1945*, Rick Atkinson, pg 398-401. Describes the cost of luxury items on the black market and prostitution in Paris after the liberation.

CHAPTER 5

8   *The Blood of Free Men*, Michael Neiberg, Pg 112. Identifies one of three Paris Police Resistance Groups known as The Gaullist Honneur de la Police.

CHAPTER 8

9   *The Deserters – A Hidden History of World War II*, Charles Glass

CHAPTER 9

10   *American In Paris*, Charles Glass, pg 396. Comments on the request by a U.S. General to the French 2nd Armored Division not to include French Colonial African troops in the liberation of Paris in August 1944.

11   *Yank Magazine*, May 4, 1945, by Sergeant Allan B. Ecker. Provides a detailed account of black market operations and other crimes committed by U.S. Army personnel in the ETO during World War II. This included crimes committed by serving U.S. Army Officers, Non Commissioned Officers and enlisted men, as well as by Army personnel who were AWOL and listed as deserters. Some of these G.I. Gangsters were so bold as to impersonate U.S. Army Military Policemen.

CHAPTER 14

12   *The Deserters – A Hidden History of World War II*, Charles Glass

13   *The Unit History of The 4ᵗʰ Convalescent Hospital*, by WW2 Medical Research Centre. Ch 14, Footnote 13, DK Eyewitness Travel 2016 Paris. Page 228, Place du Tertre & La Mere Catherine.

14   *Deserters*, Charles Glass. Chapter 23. The use of troops from the 2ⁿᵈ Battalion 38 Infantry Regiment to serve as guards on trains in France to protect vital supplies from being stolen.

CHAPTER 16

15   *World War II Story*, Robert F. Gallager,-Ch 26, Black Market. The issue of converting army script and local currency into war bonds and postal money orders is described. Also, see *Yank Magazine*, May 4, 1945, "GI Racketeers In The Paris Black Market."

16,17,18,19,20,21,22 *The Guns At Last Light*, Rick Atkinson, ch 11, pg 549. The capture and crossing of the Rhine River by U.S. Army mechanized and infantry troops across the Remagen Bridge is discussed in vivid detail. This book is a must read for anyone interested in WWII ETO history.

CHAPTER 18

23   *World War II Story*, Robert F. Gallager,-Ch 26, Black Market. The issue of converting army script and local currency into war bonds and

postal money orders is described. Also, see *Yank Magazine*, May 4, 1945, "GI Racketeers In The Paris Black Market."

24   *Hitler's Wehrwolves*, Charles Whiting, and *Werwolf – The History of the National Socialist Guerrilla Movement*, Perry Biddscombe, and *Armageddon*, Max Hastings. See Chapter Twelve, Marching On The Rhine, Page 339. See Pages 359, 360 and 499 re: Werewolves (German guerrillas).

25   *The Road To Victory – The Untold Story of World War II's Red Ball Express*, David P. Colley. See Chapter 26 for details on the ABC/XYZ Express Quarter Master Companies Long Haul Truck Lines.

26   *Army Historical Series- The U.S. Army In The Occupation Of Germany 1944-1946* by Earl F. Siemke, Center Of Military History, United States Army, Washington, D. C., 1990.

OTHER RESOURCES

Hitler's Wehrwolves, Charles Whiting

Werwolf – The History of the National Socialist Guerrilla Movement, Perry Biddscombe

The Guns At Last Light – The War In Western Europe 1944-1945, Rick Atkinson.

www.ingramcontent.com/pod-product-compliance
Lightning Source LLC
Chambersburg PA
CBHW062110170626
46813CB00002B/386